FC GOMEZ

RISE OF THE DARKNESS

Copyright © 2023 by FC Gomez

All rights reserved. No part of this publication may be reproduced, stored or transmitted in any form or by any means, electronic, mechanical, photocopying, recording, scanning, or otherwise without written permission from the publisher. It is illegal to copy this book, post it to a website, or distribute it by any other means without permission.

This novel is entirely a work of fiction. The names, characters and incidents portrayed in it are the work of the author's imagination. Any resemblance to actual persons, living or dead, events or localities is entirely coincidental.

FC Gomez asserts the moral right to be identified as the author of this work.

FC Gomez has no responsibility for the persistence or accuracy of URLs for external or third-party Internet Websites referred to in this publication and does not guarantee that any content on such Websites is, or will remain, accurate or appropriate.

Designations used by companies to distinguish their products are often claimed as trademarks. All brand names and product names used in this book and on its cover are trade names, service marks, trademarks and registered trademarks of their respective owners. The publishers and the book are not associated with any product or vendor mentioned in this book. None of the companies referenced within the book have endorsed the book.

© 2023 | FC Gomez

First edition

ISBN: 978-1-962919-01-2

Editing by Daryl Lyon
Proofreading by Martin Schneider
Cover art by Rafal Kucharczuk

This book was professionally typeset on Reedsy.
Find out more at reedsy.com

*To all you wonderful readers,
I want to express my gratitude for embarking
on this odyssey with me.
Thank you for immersing yourselves in the world I've created, for investing in the characters' stories, and for sharing in the emotions, adventures, and discoveries that unfold within these pages.
It's your presence that truly makes them come alive.
You are the greatest gift an author can receive, and I am sincerely thankful for your support.
May this book resonate with you and inspire you.*

Take courage, my heart: you have been through worse than this.
Be strong, saith my heart; I am a soldier; I have seen worse sights than this.

— HOMER

Contents

PROLOGUE	iii
CHAPTER 1	1
CHAPTER 2	7
CHAPTER 3	14
CHAPTER 4	26
CHAPTER 5	37
CHAPTER 6	49
CHAPTER 7	59
CHAPTER 8	72
CHAPTER 9	78
CHAPTER 10	82
CHAPTER 11	85
CHAPTER 12	96
CHAPTER 13	106
CHAPTER 14	111
CHAPTER 15	123
CHAPTER 16	136
CHAPTER 17	140
CHAPTER 18	145
CHAPTER 19	149
CHAPTER 20	156
CHAPTER 21	165
CHAPTER 22	172
CHAPTER 23	186

CHAPTER 24	197
CHAPTER 25	210
CHAPTER 26	223
CHAPTER 27	232
CHAPTER 28	241
CHAPTER 29	247
CHAPTER 30	257
CHAPTER 31	263
CHAPTER 32	273
CHAPTER 33	281
CHAPTER 34	286
CHAPTER 35	293
CHAPTER 36	297
CHAPTER 37	307
CHAPTER 38	313
CHAPTER 39	322
Acknowledgments	329

PROLOGUE

April 10th

As Bus 38 from New Oxford Street rolled to a stop, Dr. Armaud Dupont noticed that it was a wet, drizzly night in central London. *Typique,* Armaud muttered as he daydreamed of his sunny childhood in Aveyron. He had moved to England twenty long years ago, and he was still not accustomed to the damp weather.

Upon exiting the bus, Dr. Dupont splashed down the puddled sidewalk and automatically followed the members' entrance into the British Museum. A handful of tourists were making their way out of the sprawling Greek entrance with cameras flashing for one last picture of the magnificent architecture.

Dupont paused and marveled at the quadrangle, the site of his second home for the majority of his life abroad. *After tonight, will this structure still stand? What about the wondrous objects housed inside?* Dupont shuddered as the last stragglers exited the golden gates out onto Great Russell Street. *The last souls to visit before the new era dawns.*

"Are you alright, Doctor?" The question startled Dupont and brought him back from his reverie. It was John Allen, the museum's head security guard.

"Yes, just thinking, Allen. My apologies," Dupont replied. He desperately needed Allen to be unobtrusive tonight.

"Would you like some tea, Doctor? You look quite pale, sir, if I might add." Allen's concerned stare reminded Dupont of his mission.

Breathe, it will all be well; this is my destiny, my dream.

"No, no my dear Allen. Your concern is heartening, but do not worry. I shall be in my office if you need me." As Allen nodded and turned to begin his nightly rounds, Dupont wondered if he would need to add some herbs to Allen's tea... it would not do if he were to wander into the exhibition at the wrong time.

Clearing his head, Dupont glanced at his watch; it was fifteen past five. Four more hours to go. Heading toward the stairs, he unconsciously hastened his pace, his heart racing. *Oh, what the world will say about my achievements! My name shall be in every newspaper on earth. The headlines will go wild after I finally prove my years of research. Of course, it would not have been possible without the Clarkson boy.* Dupont shook his head. No, this was his achievement and his alone. He had researched and studied for years, suffered through endless roadblocks, sacrificed countless hours, been humiliated by his peers and yearned so much for this moment. It was his time to shine.

His office was located in the Department of Scientific Research on level minus two. Dupont locked his door and absentmindedly paced about the room, glancing at the wall clock every so often. He separated some of the papers strewn on his desk for Leo Clarkson to sort and discard if necessary. His intern, a brilliant yet unassuming teenager, was eager to please and filled with boundless energy. Dupont was shocked to realize he would miss the kid who was uncomplaining and always ready for a puzzle or quandary.

Dupont sat heavily on his desk and reached down to prize open his secret drawer. He took out the package that had changed his life and placed it carefully, almost tenderly, on his cluttered desk. He noticed the manila envelope with his latest findings at the bottom of the drawer. He wrote a note on top of it and smiled to himself. *At least Leo will get some credit for this earth-shattering discovery.*

Dupont closed the drawer and stared at the package, his pulse racing and his hands shaking. Gingerly, he opened the small cardboard box and retrieved a golden jewelry bag that was adorned with patterns of black and silver. Inside was a leather armband, styled with Greek serpents, their heads intertwining toward a small amethyst located at the center of the band. Dupont twisted the armband while examining it. It was one of the most exquisite yet unpretentious pieces of jewelry that he had ever seen. He looked at the sender's address one more time.

2 Whitehall Ct, Westminster, London SW1A 2EJ, United Kingdom

Very peculiar. Dupont once again puzzled over the label. It was sent from The Royal Horseguards in London, just over a mile away. It would have been easier, not to mention cheaper since it was labeled as an express delivery, to walk over and deliver the package directly. The sender would have saved a few pounds by just strolling into the museum and hand delivering the small cardboard box. *Why had it been sent in the mail? And why was the sender's name missing?* Dupont could not imagine why someone would send such a priceless item to the British Museum by post, and not want to receive any credit for its discovery. Maybe it was stolen. *But why not keep it? Or sell it on the black market?* That had been Dupont's first thought. This precious armband would bring a hundred thousand pounds online, if not millions from relic enthusiasts and antiquarians.

This artifact reminded Dupont of Leo's essay on "The Mystical Elements of Ancient Cultures," in which Leo depicted an armband identical to the one Dupont currently possessed. His argument was that it had supernatural if not magical curative powers, capable of resurrecting its past owners and those connected with its origin. Dupont had been called mental, bonkers and a crazy old loon a few times in his life so much so that he was convinced his true genius and erudite ways were the cause of such derogation. And for that reason, he had accepted Leo's request to be the junior curator.

Leo had his own bizarre theories and fanatical behaviors, yet his charisma and personality made people consider his studies to be a passion instead of madness. Dupont enjoyed Leo's essay so much that he published it online. Of course, he could not give credit to Leo because he had not yet graduated from high school. However, Leo did not mind. Unlike most teenagers his age, he craved knowledge rather than power or attention. Dupont was the opposite.

He had lost track of time, and when he glanced at the clock, it was almost twenty past nine. He hurriedly got to his feet, stuffing the valuable armband into his jacket pocket. He only had one chance to sneak into the exhibit alone and stay for a prolonged period, and he was determined to make the most of his time. Wiping the sweat from his brow, Dupont started toward the long stairway, feeling that if he were to take the elevator, it would make him feel claustrophobic and nauseous.

After thirty-seven shaky steps, he emerged into Room 24: Living and Dying. As he passed by Hoa Hakananai'a imposing statue, he pulled the Greek armband from his coat. It felt warmer than it had been in the office. *Must be my sweat. Get a grip on yourself, old man. No need to feel heated.* On the contrary, Dupont was feeling colder by the minute, as if the warmth around him was diminishing.

Exiting rooms 26 and 27, Dupont finally reached his destination, Room 1: Enlightenment. He looked at his watch; it was 9:28. Only seconds to go now. He knew this museum by heart, could wander the exhibitions and galleries blindfolded. He also knew that Allen's nightly break was from 9:25 to 9:40. Those fifteen precious minutes were all the time he needed to enter the gallery unobserved and undisturbed. Dupont rubbed his hands, trying to warm them. He exhaled, and his breath came out in an icy puff.

At that moment the lights overhead were extinguished, and the room was suddenly very dark. Only the reflection from the moon lighted his eyes. A shadow shifted in the corner of the room. Dupont turned quickly, but nothing was there. He squinted and saw only emptiness. He shook his head. *It's just your eyes playing tricks on you.* Still clutching the Greek armband, he reached into his pocket and took out his phone. He clicked it once, and the screen lit up.

As he turned to look around the room, he sensed that he was not alone. Heart pounding in his chest, Dupont raised his phone to shine some light on his surroundings, but nothing was there. He lowered his phone slightly and squinted at the far wall which looked oddly dark. He stared intently, straining his vision, and after a moment felt terror crawling through his body. The dark shadows shifted, molding swiftly into a single form.

As the shape was materializing, forming itself in the gloom, Dupont could not blink his disbelieving eyes. He felt a flow of ice on the back of his neck, and his heart pounded so hard that he thought it would burst. He gaped. His phone fractured with a metallic screech. A scream formed in the back of his throat; his lungs gasped for air, as he made one desperate attempt at salvation. But the silence was his last company. With a flash of blinding light, Dupont's body vanished, and the armband he was clutching fell to the floor. It rolled to a stop inches from all that remained of Dr. Armaud Dupont, his cracked and shattered phone.

CHAPTER 1

April 25th

Leo Clarkson was wrapping up his lecture entitled "Magic During the Middle Ages," and he was very stressed. It wasn't the public speaking that made him anxious; it was that Dr. Dupont had not shown up for a second week in a row. *Maybe he is deadly ill and can't reach his mobile.*

Leo pondered why Dupont had been absent without giving a reason. It was very unlike him. Usually he was punctual to the point of obsession. *Maybe he had to leave the country unexpectedly, and had no time to leave a note.* According to the local gossip, Dupont had left the school early one evening and never returned. *Maybe he decided to become a hermit and live out his life in a cave somewhere.* He shook his head. Leo had realized something was wrong when he arrived tardy to Dupont's office, and found it unlocked. Leo had feared a monologue on the virtues of punctuality, but Dupont was not there. He had not even locked his door. *How odd.*

A door opened in the rear of the packed lecture hall, and the sound brought Leo back to the present. He looked up from his lectern. "Can anyone tell me what the difference is between an amulet and a talisman?" Only a few hands shot up. Leo chose a student in the third row.

"Talismans usually have power, and amulets do not," said the student. Leo smiled inwardly. *Close.*

"Thank you, Jessica. You are correct to assume that an amulet does not have magical properties. Amulets are usually considered good luck charms. Their symbolic nature is relative to where you live, and in which time period you reside. It is believed that amulets confer protection on their possessors. The exact wording is derived from Latin." Leo turned and wrote *"amuletum"* on the board behind him. "According to Pliny's *Natural History*, an amulet is an object that protects a person from trouble. However, in some religions, amulets do have power. These are considered folk religions or paganism. On the other hand, Christians believe that amulets have no power. In contrast, a talisman is an occult object that stems from religious or astrological practices. It directly connects the wearer with the spiritual world, and provides functions such as healing and protection."

A hand was raised in the back of the class. Leo pointed. "So, what's the difference then? They both have powers?" asked another student.

"Not quite, Luke. Talismans differ from amulets because they have several more complex magical powers besides protection." Leo allowed himself a smile now. "With the decline and fall of the Roman Empire, talismans became a wonder from the past; objects that held symbolic powers, not actual magical potential. Christianity's rise prompted the popularity of amulets, including various medals and sacramentals that were believed to defend against evil because of their association with a saint or archangel."

The bell rang, breaking Leo's spell on his enraptured audience. The lecture hall burst into a buzz of chatter and conversation. Some students began closing their laptops, while others made a beeline for the doors. "Ok, everybody," Leo yelled over the cacophony, "Dr. Dupont expects your essays to be emailed no later than 11 pm on Sunday."

CHAPTER 1

A small bubble of freshmen was crowding around Leo's lectern. He looked up and immediately froze. They were all staring at him – and they were all girls. In loud voices, they were asking questions while tussling with each other for space.

"When will Dr. Dupont be back?"

"I was sick last week; could I have an extension on my paper?"

"Is it supposed to be twelve-font double spaced in four pages? Or can it be changed to two pages written in single space?"

"What are your office hours this week?"

At the back of the group of the bubbling young women, university student, David Lyon, loudly cleared his throat. The deep throaty sound made Leo sigh with relief. He strode forward with his palms up. In one confident move, he shifted to face the small crowd. "Leo will be taking over some of the history lessons for Dr. Dupont for the foreseeable future. No extensions will be granted for this paper. Enjoy your weekend."

He flashed a half-smile, his teeth brilliantly white against his dark skin. "Keep it to four pages, Jessica. Leo will be available this evening from 5 to 6 pm in his study hall, so take advantage." David waved in dismissal. The group before him dispersed like flies swatted off a cake, and a few mumbling remarks could be heard.

Leo's posture relaxed. He started collecting his scattered papers and turned off the projector behind him. "Thank you, David. I owe you one." He noticed that David was smiling as he wiped the blackboard clean.

"I swear, you could talk to a mob of lions about myths and rituals. But one small pack of girls, and your whole body tenses up." Leo flushed a deep crimson; glad David's back was turned.

David was right, of course. Leo loved talking about history and magic and mythology; really, anything that fascinated him. Yet, his power of narration was not enough to quell his introvertive personality. David was the exact opposite. A confident extrovert, he was always in control of a crowd, no matter what age or gender. No wonder he wanted to become a professor and was now a teacher at the prep school.

David regarded Leo with a broad grin. "Good job today, Leo. I'm very impressed. We won't need to get a substitute; you're doing really well." He reached over and patted Leo's shoulder. Leo's flush had subsided, but he feared it would resurface. He turned quickly and said, "Thanks. But I'm not a professor, just Dr. Dupont's assistant."

"Not yet," David replied, "but after today, you should consider pursuing a degree in education when you go to university. You're very good at keeping the students focused and engaged. And you're doing a great job, considering…" his voice trailed off. Leo hadn't envisioned himself as a professor. He was glad he could help out the school during Dupont's absence, but he was not sure teaching was his passion. Leo loved spending hours reading old manuscripts and translating ancient texts into modern-day languages. He could spend the rest of his life happily living in a museum. He would only need food to survive. He could even sleep on the floor, as long as some prehistoric artifact was nearby.

David was shaking his head. Leo studied his face, admiring the tight curls of his chocolate brown hair. His eyes were a sparkling hazel-green, like moss on the forest floor. David looked up, and Leo quickly shifted his gaze to the clock behind David's head. "It's almost time for lunch. Do you have any plans, David?" Leo's heart stopped for a second, waiting for a reply.

"Not really. I was going to grab some food from the cafe next door. Want to join me?"

"Sure, why not." He tried to sound casual, but he was nervous that David might notice his forced informality.

They headed north toward Covent Garden. David chattered

CHAPTER 1

amiably about his classes. David was an undergrad student, unlike Leo, who had just turned eighteen. They attended King's College which was both a prep school and a university. Because of the connection, the students had the option of taking advanced classes if they wished, and that was why King's College was so inviting for Leo.

As they turned on Drury Lane, the conversation shifted to the gossip of the week. "Any news from Dr. Dupont?" asked David.

"Nothing," replied Leo sadly. The first three days of Dupont's absence seemed very abnormal but not worrisome, but the situation soon worsened after he had been MIA for more than a week, and no one had a clue to his whereabouts. Dupont didn't have a partner, so there was nobody the school could contact to locate him. His last surviving family was in France, and he hadn't left any reliable information about them at King's College. The staff liked to believe he had gone there for an impromptu holiday, but it was very unlikely. Dupont was not a social person, and he had been estranged from his family for a long time.

"I wonder when he'll come back," Leo said after a quiet pause.

"You mean, *if* he comes back," David answered dourly. Leo frowned, shocked. David registered the disturbance in Leo's features and rapidly tried to amend his words. "No, no, I didn't mean it that way. I just meant that maybe he hit a midlife crisis, and started a new life away from all the teenage drama and his monotonous routine."

Leo thought about that, then continued walking forward. *Maybe, but I doubt Dupont would have just packed his bags and left.* "He wasn't really the adventurous sort," Leo replied. There was a long pause before David changed his pace into a springy step.

"Have you checked out that new section of the library? I swear, it was built for you," he said. Leo smiled widely. David was so good at cheering him up. It must have been the fact that he grew up with four sisters, the baby boy of his family. David was great at noticing moods and shifting them appropriately. Leo ran a hand through his mahogany-colored hair, his fingers twisting the ringlets at the end. They were getting long, almost to his nose.

David noticed the gesture and in mock distress stated, "You're not thinking of cutting your beautiful mane, Leo? It will drive the freshmen mad." He winked, and Leo could not help but laugh. Some of the underclass girls were definitely showing too much interest in their new "substitute" teacher. David reached over and twisted a curl around his index finger, mimicking Leo's movement. Leo's heart faltered again, but he tried his utter best to remain cool and composed. David swiftly retrieved his finger and the ringlet bounced back into its original shape; only this time it covered Leo's glasses.

"Maybe it's too long," David said as he opened the cafe door and entered with confidence. Leo let the door shut in front of him. He hurriedly fixed his hair as he looked at his reflection in the window. He was wearing his long polo shirt underneath his sweater. Wanting to fit into the "adult scene" by assuming an air of nonchalance, he left it untucked.

There was a sudden movement at the top of the window, like a shadow shifting in the sunlight. Squinting, Leo stared. Unconsciously, he took a step forward, trying to scrutinize the shape. David's booming voice could be heard from outside the cafe. "You coming, Clarkson?" he bellowed. Startled, Leo blinked and the shadow was gone.

"Yeah, sorry, I thought I saw something." Leo shook his head, wiping his glasses with his sleeve. He moved his gaze to the top of the window. *I'm just a bit tense. It's nothing,* he thought to himself. He headed into the cafe. As soon as the door closed, the shadow reappeared.

CHAPTER 2

David sauntered to the west end of the building, finding an empty table in the packed space. Leo glanced around the room, surveying the place with interest. The cafe didn't feel as large as it was; it had a warm personal aura. The table David chose was ideal. It was surrounded by people, yet the chances of being overheard were slim.

There was a small group of girls by the exit, and one of them turned and smiled at Leo. He tried his best to look interested in the menu, hoping they would not approach him. After a few moments, he heard the door close and saw the group leave. He sighed in relief. Those moments did not occur often, but, much to Leo's chagrin, there were some brave souls who had dared before.

Leo groaned, recalling the first time it had happened. It was on a weekend, and he had been in the London Library. Leo was entranced by the humongous Latin book in front of him, his glasses falling almost to the tip of his nose. He heard a giggling sound directly in front of him. Disoriented, Leo looked up and was horrified to see a group of girls coming toward his desk. The boldest one approached him, striding forward while flirtatiously fluttering her eyelashes. Leo was so dumbfounded that he did not register what the girl said. She waited patiently, but he blankly stared back.

Moments passed, the girl flushed bright pink, and Leo finally thawed. "Sorry, I didn't catch that. Could you repeat it, please?" he said, trying to sound friendly instead of petrified.

The girl gave a laugh that sounded like a nervous snort instead of the coquettish chuckle she was going for. "Do you have any plans tonight? We're having a party in our dorm and want you to come." Leo swallowed and stammered incomprehensibly. Seeing his discomfort, she grabbed a notebook from her bag. "Here, just give me your number and I'll call you." She grinned. Leo nervously reached for his pen and, carefully avoiding eye contact, rapidly wrote down the number and closed the notebook to stop his hands from shaking. The girl swiftly grabbed it, turned in triumph to her group of friends, and they all strode out of the library. Leo took a long breath, which quieted his fluttering nerves. His heart rate returned to normal. After a moment, his face turned as red as a pomegranate. He realized that he had written down his mother's number instead of his own.

Back in the present, Leo shuddered with remembered shame and glanced at David, who was thankfully looking over the menu and not at him. Van Morrison was playing through the overhead speakers. David mumbled along to a verse of "Brown Eyed Girl". Leo sighed inwardly, his eyes unfocused.

He was lost in thought when David reached over and patted his hand. Leo's eyes widened as he controlled the urge to pull his hand away. David's touch was like a small fire, sending warmth throughout his body. "I'm sorry, Leo; this must be tough for you." David's eyes crinkled in consolation. "I'll go get us some sandwiches. Do you want a coffee?" He asked softly. Leo shook his head. He knew exactly what David was thinking, and why he sounded so consoling.

The first day they had met, Leo had almost spilled all of his secrets to David. *Almost.* It was last year's faculty holiday dinner at King's College. Trying to force him out of the library, Dr. Dupont had invited Leo, who had only been his assistant for five weeks. Leo guessed Dr.

CHAPTER 2

Dupont would have preferred to have his presence there rather than face a social gathering alone, and Leo didn't really mind. He had been looking forward to meeting his new professors, and the invitation made him feel as if he belonged.

He was not an intruder at the faculty's elite party. Leo was a teacher's assistant for the semester, but most of the department just assumed he was a talented pupil. Nearly all faces registered shock when Dupont smugly admitted that Leo was also interning for him at the British Museum.

David approached Dupont while Leo was getting drinks, so he had not noticed David's arrival. He was wearing a tan suit with a white collared shirt, casually unbuttoned to show his muscular neck. At six-foot-two, he was one of the tallest people in the gathering. They were chatting about one of David's classes, and when Leo returned, he patiently waited behind them to hand a mug to Dupont.

Finally, the old professor noticed Leo and introduced him to David, who casually scanned him, glancing up and down as if assessing him. He smiled widely. "Didn't know bow ties were coming back in style," he commented.

Leo shifted his gaze downward to scrutinize his chosen ensemble. He had picked a blue shirt with a maroon bow tie that matched his socks and shoes. Seeing David's elegant outfit made him accept that he was just a school boy.

"I'm kidding. Good of you for bringing some variety and color to this party. I'm tired of seeing black and white suits."

Leo looked around; almost everyone had the same monotonous outfit on. Even the women wore black or navy attire.

Dupont cleared his throat. "I'm going to get another drink, Leo. I'll see you tomorrow at 10 am sharp."

David chuckled while shifting his stance to relax against the wall, his right leg bending at an angle. "He means see you at 9:45 am at the latest." David snorted. "Say, how long have you been interning for him?"

"Almost six weeks now," Leo said with a bit of bravado.

David raised his glass in a toast. "Congratulations. You've lasted longer with him than all others combined." They toasted, and Leo sipped his drink.

"He's a good professor," Leo said defensively. "Too into discipline for my taste, but he's very attentive."

"Can't say anything against that. His study is next to mine. The man knows exactly when I'm taking my break, and what I'm having for lunch the next day." David gave a husky laugh. He seemed to be easy going and carefree, and Leo appreciated that.

The conversation shifted to research and work. Two years older than Leo, David was starting his second year of undergraduate study at the College. Physically, Leo noticed that he was a few inches shorter than David; but David was wide and stocky whereas Leo was slender and lean.

The conversation turned to their childhoods and their families. David was the youngest son of Olivia and Maurice Lyon. He had four older sisters who had treated him like a pet instead of a brother, dressing him up in all sorts of interesting and embarrassing outfits. Growing up with only girls did have its perks. He was well prepared to deal with drama, and was very patient.

On the other hand, Leo was the only son of Charlotte Evans and William Clarkson. Leo's maternal grandmother was Italian, and that's why Charlotte had named him Leonardo, after Leonardo DaVinci. Leo's paternal grandfather was an Englishman who had fallen in love with a young, vivacious nurse during the Allied invasion of Italy during World War II. Leo was born in Scotland, the home of his father's family. When Leo was five years old, his father left him and his mother without even a note. It completely broke Charlotte's heart and Leo never saw his father again. They moved south to London, and during the holidays, they visited Leo's grandparents in Salerno.

David was a good listener, and Leo was unaccustomed to speaking so much. The easy conversation had allowed him to open up about his long-buried pain regarding his father's abandonment.

Allowing the thoughts of his childhood to retreat into his memory, Leo shook his head as David returned with a glass of water, one coffee, and two sandwiches. He put the food down in the middle of the table and silently began to eat. It was a comfortable silence, one of understanding and compassion. Leo understood that David had made the connection between Dupont and his own father. David realized that Dupont's mysterious disappearance had harmed Leo in imperceptible ways.

Ever since their first meeting, they had become close friends. *Ah. Friends.* Leo didn't know when his view of David had changed, but now he idolized him and wished they were more than friends. *Impossible; look at him.* Contentedly, David was eating his food, sometimes looking up and beaming. Often, he flashed his disarming smile at strangers in the cafe. His smile had the power to melt hearts, and Leo was sure it worked well in David's personal life.

They talked about anything and everything, except for that subject. When they had been studying late one evening at the college and headed out for some much-needed coffee, David realized that Leo found that topic very embarrassing. Leo had ordered a latte, paying with cash. The girl behind the register handed him his receipt, and without looking at it, Leo indifferently shoved it into his jeans pocket. David chuckled all through the coffee break, sneaking glances at the cashier.

Once they left the café, David told Leo to look at the receipt. Leo read it, after which David took it. Leo's face flushed a vivid red. The receipt had a lipstick kiss next to a number, and the words "call me" with a winky face drawn in ink. On their walk back to campus, David's laugh continued to mortify him.

"Leo?" David murmured quietly. Leo looked up and saw that David was peering at him with a concerned expression. He moved the plates to the side from the middle of the table.

"I'm alright. Don't worry." Leo gave him a small smile, but David was not fooled.

"You know you can always talk to me. I'm here for you, mate."

Leo felt a surge of warmth move through his body. *I don't deserve his patience or his unwavering friendship.* "Thanks." He reached over and swiftly grabbed David's coffee. "Cheers!" Leo took a gulp and immediately regretted it. The bitterness of the acrid malt made him choke, and some of the liquid escaped through his nose.

David roared with laughter. Leo was so flustered that he could not breathe, and kept choking on the coffee. David leapt from his chair, still laughing as he banged on Leo's back.

Slowly, after what felt like an eternity, Leo cleared his throat, his eyes watering painfully. Chuckling, David went back to his side of the table. Leo grabbed his glasses and wiped them on his shirt. Leo tried to frown, partly in humiliation and partly in dismay. David patted Leo's hand amiably.

Leo's grumpiness vanished, and his shoulders tensed up slightly. David's laugh shifted into an affectionate smile as his eyes twinkled. Leo moved his gaze from David's hand to his eyes. He was looking right at him, his expression serene. Leo's heart skipped a beat, and he held his breath. The tension grew. It seemed unbearable.

Suddenly, a loud vibrating sound emanated from Leo's slacks. He froze, unaware of his surroundings. His eight seconds of bliss felt like eight minutes. The world around him dissolved into just their touching hands. The insistent buzzing shook him again. David moved his hand back to his side in a casual motion as if its previous placement

CHAPTER 2

had no meaning. Leo's shoulders slumped, and he reached into his pocket for his phone. Incredulous, he looked at the caller ID. John Allen from the British Museum.

CHAPTER 3

How did he get my number? "Hello?" Leo asked tentatively.

"Good afternoon. Could I speak to Mr. Clarkson, please?" John Allen's voice sounded tense and formal. Recalling the scrupulous security guard, Leo cleared his throat.

"Yes, this is he." Leo forced his voice to sound an octave lower than usual, in order to give the impression of being mature and respectable.

"Would you be so kind as to present yourself at the museum, as soon as possible? We have an urgent matter to discuss with you."

Leo looked at his wrist watch. It was half past two. He groaned internally. He could not deny a request from the British Museum; it was the best internship he could hope for. However, neither could he dismiss his recently acquired responsibilities at the school; especially not right before a paper was due. "Actually Mr. Allen, I have some duties to attend to this evening at King's College. I am unsure of…" he trailed off.

Leo's attention was diverted as David mouthed the words, "I'll cover for you."

"Erm, as it happens, I can head over right away," Leo replied, feeling relieved.

"Good. Are you near the museum? If so, see you in fifteen minutes." The phone call ended as abruptly as it had started.

"What's up?" David asked.

CHAPTER 3

"It was Allen, the head security guard at the British Museum. They want me to come over right away... he said it was urgent."

David's eyes widened and his eyebrows shot upwards. "It must be some sort of crisis if they want you there as soon as possible. I wonder what happened."

Leo's brow creased. He was a junior curator at the museum, one of many. Why did they need him specifically? Couldn't the issue be handled by someone higher up? Could it have something to do with Dupont's disappearance?

"Don't worry about helping the kids with their essays; I'm free this evening. I'll handle it," David commented. Nonchalantly, he went back to eating his sandwich, then glanced at Leo who was lost in thought. "You don't want to keep them waiting. You know how punctual they are."

Leo nodded. "You're right. Thanks again."

David chuckled. "Sure, you can pay me back with two coffees. And give me your bag while you're at it. I'll need some context clues to help your students with their papers."

Leo shook his head, smiling to himself. David was really considerate. *And soon we can get some coffee again.* With a bit of euphoria, he rushed down the stairs and headed out. His stride lengthened as he stepped onto Maiden Lane, engrossed in thoughts of the ensuing emergency. He did not discern the movement of a darkened outline shifting out of the shade from the cafe behind him.

Leo took a shortcut to the museum through Covent Garden, moving toward Betterton Street and then onto Drury Lane. He came to Museum Street, where he spotted the colossal Greek columns rising around the well-lit institution. Crossing the golden gates, he patted down his wild hair as he approached the members' entrance, where he assumed Allen would want to meet him.

The museum's head security guard appeared outside the entrance, tapping his foot. He was a short, stocky man with his hair parted in the middle and filled with copious amounts of gel. He was wearing his immaculate black and white suit, and Leo observed that he was looking around furtively.

Allen spotted Leo and headed straight for him. "Thank you for coming so quickly. We have some issues with inventory. This way, please." He gestured with a brisk movement that clearly meant no questions or small talk would be allowed.

They entered the members' vestibule, and moved silently into the impressive expanse of the entrance hall, heading toward the stairs. The tourists, gathered around Queen Elizabeth II's Great Court, took no notice of the two figures as they were striding past, for they were clicking and marveling at the striking architecture that encompassed them. Allen and Leo treaded down the stairs, emerging onto level minus two. Allen opened two immense metal doors and signaled Leo to follow him. They stepped into a long dark storehouse, and Leo realized that this was where the museum kept many of the magnificent objects that required restoration or examination. One of the duties of a museum curator was the delicate work of caring for these majestic paintings and sculptures. Art restoration was essential to preserve the integrity and value of an original work. It was a curator's duty to protect cultural collections and ever since Leo could remember, he had been fascinated by the techniques used to conserve the multiple artwork.

Leo squinted in the dimly lit room. Throughout his internship, he had grown accustomed to the gloom, since the absence of brightness allowed the artwork some respite from the artificial lights of exhibits. Allen and Leo progressed farther into the storage room. As they walked, Leo, feeling at ease, ran his hands over the boxes. In the presence of art, his mind relaxed automatically, and his emotions became harmonious. He could only replicate that feeling of bliss

CHAPTER 3

after reading old books, completing a strenuous puzzle, or going on cross-country runs.

Allen stopped abruptly and turned to face him. Leo was startled and almost crashed into the box behind him. He was several inches taller than the security guard, and it made him uncomfortable to have to angle his neck down.

"We're looking for a missing object. Can you tell me what it is, Leo?" Allen asked in a rough voice.

"Excuse me?" Leo stammered, blinking in confusion.

Allen sighed. He sounded tired. "We need to do an inventory of this section of the gallery." He pointed behind him, to where a portion of the exhibit was blocked off with yellow DO NOT CROSS tape. "We've already done multiple sweeps, but I have orders from above that we need you to do one as well."

Leo stared uncomprehendingly, waiting for another explanation. Allen remained silent and self-assured, his gaze untroubled. Leo cleared his throat. "Ok, I can do a register. No problem. By what time do you need it, Mr. Allen?"

Allen's expression softened slightly. "By tonight. It's urgent." He picked up a box from the desk behind him, and gave it to Leo. Without another word, he turned and headed out of the dusky room.

At first Leo was disoriented and befuddled. Nevertheless, after a long moment, he smiled. *What a treat,* he thought. There were very few people in the world who would have considered it a treat to spend several hours in a dark room alone, but Leo was one of them. He would have unlimited time to explore and examine the objects around him.

He surveyed the plastic box he was holding, weighing it carefully. It was very light. He placed it delicately on the desk in front of him and opened it to inspect the contents. Inside there was a headlamp, a couple of batteries, a sheet of paper and two pencils. He put on the headlamp, adjusting the length of the strap to his head. It served as a headband as well, taming his unruly hair in a way brushes never could. He clicked the headlamp once, igniting a single beam outwards. Next, he scanned the single sheet of paper. It was a list of every object that needed to be marked. Leo beamed and commenced his work.

Outside the metal double doors by the storeroom, the intruding shadow could hear the shuffling and unpacking of boxes. It shivered with annoyance, waiting patiently for the trifling humans to finish their little game of hide and seek. Humans were slow, feeble, and so dense that they didn't even know what they were searching for. *Pathetic.* Their puny capabilities could never comprehend the power that was within their reach. Even now, after fourteen days, they still couldn't sense the menace that inhabited their building.

The electricity outside the storage room on level minus two sizzled with supplemental current. This inconsequential human was the last witness needed to conclude the game. The shadow was enraptured. The lights overhead started visibly palpitating with his anticipation. Once this mortal finished his trivial search, the shadow would have no obstacles in his way. He could commence his plan. The black silhouette raced up the wall and vanished.

After nearly four hours of meticulous work, Leo was still feeling ecstatic. The second pencil was almost down to its core, his neat sheet was full of scribbles, and his headlamp burned as brightly as when he had begun his task.

Leo sat down on the floor of the storeroom and sighed happily. He removed the headlamp from his forehead; it left angry red marks on his skin. He looked over the sheet once more. *All done.* Every object on the list was secure and accounted for. His phone buzzed. It was a text from David: YOU OWE ME. BIG TIME.

Oops. Leo checked his watch; it was almost eight o'clock. So, the freshmen had taken advantage of today's office hours. *Poor David.* Leo

CHAPTER 3

grimaced, but then he remembered David's resounding laugh at Leo's coffee incident in the cafe, and his frown turned into a grin. *We're even now.* He checked his phone, and noticed two missed calls from Allen. He dialed the number, and Allen's hoarse voice answered. "Leo. How was it?"

"Mr. Allen, sir, I'm done with the sweep. Every object was in place and unharmed." Leo could hear the sigh of relief from the other end of the line.

"Very good. Meet me in Dupont's old office. I have something to discuss with you." Allen ended the call.

Well, he is nothing if not succinct. Leo folded the registry sheet and placed the headlamp back in the plastic box. He walked slowly out of the storage room, wishing it had taken longer for him to finish. If he could do multiple sweeps every week, he definitely would.

The massive white metal doors groaned as Leo closed them. He squinted in the light. The room was dimly lit, yet its low glow felt as powerful as the sun. Leo closed his eyes for a moment, adjusting them. Once he felt it would be safe, he opened them a tad, perceiving that his vision was still a bit cloudy. He walked slowly toward the offices in the Center of Learning. His vision cleared by the time he felt the change of the flooring.

The museum was mostly covered in granite with stone flooring, but the offices were carpeted. He picked up his stride and reached Dupont's old office in a matter of minutes. The door was already open, and Allen sat in the heavy chair behind the desk, his back toward the door. Leo could barely make out that Allen was holding an object in his hands as he cautiously examined it. Leo knocked quietly, not wanting to disturb him.

Swiftly, Allen moved his hand to the inside of his jacket. His voice was less gruff now, his tone amiable. "Come in, Leo. Take a seat." He turned and gestured to the open seat across the desk. Leo walked in, peering around the office. It was nearly empty. Most of Dupont's possessions had been cleared out, and were now stored in the boxes strewn across the room. Dupont's academic books were the only objects allowed to remain on the shelves. Leo sat apprehensively, his earlier glee stored deep inside him.

"I have some lamentable news. Unfortunately, as you well know, Dr. Dupont has been missing for fourteen days now. I saw him two weeks ago here in this very building..." Allen trailed off, with a bit of pain in his voice. "Anyway, the museum has a strict policy. One week of absence without prior notice is concerning. It could be excused for those highest in our department, and yet, Dr. Dupont has been gone for two weeks. The museum considers this unacceptable. Our board of directors has reason to believe Dr. Dupont will not return to work. We will be searching for a new senior curator, and Dr. Dupont's work will be shelved for the foreseeable future." Leo's eyes widened with shock, and his hands clenched the arms of the chair.

"Nevertheless," Allen continued, "we wish to retain you as a junior curator. We shall place you with a new senior keeper as soon as possible." Leo looked at the boxes dispersed around the floor. Half a year of work with Dupont, carelessly tossed into unmarked packages.

Sensing his tension and pain, Allen said, "You might be able to continue your internship research if your supervisor approves it, but that is dependent on his decision, not mine. You will still have access to the museum and the research center while we find you a supervisor."

Leo's eyes were watering. He felt as if he had been punched. *All those hours, all that work. And Dr. Dupont... How sad.*

Allen took a long breath as if trying to phrase his next words. It looked as if he were having an internal battle. "We required a sweep tonight in order to prove that nothing had gone missing. The board needed to be absolutely certain." Looking uncomfortable, he added, "Leo, I know you. You're a good kid. You deserve to know the truth."

CHAPTER 3

He paused. "What I tell you now must never leave this office." Leo nodded in speechless acknowledgement.

Allen put both his hands on the desk, clenching and unclenching them. He seemed lost in thought. The delay was unbearable; it made Leo's heart pound.

"I was on duty the night Dupont disappeared. I didn't hear anything strange, so I didn't have a reason to suspect foul play." He shook his head sadly. "I feel like it is my duty to take care of the museum, including everybody and everything inside it." Allen's voice was soft now, almost a whisper.

"When I finished my first break of the night, I noticed that the lights in Room 1, The Enlightenment Gallery, were out. Before I headed down, I checked the control room, but there was no tampering. I figured it was a break in the voltage. Uncommon, but not unheard of. I turned on the lights and went to check the room. Everything seemed fine. Nothing was out of the ordinary.

"However, as I checked the room closely, I found Dupont's phone on the floor, completely destroyed. The screen was unreadable, as if it were burnt from the inside. I looked around but Dupont was nowhere to be seen, and it was then that I got worried. His office was empty. He wasn't in the research center or in any of the rooms. There was no trace of him anywhere.

"I got my team to examine the night's footage, following Dupont's every move since he had entered the building. Dupont left his office, moved up the stairs and exited Room 27 to enter Room 1. And that's when the trail went cold. We couldn't find him after that. No windows were opened, no doors left ajar, nothing. It was as if he had vanished into thin air."

Allen was shaking his head, puzzlement and torment in his eyes. "I'm sorry, kid." Slowly, he stood up as he said these words. He closed the distance separating him from Leo and patted his slumped shoulder.

Then he straightened and resumed his efficient, composed manner.

"Here," he said, taking a small object from his suit. "This was next to Armaud's phone the night he vanished." Allen placed what seemed like a thin strap on Dupont's old desk. "I thought you might want to keep something of his. Initially, we weren't sure to whom it belonged. We checked our archives, and it does not belong to the museum. Your sweep confirmed it this evening." Allen took two deliberate steps toward the door and reached for the handle. He looked back at Leo who sat rigid in his chair, his eyes staring at the object without truly seeing it. With a sigh, Allen left the room.

Leo was beyond disturbed. So that's what really happened to Dupont. But how? Who did it? Why would they do it? He assumed Allen's anecdote would provide answers to Dupont's mysterious disappearance, but instead of that, more questions materialized. Searing questions. Why Dupont? And how did it happen in the museum? If whoever did this was planning a kidnapping, it would have been easier to wait for Dupont to leave and assault him in the empty, nocturnal streets of London. The museum seemed an unlikely place for an abduction. It was well guarded, secure.

Unless this was an inside job. Leo wondered nervously. *No, it couldn't be an inside job.* If it was, Allen would not have strayed from the public pretense of the disappearance. There was no need to tell Leo the truth. Allen's revelation proved the museum's lack of involvement. Someone had abducted Dupont, there was no other explanation. If Dupont wanted to disappear, he could have just left, fled the country. The board of directors could not involve the police. There was no theft, no ransom note, no evidence of breaking and entering. *And what was that about the missing object?* Allen confirmed that every artifact in question was accounted for.

Maybe the museum assumed it was a burglary orchestrated by Dupont. But, upon second thought, this seemed unlikely. Dupont

CHAPTER 3

enjoyed limitless access to the entire museum. If he wanted to steal something, he could have easily requested that the piece be sent to the Rijksmuseum in Amsterdam, or to the MET for restoration. Once in transit, he could have taken the object for himself and discreetly disappeared.

Leo knew Dupont was an ambitious man, but he was not covetous. Dupont wished for power, but it was power of knowledge that he craved. Nothing as mundane as money. *So, who took Dupont and why?* He must have been their target, since everything was accounted for. Leo was dumbfounded.

Ever since Allen's declaration, Leo barely noticed his surroundings. Now, he finally realized what he was staring at. His mind was so lost in thought that he hadn't seen the object clearly. Allen's parting gift was a slender leather armband with Greek serpents intertwined around an amethyst. Leo stared at it, incredulous. *This can't be real.* The object was beautifully crafted, probably millennia old. What did Allen mean when he said that this object was Dupont's?

A realization came to Leo. This was the object that caused the commotion in the museum. The board probably assumed Dupont was stealing it, but could not locate it in their archives. Its owner was a mystery. To the average eye, the slender armband could have passed as being ordinary. It looked faded and worn, as if it had been utilized daily. It was exquisite to be sure, but its appearance did not seem to merit being housed in a world-famous museum. After days of scrutiny, the other curators must have concluded that it was a personal item from Dupont's many travels; the object's true pricelessness was obscured.

Leo was shaking now. The intertwining snakes… he knew what their presence meant. His breath accelerated as he understood exactly what the armband signified, and to *whom* it belonged. He sprinted out of the office with the talisman in his hand, remembering long hours in the London Library, pondering the symbolism of lost artifacts and the possessions of powerful deities. He had based his entire term paper for Dupont's class on several talismans, ranging from The Eye of Horus to Japan's Omamoris. His brain recognized this armband straight away. With rising trepidation, Leo registered its mystifying meaning.

He did not have time to focus on the questions that raced through his mind. How did Dr. Dupont get this? Why didn't he tell Leo, who had introduced Dupont to the mystical world of supernatural objects? Instead, he concentrated on more pressing concerns. He knew the museum inside and out, like the back of his hand. He could find every object with his eyes closed. Before today, it never crossed his mind that a small piece of *her* could be here. No wonder Dupont headed straight to Room 1. That's where the Greek statues were stored.

Suddenly, Leo paused, wondering if this talisman was connected to Dupont's disappearance. Allen had said the armband was found mere centimeters from Dupont's burnt phone. Leo's hands started shaking. This could be hazardous, even disastrous. On the other hand, this would provide all the answers to his burning questions. *That's if it works.*

Leo's research was mostly theoretical, nearly impossible to prove. But now, he held, in the palm of his hand, actual physical proof. He flexed his arms and took a deep, steadying breath. *I can do this.* He resumed his sprint to the storeroom. Behind him, a light bulb shattered in the far corner of the gallery.

By the broken shards of glass, the shadow curled in anger. *So, this precocious child knew.* The shadow was enraged. He had lingered in this pestilent place for the irksome humans to dispose of this hindrance. None of those idiotic mortals understood the power that the armband could unleash. And yet, this insignificant speck of dust did. Another light bulb fractured, its light dissipating. The shadow was pleased that the building was empty and dim. His presence would remain unnoticed as he shifted about following the boy. This creature was mortal, breakable. He would be easily overpowered – not even a challenge. The energy it would take to stop him would be worth the effort. *Unless he woke her.*

A row of light bulbs exploded overhead. No, the boy must be stopped before it happened. The shadow vanished upwards, rapidly scanning the museum. He moved through the darkness like a water snake slithering in a river. Finally, he found it, two floors above and directly south of his prey. The unnerved silhouette gleamed as if his darkened shape could reflect malice and excitement. The lights went out as the gallery was shrouded in darkness.

CHAPTER 4

Panting, Leo reached the white doors, his palms sweating and his heart racing. If Allen hadn't allowed him a sweep of the storage room, he would not have noticed that there was a pristine, sealed timber crate from The Metropolitan Museum of Art. It was seven feet long and three feet wide. The words "HANDLE WITH CARE" were inscribed in bold, red letters directly above the crate's label, which was inscribed with the same intertwining snakes as the armband.

Leo wiped his brow with his sweater sleeve and tried to smooth back his hair. He wanted his vision to be clear and unobstructed. This moment was the culmination of his entire research – no, of his life!

Leo took a long, deep breath and kneeled next to the enormous wooden crate. Gingerly, he placed the talisman on top of the immense box. He closed his eyes and tried to steady his pounding heart. He waited a few moments in utter silence. Nothing happened. Leo concentrated harder, but he could only make out the slight buzz of electricity that was nearby, most likely from the lights from outside the storeroom.

Please, please, please. He hoped with all his might; yet the silence endured. He opened his eyes slightly, wishing there were some alterations to his surroundings. The room was exactly as it had been the minute before. Disappointment rushed through his body. *This*

CHAPTER 4

won't work. I was kidding myself.

With a sigh, he retrieved the armband from the crate and held it in his hands, inspecting it. As he peered at the violet amethyst, the crate in front of him gave a small shake. Then suddenly, it trembled violently as if trying to break apart. Leo rose to his feet and gasped. As he did, the timber box gave a great groan, and the top of the crate flew across the room. Leo fell back with a cry of fright, accidentally tripping over a metallic package.

He puffed as he toppled backwards, dropping his arms to protect himself from the fall. He released the armband, which landed a few centimeters behind the titanium, meter high cube. Leo crashed down, hitting his head on the floor as his legs splayed in the air. He took a moment to assess the damage. Gently, he prodded his head, feeling for lumps. Apart from minor bruises, he did not think much damage had been done. His glasses were askew, and he automatically aligned them. As his vision cleared, he remembered what had caused his fall. *Oh, shit.* Tentatively, Leo looked around the metal cube and focused on the broken crate. Where the wooden crate had stood, only splinters remained.

A statuesque figure was standing over the shattered crate while looking around the room. Leo gasped, and the figure turned rapidly in his direction, her movements resembling those of a panther. She was a tall, lean woman. Her eyes were greenish-gray with a tinge of sea blue. Her hair was dark gold with light brown shades. It curled about her face and down to her chest in loose ringlets. She was wearing bronze chest armor that accented her powerful figure. A reddish-gold cape was draped across her back and tumbled to her feet. Her leather skirt almost reached her knees, and her shin guards were the same bronze as the rest of her armor. Her sandals extended to her calves in intricate swirls, and her galea lay at an angle on her head, the helmet exposing her exquisite face. A coarse, dark, red mane formed a line from the forehead to the neck of the galea.

Her jaw was clenched and her glare reflected uncertainty, as if she were assessing an opponent. Her right hand was gripped over a sharp spear, ready to strike. In her left she held a bronze shield with the face of a screaming woman with serpents in her hair. This could only be one person. *Correction: goddess.*

Leo was paralyzed. His mind screamed for him to run, but he was frozen. The Greek Goddess of Wisdom, Athena, took one step toward Leo. She was as graceful and dangerous as a leopard nearing her prey. Her gray-green eyes, drifting slowly over every inch of his body, scrutinized him from head to toe. Her gaze fell on the armband near Leo's hand. He felt he was being analyzed. It was as if with one glance this divine warrior knew exactly what his strengths and weaknesses were. And how to kill him.

Leo minutely shifted his weight. Athena's head snapped in his direction so quickly that his body moved involuntarily backwards. She took two steps forward, towering above him. Eyes narrowed, she noted the metal cube that had caused him to fall.

Athena spoke slowly, but Leo was too stupefied to understand. Fascination mingling with trepidation, he realized that she had spoken in Attic Greek, the purest form of the language. As Athena waited, Leo's mouth opened and closed wordlessly, struggling to reply in the same language. Athena shifted her head from side to side as if trying to get a glimpse into Leo's brain. She stopped after a few moments, and her posture relaxed a fraction.

"Who are you?" she asked in a slow, clear voice, flawlessly enunciating every word.

Leo could feel his body loosen, and knew that Athena somehow had calmed him. "I... umm... I'm Leo. Leo Clarkson," he stammered, unsure how to address this unearthly being. Athena's expression did not change.

CHAPTER 4

A sudden boom made Athena's head snap upwards, her posture tense and ready to strike. Leo looked around. It sounded as if a massive rock had been shocked with a bolt of electricity. The storage room was in the middle of the museum on the bottom floor. Whatever that noise was, it came from inside the building. A cavernous roar erupted overhead, and Athena sprinted toward the door.

Leo blinked. What was that noise? He couldn't understand why, but he had the sudden urge to dash after Athena. He stood up and followed the retreating warrior. Her cape billowed like a flash of sunshine behind her. She stopped in front of the white metallic doors and hurriedly threw them open. After a momentary pause, Leo rushed after her, trying to close the gap between them. They bolted up the long stairs, following the receding roar.

Athena arrived at the Great Court only seconds before Leo. She stood as still as a statue, her muscles flexing as she surveyed the scene in front of her. Leo, panting with effort, stopped one step behind her. He looked around the huge marble hall, and his mouth dropped in disbelief and horror.

At the center of the British Museum sat the largest covered public square in Europe, the Queen Elizabeth II Great Court. Twenty years after its remodel, the Great Court became a two-acre space enclosed by a spectacular glass roof with a gigantic tube-like reading room in its center.

As incredulity transformed into alarm, Leo saw a beast at the far side of the white marble court. "What is that?!" He murmured to Athena, his voice crackling with agitation.

Athena was assessing the beast with her keen eyes. Quietly, she moved her spear toward her shield. Noiselessly, she pulled her bronze helmet down over her head and glared across the court. The helmet had a horizontal slit through the middle, allowing her eyes an unobstructed view of the creature in front of her. "Manticore" she said, her voice expressionless.

Leo's lunch threatened to resurface. He felt the blood drain from his face. Athena extended her right hand toward him, palm up. Feeling nonplussed, Leo looked at her. Athena's hand shook with impatience. *What does she want? A high five?*

"The armband," she whispered. Leo remembered dropping the precious talisman in the storeroom during his fall. The manticore's growl could be heard from across the room. Athena stared at Leo, her combative eyes gleaming with expectation.

"I'm sorry. I dropped it," he stammered.

Athena blinked once, her expression unchanged. "Do you know how to wield a sword?" she asked, her voice calm but with a hint of frustration. Leo quickly shook his head. Athena set her jaw. "Here," she said as she unloaded the heavy shield from her left arm. "This will protect you."

She swiftly surveyed their surroundings, assessing the immediate perils. As she did so, she strapped the aegis to Leo's arm. "I need you to go and get it. Run." She enunciated the last word with urgency, and Leo knew his life depended on that armband. He nodded, and Athena let go of the shield. It was very heavy, close to forty pounds. Leo felt his arm drop, and he raised the aegis with both arms, astonished at how effortlessly Athena had maneuvered it.

As he turned to run, he saw another manticore entering the Great Court. Athena spun around to face the approaching beasts. She rotated the spear in her hand, pointing it at the beasts.

Leo dashed back to Room 24, running at full speed toward the west stairs. Hearing a hum of electricity as he reached the first step, he turned just in time to see a bolt headed in his direction. With a massive effort, he raised the shield in front of him. The aegis absorbed the blow, making it ricochet back to his attacker. Leo risked a peek at his assailant, but he didn't see anything. He kissed the top of the shield,

CHAPTER 4

and resumed his downward sprint.

He was panting loudly as he approached Level Minus One. The shield vibrated slightly as if sounding a warning. Instinctively, Leo raised the shield at the exact time a second bolt struck. The aegis deflected it in the nick of time. Leo continued his downward rush, holding the shield to his side and bending low to protect most of his body. Only his feet were visible below the shield.

He reached the opened, massive doors and ran straight in, tripping over boxes as he rushed by. He saw the armband lying where he had dropped it, in front of the shattered wooden crate and next to the cube he had tripped over. His outstretched hand reached for it.

He heard the buzz before he had time to react. The shield felt suddenly heavier, and his weight shifted back as if pulled by the aegis. The bolt flashed past the spot where Leo's hand had been mere seconds before. With a screech, it collided with the metal cube. A shower of razor-sharp titanium fragments erupted around the storeroom. Leo crouched, putting the shield in front of him. Breathing heavily, he held onto the aegis for dear life. His muscles ached from the strain as the shards hit the shield like a wave crashing against the shore. The blows struck unrelentingly, but the shield held its ground.

Leo felt the temperature around him drop, and his breath came out in icy puffs. After what felt like ages, the tempest abruptly ended, and in unison the dim overhead lights shattered, leaving the room in darkness. He remained in his crouch, the shield covering his body. The silence around him continued. He waited to hear the hiss that signaled an attack, but nothing could be heard.

After a moment, he felt warmer. He tugged on the shield, and it yielded easily. It felt much lighter than when he first held it. He stood up and squinted into the darkness. The only light he could see came from the vestibule at the far side of the room.

He heard a roar and the sound of steel striking stone, and he remembered his task. On his hands and knees, he patted the floor around him to find the armband. Titanium fragments cut into his hands. Cursing, he continued the search.

Finally, he felt a small, cold stone surrounded by leather, and his bleeding hand closed around the armband. He thrust the armband into his pocket and raced toward the light, colliding with various objects as he ran. The lights around the stairs had diminished as if the current somehow had been sucked out.

As he neared the top of the west stairs, a movement caught Leo's attention. A silhouette seemed to be lingering in the shadows, shifting according to the growls and scrapes heard from the fight. Leo could make out that it wasn't an ordinary shadow; its movements were unnatural, too fluid to be a reflection.

A loud crack emanated from the court, followed by a roar of pain and anguish. The dark silhouette expanded visibly as if enraged. The dimmed lights around the stairs fractured instantly.

Leo raised the shield to protect his head from the falling glass. The shadow turned toward the stairs, and Leo locked eyes with the silhouette. He felt utter terror as he stared at the figure. It looked as if it were made out of flames. The shadow's arms curled with long blazing fingers. If hatred and malice were palpable, Leo felt sure that this would be the visible representation. Snarls were heard from the continuing fight in the Great Court. The shadow followed the noise and vanished.

Leo put his hand on his head to see if he had a fever. *Maybe this is all a dream. Maybe I hit my head pretty hard, and I'm hallucinating.* As if in response, the aegis strapped to his arm tugged him forward, urging him on. *Ok. This is definitely not real,* Leo thought as he finished his run up the stairs.

He paused as he exited Room 24 and moved into the marble entrance hall. Rubble was strewn across the court. Athena's back was to

CHAPTER 4

Leo, and she was guiding three manticores away from the entrance, incessantly prodding them with her spear. Roaring in displeasure, one of the large beasts tried a swipe with its enormous paw. Athena thrust her spear at the approaching monster, and the sound was that of steel on stone. At first glance, Leo thought the beasts resembled living lions, but now he realized that they were actually made of a sandy brown stone.

The one farthest away from Athena menacingly twitched its tail. Leo recoiled. It wasn't a lion's tail; it was a scorpion's tail. The body was indeed of a lion, yet its fearsome face resembled a human's scowl. The creatures growled in unison, baring long fangs and several rows of serrated teeth. Athena danced backwards and the manticores followed suit, their huge paws shaking the floor with each step they took. Their claws were abnormal, as long as kitchen knives and probably as sharp.

Leo gulped. The closest manticore risked another step, and its tail flashed forward in an attempt to strike. Athena's movement was lighting fast; she cut into the tail with a quick arc of her spear, severing the poisonous tip. The manticore roared, and its pack viciously attacked, shooting the tips of their tails like arrows. Athena shifted her arms to hold the spear in front of her like a slender shield, lithely deflecting the tails. In one nimble motion, she returned the spear to an attack position. The cut tail of the manticore regenerated without a scratch, and the creature prepared for another attack.

"Manticores are indestructible. Their name was derived from mantichoras... meaning man-eater." Leo cursed out loud. All three beasts turned to assess him, their murderous eyes blazing red. Athena stepped forward in a flash and impaled the closest manticore through its snarling mouth. The beast seemed momentarily stunned and tried to attack with its tail, but Athena was quicker. She brought the spear down in a semi-circle, severing the head of the enormous beast. With a loud crack, the manticore disintegrated into rubble.

Growling, one of the remaining beasts lunged at Athena. The other raced toward Leo, baring its teeth. Not believing that he could defeat it, Leo lifted the shield. He felt the manticore crash into him, throwing him backward onto the marble floor. His right leg fractured with the impact, and he cried out in anguish. The animal was on top of him, its weight crushing him. He heard the snarls and strikes as the manticore prodded the shield for a weak spot. Leo screamed in agony.

Suddenly, he heard a whooshing sound and the weight was lifted from him. Under the shield, he saw a spear skewered in the manticore's jaw. Just inches from Leo, the beast was twitching its colossal frame and writhing in pain. Its tail was sweeping wildly, haphazardly shooting poisonous arrows. Leo pushed himself into a sitting position and raised the shield, bringing it down with all his might onto the beast's head. As the shield crashed through the stone, the manticore instantly fragmented.

Leo grunted in relief and pain. He frantically looked around and saw with horror that another manticore was exiting the Persian exhibit and rapidly stalking toward Athena. She looked to her spear, which was twenty yards away, then stared at the approaching beast as it bared its teeth and charged.

Athena was slightly crouched, her knee bent forward as if ready to meet the monster. As it lunged, Athena reached across her body and pulled her short sword out of its scabbard. The steel hit the manticore's jaw, shattering it upon impact. Athena stood unmoving as pebbles rained down around her. She snapped her head to the side, and Leo was appalled to see the shadow.

With a sudden hiss, the shadow shot bolt after bolt at Athena. She whirled backwards, lifting her short sword in defense against the bolts. Leo heard a frightening growl and turned his attention to the Persian exhibit. Bile filled his throat as another manticore crashed out of the gallery at full speed. Its body collided with the opposite wall in its sharp turn, then it lunged at Athena.

"Watch out!!" Leo screamed, but he was a second too late. Athena turned to face the beast and raised her left arm. But her shield was not strapped to her arm, and Leo heard a deafening crunch. The manticore's teeth bared into Athena's flesh and hurled her around until she landed at its feet.

As the two tangled bodies hit the marble floor, the edge of Athena's sword erupted from the manticore's side. With a booming roar, its jaws unclenched momentarily, and Athena was able to maneuver from under the beast's grasp. She jumped upwards, rapidly raising her short sword. With all her strength, she brought the sword down, bending her body to behead the beast. The animal disintegrated, and Athena was left half-kneeling over a pile of rocks. Leo looked at Athena's arm and vomited. Blood was pouring from the many puncture wounds, and it was obvious that many of her bones had splintered. Unsteady on her feet and looking ghostly pale, she rose.

The shadow hungrily stared at Athena. Leo could feel the deadly energy emanating from the darkness it reflected. Another roar caused both Leo and Athena to glance toward the Persian exhibit as one last manticore made its fatal approach. Athena dashed toward Leo, clutching the short sword while her useless left arm swayed like a bloody rag at her side. "The armband!!" she bellowed, as the shadow shot electric blasts at her darting figure.

Leo gaped at the charging manticore and reached into his pocket for the talisman, his hands shaking uncontrollably. Athena was sprinting toward him as fast as was physically possible. He tossed the armband with all his remaining strength. Athena dropped the sword as she jumped up to catch the talisman. Her fingers closed on the leather edge of the armband. When her feet touched the floor, she tensed in anticipation.

Half a second later, the manticore collided with her. Leo expected her body to be crushed by the rushing stone monster, but Athena was intact as she stopped the beast's rush. Her left arm healed as soon as she touched the talisman. She wrapped her body across the beast, and squeezed with all her divine strength. With a screech, the manticore burst into a storm of stone pebbles. She held its decapitated head in her grasp and crushed it until it became sand.

The lights around the museum burst into a whirl of luminescence. Leo saw Athena rush toward her spear. She grabbed it and twisted her body to hurl it at the wall where the shadow had lurked moments before. The spear whooshed in a flawless line. Leo was sure it would hit its intended target. The shadow reacted faster than was humanly possible, moving out of the way a mere instant before the spear penetrated the wall. Malevolently, it glared at them. In a flash, it raced out of the museum, leaving in its wake of destruction piles of broken stones and fresh blood.

CHAPTER 5

The Greek goddess was staring at the exit where the shadow had vanished, her eyes reflecting hatred and loathing. Leo cringed at her expression and glanced at his leg. He regretted it immediately. The blood was pooling under him, and his leg was sprawled at an awkward angle. He screamed, but his cry was cut short as Athena rushed at him and put her hand over his mouth. Her eyes were calm as she signaled him to be still. Leo nodded, his face wet with sweat. Athena kneeled next to him and, placing her left hand firmly over Leo's heart, she started chanting under her breath. The amethyst in her right hand glowed bright purple as she chanted. Leo was so mesmerized that he momentarily forgot the pain in his shattered leg. Then he realized it wasn't his fascination that made him disregard his anguish, he didn't feel pain anymore. He risked a glance at his smashed leg. It was normal, its previous dreadful state replaced by a straight line. The only sign of harm was the blood that remained on the floor and stained his pants. Seconds later, the blood had vanished as well.

Tentatively, he bent his leg, and it moved without any strain. Athena released him and placed her hand on the floor as the amethyst glowed even brighter.

The damage to the Great Court vanished instantly. The columns that had been disfigured by the manticores' assault returned to their original shape. The eight piles of rubble were transformed into distinct clouds of sand that faded toward the Persian gallery. The wall that had been pierced with her spear became smooth.

Leo was astonished as he looked around the court. There was not a trace of the damage and devastation that had occurred only moments before. He was about to ask a question when he saw the look on Athena's face. She was surveying the building, her eyes missing nothing. She silently placed her mystical talisman across her left bicep. The armband seemed to glow as it securely attached itself to her skin. She snapped her fingers, and her spear materialized at her side; her short sword was already in her scabbard. Her intense stare was fixed on the west stairs. "We need to go," she said, reaching for the bronze shield on the ground.

Leo heard footsteps, and understood the urgency. "Do you know of another exit?" she whispered. Leo nodded. He got to his feet and was surprised by how agile he felt; it was as if his leg had never been broken. He started running toward the north side of the Great Court, and Athena instantly followed. They turned into Rooms 26 and 27: North America and Mexico, then raced to the stairs, jumping down two by two.

Once they reached Level Minus One, Leo spotted one of the secure member exits. With all his strength, he attempted to push the door open, but it was firmly locked. Athena inspected the door, looked over her shoulder and took a step back. With the grace of a ballerina and the ferocity of a boxer, she kicked open the metal door. It flew from its hinges as she strolled out of the museum. Leo dumbfoundedly gaped at the foot-sized dent in the huge door.

"Come on!" Athena urgently whispered. Leo ran outside into the cold night air as Athena easily lifted the door and placed it back on its hinges, while murmuring an incantation. Her violet amethyst glowed in the night; the door straightened and locked in place.

CHAPTER 5

The cold wind brought Leo back from his daze. "What just happened? How did you do that? Those manticores," he shuddered. "And what was that shadow thing?!" He screeched, a sense of panic and dread washing over him every time he pictured the fiery being.

Athena placed her hand on Leo's shoulder, and his panic subsided. "I can't explain it here. Not now," she said as she eyed the surrounding building. "Is there somewhere private we can go?"

This is London – nothing is private. The only place Leo could think of was his study back at King's College. It was Friday night, and most of the students would either be in their dorm rooms or out partying. His tiny room would be anything but private. Leo blew on his hands to warm them. Athena looked expectant. Leo was thinking fast.

When he first met the goddess, Leo was convinced she wanted to kill him. And now, she wanted to go somewhere private. *Why? To kill me?* No, she had protected him during the fight. Even after the talisman was well within her reach, the goddess of bravery and courage had risked her life to save him from being crushed by the manticore. *So, what does she want with me?* He looked at her mesmerizing gray-green eyes. They reflected no emotion, only expectation. He observed the bronze shield strapped to her left forearm. "Yeah, I know somewhere safe and private. But I don't think you can go dressed like..." He trailed off, gesturing at her soldierly armor. Her eyes narrowed, as they bore into his. Leo once again felt as if she were inspecting his soul.

Without breaking eye contact, she flexed the hand that was holding her spear and jammed it into her arm. Instead of piercing her skin, her nearly eight-foot spear shrunk to an exact replica that was only three inches long. She attached it to her armband, and it fit perfectly with the design. She did the same with her short sword. With her free hand, she unstrapped the shield, and it vanished. Leo looked around, wildly trying to see where it had gone. Athena chuckled once, holding up her right hand. Leo could see that she was wearing a circular ring.

Without thinking, Leo grabbed Athena's hand and gaped at the now-hidden shield, his index finger tracing the petite and intricate snakes. Athena cleared her throat. Leo swiftly released her hand. "My apologies," he stammered, as he did not know the proper way to address this important divinity. He tried to bow his head.

"Come on!" She pulled him roughly, and they both trotted onto Montague Place. Leo mindlessly walked toward King's College. He made this trip every week, so he could find his way blindfolded. The night was chilly with icy winds. Leo would have preferred taking the metro, but the beautiful goddess next to him would undoubtedly have attracted attention, and that was the last thing they needed.

Every so often, Leo would glance at Athena and then hastily look down at his shoes. She looked real enough. She had covered her bronze body armor with her golden red cloak, and she casually held her helmet in her hands. Her appearance resembled that of a student or actress on her way to rehearsal. They approached the college in silence, both lost in thought.

Following his usual route to his study, Leo entered Strand Campus. Athena glided like a quiet shadow behind him. His office light was on, and the door was unlocked. He heard David's voice coming from the open door: "Leo, is that you?" and his concern turned to relief. Reassured, Leo looked at Athena. And just as suddenly, his relief turned to dread.

He realized what their presence would seem like. He was bringing a stunning young woman to his study on a Friday night. *What am I going to say?* As Leo heard David moving toward the door, sweat started beading on his brow.

David opened the door, perhaps hoping to catch some students sneaking around. His expression lightened when he saw Leo, and then he registered the figure next to him. His mouth dropped open slightly and he blinked several times. Leo was looking from Athena

CHAPTER 5

to David, and seeing what his friend was seeing.

Athena was one of the most beautiful creatures either of them had ever seen. Her flawlessness was elegant and intimidating at the same time. Leo didn't really care about physical appearances, but now that he could really look at Athena without fear of dying, he noted how attractive she was. Her beauty was otherworldly.

Leo cleared his throat and David seemed to recover himself. "Excuse me, miss." He flashed his striking half-smile. "I'm David." He extended his hand to Athena, who turned to Leo.

"Um, this is... Um Ath..." he started to mumble, but Athena cut him off.

"Alexandra," she said as she shook David's hand. Leo was surprised at how quickly Athena had gone from assessing David for weaknesses, to cordially introducing herself. "I'm Leo's sister," she announced, assuming an air of nonchalance.

"He never mentioned having a sister," David retorted.

"I'm his half-sister," Athena said, and for a moment even Leo believed the lie.

"Oh, no wonder. You must be another Clarkson then." David was still shaking her hand, his regard contemplative. He was staring into Athena's eyes with wonder and... *lust?* Leo thought.

He stepped forward. "Um, Alexandra? Can you please wait for me inside my study?" Leo pointed to the open door. "I'll be there in just a second."

Athena nodded and smiled at David. "Nice to meet you, David." She floated by Leo and, with a swirl, shut the door behind her.

As soon as the door closed, David punched Leo's shoulder. "You never told me you had a sister!" He looked at the closed door and whispered, "And a hot one, too. What else are you hiding from me, man?" He laughed.

Leo thought. *Oh, nothing. I've truly had a wonderful evening. I woke* the Greek goddess of war. *I was almost a chew toy for a bunch of ravenous manticores, and oh, yes, some random, demonic shadow wants to fry me alive.*

David's smile turned into a frown. "I'm sorry, I didn't mean it like that. Of course you're protective of your sister. I swear, I wasn't hitting on her."

"It's okay, David." Leo shook his head, trying to clear his mind. He placed his fingers on his temples and lightly massaged them. *I have no idea what to do.*

"Hey, it'll be alright. I know these last few days have been stressful. Feel free to talk to me whenever you want," David said as he patted Leo's shoulder. "By the way, you had thirteen freshmen come by. I think half of them just wanted to see you because as soon as they saw me in your office, they bolted. What happened at the museum? Was everything alright?" He sounded a bit concerned under his facade of cheerfulness.

Leo chewed his lip as he mulled over what to tell his friend. He needed to talk to Athena as soon as possible to get answers to so many questions. He decided to be honest but brief with David. "Yeah, everything is good. They just wanted a quick sweep of the ancient artifacts in the storeroom. I stayed over a bit longer; you know how much I love sweeps. John Allen said Dupont won't be returning anymore, so I guess I have free time now. My internship research has been put on hold."

David said, "Oh. I'm sorry about that. What about your sister? I guess you have some time to hang out with her now. Why didn't you tell me she was coming? Or that she even existed."

"Actually, I hadn't met her before. I knew of her, but I was shocked when I saw her at the museum," Leo replied, avoiding the most important facts. "I'm not sure how long she wants to stay, or what she wants with me. I guess I'll find out tonight."

CHAPTER 5

"Well, you still owe me a coffee." David lightly punched Leo's shoulder. "Then you can tell me all about your undisclosed relatives." Leo ran a hand through his wavy hair. After a pause, he said, "I definitely owe you for covering for me. Thanks."

"No problem." David turned toward the office and knocked twice. "I just need to get my backpack," he called as he slightly opened the door. Leo followed David into the study. Athena was standing by the far wall of his small cluttered workplace. She was staring at Leo's maps. Clearing his laptop and notebooks from Leo's desk and placing them inside his backpack, David said, "It was good meeting you, Alex. We should get some dinner while you're in town."

Athena had moved silently to the other side of the desk. Leo gave a start. *She really does move like a panther.*

"That would be fun," she said. The atmosphere in the room felt light and untroubled. Leo once again wondered if Athena had some sort of calming aura.

David's expression was a bit dazed. "See you on Monday, Leo," he replied as he closed the door behind him. Athena was looking at the door with a soft smile filled with innocence and merriment. However, as soon as she heard the footsteps fade, the smile disappeared and her dangerous demeanor returned.

"How did you do that?" Leo stammered.

"I couldn't have him notice what I was wearing, now, could I? I altered his focus on what I wanted him to see – which, unfortunately for him, was the only thing I didn't have covered in bronze armor," Athena said as she moved to the front of the desk. She placed her outstretched arms on the desk and put her helmet between them in a menacing manner.

"Why is that unfortunate for him?" Leo asked. Athena indicated the empty chair. Intimidated, he cleared his throat and sat down.

Athena fixed her gaze on her helmet. Carefully, she stroked its mane.

"Let's just say he'll be a bit disoriented for a while. I'll be surprised if he can recall my features tomorrow morning." Her face shifted to Leo's so quickly that Leo recoiled under her scrutiny. "Now, I've been honest with you so far. I want you to be honest with me. I'll know if you're lying."

"What do you want to know?" Leo spluttered.

"How did you get my armband?"

Okay. Here goes nothing. Leo retold the story about the evening's events and about Dupont's disappearance. He included John Allen's revelation about Dupont's mysterious escapade, and how John had found the armband by Dupont's broken phone. He talked about the sweep, and how he had imputed the talisman's significance when Allen stated it was not included in the museum's inventory. "And that's how I found you," Leo concluded breathlessly.

Athena asked, "How did you know the armband was mine?"

"Well, I wrote my term paper last year on 'The Mystical Elements of Ancient Cultures'. I dedicated four pages of it to your talisman," Leo gulped.

"Your term paper?" Athena asked blankly.

"Yes. It's around here somewhere. Let me find it." Leo got up from his chair and rummaged around the shelf behind his desk. He found the manila envelope where he kept a copy of his paper. "Here it is." Adoringly, he handed Athena the envelope, offering up his most precious possession.

Cautiously, Athena took the envelope and, without breaking eye contact, opened the folder. She took out the heavy manuscript and began to peruse. The more pages she turned, the more the atmosphere of the room lightened. Leo felt calmer as he studied Athena's face. Her eyebrows were creased in concentration.

She looked away from Leo's essay and asked, "You wrote this?"

"Yes. It's my pride and joy."

CHAPTER 5

Athena put the paper down and placed her hand on her chin. Deep in thought, she looked out the window, her eyes moving rapidly as if seeing something far away. Leo did not dare move a muscle. He peered at Athena's imposing face and looked away, fixing his gaze on her helmet. From far away it looked crude, but up close, it was beautifully carved. Snakes, moving down and across the frame as if ready to strike, adorned the bronze eye slit.

Athena sat back, her posture relaxed as her fingers drummed on the table. Her other hand still held her chin, her long index finger reaching from her jaw to her temple. She inspected him quizzically, and as her eyes moved around Leo's body, he realized that she was reaching deep into his soul.

"So you know all about talismans and their magical powers to protect and bring good fortune?" she asked.

"Yes, I've been focusing my research for the last couple of months on discovering authentic talismans. My report focuses mostly on objects mentioned multiple times in ancient texts that must have belonged to a god, and had otherworldly powers. I've only been able to find two or three, but I've written about the ones known in various cultures. There are hundreds of them."

Athena's eyes were glowing with keen interest. She seemed as intrigued by the talismans as Leo was. "So if I showed you one, would you be able to identify it? Who it belonged to, and where to find its original owner?"

"I think so," Leo answered "Why?"

Athena's features transformed; she smiled broadly and her eyes shimmered with an emotion Leo had not yet seen on her ethereal face. They seemed to express hope. "Before I tell you, I need you to promise me that you won't reveal to any mortal what I'm about to tell you."

Leo nodded.

Athena drew her sword from the armband in one swift motion. "Blood oath," she said, her expression serious and intense.

Leo felt a bit nauseous. The sharp sword looked as if it could cut through steel. He took three long breaths. Athena waited patiently with the sword, which she had placed in between them. Leo lightly grasped it with his hand and closed his eyes, feeling the cold metal on his fingertips. He exhaled and squeezed. As the sharp metal cut into his skin, he cried out.

Slowly, he raised his bloody hand, and said in a clear voice, "I swear, I will never reveal your secrets."

Athena held out her hand to him as if to shake it. Leo hesitated for a second, and then he reached for her hand. Her touch was like fire to his skin. It burned through him, and he felt a gust of light between their clenched hands. After one firm shake, Athena released her grip.

Leo eyed his hand. It felt as if fire ants were crawling under his skin. He was alarmed to see that the blood was gone, and in its stead was a sort of burnt tattoo made up of intertwining snakes. He looked at it from several angles. The snakes seemed to be alive. When he turned his hand to the back side, it seemed normal. No snakes were visible.

Athena explained, "Blood oaths are sacred. Only those sworn to the secret can see our pact. If you break the bond, these snakes will eat you from inside."

Repulsed, Leo gulped and gawked at his hand. Athena grabbed his arm and waved her talisman over the tattoo. It vanished and she let go of his arm.

"About half a year ago, the Council of the Elders met and elected one representative from each divinity. I was chosen by the Greeks. We were tasked with discovering the mysterious disappearances of some of our deities. When I say deities, I mean ones in every culture that has existed on this earth. Battles between gods were the norm, as my own history attests. There was the Titanomachy, in which the contemporary Olympians fought the age-old Titans, and so on. Yet... this was no battle. The Council decreed that I was to find the culprit of a slaughter."

Leo was speechless. Athena continued without pausing, "Our terrestrial energy is stored in talismans. With these objects, while we are on earth, we can project ourselves and take on desired forms. Some cultures worship shape shifters, while others worship elements. It varies. When we project ourselves in human form, we store our divine powers in our talismans. Without them, we are weak and vulnerable, as you probably noted in our clash with the manticores."

Athena noticed Leo's uneasiness, and she smiled reassuringly. "I wouldn't have been killed. I am not mortal. But my destruction would have caused me to remain in a state of limbo, trapped within my talisman. We were woken and allowed to return to Earth by the Council, and only the Council can ask us to return to our somnolent existence." Athena paused, making sure Leo understood so far.

"So... the manticores. They hurt you. But they can't kill you? I don't understand," Leo said.

Athena half-smiled. "They were certainly close. But no, I wouldn't have died. My current physical state would have vanished, and you would have had to find another one of my statutes and woken me with the same ritual you used the first time."

"I still don't understand... So within the talisman, there are many of you?" Leo asked.

"No. There is only one of me." Athena looked around, trying to explain. She pointed to one of his pictures on the desk. "Is that you?"

Leo nodded.

"But you are in front of me. Are there two of you?" Athena asked patiently.

Leo felt that his brain was beginning to work again as his comprehension returned. "I get it. So if your current physical state dies, I would just have to find another object representing you, and wake you."

"Exactly," Athena replied. "The power of my talisman is restoration, so it is very difficult to destroy me as long as it is in my possession."

"Why wasn't it in your possession? Why did Dr. Dupont have it?" Leo asked.

"I sent it to him."

CHAPTER 6

Leo sat dumbstruck. *I definitely did not see that one coming. Why in the world would a divinity send her "life-support" to a museum curator?* "Why?" he blurted out.

"It was part of a trap." She looked away toward the window. Almost imperceptibly, her features shifted, and she appeared to be in pain.

Until now, Leo had been clasping his hands together, too tense to relax. But there was something in Athena's pained expression that effaced his fear. He reached and touched her hand. This gesture reminded him of when, earlier in the evening, Allen had tried comforting him in the same way.

In a flash, Athena reached for the sword that sat between them. Leo was too stunned to recoil in alarm. He retrieved his outstretched hand without breaking eye contact.

Athena sighed and let go of the sword. She stood and turned away from the desk, her hands in tight fists. Instead of fearing reproval, Leo wanted to comfort her. Any sane person would have escaped. Athena exuded anger and resentment, but deep down Leo felt that her suffering was not directed at him.

"I'm sorry," he said. He wanted somehow to ease her pain, as she had healed his broken leg at the museum. Yet, he didn't know how. Clearly, his touch had startled her. *Well, she is a goddess, I shouldn't be touching her in the first place. I should be bowing respectfully.* Still,

Leo felt bonded in some way to this unearthly being, as if the night's events and his blood oath had forever tied his fate to her.

Athena's posture slumped; her fists unclenched. "I should have been there. He was getting too powerful, his evil influence was spreading without control," she whispered almost to herself. Athena straightened and returned to her usual daunting self. "We were paired off by the Council. The combination of two powerful deities would surely be enough protection for our quest. We were the new generation of guardians. And one by one, we were taken out. We could sense him coming for us, coming to steal our talismans. The problem was, we didn't understand why he was collecting them, or what he was planning.

"I decided the safest way to travel would be to assume human identities. I was sure he would not search for us among mortals. And thankfully, we were safe for a while. One day, though, he found us." Athena's voice cracked with sorrow. "And I was left alone."

Leo could tell that Athena was not used to expressing herself to humans. She was a goddess, not an emotional earthling. She continued. "That's when I started doing some research of my own." She tapped the essay on the desk. "I came across your paper published in a King's College Journal under Dr. Armaud Dupont's name. It was very enlightening."

She gracefully sat down, and reaching for the paper, she scanned it and found the page she was looking for. Without looking up, she continued, "It was a new perspective, and it was intriguing. If the author of this paper knew about talismans, then he could easily find me, if given the correct clues. So I set a trap for our would-be thief. It cost me my life, but it was worth it. I stripped him of some of his powers, transforming him into a one-dimensional shadow of his former self."

Leo gasped, "So that thing in the museum! That's the talisman thief!"

CHAPTER 6

Athena smiled. "Yes. That's what remains of him. Ex Nihilo, that's the nickname we gave him. It means 'out of nowhere'. That's how he operates; he strikes from the shadows and attacks without warning. He's the embodiment of evil. Now that you've seen him at his lowest and weakest, you can imagine how powerful he was in his full form."

Leo unconsciously shivered. That thing had nearly destroyed the entire museum, and put him into an early grave. Leo rubbed his hands together and bit his lip before asking, "So, Dr. Dupont… is he alright? I found your talisman today, and that is why I went to wake you. It was in Dupont's possession before he disappeared nearly two weeks ago. The only remains were your talisman and his shattered phone. Could he still be alive?" He unconsciously knew the answer, and was dreading Athena's response.

Athena looked sadly at Leo. Her voice was filled with despondency as she answered, "I don't believe any mortal could have stood a chance against the wicked Ex Nihilo. He would not have seen human life as having any value. He would have exterminated Dupont without a second thought."

Leo's face paled, and he looked down at his clenched hands. Nothing in his life had ever prepared Leo to face such malevolence; it was inconceivable. Dr. Dupont was dead, just because he was in the wrong place at the wrong time.

Athena's dejected expression was replaced by a seriousness that was almost business-like. "I need your help," she said. *This must be the first time she has ever said those words. Especially to a human,* Leo thought.

"I don't know what he is, or what he wants. But you might," she added.

Leo gulped. "Do you recognize him from my essay?"

"No. If I did, I wouldn't be here." Athena sounded annoyed. "There's no trace of him. I've memorized your entire paper, and there isn't a single clue about him."

Flustered, Leo asked, "If there's no mention of him in my paper, why do you think I can help?"

"I've lived many eons, traveled the world, and read countless transcripts. I know every language in existence. And yet... I have no insight into this creature. But your view is different from ours. Your outlook and mine are so dissimilar. You write about us three-dimensionally. And *theoretically* you've discovered more talismans than I would have believed a mortal could." Ruefully, she chuckled. "I couldn't find him before, but I might now. If there is one thing I know about that *thing;*" she said the last word with contempt and hatred, "it is that he underestimates humans. That's his weakness."

"So you want to work together and find out who or what he is?" He couldn't believe he was being offered the chance to work with one of the most intelligent beings on Earth, on an enigma that even she couldn't crack.

"Yes. We need to find him, and we need to take back all the talismans he has stolen. In doing so, we will take back the power he has wrestled from us. The Council sent me here to deter him from his destructive path, and I will not rest until I complete my mission," Athena replied. "And I must warn you, this is one of the most dangerous expeditions you will ever undertake."

Leo smiled. *Worse than high school?*

"You will probably die," Athena solemnly continued, noting Leo's unwarranted glee.

I might die. But I'll get to live. "I'm in," Leo said, thrilled about the challenge.

Athena's seriousness faded. She returned Leo's smile, all traces of her threatening tone gone. She stood up briskly. "Let's go then. Gather your things. We leave at first light."

When Leo stood, his legs were trembling. He felt overjoyed. *What do I need from here?* He looked around the study as if inspecting it for the first time. He grabbed his essay from the desk and placed it in his backpack. He opened all his drawers and shuffled around, but didn't find anything useful, apart from an old compass he used to take with him on trips. He shrugged and placed it in the pack, then added a few books that he thought might be useful for the adventure.

Zipping the bag, he turned to Athena who stood waiting by the door. Leo looked at her bare legs and shivered. By this time, London would be close to freezing. He didn't think she might need a jacket for warmth, but people would definitely stare at a beautiful woman with a perfect physique, striding along bare-legged and dressed as if ready to join a battalion. He reached for his coat and handed it to her. It was black and long, stretching down to his knees. Athena narrowed her eyes. She looked at it for a moment as if debating whether to rip it to pieces or throw it out the window.

"To prevent unwanted attention," Leo said in a quiet voice. Reassuringly, he smiled, wondering why Athena looked as if she had been offered a cockroach.

She took it. "Good point." She moved her golden red cloak from around her shoulders to her legs, draping it like a toga. Then she put on Leo's coat, and buttoned it. She swiped her hair out from under the coat, causing her dazzling golden ringlets to cascade down her back.

Athena opened the door and stared at Leo. She hesitated before she asked, "Is your resting place here at the university?"

Rest? What does she mean? With a bit of annoyance, she said, "Don't humans usually have a home or somewhere to sleep?"

"Oh, yes, of course. My apologies. We can head to my dorm and rest, if that's alright with you," Leo timidly answered.

Athena nodded and Leo gestured for her to follow. He remembered how highly the Greeks valued hospitality. Leo recalled one famous instance involving Zeus and Hermes, Athena's powerful father and her trickster brother. The duo had traveled incognito to Tyana, where almost every townsperson had rejected their request for a place to sleep that night. An old married couple, Baucis and Philemon, were the only ones who welcomed the disguised gods. By the next morning, the elderly pair were the only townspeople to survive Zeus's retaliation. Leo shuddered. He wished he'd cleaned his room that morning.

They exited through Surrey Street and turned toward Strand Campus. Leo led the way to the dorms. While they walked, he blew on his hands to warm them. Athena stayed close to him, menacingly scanning her surroundings. Even with a battered old coat and a scowl on her face, Athena made the garment fashionable. Leo felt self-conscious. He hoped his humble room wouldn't upset Athena.

He cleared his throat. "Can I ask you some questions?" Athena nodded.

"So, I think I understand so far. A bunch of deities came to earth to find this shadow thing, but they were taken out. Do you know how many?"

Athena shook her head. "For safety reasons, we weren't supposed to contact each other. We could communicate with the elders, but our identities were supposed to be kept secret. I don't know who or how many were summoned."

"And each representative has his own talisman?" Leo asked. Athena nodded. "So if someone lost his talisman, he would be weaker?"

"Technically. That deity would have lost one of his or her main weapons." Athena replied.

"And the way to destroy deities is to steal their talismans?"

"Not necessarily. It takes a very powerful being to destroy us – or multiples working all at once, like an assault."

"But why would someone want your talisman? To take your power and use it for themselves?"

CHAPTER 6

"No. It doesn't work like that. Talismans are unique; they work only for their owners. I can only guess that he wants to rob us of our powers and weaken us."

"And you were attacked by Ex Nihilo before? Your partner didn't survive?"

Athena grimly nodded and looked away. Leo sensed that she was close to tears. He mentally noted that he should never ask about her divine friend again.

As they passed by a drunken group of men, one of them whistled and the others hooted and laughed. Athena threw them a menacing glare. Her intense glower immediately sobered the men, and at once they stopped their misbehavior. Leo was impressed. *No wonder she was feared. If looks could kill....*

They were silent for most of the walk, as Leo pondered the night's events. What started off as a nightmare turned out to be a pretty exciting adventure. Of course, there was the chance that he would die. Maybe he'd get eaten by some sort of mystical creature, or even electrocuted by that awful Ex Nihilo. He wondered what Ex Nihilo was... what he wanted. All he knew was that he was collecting talismans and taking no prisoners. His mind raced with possibilities. It definitely wasn't Erebus, a Greek primordial god of darkness; Athena would have recognized him immediately. Could it be Nocnitsa? He thought not. Nocnitsa was a nightmare spirit from Russian and Slovak folklore, but she usually only tormented children. Ex Nihilo was definitely straight from a nightmare, very potent and very driven.

If Ex Nihilo was looking for talismans, why didn't he just snatch it from Dupont? It seemed so easy to take it from non-supernatural humans. Unless... maybe Ex Nihilo couldn't hold onto objects in his current state. Maybe he was made out of deadly energy that couldn't be dimensionalised.

His mind had wandered so far, he barely registered that they had arrived. He grabbed his keys and typed the entrance code into the gate. The door buzzed, and they entered together. Leo continued toward the elevator, and it opened immediately. *Huh, that never happens.* He checked the time on his watch: it was 23:46 pm.

"Oh goodness!" he exclaimed.

Athena reached for her shield ring and menacingly glanced around.

"Look at the time!" Leo said as he walked into the elevator. He heard a sigh of exasperation behind him and turned to see Athena's glare.

"What?" Leo asked. He clicked Level 6 and shook out his wet hair, then wiped his glasses with his shirt. Athena silently walked into the elevator.

As the lift glided upwards, Leo's stomach groaned. *Geez, I haven't eaten since lunch. I'm starving.* He looked at Athena. He knew that some deities indulged in mortal food, but he was unsure if they required it for survival as he did. *I'll know soon enough.*

The elevator jerked to a stop. Leo gestured for Athena to exit first, but after sensing her glare, he cleared his throat and walked toward his room. Again, he wished he had cleaned up before leaving. He opened the door. "Welcome to my humble abode!" he nervously announced.

Athena strolled into his room and surveyed his living quarters. The tiny kitchen was separated from the combination living/dining area by a breakfast nook. There were two doors, one was the bathroom and shower, and the other was Leo's bedroom. His walls were plastered with tapestries and maps. Most of the tapestries were landscapes of places he wanted to visit. The maps were scribbled with red sharpie, symbolizing geographical excavation sites where objects from his research appeared.

Anxiously, he rushed to pick up textbooks and notebooks from his sofa. He stacked them by his desk in the corner, then cleared the little dining table that functioned as an eating and working space. He didn't

CHAPTER 6

feel Athena's proximity until he heard her clear voice. "Thank you," she said, holding out his black coat. Her tone had softened somewhat. "It's nothing," Leo replied. He took the coat and ran his fingers through his hair. "It's not much, but it's home. My bedroom is that second door. I'll take the sofa."

"No, it's alright. You should stay in your room," Athena replied.

"No, no. I insist! Mi casa es tu casa!" Leo said in broken Spanish. Athena opened her mouth to reply, but at that moment, Leo's stomach gurgled.

"I'm going to cook dinner. Would you like some food?" he asked, embarrassed.

"Certainly." She turned toward one of the frayed maps near the door and began to closely examine it.

That's my cue. Smiling, Leo moved into the kitchen. He loved to cook. When he was younger, his Italian grandmother had taught him the basics, and ever since then it was one of his life's passions. Happily, he grabbed his chef's apron from the drawer, then washed his hands.

Thirty minutes later, all his veggies were cut, the meatballs were almost done, and he was lost in thought while buttering his fettuccine. Intrigued, Athena was watching him, but Leo was oblivious. He took out a loaf of bread along with a knife, then checked how his sauce was doing. It was simmering nicely. He added a pinch of garlic, and mixed it in. He remembered the bread and turned to cut it; however, it was already neatly carved and stashed in a bowl. He blinked rapidly and looked around in bewilderment. Athena was by the stove, examining the contents of the pots and the spices.

"Ah!" Leo cried out.

Athena didn't even turn. She said, "Did I startle you?" as she smelled his spices, then she sniffed the sauce. "Let me guess: garlic, pepper, onion, basil, tomatoes, olive oil." She sniffed again. "And parsley."

"Wow. That's very impressive." He took out two plates, served large portions on each, then placed them on the table.

"Perfect," he mused. He gestured for Athena to join him. Sitting down in companionable silence, Leo realized that today had been surprisingly chaotic. Reaching for the jug, he poured two glasses.

He raised his and toasted, "To not being a manticore's lunch."

Athena chuckled and reached for her water. "To surviving another day."

CHAPTER 7

April 26th

A thena opened her eyes and looked around the dark, quiet bedroom. She became aware of heavy breathing coming from the living room. Straightening, she flexed her back, moved toward the window, and she cracked open the shutters. The sun had not yet risen, but she calculated it was twenty-five minutes away. *Time to work.*

She soundlessly glided into the living room. Athena was used to silently moving around, so she was not surprised when Leo did not stir. She squinted her eyes and examined his posture. The youth was sprawled on the sofa, his lanky features covering most of the love seat, and the sheets were in tangles around his waist. For some reason, he reminded Athena of someone she had known.

She raised her eyebrow. *Ganymede. Very interesting.* There were definite similarities between them. Both were slender and good-looking. This teenager was taller, however. His hair was dark instead of light, his eyes brown instead of blue. There was something else that was different as well. Leo was lovely, but not alluring. The differences between the boys were comparable to Aunt Aphrodite and her. Athena's attractiveness was expressed in aesthetics; her beauty derived from thought and strength of character rather than the more physical and superficial kinds of love that her aunt exuded.

Athena wondered about Leo's character; would he be brave enough to survive the challenges that lay ahead? A human with his face surely must have many who had loved him. Be that as it may, last night at the college, Athena had realized that he was in love. Relief flooded through her because, if this were true, there would be less complications and unnecessary drama. Inwardly, she shuddered as she remembered how many male suitors she had rejected. The worst case had been her half-brother, Hephaestion. She gagged, repulsed by the memory.

Leo shifted in his sleep; his face was turned upwards and his mouth was open. There was something shiny near his bottom lip. *Drool? Ugh, humans.*

Athena decided to start the day's preparations. She needed to free the young man of any tasks that linked him to London. That could easily be accomplished with the right word in the right ear. His absence would never be questioned.

She headed into the small kitchen, still thinking about Leo who was technically considered an adolescent. Notwithstanding his youth and his lack of experience, he was courageous. Not as brave as Perseus, of course, yet there was some potential. Now that she considered the matter, Leo's character did remind her of Perseus; both were intelligent, resourceful and compassionate – a rare quality in mortals.

As she pondered Leo's strengths and weaknesses, she prepared breakfast. For a young adult, he was skilled at preparing food. She mused that he must have acquired this talent from his family; therefore, his gift was inherited. She disliked how some societies frowned on boys and men who cooked. It was a utilitarian skill, practical in the most important sense. She considered human pride the culprit. *Hubris,* the downfall of many would-be heroes.

Opening the fridge, she took out a number of jars, then washed and

CHAPTER 7

cut all the fruit found in Leo's pantry. She examined the remaining provisions, and separated out the ones that would be valuable on a day of travel. Humans needed to constantly eat to maintain energy, and this excursion would surely be taxing. She finished cutting the bread into halves, dripping olive oil and honey on half, and packing the other half in little plastic boxes that humans use to carry food.

Athena sighed, pleased with herself. She squinted in the gloom and realized that Leo had not even begun to wake. She moved slowly to the window and opened it. The rays of sunlight beamed in, causing Leo to groan while trying to hide his face under his pillow. Athena cleared her throat to catch his attention. Nothing. She repeated, but louder this time. Leo sleepily peeked from under his pillow, then cried out in alarm. Raising her eyebrow, Athena walked back to the kitchen and started setting the table. Leo wrapped himself in the blanket and slowly stood up while cleaning his glasses and wiping them on his sleeve.

"I must be dreaming," he mumbled.

If he were asleep, this wouldn't be a dream; this would be a nightmare. "Get your belongings ready. Pack only the essentials," Athena calmly commanded.

"Where are we going?" Leo asked as he rubbed his eyes.

"I'll explain over breakfast. Go," she said in a tone that invited no argument. Leo stumbled into the bedroom and quietly shut the door.

Where *are* we going? Athena mused. She sat down and grabbed a chunk of bread. Gently, she dipped it into the wine bowl and took a bite. Before heading out, she told herself that she needed to collect her possessions from around London. Human necessities mostly: identification cards and money. They would go to the market for clothes, as well. Once they were ready for the journey, they would know where to go.

You'll find me.

Athena shuddered. She recalled every painful detail from that dreadful evening. It was one of the few times she had truly lost control. As if back in that gallery, Athena remembered running as fast as she could toward the screams. She recalled her racing heart and could hear the scrape of her armor on the floor, the swish of her spear, the weight of the electric shocks on her gorgonic shield, the metallic smell of death. She felt the tears that rushed down her face. The heartbreak.

She remembered the feeling of the dying goddess' skin on her own; how she reached for Athena as she perished. Athena recalled the feel of the cold steel of the necklace as it was wrapped around her shaking hand. Her voice, normally so strong and fierce, feebly whispered, *"You'll find me."* Then the light vanished from her eyes. Athena had tried to hold her, but her body evaporated. Gone. At that moment, Athena's control vanished. Her howl was filled with agony. She hurled her spear in the direction of Ex Nihilo as she braced for an attack, but he was gone. They were both gone, and Athena was left alone with her pain.

Leo's footsteps from the other room were getting louder. She heard him reach for the knob, and forced herself to clear her mind. The door creaked. Timidly, Leo approached the dining table and cleared his throat. "I've packed my passport, my student ID, and some books that could help us," he shyly declared. He tried clearing his throat. "I packed all the cash I have. Do you know how much we will need?"

So that's what he's worried about. The night before, when he had offered his coat, she realized that he was genuinely concerned about her well-being. Athena added "gallant" to her mental notes on him. Smiling gently, she said, "Do not trouble yourself with such matters. I am well equipped and prepared for this endeavor." She gestured to the seat next to her.

Athena picked up his plate and filled it. She said, "We need to visit two locations in London today. There is a market on our way. We

CHAPTER 7

will prepare for our travels there. Tell me, Mr. Clarkson..."

"Call me Leo," he interrupted. He sat down on the chair next to her and reached for the plate in front of him, then filled his mouth with sliced fruit.

Athena noted his change of stance. *Interesting. Respectful, yet practical.* "Very well then, Leo, for the foreseeable future, we will be traveling around the globe. Can you tell me how two young "adults" would inconspicuously travel with few belongings, and without attracting attention?"

Leo swallowed his food. "That's easy, as backpackers."

"Correct," Athena said. "We will backpack around the world until we fulfill our duties. I've found the perfect company to help us with our journey. It is called 'Patagonia'." Happily, she took a chunk of bread and buttered it. "I was convinced by their products last time I was on Earth. They are very durable, and apparently you can return certain items and get them fixed at next to no cost."

Leo chuckled and quickly covered his mouth. Athena uncomprehendingly observed her travel partner.

"I'm sorry. It's just that..." stammered Leo. "What I mean to say is, you find human life or the human experience fascinating, do you not?"

Athena was surprised by the question. "I do. Humans are very intriguing creatures. I've always found them most entertaining and complex." She pondered his remark. "Do you find that odd?"

"No, no," he replied. "It's just that I've spent my entire life reading about divinity and mythology. For me, it's a shock to see you acting and talking about your everyday life. This isn't a conversation I could have dreamed of having with an Olympian."

Athena smiled to herself. There was no denying that she did enjoy the company of certain humans. It was as if a book came to life before her eyes, and she could play both author and character. It was exciting to watch their lives unfold. Each person was so unique, and everyone's story was so intricate. Admittedly, she had a soft spot for the vulnerable mortals, and she appreciated the varying cuisines Earth had to offer. She was also looking forward to the next chapter in her perplexing battle with Ex Nihilo; she had outsmarted him once before. She would do so again.

As they finished their meal, their excitement grew. Athena collected the various items she had prepared, and neatly packed them in Leo's bag.

"Do you know how to get to The Royal Horseguards?" she asked as he politely opened the front door.

"The hotel by the London Eye that looks like a castle? Yeah, sure," Leo curiously replied. He shut the door behind himself and locked it, then closed his eyes. He kissed the door and slammed his palm against it.

Athena raised her eyebrow, causing Leo to shrug. "It's a form of good luck for me. It means I will return someday – alive." He gulped and ran a hand through his hair, then hurried toward the elevator. "What's at the Royal Horseguards? Why are we going there?" Leo casually asked as if oblivious to his previous consternation.

"You'll see," Athena answered. Once opened, the package awaiting her return was rather self-explanatory. There were more important details to discuss. "Apart from your studies at the school, do you have any other arrangements I should be aware of?"

Leo scratched his head pensively. "Besides my internship at the museum, nothing really. But I've been placed on hold since Dupont won't be coming back. By the way, there's a store nearby called The Brokedown Palace where they sell Patagonia gear."

"Splendid! We shall commence our journey with a stop there." They exited the building and walked toward Kingsland Road. The mention of Dupont's name reminded Athena that the death of this erudite

CHAPTER 7

man was indirectly her fault. She had placed him in peril by sending him her talisman. Yet, if he had been honest and transparent about his research, he would not have been evaporated by Ex Nihilo. The fact that he took credit for Leo's paper and did not ask for his pupil's assistance, despite the fact that he was ignorant of the meaning of her message, peeved her. Dupont would be alive today, if only he had asked for a little help.

Entering the quaint store, Athena glided down the aisles searching for what they needed. She instructed Leo to grab items similar to the ones she was collecting, but in the style or color he preferred. Together, they chose two 65L packs, hiking shoes, two sleeping bags, two ultralight mini-hip packs, various towels, durable water bottles, water treatment supplies, and a three-person tent (some extra space never hurt). Lastly, Athena picked weatherproof clothing, ranging from Parkas to UPF-rated clothes, to protect them from exposure and extreme heat.

Leo raised his eyebrows as he took in the scope of outdoor wear. "Where exactly are we going?" he asked as he tried stuffing a woolen ski jacket into his 65L pack. Athena's own pack was already neatly arranged, every object perfectly organized. For safekeeping, she put most of Leo's books in her pack.

"I don't know. We might go to the Arctic, or we might go to the Sahara. That depends on where our dear friend goes." She pronounced the word *dear* sarcastically. Approaching the counter, she fluttered her eyelashes and smiled politely at the cashier. She mumbled something about being forgetful and leaving her card at home. "I am so scatterbrained; this is not the first time this has happened to me. Thankfully, I do remember my card details. I hope that will be sufficient for our purchase." She smiled warmly, and the cashier typed in her card number without question.

Collecting her belongings, Athena stared intently into the man's eyes. She smiled once more, taking her leave of the store just as Leo lifted the heavy pack onto his shoulders. The cashier waved slowly at Leo's back as he departed. The only thing the cashier would remember of the last half hour would be the presence of a young couple preparing for a trip. In the next day or so, he would not even be able to recall their faces. The only memorable occurrence would be that it was his biggest sale of the year.

They took the bus back toward the city center. Athena surveyed the passengers around them. She and Leo were not receiving the odd and leering glances they had endured the night before. Instead, most people assumed they were two youths embarking on a trip. Only a few noticed Athena's striking beauty. At Aldgate East, they exited the bus and walked to the tube.

A few minutes after exiting the underground, they turned left onto Whitehall Court and headed toward the entrance of the hotel. Frowning at first, a sleepy porter squinted at them in the morning sun. He shifted his glance from Leo to Athena. For a moment, as his eyes focused on her, he looked stupefied, and then he immediately straightened, happily greeting her.

"Ah, Ms. Pallas! You're back!"

"Good morning, Geoff." She gave him a smile as she glided forward. Beaming, Geoff gave a little bow. He hastily opened the door as Athena stepped inside and Leo shuffled in behind her. She reached the front desk in three quick strides and assumed a relaxed position at the counter. Leaning on the table, she tapped the bell. The hotel guests were sleepily meandering around the lobby, paying her no mind.

Getting their travel packs ready and changing clothes before collecting her packages was a smart move. She praised Leo for his cleverness and noticed that he was inquisitively surveying the hotel. A door opened behind the front desk, and a young woman emerged holding a visitor log. Furiously writing notes, she furrowed her brows

CHAPTER 7

in concentration. Athena glanced at her new Garmin watch. It was nearly a quarter till nine.

The receptionist looked up from her notebook, and her mouth opened in surprise. Athena smiled cordially. "I'm sorry I'm late, Monica. I'm back to retrieve my package."

"Oh, yes," Monica answered, seeming flustered. "I was expecting you earlier, Ms. Pallas. We were worried you would never come back."

Athena forced her voice to be nonchalant. "We?" she asked, wondering who else knew of her whereabouts.

"Just Geoff and me. Don't worry! We didn't tell anyone of your stay with us. Complete secret." Monica raised her finger to her lips. "I sent your box by express mail as you instructed. I hope it arrived safely!"

Athena continued to smile, but she could sense a lie. How deep could this deception be?

Behind her, Leo groaned. Alarmed, Athena rapidly turned toward him, but he was only putting his pack down and stretching his arms. Monica noticed his presence. "Good morning. Welcome to the Royal Horseguards." The receptionist's face became blank as she looked Leo up and down, then she frowned. "I'll go get your package, Miss," she announced as she retreated to the back of the reception area.

Athena studied her retreating figure, a smile playing on her lips. As soon as her footsteps faded, her smile vanished. Leo approached the desk and eyed her with concern. She answered his silent question with "There's deceit in the air." Athena flexed her left bicep, readying herself for a possible altercation.

Monica reappeared from the back room, holding a large brown package. Her expression remained blank and distant while she gingerly placed the bundle on the desk. "Here you go, Miss Pallas. Would you like two rooms today, or just one?" She glanced at Leo as if noticing him for the first time. Athena stared at the package. She ran her palm across the top and sniffed her fingers. Her jaw tightened.

"Did anyone handle this package after I gave it to you?" Athena asked, while maintaining a calm voice. Monica shook her head, her expression unchanged. Athena flashed her piercing green eyes at her. The receptionist seemed momentarily taken aback by this menacing glare, and just as suddenly she looked exhausted. Athena concentrated hard in order to see into Monica's mind. She noticed with mounting concern that it was murky.

Showing no emotion and persisting with her eye contact, Athena inquired, "Who asked you about the package?"

"No one, Miss," Monica replied in a monotone. "We placed it under lock and key, as you instructed."

Athena realized the deceit was hiding inside the truth. *Her memory's been tampered with.* She blinked, breaking the insight, and took the package from the desk. Monica was looking around in bewilderment, as if she had been dozing for the last ten minutes.

"We'd best be heading out," Athena quietly said to Leo. "Thank you for your discretion, Monica." The young receptionist seemed to sway, and Athena reached across the counter to steady her. Under the heavy coat, she felt the pulsating energy of her gleaming talisman.

Monica blinked and tried to reply, but she slurred her words. "Goodbye, Miss Pallas... Miss Pa... Miss." Monica's swaying abruptly ended. She straightened, reached for the visitor log on the desk, and began scribbling. Athena signaled to Leo who, without saying a word, followed her to the exit.

The doors inched open, and Athena approached the cheery porter. Without a sound, she rapidly placed her palm on the back of his neck and strolled past him. Feeling confused, the porter looked around. He seemed oblivious to Athena's presence, but registered Leo, who was briskly exiting the hotel. After a long moment, the porter waved goodbye, yelling, "Good day!"

Athena retraced her steps toward Embankment. There was no

CHAPTER 7

mistaking the divine scent that was unrecognizable to humans. The question was... Who was it, and for what was it searching? It troubled her that someone knew the location of one of her hiding places. The only other celestial being that had paid a visit to the hotel was Ex Nihilo; why would he return to the place where he was stripped of his corporeal self?

Leo made his way to Athena and gently touched her on the shoulder. "Are you alright? What happened?"

"We must be careful; someone or something visited the hotel," replied Athena. She leaned close and whispered, "Immortals."

Leo's face was pale. Athena touched his arm, instantly soothing him. "We have no time to lose. We need to go to London Heathrow," she said in her measured voice.

He nodded, visibly relaxed. "Let's take the underground from Leicester Square. The Piccadilly Line will take us straight to Heathrow Airport."

One hour later, Leo and Athena hustled through the large crowd of people that filled Terminal 2. Instead of approaching a counter, Athena left the building and walked across the parking lot to a baggage storage locale. The line was short, and they waited just briefly before it was their turn.

"Finally," Leo huffed. Well, it was a short time for her. Patience was one of Athena's virtues.

She smiled as she approached the counter. "Good afternoon. I'm here to collect a small bag."

"Name?" asked the disgruntled worker.

"Alexandra Pallas."

"Hmm. Seems like you left your bag overtime. There's a fine for that. The total is 97.5 pounds." The man looked up from his computer, his expression smug. He finally focused on the goddess, and his mouth dropped open in shock.

Athena reached into her fanny pack; on the train ride she had stowed the contents of her package in the small, easily portable bag. It was comprised of various identification cards, a passport, differing currencies and multiple international debit cards. She took out one of the cards and swiped it. The payment was approved. She sensed that the man's gaze was still on her face.

Leo cleared his throat. "The bag, sir?"

"Oh. Right," replied the stupefied man. He handed Leo a compact square container. Athena took it and held it close to her chest.

Outside, in the parking lot and away from curious eyes, Athena opened the receptacle. It was neatly packed with a few clothes and a blanket. To anyone else it would have looked like an ordinary handbag. Carefully, she put her hand into the deepest pocket and felt around. She found a papery texture and pulled it out. Handing it to Leo, Athena reached back inside and felt the cold steel of a necklace. *The vegvisir.* She clutched it tight, her heart racing. Pulling it out of the depths of the bag, she carefully placed it around her neck. Then, she opened her travel pack, inserted the hand bag, and closed it.

Although the vegvisir was a tool that had once belonged to Athena's Norse companion, it was now tainted with Ex Nihilo's scent, and she could utilize it as a compass to his location. The vegvisir was an immensely powerful Icelandic magical stave. In old Norse, visir meant "to show or to indicate." Vegvisir signified "to point the right way." The necklace would guide her on her quest.

Leo was looking over the paper map, perusing every angle. "Beautiful map. Are we going to use it to find out where we're going?"

"Yes," Athena replied.

She closed her eyes and held the necklace tightly in her palm. *You'll find me.* The remembered words stung her heart. As she felt the cold metal on her skin, she placed her faith in the vegvisir. It would guide

CHAPTER 7

her in the right direction. She breathed deeply, trying to concentrate on Ex Nihilo. She pictured him, visualizing the murky figure stalking in the darkness. She felt movement against her fingers and cautiously opened her palm and her eyes at the same time. The necklace was made of stainless steel with a lone ring attached to the middle. Norse symbols covered the outer layer of the ring, and in the center a variety of arrowlike characters pointed in every direction. The ring began turning rapidly as if spinning out of its axis. Athena and Leo looked on in amazement.

Suddenly, it stopped. Athena cautiously stroked one of the arrows that had a circle on its edge. It remained motionless. Silently, she moved the necklace forward toward the map that Leo was holding. The arrow, like a compass, spun and shifted. She followed its movement until the arrow was stationary once more.

Athena exhaled in triumph. The arrow was pointing at a precise location on the map. Leo fixed his glasses and gaped at where the arrow had landed. Madrid!

CHAPTER 8

The next available flight to Madrid from London Heathrow was leaving at 6:50 pm and landing in Madrid around 10:10 pm. Athena checked her watch. It was half past 2 pm. They would have to wait a while, yet the risk was worth the reward. They obtained their tickets at the counter and passed through security without fuss.

Athena made sure Leo was eating properly for the upcoming excursion. The safest option for him was to stay close to her, no matter the danger. If they were separated, she would not be able to protect him. Athena considered that it might be time to start showing him the basics of self-defense, just in case Ex Nihilo decided to target him in the approaching showdown.

Leo was consuming his third sandwich of the day as they sat together waiting for their gate number. Between every bite, he pensively looked around. "I don't get it," Leo said. Athena diverted her attention from the book she was reading, *Critique of Pure Reason* by Immanuel Kant. "If you were able to curse him, why is Ex Nihilo a shadow? Why wasn't he destroyed? How come he retained his form?" Famished, he continued devouring the sandwich.

Why indeed? Athena closed her book. Even though she was enjoying Kant's claims of understanding, she wanted to ponder Leo's questions. The young man was insightful. He was quick to ask why, and most of

CHAPTER 8

all, he was not afraid to admit his own ignorance. It was an important quality for someone seeking knowledge. It was often those who believed they knew everything, who truly knew nothing.

Athena had told Leo about the aftermath of Ex Nihilo's attack. She recounted the story at the beginning of Ex Nihilo's flight, avoiding the ambush that had killed her divine partner. It was painful for her to even think about that experience, let alone relive it. The ambush happened one late afternoon, six weeks before.

With sorrow, Athena recalled the events of that fateful day as she took out her passport and caressed the cover. Leo eyed the document quizzically and then raised his eyebrows. "Finland?" he whispered.

"We were near Oulu when we decided this was the safest way to travel. And it's one of the most powerful passports in the world." She kept her Norse partner's passport deep in her traveling bag, not because she believed she would be needing it soon, but as a reminder of her; something of hers that wasn't tainted by the creature's scent.

The last time she had been in an airport, this magical artifact had pointed to Manchester, England. It was the beginning of the end for the divine duo. Their hope had been to find any information that could provide some knowledge about the evil deity.

Athena lost herself in her memories. She remembered the long days of scrolling through endless books. It was after three days of non-stop research in the John Rylands Library that she had decided to pay a visit to Chetham's Library, which was within walking distance. Her partner had chosen to remain at John Rylands and continue their search. Parting ways for mere hours seemed safe, and Athena decided it would help to divide their time.

At Chetham's, she found various old texts on curses and maledictions, but there was nothing close to what she was searching for. Lost in between the dust and the endless rows of books, Athena felt a tremor passing through her body. Her neck felt icy and her skin burned with the sensation of approaching doom. In one swift motion, she slid her index ring onto her left forearm, bringing to life her magical shield. The next moment she heard an ear-piercing scream that humans would be unable to recognize. It was the distress of a dying goddess.

She avoided recalling these painful details and sharing them with Leo, choosing instead to recount how, when she had run back to John Rylands, she tossed her spear in self-defense and was surprised to see that the action had indeed caused harm to the deity. It wasn't until the evil creature vanished from the library that she noticed the spear was coated with a liquid. She examined with growing eagerness what she came to realize was blood on the spear: black, thick and foul-smelling. She gauged that in total, the blood equaled less than half a small test tube, a mere graze. As she was analyzing the liquid, a droplet fell to the floor, and Athena fixed her gaze on the crumbled sheets of paper. She had accidentally stepped over them in her haste to examine the odd liquid. There was red, hot blood on the corner of the sheets. The title of the essay was circled next to a note in untidy black ink. Hastily wiping her tears, Athena read it. *"He knows!"* was the only sentence scribbled on the note. Athena cleared some of the blood from the title of the paper: "The Mystical Elements of Ancient Cultures" by Armaud Dupont. A plan began to form in her mind.

Returning to the present, Athena noticed that the screen in front of them flashed bright red, signaling an opening gate. She saw that the international flight to Madrid would be boarding in 45 minutes.

Athena and Leo collected their belongings, and as they walked, Leo began unwrapping a new sandwich. "Maybe it's because Ex Nihilo had many stolen talismans," said Leo. He continued, "You said that each deity chose a talisman to store their divine self. Maybe your curse didn't totally destroy him because he had loads of them to spare."

Athena was certain Ex Nihilo's immense potential was directly

CHAPTER 8

related to his thievery, but how much of his potency was correlated with the talismans, and how much of it was his own power?

"And how come you can restore yourself? I wasn't aware that you could. I thought you were more," Leo pointed to her book, "into wisdom and the arts."

Athena smiled. "My brother, Apollo, is the God of Healing. When I was chosen by the Greeks for the Council and sent to Earth, Apollo offered to bless me with powers of restoration. And, of course, I took his offer. Healing compared to weaving is a more effective tool in combat."

Athena reflected that of the twelve Olympians, after her, Apollo would be the second choice to represent the Greeks. Apollo was lord of reason and logic, enlightenment and medicine, as well as many more. He was also prophetic. He must have had an inkling that Athena would require healing on her dangerous journey. Apollo was radiant, and only a fool would mistake his golden beauty for a sign of weakness. Apart from being a supreme archer, Apollo was a fierce fighter.

In contrast, Ares was also an extraordinary warrior, but he was too savage and hot-tempered. He lacked self-control, and would rather watch the world burn than put out the flames. Artemis was too independent; she cared little for the human race. Actually, Athena corrected, she cared little for men, as she severely punished any male who presumed to approach her. After further consideration, Athena decided that her younger sister was the complete opposite of her. Athena loved to cultivate, to craft, to think things through; while Artemis was instinctive and untamed.

To be sure Hermes was quick, witty and clever. But he was also impulsive and deceitful. Hermes was the god of rascals and thieves, liars and storytellers. Father had been wise to prevent Hermes from volunteering for this mission. Hermes was so charming that he could convince anyone to do whatever he pleased, but the dire perils he would have to face were more than he could handle. Her despicable uncle, Poseidon, was the most moody, foul-tempered and vindictive Olympian. He was a clear no. Her other uncle, Hades, was not considered an Olympian; plus he rarely left the underworld. Aunt Hestia and Aunt Demeter were too kind and placid, Hera too proud and imperious. Next was Aunt Aphrodite, but anyone could see that she was not a fighter. She was beauty itself, the symbol of perfect love. Hephaestion was lame, and Dionysus a drunk.

That left Apollo and her. Athena was glad Apollo was unable to lie; afterwards she asked him about his feelings regarding the unanimous vote, and he fervently stated that he held no grudge, while wishing her safe travels and even granting her the power of healing. Athena had many siblings – more than fifty – but Apollo was one of her favorites. He was noble and congenial. Of course, he could be cruel and brutal, yet every Olympian had that potential, including Athena herself.

The loud voices of the people in the airport brought Athena back to the present. It was already crowded with tourists, so Athena and Leo took a seat and waited for the agent to call for passengers to prepare for boarding. Athena extracted her boarding pass and documents. She caressed the maroon document, then sighed as she clutched it in her hands.

The plane was almost full, so Athena and Leo had to share a row with an elderly, talkative lady. As soon as she grew quiet, Leo promptly reclined his head and fell asleep. Athena did not wake him. It was going to be a restless night. She kept her eyes on the window, thinking over the upcoming battle.

Ex Nihilo would need to be ambushed. If he spotted them before the attack, he would quickly evade them and the chase would begin again. The question was, how should he be ambushed? A little voice inside Athena's head started a more important inquiry. Why was Ex Nihilo

CHAPTER 8

in Madrid? Could he be looking for another weapon? She thought not. His electric shocks were extremely effective and powerful enough to wake manticores...

With a jolt, she straightened. He could be creating an army, waking several kinds of beasts for an attack. It would be extremely foolish of him to do so without her nearby, for how could he control them? Except... Ex Nihilo was able to anger the manticores, which in turn attacked Leo and Athena. Their ferocity and their hostility were unnatural, even for legendary man-eaters. Back in the museum, Ex Nihilo had bided his time, waiting for her to wake. Perhaps he did so in case the true owner of the essay was never found. If he killed Dupont for merely holding the talisman, what would he do to Leo?

Athena knew that, in fear of retaliation, Ex Nihilo had avoided attacking Leo in the storage room. As soon as she was free to pounce, he vanished. So maybe in this form, he was susceptible to defeat. What was his plan now? Would he continue stealing talismans while she was hot on his trail? Ex Nihilo wouldn't know that she had the capability to find him. She racked her brains, as she often did when considering the evil creature's next move.

The plane jolted and descended at an angle onto the runway. Soon she would be able to figure out what Ex Nihilo was planning. Soon she would have her revenge.

CHAPTER 9

As the sun dropped to the edge of the horizon, dusk's golden fingers crept over the sky, shadowing Europe's third largest city with darkness. In the heart of the bustling city of Madrid, a shadow moved silently through the darkening streets. The Crystal Palace, situated in El Retiro Park, glistened with the soft radiance of the setting sun. Twilight settled over the park, inviting the darkness in.

The electric lights were bright inside the grand Museo Nacional del Prado, as they illuminated the neoclassical architecture. Housing one of the world's finest European art collections, the towering edifice is home to a great many artists including Bosch, Titian, Velazquez, and Goya.

Antonio Canova was fifty-seven years old in 1815 when English King George IV commissioned him to create a marble sculpture. This was not an unusual task for the Italian sculptor whose portfolio included Perseus Triumphant, Theseus fighting the Centaur, and The Three Graces. However, Canova would never know that his depiction of Mars and Venus would have such important repercussions for the 21st century.

In the foggy gloom, the outline of the museum was visible. Outside the lone cafe and toward the back of the edifice, two men stood smoking cigarettes and shuffling their feet from side to side to stay warm. Their light banter was a perfect diversion for Ex Nihilo, whose crouched silhouette by the fence line of the museum remained motionless and unsuspected. After a few minutes, the two men threw down their cigarettes and sauntered inside to the warmth of the cozy restaurant. The door closed, and in an instant Ex Nihilo crossed the small space, racing into the Prado Café. Ecstatic, he continued through and into the confines of the main gallery. It was only a matter of time before the building emptied and the mayhem began.

Time was not something that concerned Ex Nihilo. For him, centuries were ephemeral. Before his debilitating clash with the heinous Greek female, he had had the power to strike down divinities as he pleased. He was on a quest to restore himself to his past grandeur. In the beginning, he had moved about the earth as a powerful shape-shifter, a force that could not be overcome. His power was unmatched. *If that deceiving woman wants war, so be it.* She had foiled his plans once, but she would not do so again. What an irritating nuisance she had become. If all went according to plan, she would be dead soon.

Ex Nihilo bristled with resentment, causing one of the overhead lights to shatter. A startled tourist glanced away from *The Marchioness of Santa Cruz* and looked up, seemingly wanting to know what had just happened. Then, unaware of the danger, the tourist returned his attention to Goya's stunning canvas. Hiding behind the priceless painting, Ex Nihilo remained unperturbed. Humans were easily diverted and unaware. They were so weak, so foolish. War was raging around them, and yet they continued with their frivolous lives. Ex Nihilo could feel the magnetism of his next victim. He was so close, his appeal so alluring.

As the smell and proximity of humans evaporated, Ex Nihilo knew it was time to implement his plan. For the next few moments, he needed to be extremely careful; it was crucial to get this transformation right. While exploring and probing the sculpture of Mars and Venus before him, he observed the minuscule alterations in the stone.

If this powerful god could be convinced that Athena was the culprit behind the deities' mysterious disappearances, then she would cease to be a nuisance to him. Everything he knew about this pugnacious and violent deity convinced him that he was the ideal weapon for her destruction.

As he scrutinized the statue of the interlaced lovers, another plan formed in Ex Nihilo's mind. His energy sizzled as he formulated what to do. Creeping into the middle of Room 075, he concentrated with all his might, expanding his shadowy mass across the darkened floor. Abruptly, he shifted upwards, becoming a solid three-dimensional shape. His form seemed to vanish, dissolving into a confined ball full of his deadly, potent energy. The sparks around his form multiplied. A thunderous bolt catapulted into the overhead lights situated directly above the marble sculpture of the intertwined lovers. The metallic structure sizzled and detached from the ceiling. Time seemed to freeze. As the lights fell toward the lovers, the dank mass shot another mighty bolt into the marble structure of the Greek God of War.

The bolt and crash were nearly instantaneous, and caused a sequence of events. The merged figures separated, and the likeness of the Goddess of Love shattered into a million pieces. Next, the lights struck the now sinewy leg of Mars, also known as Ares, who opened his eyes at the sound of the collision. In an instant, Ex Nihilo transformed from a mass of electric voltage into a shadowy figure, then hid behind a canvas.

Ares blinked once, flexing his mighty muscles and, like a menacing lion, craned his head to observe his surroundings. His eyes fell on the scattered remains of his eternal love. Incredulity became confusion, then grief, and finally pure rage. His whole body emanated savagery, violence and wrath. His hand clutched, then shattered the wooden spear that he held. With a nimble leap, he descended from the podium

CHAPTER 9

with a roar that shook the exhibit. The polished floor shook so violently that it cracked.

Ares stood motionless before the remains of his life's love. From behind the canvas of *The Marchioness of Santa Cruz*, Ex Nihilo moved into the exhibit. "She did this," he whispered. "Athena killed her."

Ares' hands hung rigidly by his sides, his fists clenched. His whole body shook with rage.

"She was jealous. She wanted to destroy her, to hurt you." Ex Nihilo's slimy voice snaked into Ares' head.

"No," was all that Ares could muster. His voice cracked with pain.

"She's laughing at you now. Behind your back."

Ares reached his trembling hand forward to stroke the marble scattered on the floor. His whole frame shook violently, as if he was about to explode.

Ex Nihilo knew he was almost there. "She killed your lover. You don't matter while she still breathes. She's your father's favorite child. You are nothing. You are meaningless." Ex Nihilo's voice was crescendoing, filling Ares with poison. "Aphrodite's gone. She'll never come back. She'll never love you again."

"Nooooo!!" Ares screamed at the top of his voice. His massive fists clenched, and he threw himself onto his knees, smashing his hands on the stone floor. The impact of his powerful muscles cracked and splintered the flooring, causing the building to quake.

His chest expanded as his breathing accelerated. His eyes bright red and full of bloodlust, Ares lifted his head and shouted. "Athena!!!!!!"

CHAPTER 10

It was 10:45 pm at the Madrid Barajas International Airport when the ground shook so violently, it felt as if an earthquake had hit the city. The lights around the airport flickered in the gloom. Everyone in the airport collectively held their breath until the vibrations ceased. Then the screaming began.

Athena had pushed Leo to the ground before the earthquake hit. She felt the tremor approaching them, and had only seconds to brace herself. She threw her body on top of his to protect him. The trembling lasted only fifteen seconds; just enough time for Athena to realize that the quake was abnormal. What could have caused such a tremor? Or who?

She put her palm on the ground and whispered the necessary incantation in Attic Greek:

With this touch I restore thee
Go forth and be set free
For your loss and your pain
Are cured in my domain

Athena's armband flashed violet, and she felt the light emanate from her palm and travel all the way across the floor. It repaired cracks and broken windows as it restored the airport to its former self. The people who had fallen on the floor were looking around in confusion. It was obvious by their dazed expressions that many thought the

CHAPTER 10

earthquake had been a hallucination.

Athena crouched over Leo, giving him a quick examination. He looked uninjured, but he was intently studying his hands. "Are you alright?" she asked.

"Yeah. I could have sworn I cut my hand, but it's fine now." He held it close to his face.

"Good. Get a cab. We're going to central Madrid. We have no time to lose! It might strike again."

Leo ran toward the street and stretched out his hand, frantically waving. At that moment, another tremor shook the ground; not as potent as the first, but strong enough to make him lose his balance and fall backwards. Every car and bus stopped. In panic, the people in the airport started screaming.

Athena gritted her teeth and approached a Peugeot Traveler Van with a neon sign that said, "UBER." She wrenched open the front door to find the driver sitting in the passenger seat, smoking a cigarette and listening to the radio.

"¡Oye!" said the man in Spanish.

"I need to borrow your car," Athena said, also in Spanish.

The man seemed about to argue, so Athena placed her hand on the driver's head, sending him into a deep slumber. The Council had given each divine representative two magical powers in order to protect the humans from exposure; one was the ability to alter memories, and the second was dreamless sleep.

Athena reached over the seat, grabbed the man's keys, and latched the seatbelt around him. Leo had joined her, and was staring at the stunned man.

"Do you know how to drive?" she asked Leo.

"Um, yeah, but not on this side of the road."

There's a first time for everything. She ran around the car and opened the driver's door. "Get in!" she yelled at Leo while she adjusted the driver's seat.

Leo opened the sliding door and stepped into the back of the van. "Do *you* know how to drive?" he questioned.

"No. Explain the basics really fast," she demanded as she fumbled with the mirrors and the seat belt.

Leo attached his seatbelt and made a quick gesture up to the sky. "Ok, so there are three pedals. The one on the right is for accelerating, and the one in the middle is for stopping. You turn the key in the ignition, and that starts the engine. You fidget with the gears since this car is manual, and the faster you go, the more you have to switch gears. Press down on the clutch," he signaled the left pedal, "and that's how you switch gears. The wheel is pretty straightforward; you turn it in the direction that you want to go," he breathlessly concluded.

Athena started the engine. "Anything else I should know?"

"Don't go above a certain speed. Um, try to go at an average speed or less than the fastest car. And turn your lights on!"

Athena pressed the right pedal, and the car jerked forward. She continued playing around with the wheel and the gears. *Ingenious,* she said to herself, as the old van headed southwest.

CHAPTER 11

As they sped along Madrid's highways, Leo prayed, although he didn't know to whom or what he was praying. Athena was driving just below the speed limit. Every once in a while, she would glance down at her vegvisir necklace and adjust the wheel to turn in the direction it indicated.

"You have to stay in the lane!" yelled Leo as the driver in the car behind them honked aggressively.

"You didn't mention that," Athena coolly said.

Leo sighed and tried to keep calm. Driving lessons with his mom certainly did not prepare him for this. "The white and yellow lines mean that you can't move out of your lane. You can change lanes only if you use your blinkers."

"Where are those?"

"They should be to the left of your wheel. Move it up to show you're going right, and down to show left." He wiped sweat from his brow.

Athena focused on the road ahead while moving the signals next to the wheel. She even tried the windshield wipers.

Leo was starting to feel slightly calmer. His panic stemmed not only from being in a car with someone who had never driven before, but it was also night time, and they were on one of the busiest highways in Western Europe. He tried to relax. Closing his eyes, he whispered to himself, *deep breaths, one, two, three.* His heart rate dropped minutely, but he felt more in control. *It's going to be alright. I can do this. We'll be fine.*

He heard the sound of the blinker and opened his eyes. So far they hadn't crashed. They were still alive. He sighed and looked out the window toward the bright buildings on the horizon, which seemed to be shaking slightly. Leo grabbed his glasses and wiped them clean with his shirt. He squinted toward the buildings once more. Now the structures were violently shaking, flooding outwards and speeding towards them.

"Ah! Ahh! Athena!!!" he screamed as he pointed at the quaking skyscrapers. She rapidly turned to spot the danger.

Flashing her left turn signal, she drove the van onto the shoulder of the highway. Opening the window, she reached toward her left bicep and took out her spear. It transformed from a tiny replica into a massive, almost seven foot long blade. In one swift motion, she jammed the end into the ground and rapidly began her incantation.

The streets broke apart as the shaking tore through Madrid, and the cars around them violently screeched to a stop. Athena's talisman was shining brightly through her clothes, and Leo could feel an invisible energy emanating from her spear, colliding against the remaining vibrations of the temblor. Her powerful healing energy automatically repaired the shattered roads and separated the cars that had collided. Athena groaned as she continued to recite her incantation, her brow furrowed in concentration.

"Leo," she said, "I need you to hold onto my spear." Leo gulped and unbuckled his seatbelt, then crawled over their packs to sit right behind the driver's seat. Forcing the door open, he reached over and clutched the wooden spear in his left hand.

"You're going to have to touch my shoulder while I drive. Do not break the connection," commanded Athena. Leo held onto her shoulder with his right hand. He felt the energy flowing through his

CHAPTER 11

body as it progressed toward the spear. "Ready?" asked Athena, her eyes focused on the cars in front of her.

"Ready," answered Leo, his voice breaking.

Athena changed gears and sped forward, veering from lane to lane in order to avoid the stopped cars and buses.

For the rest of the drive from the Madrid-Barajas Airport to the city center, Leo held on for dear life to Athena's wooden weapon. Somehow he knew that the spear would not fall or shatter, even if he let go of it. Yet he would never break one of Athena's commands; he feared the repercussions more than anything else in the world. For the remaining ten minutes of the drive, the spear sent out sparks that collided with the van's exterior. Within the same second, however, the spear repaired itself and the ground around it. The cuts that it made in the road disappeared immediately. Athena's armband burned brighter and brighter as they approached the city's center, flashing past tree after tree that, because of her healing powers, now stood tall and erect.

Once the van turned onto Paseo de la Infanta Isabel, Athena signaled and the van sped toward Calle de Alfonso XII. Carefully braking in front of the massive Retiro Park, Athena jumped out of the driver's seat, took the spear from Leo's trembling hand, and went to check on the sleeping man in the passenger seat. She opened the backdoor, waved Leo out, and hitched her Patagonia pack across her shoulders. Grabbing a 50 euro note, she placed it in the man's hand, and signaled for Leo to follow her.

Leo squinted into the darkness. The lights around the park were unnaturally dim, as if the electric power had been cut. Holding her spear, Athena crouched in a defensive position.

Then they began to follow the vegvisir north through the park. They reached a massive clearing just as the mystical tool pointed northeast. Athena unbuckled her pack and motioned to Leo to do the same. He did, and then reached into his bag and pulled out a headlamp which he placed on his head.

Athena raised a finger to her lips. She slid under the bushes and analyzed the field in front of her, then let out a gasp of surprise.

"What is it?" Leo whispered. He pictured enormous beasts with fangs that dripped poison, or giant, hairy creatures that could kill them with one swing of their mighty arms.

Athena did not respond. She seemed to be concentrating intently. Leo was burning with curiosity, and slowly he peered out over the bushes, trying to find the source of her alarm. He couldn't see anything beyond a couple meters. His hand reached upwards to turn on the headlamp when Athena quickly pulled him down.

"I'm sorry! I wasn't going to turn it on," he whispered.

"We need to be really careful. We can't frighten him." Athena's eyes were pleading as if trying to defend the creature. "Here. Hold my spear," she commanded.

Taking the talisman from her bicep, she wrapped it around the spear, then rapidly whispered another incantation.

My foes and enemies I curse
To trap inside this shield of force
With no way to disperse
For only I can reverse its course
And free you from your worst

Leo was in awe, half in protest, knowing that Athena depended on the talisman for survival. Then he heard a noise in the distance that sounded like sobs. His first thought was that someone nearby was in pain, or possibly being devoured by the monster. As he stood up, the sobs became piercing screams of anger, then a deep throaty release of pain.

"Focus, Leo!" Athena shoved him down. "Now listen very carefully.

CHAPTER 11

Avoid looking at him; do not let him see you! You need to circle us. I'm going to distract him while you keep the spear on the ground and draw a circle around us. Do not break the line; keep the spear on the ground."

Leo nodded. *Draw a circle, and don't look up. Got it.* Athena straightened as she prepared to enter the clearing. Leo followed closely behind her. After fifteen paces, he turned away from the sobbing.

Once he was far enough away, he peered into the night and saw a kneeling silhouette that resembled a naked man. His arms were over his head, and his huge chest was expanding rapidly. Leo felt pity for the creature. It was clearly in distress. The man gave another even more piercing scream of anguish as he pounded his massive fists on the ground. The impact threw Leo backwards, and he fell, almost dropping the spear. The man hit the ground so hard that the earth shook, and the trees snapped in half.

"Noooooo!!" the man hollered at the top of his lungs.

Leo's heart was pumping fast. Fixing his glasses, he stared at the man and noticed the outline of Athena who was slowly approaching the crouching being with caution. Her hands were outstretched in a signal of helplessness. The man's head snapped upward like a ferocious lion whose meal was being threatened.

"Youuuuuuuuu!!!!" he bellowed. His booming voice sent shivers down Leo's spine.

"You did this!!!!!" he continued, rising to his feet. Leo clearly could see his outline. His skin was shining in the moonlight, his muscles bulging with tension. In the cold, steam rose from his exposed skin.

"You killed her!! I will destroy you!!" The man grabbed the nearest tree and hurled it at Athena, who easily avoided it.

Leo's hand slipped down the spear, and that movement helped him remember his mission. With all his might, he stuck the wooden weapon in the ground and slowly began walking behind the fuming man, careful to keep himself out of sight.

"Ares," Athena calmly said, "What happened, brother?"

"Don't you brother me!! You did this!! You killed her!!" Ares was screaming at the top of his lungs. He tried charging Athena, and stomped the ground so hard that Leo's bones shook. He clenched his teeth to stop them from chattering, and continued making the circle.

Athena moved slowly, trying to lure Ares toward her. Her voice was soothing and reassuring. "Ares, who did I kill? What happened?"

"You did this!! You killed Aphrodite!!" Ares bellowed, throwing his fists toward the sky. "By Zeus, I will kill you!!!" Ares glared at Athena. His eyes were a bright red that resembled blood. He was an angry bull about to charge. Instead of attacking, however, he struck the ground with all his might. Leo was able to grab hold of the spear before the collision, and he remained on his feet. The trembling that resulted was unlike any that had come before. It was three times as hard and as savage. Even Athena had to place one knee on the ground to steady herself.

"Ares, please, calm yourself. How could I have killed Aphrodite? I haven't even seen her since I left! Tell me what happened."

Instead of answering, Ares threw a massive boulder at Athena. Nimbly, she rolled out of the way before it shattered on the ground, missing her by inches.

"All I know is that I looked down, and she was gone!!!!"

"Ares! You are not making sense! Calm down!" Athena ordered in a commanding voice.

"She's gone!!!! First Hephaestion, and now you!! I will destroy you!!"

Leo was halfway done completing the circle, but was getting too close to Ares's peripheral vision. Athena glanced quickly at him and then back at Ares.

"For the last time, what happened?!" she yelled.

CHAPTER 11

Ares' tantrum was only beginning. His chest heaved and he bared his teeth. Once more, he prepared to strike the ground with his massive fists, yet Athena intervened before he could cause another quake. Grabbing a few of the shattered rocks, she hurled them at Ares, each hitting its mark.

"If you want a fight, I will give you a fight!" She declared, pulling her shield from her bicep and locking it in front of her. Filled with deadly wrath, Ares stared at Athena. He was so blinded by frustration and loathing that he did not see Leo creeping up behind him to complete the circle.

Athena refrained from drawing her sword, but kept her shield in place as she stalked forward then shifted sideways, forcing Ares to mirror her movement. Leo was about to close the ring when Ares charged Athena. He ran at lighting speed with his head down. Athena had no choice but to lunge sideways to avoid a collision. After one last sprint, Leo finally was able to reach his starting position. He felt the spear tremble as he pulled it from the ground. As he lowered the spear a fraction, it snapped backwards.

What was that? Tentatively, he put out his hand and moved it forward. In front of him, an invisible shield was now separating him from the fighting deities. He stroked the undetectable wall and then hit it with his fist. It did not bulge. He hooted in triumph.

"Oh, shit." He covered his mouth with his hands, but it was too late. Both Ares and Athena were looking straight at him, one with concern and the other with loathing. Ares let out a war cry and charged toward Leo. His eyes burned bright red, and his snarl made him look rabid. Leo froze, hoping that the invisible shield would somehow withstand the rushing Ares.

Athena was closing in on Ares, yelling for him to stop. He was meters away now, and Leo closed his eyes in dread. For the second time that day, he prayed. He caught the sound of a body colliding with a solid mass, then heard Ares' roar of distress. Cautiously, he opened his eyes and discovered Ares standing right in front of him, staring straight into his eyes. In vain, he pounded the wall between them, trying to break his way through. Standing behind Ares, Athena raised her shield and smacked her brother across the back of his head, knocking him unconscious.

Leo felt his heart racing. He slumped and collapsed onto the ground. Athena felt for Ares' pulse. Satisfied, she sighed and walked through the shield. She knelt near Leo and placed her palm on the ground, reciting her healing incantation. Around them the boulders returned to their original shape, while the trees regained their full stature.

The eerie silence was broken by faraway shouting. Leo tensed and searched for their source.

"Get down!" Athena hissed. She gracefully lowered herself while she analyzed the approaching figures.

Leo threw himself on the ground and, unable to close his eyes, he stared up at the night sky. He could make out muffled yells from the men whose voices grew louder by the second. As he tried to control his breathing, a new sound caught his attention.

It was a flutter of wings, as if a bird had come to observe the spectacle. Leo realized that Athena was also aware of the bird. He followed the goddess' gaze and squinted into the dark. At the top of one of the tallest trees, a lone falcon rested. His dark eyes were surrounded by bright yellow flesh, making them glow in the night. The magnificent creature regarded them with curiosity. After what felt like an eternity, the falcon's head turned away, and then back to the group on the ground.

Leo could clearly make out the voices now. Four to five men were approaching the clearing, their heavy footsteps echoing in the gloomy night. Suddenly, Leo saw a bright flash of light and groaned inwardly. The men were security guards investigating the recent scuffle.

CHAPTER 11

"Over here, over here!" called one of the guards in Spanish.

Athena was still staring at the wonderful bird. With one flap of its wings, it disappeared into the night. Out of nowhere, the men's shouts of encouragement turned to shrieks of panic.

"Get him off of me!" they screeched.

"Run!" yelled one of the guards. The lights faded into the distance. Athena tapped Leo on the shoulder and murmured, "Get the packs."

Leo nodded and crawled toward the bushes that hid their belongings. Strapping his bag to his waist and adjusting it on his back, he headed back to Athena, who was crouched over the sleeping Ares, trying to figure out the best way to carry him.

"He's so heavy," she groaned as she tried to push him up. Now that he was closer to the God of War, Leo was able to examine the deity. Ares was muscled like a bull; every tendon in his body bulged. Leo grabbed one of Ares' arms and puffed with the effort.

"Geez, how much does he weigh?" he wheezed. In stature, Ares was a couple of inches shorter than Leo, yet at least sixty pounds heavier. Leo guessed Athena must be one hundred pounds lighter than her half-brother.

While trying to figure out how they would be able to move this colossal being, Leo averted his eyes. Holding his glasses out in front of him, he coughed. "Um, Athena? I'm not sure we can take Ares anywhere in this state," he mumbled.

"I know he's heavy, but we'll find a way to move him. We need to get the truth out of him," said the goddess, oblivious of Leo's discomfort.

Leo awkwardly harrumphed. "I meant that he's not wearing any clothes. If someone were to see us carrying him around, they would charge us with public indecency."

"Oh." She was quiet for a moment.

"I'm sure I have something that might fit him."

"Yes, yes. I shall help you."

In clumsy silence, the pair tried wrestling the hefty Ares into a variety of outfits. After a long struggle, they were able to dress him in dark gray joggers and a white t-shirt. The shirt was so tight that it seemed almost invisible, and as they shifted Ares to a sitting position, it ripped in the back.

"If we carry him by his arms and legs, we might get somewhere," Leo dubiously offered.

"Our hands might slip and we will drop him," cautioned Athena. She paced around the clearing.

Suddenly, her eyes glowed. "I know how we can carry him! But you must never mention it to anyone. Ever. Ares might dismember you on the spot."

Lifting her spear from the ground, Athena knotted Ares' hands together with rope from her pack. She moved to his legs and attached them to the bottom of the spear. "The wood won't bend, and we'll be able to use most of our body strength."

"Ok," said Leo skeptically. At the sight of the belligerent god tied up like a pig for roasting, he felt like bursting out in laughter. Athena words rang true, however, Ares would eliminate him instantly.

"Where should we take him?"

"Let's go somewhere in the open air, surrounded by people yet with some privacy. With me around, Ares will hesitate to throw a tantrum in front of mortals."

Together they heaved and hoisted the spear onto their shoulders. Their height difference forced Leo to bend his knees slightly. Leo was in the lead and following Athena's commands. Moving along the pedestrian route, they slowly walked north on Calle Nicaragua.

"We can't walk with him like this in public," called Athena as Ares' body swayed from side to side.

"You're right. Let's take him over there," Leo said in between gasping breaths.

CHAPTER 11

They were nearing a massive pond where a sprawling monument had been erected for Alfonso XII. It was filled with statues, and had steps leading down to the pond where, during previous visits to Madrid, Leo had seen tourists resting and picnicking.

Leo's muscles shook as he tried to gently set down the snoring god. Exhaling with triumph, he lowered himself onto the steps and rested his head on his knees.

"Are you sure we'll be indistinguishable here? It seems empty," questioned Athena.

"These steps are a very popular spot to watch the sun rise and set. Sunrise will start in about five hours, and it will be full of people by then. We'll blend right in. We look like average backpackers. Well, maybe not average, but we will be fine here."

Opening his pack in search of food, Leo found his phone. He hadn't checked it since they left London. He had a few missed calls and texts, and he skimmed through them. His heart fluttered as he read David's lone text:

"Hey, Leo. Hope you are having fun with your sister. Let me know if you want to hang out soon. Would love to show Alex around London."

Deep in thought, Leo tapped his phone. He erased each sentence he managed to type. He was unsure of what to say, and kept getting lost in his words.

"You should rest," said Athena in her soothing voice.

Up until that moment, Leo hadn't realized how exhausted he was. Laying his head on his pack, he fell into a deep slumber.

CHAPTER 12

April 27th

Again, Leo was dreaming of his father. He must have been five years old when his father disappeared. In his dream, young Leo sat at the kitchen table drawing on a wrinkled piece of paper. He was near the window and noticed it was cold; it must have snowed during the night. He could hear faint shuffling and loud argumentative voices from above. He kept on drawing. Fights between his parents were commonplace.

Two looming figures headed down the stairs, their argument getting louder and louder. At the bottom of the stairs, his father turned sharply, hitting his shoulder bag against the table. Leo was not surprised when he heard the Italian vase shatter. "Well, you've done it again!" cried his mother, her voice crystal clear.

In his dreams, like in real life, Leo could not remember what happened next. Sometimes his father calmly walked out of the house without any hint of emotion. Other times, his father yelled and threw objects across the room.

This time, however, his father looked directly at Leo. His father's eyes were on his young son's face as if burying deep into his soul. Leo shrank at his forceful gaze. Had he really looked at him before he left? Leo wasn't sure. He could barely recall his father's features. Even

CHAPTER 12

in this lucid dream, his father's face was unrecognizable. It seemed darkened, as if masked by hatred and loathing. His eyes were shining with a malice that made the hair on Leo's skin stand up.

"You are not my son. You are an insult. I never want to see you again." His father's voice was soft, and the faint sound made his words crueler than if they had been shouted.

His father dissolved into a black fog, and the scene around him changed. Leo was sitting in a large school room with an old notebook on his lap. His uniform pants were gray, and his shirt was maroon. Slowly, he fixed his curls behind his ear and tried to focus on his work. He heard sneers from the boys in the front of the classroom.

"I bet that's why his father left him," one of the boys said.

"Stupid faggot," responded another.

Leo swallowed hard and pretended to be oblivious to their comments. Absently, he kept doodling in his notebook, not truly seeing what he was drawing.

"I'd wager he's not even a boy. Look at him. He's probably a girl or some sort of strange hybrid," remarked the tallest of the gang. The group sniggered and pointed, making sure they were loud enough for Leo to hear.

Leo closed his eyes and sighed. *Don't listen to them. Don't listen to them.* When he opened his eyes again, he noticed the picture he had drawn. It was a fiery demon, dark and mysterious. His eyes, filled with murder, blazed. Leo yelled and tossed the notebook away, feeling as if his hands were burning.

"Leo? Are you alright?" The soothing voice brought his mind back from the nightmare.

Opening his eyes, Leo straightened. "Agh. What time is it?" he asked. The sun was shining brightly.

"9 am. You're sweating. Are you alright?" repeated Athena.

Leo put his palm to his face and realized he felt clammy. He looked down and saw that his shirt was drenched in sweat. "I'm not sure. I...."

Nobody apart from David knew about his nightmares. It had taken a lot of time for him to open up about his recurring fears. Even if years had gone by, the sting from his childhood felt as fresh as a slap on the face. He wavered between honesty and shrugging it off.

Athena laid a hand on his shoulder and gently squeezed. "You don't have to tell me if you don't want to. I'm here for you," she said.

He felt a deep sense of gratitude toward her. "Thanks, Athena. Really, it was just a nightmare," said Leo. Yet something in the back of his mind irked him. There was something distinctly different about this nightmare. What had he seen that was odd? What was it that made his skin crawl and his heart pound?

He heard a large exhale next to Athena. Ares' massive form shifted toward them. The God of War snored peacefully, looking like a contented adult napping in the sun.

"He hasn't woken up?" Leo whispered.

"He'll be up any time now. We'll need to be calm and soothing," Athena said. "Can you pretend to be asleep? He'll find it more comforting to know that you won't be privy to what he has to say."

"Of course. I can leave and go on a walk if you want; I don't mind," said Leo.

"No. You should be here. You might pick up on something I miss. You're important to me." Athena gave him a kind smile and squeezed his hand.

"Sounds good. I'll roll over in case I make a noise." Adjusting himself on the stone steps, he nestled in, using his pack as a pillow. Athena trusted him! She said he was important. If he could cry, he would. But he was afraid to wake the sleeping Ares. Faintly, he smiled. *Sleeping beauty.*

As a student of history, Leo knew the reputation of the Greek

CHAPTER 12

Olympians. They were all stunning, splendid and alluring. Wars had been fought over who was the most beautiful, as was the case in Paris' ill-fated judgment when the sparring queens of heaven argued over who was the fairest of them all. In the end Paris gave the golden apple to Aphrodite, the goddess of love, beauty and fertility, who swayed him with promises of rewarding him with the most beautiful woman on Earth. These events subsequently triggered the famous Trojan War. If only he'd known what the consequences of his actions would be. But then, how could anyone know?

Leo was reminded of something he had not truly considered until now. He was glad he was allied with Athena, for she rarely lost a fight. He wondered what the cost of his alliance would be, and how it would affect his family. Surely they would be safe. As intimidating as Ares was, Athena was someone you did not want to cross. Her poise and perfect manners were but one small layer of her personality. Leo felt that Athena was highly motivated, driven by the need to succeed and willing to prevail at any cost. In most Greek myths, her favored heroes did enjoy everlasting glory, but the price for legendary immortality was high.

Odysseus provoked Poseidon, and he was cursed to spend ten years at sea, separated from hearth and home, wife and child. Heracles or Hercules, his Roman counterpart, was considered the greatest of the Greek heroes, yet he was tricked by an angry Hera into slaying his wife and children. To expiate the crime and clean himself from familicide, he was at first forced to complete ten labours by his arch-enemy. Later it was increased to twelve.

It was crucial for Leo to stay on the good side of these immortal beings. One wrong step with either Athena, or more likely Ares, and he would be cleaning the entire universe with a toothbrush. He swallowed and eased himself into a meditative state, waiting for the god to awaken.

While he meditated, he thought of David. He should give him a call tonight, or else David might get worried. *At least I hope he worries.* His relationship with David was more than just friendship, but they had never spoken about such matters. Leo wondered if it was all in his head – the glances, the soft smiles, the winks whenever they were in a crowd of strangers. Next time they spoke in person – if he ever saw David again – Leo would summon up the courage to ask him out. He hesitated. Maybe he should wait and talk about romantic interests first. What if David rejected him? What if……

Leo's thoughts were interrupted by a loud groan. He shut his eyes tight and tried to control his breathing.

"Where… What… How…" mumbled Ares.

Leo heard a loud cracking sound. He guessed that Ares was stretching his entire body and waking his powerful muscles.

"Ares, brother. You are safe now," entoned the calm voice of Athena.

"You killed her," slurred Ares. "I saw her remains."

"Brother, I would never purposely hurt Aphrodite. She's family, and no matter our differences, you know I would never kill her."

"But the voice. It said you did it, and she was gone. You hurt me. I know you did it because you've hurt me before," whimpered a shaky voice that Leo was astonished to realize belonged to Ares. Leo could discern another sound; was someone crying? Leo imagined that Athena might be trying to soothe her belligerent half-brother.

"There, there. I know we've had our differences, but this is bigger than anything we've faced before. We were enemies in Troy, and look at where that got us. We are never strong divided, Ares. I wouldn't want you as my enemy. So why would I hurt her? When we are allies, we are powerful and indestructible."

"So you didn't hurt Aphrodite?" said Ares.

"Of course not," Athena said.

Ares raised his voice to an alarming boom. "Then who killed her?"

CHAPTER 12

"Calm down, please. We're in public. Lay back down, and I'll tell you everything I know," Athena promised.

Grumpily, Ares set his head down on Athena's lap, and she began stroking his hair. "I haven't seen Aunt Aphrodite since I left Olympus three moons ago. I was unaware that more of us could come into this world without the express consent of the Council. How did you get here?" Athena asked.

"I don't know. One minute, I was enjoying myself in the company of Dionysus and Hermes the next, I was in this miserable place," grumbled Ares.

"You mentioned a voice. What voice are you talking about?" Athena asked.

"The one that told me you hurt Aphrodite," said Ares in a tone that was both petulant and sardonic.

"Yes, I understand. Where did you hear that voice? Whose voice was it?"

"I don't know; it was in my head! I couldn't recognize it. But it made me so angry, I just wanted to rip your head off and stuff it with...."

"Yes, I can see how that voice made you feel. There, there," interrupted Athena. She continued playing with his hair, not breaking physical contact. Leo could feel the tension ease, and he heard Ares' breathing return to normal. He wondered if he should snore to pretend that he was still asleep, but realized Ares had not even noticed him.

"Let me guess. Nod your head if I'm correct. You woke in a room full of pictures or paintings. There was no other person or creature in sight. You've mentioned Aphrodite was killed. Yet there was no sign of injury, correct? No blood or flesh visible. As you say, she was shattered. Did her remaining pieces look solid? Maybe even white as marble?" queried Athena.

"How did you know that? You were there," accused Ares.

Athena ignored his scalding tone. "Then I am happy to confirm that Aphrodite is safe and sound. She is still up in Olympus, and did not journey here with you. As for your presence, I can only assume that whoever brought you here wanted to provoke you into an uncontrollable rage."

"So my love is safe? She's alive?" asked Ares, his voice shifting from testy to cheerful.

"Yes. She's unharmed. In addition, I am sure Father would have come down and mercilessly attacked whoever harmed her," replied Athena.

"I'm not so sure about that. We all thought you were dead a couple weeks ago, and he was livid. He raged and threw down thunderbolts. You know how much he loves you in comparison to everyone else. He often says, 'My favorite child.' But even the great Zeus, Lord of the Skies, did not come down to avenge you," responded Ares haughtily.

Athena was stunned into silence. She momentarily faltered and stopped toying with Ares' hair. "He must have been relieved when I awoke two days ago," she replied with forced casualness.

"Eh. He might have been pleased, but he was pretty angry at Apollo."

"Why? What did Apollo do?"

"Hermes told me the story, but it was really long and I didn't pay much attention. But apparently when Father heard the news that you were dead, he got intensely angry and went off on his own. Artemis raged and wanted to avenge you. So, in truth, did I. Nobody gets to kill you except me. Hephaestus and Demeter were panicking as usual, blithering fools. But Apollo disappeared. We found out later that he came to Earth. He didn't ask anyone; he just puffed and vanished. Hera raced to tell Father, and he was horrified. He forbade us from following Apollo down to Earth, and just in time, because Artemis was already done packing her special arrows," concluded Ares.

Leo was awed to hear Ares and Athena chat about the Olympians in

CHAPTER 12

such familiar tones. The realization that Apollo, god of the sun and light, music and poetry, healing and plagues, prophecy and knowledge, order and beauty, among many others, was also on Earth, struck him a blow. He wondered if he had been captured like the others, or if he was gone forever.

Athena was silent for a long time. Ares sat up and moved next to her, cracking his knuckles. Athena finally broke her silence. "When did Apollo come down?"

"Hm. Maybe a day or two after your supposed death. I'm not sure, I don't keep tabs on the golden boy."

"Did you see him die like you saw me?" asked Athena.

"No. I didn't see you, either. Helios told us about your accident, that snitch. I'll wring his neck one day," fumed Ares.

Leo recalled that in Greek Mythology, Helios, the Titan personification of the sun, had told Hephaestus about Ares and Aphrodite's love affair. In revenge, Hephaestus, who was married to Aphrodite, had trapped the lovers in a net and humiliated the embracing paramours.

"Maybe Apollo is still alive. I'll check," said the goddess as she reached for her necklace.

"Huh?" grunted Ares. He stared at her magical stave. Leo heard Athena give a triumphant hoot.

"He's still on Earth!" she happily exclaimed.

"How do you know?" Ares asked.

"This is a vegvisir; a mythological Norse talisman. I was looking for the evil creature who woke you, the voice in your head that tried to pit you against me. I call him Ex Nihilo. The vegvisir showed us that he was here in Madrid. Now we know why: he was trying to get us into an epic fight. I'm thankful we found you just in time." Athena wrapped one arm over her half-brother's massive shoulder.

"This necklace points to the object or person for whom I'm searching. Here, come closer. Notice that the arrow is about to change;

it is because I'm thinking of finding you. So now the arrow is pointing directly at you. If I search for Aphrodite or any of our family, the arrow will not stop spinning, since they are not here on Earth. See? But if I think about Apollo, and I picture him in my mind's eye... Ah! There! The arrow is pointing northeast."

She turned and shook Leo, whispering for him to wake up. Leo pretended to be oblivious, even though he had been following their conversation. He shook his head and rubbed his eyes for dramatic effect. Sitting up, he turned to look at Athena.

"Brother, this is Leo Clarkson. He's accompanying me on my journey. He's been studying mythological talismans," said Athena.

Leo fixed his glasses and stared at the imposing figure of Ares. He could not believe that he was sitting down on the steps of the Retiro Park with two gods of war. Their differences were striking. Athena was slender and graceful, whereas Ares was massive and intimidating. Athena's gray-green eyes reflected strength of mind, while Ares' black eyes reflected distrust and hunger. It felt as if whoever stared into them would lose self-control. Leo's heart raced and a need to fight took over his body like a drug. Ares' unnerving stare was enough to make Leo's skin crawl. He wondered how in the world the goddess of beauty, of love, of pleasure and passion, could have fallen for such a menacing being. It was true that Ares was good-looking in his own way, but all Leo could see or feel was uneasiness mixed with bloodlust.

Athena gently touched his knee. The motion made Leo blink, causing him to break the grip that Ares had on him. He cleared his throat and extended his hand. "Nice to meet you. I'm Leo," he said. He had no idea where he had gained the courage to offer his hand to this domineering god. He wished he could take back the gesture, but he knew that the action would demean him in Ares' eyes.

Ares glared at Leo, and then at his outstretched hand. His mouth curled into a snarl. He seemed to be weighing the possibilities of

CHAPTER 12

fighting Leo without angering or provoking Athena. After what felt like a lifetime, Ares reached out and shook his hand.

Leo moaned inwardly as he felt his hand being crushed, but after looking at their linked hands, he realized that Ares was barely touching him. *This guy is seriously strong.* Ares released the handshake and scornfully said, "Another one of your human pets, Athena?"

Flipping her hair to one side, Athena raised her head high. "He's not my pet. He's helping me on my journey."

Ares raised an eyebrow. "Sure. So what do you do? Are you a fierce warrior? A capitan? An army commander? A navigator?"

"He's a wayfinder and a researcher," Athena answered quickly. "Leo, my half-brother Apollo is missing. We need to find him as soon as possible; he might be in peril. Can you tell me where he might be?"

Ares looked at Leo and snorted; as if this speck of a human could ever find someone as important as the golden Apollo.

Leo understood Athena's hint. Once more he was grateful; she was letting him show Ares his worth. He searched his bag for the map Athena had entrusted to him. Carefully unrolling it, he pointed to the vegvisir and politely asked, "May I?" Athena nodded, and Leo held the vegvisir in his palm. He moved it slowly across the map in a northeasterly direction until the arrow shifted minutely, signaling that he had passed Apollo's location.

"Oh," was all Leo could say. Apollo was in Paris.

CHAPTER 13

Nestled in between the South China Sea and the Philippine Sea, the island of Luzon is home to the Sierra Madre Mountains. This magnificent mountain range makes up approximately 40 percent of the country's total forest cover. The largest governmentally protected area of the Philippines is the Northern Sierra Madre Natural Park of Luzon.

One of the natural wonders of Luzon is Mount Cagua, located in the northern part of the island. It is considered an active stratovolcano, even though the most recent eruption was during the early years of the twentieth century. It has a circular summit crater of about a mile in diameter with steep, 200 foot walls. Locally, the volcano is known as "Fire Mountain." The local population was not wrong to name it so.

Racing through the bright green jungle of his native habitat, Ex Nihilo pondered his next move as he approached his destination. He was heading to one of his ancient lairs, Mount Cagua, which loomed in the horizon, dark and imposing.

So the goddess survived. It was time to stop underestimating her stubbornness and her will to live. She was shrewd and patient, two bothersome qualities in an enemy. Back in Madrid, Ex Nihilo had hoped that the incredibly powerful Ares would somehow weaken her, maybe even detain her from pursuing him. However, she was able to subdue him... but not without the help of that insignificant human. Before these recent events, Ex Nihilo had not considered humans as effective or even useful.

To him, humans were nasty creatures, intent on delusion, selfishness and self-destruction. They were the dust on the bottoms of his feet. No other creature could show as much envy and greed as a human. When he commenced his plan, he avoided their reeking presence, deeming them so far below his interest that he could have killed entire populations without even lifting his finger. It had been very clever of the goddess to hide her presence among them. How she could stand their ignorance and their stupidity, he did not know. Even after her defeat, he did not think his foe could sink lower, but the Greek was full of surprises. She took advantage of a human, and used him as a pawn to bring herself back into the world. It was brilliant, and Ex Nihilo bristled in resentment.

He followed the crater's edge to the entrance of his cave. A smoking hot spring with sky-blue and lime-green moss signaled the entryway. "Massok," he hissed. At the sound of this access key, a stone vault opened beneath his silhouette. This hidden entryway was how one could access the outer layers of the Kasamaan. Ex Nihilo dissolved and slithered into the crevice leading to his elusive cave of pandemonium.

For centuries his cave had been silent, his agents quieted by time and repose. But not for long. If Athena would ally with the humans against him, he would destroy them in return.

The rocky crevice was completely black; not a sliver of light was able to seep through the stone. He focused his energy and flared, lighting the twelve wooden tapers that surrounded the cave. First, he would summon three of his agents of chaos. The fourth and most deadly, he would save for last.

Staring at the carved figures of his devotees, he summoned all his hatred and power to shoot three electrifying bolts of plasma into the stone-like beings. With a crash like thunder and a groan that split the wall of the cave, his pupils awoke.

The first to react was Manggagaway. She stretched and yawned, moving her shape from side to side in the process.

"Transform yourself," commanded Ex Nihilo.

Manggagaway nodded and reached her hand to the other two shapeless beings next to her. In an instant, the three stood in human form, each admiring his own flesh and figure. Manggagaway was slight of build, with snowy white skin and dark squinting eyes. Her hair, black as ink, cascaded down to her waist. She appeared focused, ready to follow whatever command was given.

His second agent was Mangkukulam. He flexed his hands and ardently examined his fingers. In one swift motion, he placed thumb to forefinger and snapped them. Flames erupted from his fingertips. Mangkukulam smiled. His teeth reflected the same orange glow that emanated from his skin and eyes. He turned and bowed to Ex Nihilo. "Master. We have missed you," he purred.

The third agent of chaos was Manisilat. She cackled a high, screechy laugh that would cause a child to cry. She moved her hands toward her head, feeling the tight, helix shape of her hair. She pulled her head back and roared in contentment, quickly caressing her body and beaming at her companions. "We're back!" Manisilat's voice was low and deep, full of mirth and mischief.

Manggagaway looked toward the fourth stone figure and cocked her head to one side. Ex Nihilo did not miss this silent question. "I have a different task for Hukluban," his voice sounded in her head.

Manggagaway straightened her head without changing the expression on her face. The two others did not notice the exchange. Manggagway expectantly looked around, waiting for the next command.

"We are preparing for war," said Ex Nihilo in a tone that allowed for no argument. Of course there would be no argument; it was for

CHAPTER 13

destruction and chaos that his agents were created.

Manisilat hooted and slapped the air with her fist. Mangkukulam smiled a ghastly, slimy smile, curling his lips upward without showing his burnt teeth. Manggagway waited without so much as moving a muscle.

"You will be sent to different corners of the world. There you will be free to do as you please, with only two rules," commanded Ex Nihilo.

The three figures stood expectantly. Manggagaway leaned forward. Mangkukulam opened his eyes so wide, they seemed about to explode, and Manisilat excitedly bounced up and down on her toes.

Ex Nihilo continued. "One: if you have the misfortune to encounter another deity, do not fight them. Do not engage, do not even acknowledge. Keep your true nature and identities a secret." Ex Nihilo stared at each until they nodded their heads. He wanted to create chaos, he craved pandemonium, he desired calamity. He would spread his corruption throughout the world and taint the earth. "Two: destroy everything and everyone you can."

Manisilat shouted in anticipation, then laughing, she darted out of the cave. Mangkukulam's eyes blazed a fiery orange as he bowed his head in respect, then vanished. Manggagaway allowed herself a brief smile before crossing her arms over her body and dissolving into a mist.

Ex Nihilo turned toward his last agent of chaos, Hukluban. She was his secret weapon. With one last jolt of energy, he struck her stone figure, waking her from her sleepless slumber.

Hukluban was wrinkled and stooped. Her matted gray hair covered her weathered face. Her bony fingers clutched a splintered staff. Around her neck and between her sagging breasts, a lone white skull dangled. She looked up with her mismatched eyes and met the penetrating gaze of her lord.

"I have a task for you. Guard the Kasamaan against any intruders.

My guests must never escape."

Hukluban blinked and turned on her bowed legs toward the exit.

"Wait. Before you go: if anyone stands in your way," Ex Nihilo paused as he looked over his best pupil. "Kill them."

CHAPTER 14

April 28th

Ares was staring out of the window of Train 8530 from Gare d'Hendaye to Gare de Lyon. The train was half-empty with passengers scattered around the second-class cabin. His head was resting on the window, his eyes focused on some point on the horizon. His black hair shone against the afternoon glow that reflected into the speeding train.

Casually, Athena lowered the book she was reading. It was Darwin's *On the Origins of Species*. She found the book fascinating; it presented a body of evidence that the diversity of life arose from a common descent through a branching pattern of evolution. She saw that Leo was tapping his fingers on the table that separated them from Ares. Leo kept glancing from the compartment door to his phone.

It was understandable that Leo was tense. When they discovered that Apollo was in Paris, Ares stubbornly refused to leave Earth until their brother was found. Athena realized that no amount of coaxing could possibly change his mind. Athena trusted that the vegvisir was leading her to Apollo. Although guided by the mystical object, she still felt somewhat lost, but knew that Apollo would be able to provide answers.

Athena stared at Ares and shook her head silently. Not even the lack of a passport could deter him. She knew her brother well, and did not fight him on his decision. He might even be some help in discovering where exactly in Paris Apollo was and why. Once they did find their golden brother, however, she would need to conceive of a plan to send Ares back to Olympus. There was just one snag: how would she send him there? The only way she knew was to have the direct approval of the Council, plus a talisman. She would need to ponder this further, but did not feel any misgivings; she was nothing if not resourceful.

"I can't believe we got away with it," whispered Leo.

Athena chuckled. "That was a very precarious plan I created," she acknowledged. But there had been no other choice. Without a passport or a European identification card for Ares, crossing the border would have been too difficult. So that ruled out the fastest way – a flight. And so they chose the next quickest manner of travel, which, even though it took ten hours, was a train trip from Madrid to Paris. Trains required less documentation than planes. The last option was driving, but that would have taken around twenty hours, so they rejected that option. Together, they had agreed that taking an indirect route by train to France's capital would be the best option.

Traveling from Madrid Chamartín Station to the Spanish city of Irun, they came up with a plan to cross the border from Spain to France. The manner and timing had been perfect. First, Leo had approached the border patrol office and shown his documents. Right after he got the ok to pass, Athena, who was standing in line, had fainted. The officers, enamored by her beauty and grace, assisted her. Even the border patrol officer stepped forward to survey the commotion. While all three men were enraptured with Athena, Ares casually walked by and joined Leo on the French side of the border. Tripping over their feet to aid her in any way possible, the men assisted Athena with her documentation and her traveling pack. Innocently,

CHAPTER 14

she fluttered her eyelids as she waved them goodbye and climbed onto the direct train to Gare de Lyon in Paris.

Although ingenious, she could not take credit for the originality of the scheme. A couple of eons before, Pandora had swooned in the exact same way to win the heart of the titan Epimetheus, brother of Prometheus. Athena simply mimicked Pandora's actions, and to her delight, it worked.

Contented, she closed her book and stretched. Ares continued to stare out the window, deep in thought. He was still wearing the torn white t-shirt and the gray joggers that they had dressed him in the night before. He had refused any other clothes, but at least he'd accepted some shoes. Back in Madrid, when they were on their way to the station, Athena had bought him leather work boots. Hopefully, they would last a day or two. Ares was so strong and he moved so forcibly that the only clothes he could wear were made out of bronze. Unfortunately, they were out of style.

Sitting beside Athena, Leo cleared his throat. "Um, Ares?" The god grunted in response. "If you're bored and want to watch a movie or something, I have a couple downloaded on my phone."

Ares shifted his head, intrigued by Leo's offer. "What's a movie?" he asked. Athena knew this interaction between them was going to be either entertaining, or devastating. She observed Leo as he tried to explain the basics of human technology to a centuries-old deity.

"So, it's a film. That is to say, basically, just like in the ancient Greek dramas, actors perform in a play, but the play is recorded, and you can watch it as many times as you like," explained Leo.

"What's a phone?"

"Well, it's this gadget," Leo said as he timidly moved closer to Ares. He extended it so that Ares could see it up close. Ares didn't turn his body, but his eyes were intently following Leo's movements.

"You can use this to call, um, humans and so on, to send messages, take pictures or watch videos. I have a couple of them saved, in case you want to watch something. What genre do you prefer?"

"What's genre?" Ares asked.

Athena was tempted to roll her eyes, but she controlled herself. She did not want to show her exasperation. Ever since their permanent move back to Olympus, Athena had kept a close eye on humans and their development. She was fascinated by the way they adapted and survived in all types of climate and situations. Over the last century, their technology had accelerated at an impressive rate. She knew that a few of their new discoveries alarmed some of the gods, but they were under strict orders not to influence or intervene with humans and their progress.

She recalled what had happened to Prometheus after he disobeyed Zeus and gave the early people fire. The Divine Fire, it was called. Poor Prometheus was tied to a rock, and every night his liver was devoured by vultures. Each morning his organ would regenerate, only to be eaten again at dusk. The torment did not end until Heracles saved him from that endless nightmare.

She thought about modern-day humans with their electrical grids and nuclear bombs. They were both blessed and cursed. They had so much power and privilege, yet they were blinded by their circumstances. It drove them to want more and more in a deadly, never-ending cycle. *Not unlike my family,* she considered.

Some of the Olympians had followed humanity's progress. Hephaestus was obsessed with the advancements of metallurgy and assembly. Artemis had an incredible weaponry collection from the 15th century. Dionysus loved his world- wide collection of wine and alcoholic beverages. Even Aunt Demeter was pleased by how humans had figured out how to improve agriculture and the cultivation of crops. Athena shouldn't be surprised that, out of all her family, Ares ignored human progress. If he couldn't play with them, he wasn't interested.

CHAPTER 14

She saw with pleasure that Leo was being incredibly patient; he even allowed Ares to briefly hold his phone, then he gently took it away as the screen cracked under Ares' touch.

"So, some examples of genres are comedy, science fiction, thriller, romance, mystery... Oh! I have *Troy* downloaded; it's a classic. Do you want to watch that?" Leo asked.

Ares glared at Athena. She opened her book and pretended to read. Troy was a touchy subject for her siblings. It was one of those family dramas that never ended. She turned to the next page and feigned intense interest.

"Does it show us?" questioned Ares.

"Ummm, I don't think so. I'm pretty sure it's just about Helen, Paris, Achilles and Hector," responded Leo.

"Sounds boring. Put it on and maybe I'll watch," Ares said. Athena knew he was intrigued, but he didn't want to show it.

Leo got up and sat next to Ares; then he put his phone on the table in front of them and took out a snack. He seemed happy to interact with Ares. Athena knew that Ares was a ticking time bomb that could go off at any minute. But at the present, he seemed controlled; he wouldn't cause much trouble. In his own way, Ares could even be companionable. She went back to her book.

Ares commented throughout the entire movie. Repeatedly, he mentioned that a certain scene was not historically accurate:

"That's not how it happened."

"That doesn't sound like Menelaus."

"He wasn't killed by Hector."

"Ha! That was a good move."

"This is going too fast. Troy lasted ten years."

"Why won't they show more fighting?"

"That's not how it happened."

"He wasn't killed by Hector!!"

This last exclamation alarmed nearby passengers, and made Leo jerk backwards. Athena shot a pleading glance at Ares.

"What? He wasn't. Hector didn't kill Ajax; he committed suicide. Plus, in order to avoid a confrontation before finally facing Achilles, Hector spent hours running from his fate. You can't kill someone's lover and expect to get away with it," said Ares. He looked at Leo, who was still trembling. "Can you replay that scene? I liked that. Wish there was more blood, but it was good."

Leo gained control of himself. "You mean the fight scene between Hector and Achilles?"

Ares nodded, and reached over to grab some fruit and bread. Athena had to restrain herself from laughing. Her brother resembled a little kid getting popcorn at a movie theater. *Well, this is going better than expected.* She glanced at her watch; it was almost 3 pm. Four more hours, and they would reach Paris.

Athena looked out the window at the fields that were flashing by. The countryside was so peaceful. It reminded her of Greece and her beloved islands. She wished she could visit again one day, instead of seeing it from Mount Olympus. She understood why divinities were not allowed to prowl the earth, but she felt as if it were a gift that she could no longer use. She longed to stroll about in the Kesariani Forest. Unconsciously, her hand traced the outline of the vegvisir resting close to her chest. *I wanted to take you there one day.* She closed her eyes and envisioned the bright autumn colors of the leaves at sunset. She felt the presence of the magnificent oaks surrounding her and the soft, fertile mud between her toes as she hiked to the top of Mount Hymettus.

"I'm not sure I have more war movies." Leo's voice sounded distant. Athena opened her eyes and cleared her mind. "Oh! I have some rom-coms, if that's ok with you."

"What's a rom-com?"

CHAPTER 14

"Romance-comedy movies. I can look for a different genre."

"No. Put that one on," commanded Ares as he pointed at Leo's phone.

"Ok. I must warn you though, it's a bit corny."

Ares huffed in response. Entranced by the screen, he settled back into his seat.

The rest of the train ride went without an incident. Leo and Ares sat together, absorbed by whatever they were watching. Athena's mind was too full to read. She kept strategizing and then discarding plans. There were too many variables out of her control. She came up with a number of options, but without certain pieces of information, each was futile. No matter what the cost, there was one thing she had to do: send Ares back to Olympus. He was quite useful in a fight, even if he was belligerent and hostile, but he could become unhinged. If he were provoked, all hell would break loose. She needed him on her side, but out of her way, somewhere he could be useful without being obtrusive. Maybe she could assign him some important task. That was all well and good, but how exactly was she going to send him back? She didn't have a magical elevator to Olympus. A determined expression came over her as she told herself, *I'll figure it out. First find Apollo. Then I'll know what to do.*

As the train approached Gare de Lyon, Athena kept her eyes on the vegvisir. For most of the ride, it seemed as if the arrow was pointing in the direction that the train was heading, but as soon as the train crossed the Seine, the arrow shifted northwest. *Where are you?* Athena wondered.

Exiting the train station, they walked northward, following the vegsivir's directions. After a few seconds, Athena realized that this might not be the most efficient way to find someone in a large city of roughly 49 square miles. Maybe there was a mode of transportation that could pinpoint the location better. She eyed the passing cars and shook her head. She needed something faster.

Across the Boulevard Diderot was a metro station sign. Athena reasoned that they could follow the metro along the Seine, and double back as soon as the arrow shifted again. She hoped Apollo was not on the move.

"Follow me." Athena jogged over to the metro and purchased three single-day tickets. Hopping onto the Red Line, Ares grunted as people crowded around him, squishing themselves into the tube. His expression showed deep dislike at having so many humans nearby. Leo placed his pack on his chest, holding it tightly to his body. Athena smiled, she had learned about pickpockets on her first earthly trip. However, she was unconcerned. Whoever dared approach her personal space would be sorry. She had an intangible aura that intimidated passersby.

After a few minutes, the train reached the first stop, Chatelet-Les Halles. Athena checked her vegvisir for any changes, but the arrow remained steadfast. Some people jostled their way out, while others pushed in. The metro began moving, then suddenly, it jerked to a stop. The passengers jolted and some fell violently. Both Ares and Athena easily kept their balance. She was surprised to see that Ares had held onto Leo's backpack, saving him from falling. Athena met his eyes. Ares let go of the pack, leaving a dent the size of his massive hand on the top of Leo's bag.

An expressionless voice echoed from the speakers, "Mesdames et Messieurs." Athena raised her hand to touch Ares's arm. "Ce train est arrivé à destination. Veuillez noter qu'il y a des manifestations autour de la gare. Ce train n'est plus en service. Si vous souhaitez rester dans le train, vous pouvez le faire pour votre propre sécurité."

A protest. Could this be Ex Nihilo's doing?

"What did it say?" Ares asked irritably.

"There's a protest outside the station," replied Athena.

CHAPTER 14

"I'm not surprised. Paris has protests every week," Leo said.

"Really?" Athena asked.

"Oh, yes. It's not uncommon here."

"So this is human-made. Do you think it's safe to go out?" Athena asked.

"Well, I've seen you in combat before. I think the protestors should be afraid of getting in your way," Leo joked. He did have a point. If this was just human coincidence, then they would be far from harm's way. "Alright. Come on. Let's find Apollo."

They exited the station onto the street. The roads surrounding Gare Auber were being blocked off, and tourists crowded around the fences that were put in place by the city's police units. Some people were jumping the fences and jogging toward the protests. Athena checked the vegvisir. To her consternation, the arrow was pointing south, straight toward the commotion.

She groaned. *Apollo, please. Don't let this be you.* Motioning the others forward, she swiftly jumped the fence and waited for Ares and Leo to do the same. "We need to be inconspicuous," she instructed them. She calmly walked by the hordes of people who were observing the protest.

Behind the crowd of onlookers, thirty or so women were yelling and waving signs over their heads, refusing to stand down as police officers tried to coax them out of their defensive positions. Athena read the signs they held. "My body, my choice." Another said, "History is HERstory." She tapped one of the observers in the crowd and asked, "What's happening?"

"Looks like they're protesting inequality. They should protest every day!" the man replied.

Puzzled, Athena turned to her companions. Leo was flushed, and he tried to avert his eyes from the protest. Ares was pensively looking at the women, eerily calm for someone who thrived on discord.

"Are you alright, Ares?" Athena asked.

"They remind me of my daughters, the Amazons," Ares replied.

It was intriguing to hear Ares talk about his children in such an adoring way, especially his Amazons. The Amazons were members of a strict women-only society in which men were unwelcome, except for breeding purposes. As daughters of the god of war, they preferred activities such as horseback riding, hunting and warfare. Sometimes they would capture men during battle and sleep with them in order to procreate. When they were done, the Amazon women, just like female spiders, would kill their mates.

Athena looked at the protesting women. It was good for them to exercise their rights as women, especially if they felt cheated or... *Dear me.*

Living most of her existence in Greece, Athena was used to nudity in all aspects of the word. She had momentarily forgotten that they were not in the ancient times. She noticed that the crowd surrounding them was mostly composed of men.

"Why are they protesting?" asked Ares.

"Apparently they want equal rights and equal pay," said Leo as he tried to read the signs of the half-naked women without seeming to leer at them, like many of the men were.

"What?!" Ares bellowed. "They don't have equal rights?! What type of society is this?" In one stride, he parted the crowd and moved toward the protestors. Some of the women continued yelling, unabashed and confident. A few cowered as an angry Ares approached them. Just before reaching their line, Ares turned and yelled at the officers and the crowd. "Equal rights!! What will you do when you go off to war? You will crumble!"

Athena smiled. She knew that even though Ares was male, he was very much a feminist. The fact that women were not considered equal to men truly maddened him. Sparta was one of the cities in which Ares was venerated. Since Sparta was also a very militaristic state, and as men were drafted into the army, women assumed the roles of traders, guards, craftspersons, and so on. Ares had great pride in Sparta, and he encouraged women to take on roles that were normally reserved for men. His belief that women were as capable as men made him an advocate of feminism. He might be combative and hot-tempered, but at least he was true to his beliefs when it came to war, or to himself and Aphrodite. Athena reflected proudly that Ares had never assaulted any of his partners, unlike her despicable uncle, Poseidon, and sadly, her father, Zeus.

But this was not the time to get involved in a protest. Athena rushed over to Ares before he got into an altercation with the police, who were now harassing the protestors. The crowd was turning violent; some fought for the protestors, and some against. Athena was sure it was Ares' aura that drove them toward brutality. As she tugged on his massive arms, she heard a loud screech.

Staring down from one of the towering poles was a beautiful and elegant falcon. Its unblinking eyes studied Athena. For the briefest instance, it turned its head in a westerly direction toward a point behind Athena. Just as suddenly, it looked back at her, then it flew off the pole, accelerating past the crowd and flashing by the goddess. *Interesting*, Athena thought.

As she marveled at the creature, she had the urge to follow it. Tugging at Ares, she half-dragged him in the falcon's direction. After a few moments, Ares stopped fighting her. Panting, Leo followed them. "What was that?" he asked.

But Athena's attention was elsewhere. She was staring at a flier attached to one of the city's notice boards. At once, she knew just where Apollo was. "Over here! He's over here!"

The sun was sinking on the horizon, shining its powerful rays over a huge neoclassical building. Its Greek columns were supported by

Roman arches, and between each column stood a statue that looked over the Parisian city. Golden letters radiated across the building: Académie Nationale de Musique. Two gleaming statues flanked the crown jewel of the building; a life-sized sculpture of Apollo holding his beloved lyre high above his head.

CHAPTER 15

The Palais Garnier, or Opera Garnier, is a 1,979 seat opera house at the Place de l'Opera in Paris, France. The building of the Paris Opera, at the behest of Emperor Napoleon III, began in 1861, and was completed in 1875. At its inauguration, it was referred to as "The New Paris Opera." It soon became known as "Palais Garnier" in acknowledgement of its architect, Charles Garnier. Garnier's plans and designs were representative of the style of Napoleon III, a highly diverse style of architecture. Until 1989, it was the primary home of the Paris Opera, but now Palais Garnier is utilized mainly for ballet performances.

Athena, Ares and Leo made their way through the elegant Grand Escalier toward the Amphitheatre of Palais Garnier. Leo marveled at the intricate designs, the life-like statues, and the ceiling's painting that adorned the Grand Foyer. Its magnificence was overwhelming. Athena was trying to catch up with Ares, who was thundering forward, racing down the hallway looking for a way into the theater. As he ran, he bumped into priceless artifacts and busts, and Athena tried to catch every one that he dislodged. She was able to save five of them before Ares reached the wooden doors of the theater.

"Ares, no! Wait!" she yelled. But Ares had thrown open the doors and banged his way into the opera house. Athena raced in behind him. She almost crashed into him, but at the last moment, she stepped to one side and put her hand on his shoulder. She followed Ares' gaze and did a double take.

Leo finally reached them and said, "Did you guys see this place? It's incredible. It's absolutely..." Leo stopped, finally noticing the scene before him. His mouth hung open in disbelief.

Apollo had that effect on people. It was easy to spot him, even from a distance. They were separated by about fifty rows, but his radiance was bewitching, his golden aura like rays from the sun that warm the skin on a summer's day. His proportions and his features were the ideal of male beauty. Two elegant braids conjoined at the back of his head, allowing his face to remain unhampered by his wavy, honeyed hair. His smooth skin glittered in the light. Even his eyes were bright gold.

At the center of the stage, Apollo was instructing a small group of ballet dancers. He would twirl effortlessly in the air and land on one foot, as softly as silk. When a dancer attempted the move, Apollo would stand back and, if necessary, correct the dancer. He applauded the efforts of some of his pupils, but no one could compare to his incredible agility and skill. He was wearing white tights that stretched from his ankles to his belly button. His bare feet made only the slightest sound when they touched the stage. After a few pirouettes, he grabbed his shirt, pulled it off and tossed it aside with a flick of his wrist. One or two of the dancers swayed and had to prop themselves up on their neighbors' shoulders.

Standing beside Athena, Leo sharply inhaled as he observed Apollo's polished chest, his muscles perfectly defined. Athena placed a steadying hand on his shoulder, but the momentary loss of contact with Ares was enough to unnerve him.

"That's it!" He lunged forward and began running toward the stage.

"No!" Athena yelled. She rushed after him, trying to touch any part of his body in order to calm him. But Ares was too fast. He bounded

CHAPTER 15

onto the stage, and lunged at Apollo.

Instead of cowering, Apollo deftly twirled away from him. Turning to his dancers, Apollo commanded, "Look here. Tchaikovsky's *The Nutcracker*. Act 1: No. 2."

Athena reached the stage the moment Tchaikovsky's composition began to emanate from the overhead speakers. She looked on in horror as Ares' eyes transformed from dark onyx to blood red. Like a maddened bull, he charged Apollo head-on, but Apollo calmly twirled out of Ares' path. He moved around the stage in synchronization with the music. Ares charged again and again, but to no avail. He was about to seize Apollo when the latter leapt so high that he was able to touch his toes. This infuriated Ares even more, and he stomped so hard that the floor planks cracked.

It was time to intervene. Untroubled by the gaping ballet dancers, Athena rushed onto the stage. When Ares charged again and Apollo smartly danced out the way, Athena wrapped her arms around her outraged brother and whispered her incantations to soothe him.

Apollo stopped twirling, and his eyes locked with Athena's. There was no recognition there, only curiosity. His honeyed eyes seemed cloudy as he gazed at them quizzically. Athena saw his lips move without making a sound. *Oh, no.* She lost control of her limbs, and began twirling to the music as if in step with Apollo. Facing Athena, Ares did the same; he moved in unison with her, colliding and intertwining. She gritted her teeth in frustration, and planned her next move as she swayed and twirled.

So Apollo didn't recognize them. What had happened to him? His memory had been tampered with, just like Monica, the receptionist from the Royal Horseguards. The easiest way to retrieve his memory was to heal him, and the best way to heal him was to touch him. Her talisman was infused with his curative powers, and one touch would surely remind him of who he was.

She felt someone grab her waist, and then her body floated through the air, landing smoothly and gracefully on one knee. She forced herself to look at who had lifted her, and to her dismay, she saw that Leo was now one of Apollo's dancing puppets. The dancing trio was smiling broadly as if nothing in the world was more enjoyable than capering through Tchaikovsky's composition.

"I need to touch him," she mumbled. Ares huffed in frustration. Unable to control his movements, he continued spinning. His smile seemed like a permanent fixture on his face, but it did not reach his blood-red eyes.

Before being forced to do a third arabesque, Leo's eyes briefly met Athena's. The music's tempo changed, and Athena noted that she would have her best chance if, close to the song's ending, she did a triple pirouette. She tried to move toward Apollo, forcing herself within his arm's reach. Apollo kept twirling and spinning to the music, enjoying his new pupils' dancing.

Finally, her opportunity came. She raised her arms and turned, once, twice, three times. Landing lightly, she reached out for Apollo, her fingertip glancing off his heaving chest. The touch was enough to break Apollo's trace. Immediately, the group stopped dancing, and in a snap Apollo's eyes became clear. He smiled broadly.

"Sister! You're alive!" he trilled. His melodic, sing-song voice was music to Athena's ears. He was alive and well.

"Brother," she announced calmly. She opened her arms wide and warmly embraced him.

"You bastard. You swine," growled Ares. Athena held Apollo's hand and moved quickly to hug Ares. Apollo followed suit. Ares fought against the caress, but his frame stopped vibrating.

"He's alright, Ares. Apollo's memory was tampered with. He had no idea who we were, or who he was," Athena explained.

"That's a good enough excuse." Ares confronted Apollo. "We're in a crisis, you know. We've spent days searching for you, and then I see you twirling around like an imbecile; it makes me want to rip your head off."

"Yes, brother of mine," Apollo chimed in. "I missed you, too."

"What are you doing here, Apollo?" questioned Athena.

"It's a long story." Looking over his shoulder, he approached the stupefied group of dancers. "My wonderful muses, it was an honor and privilege to dance with all of you. I shall see you soon, my lovelies, but for now I have found my family once more, and I shall return to my duties as guardian of the light." A single tear rolled down his cheek. "I will greatly cherish our time together."

A few of the dancers started sobbing, while the rest gaped at Apollo in awe. Athena was sure they had not listened to a single word Apollo had said. They were so entranced by his beauty that they merely gawked at him. Many mortals had fallen in love with her magnificent half-brother, but if Apollo's memories were gone, would he have slept with one or two of them? The Council had issued strict orders that they were to avoid any interference with humans. Having sexual relations with them was absolutely forbidden. She glanced at the sobbing dancers, realizing that Apollo might have been involved with more than half of them. Her brother was notoriously passionate, like her father and most of the Olympians. She would have to erase their memories.

Approaching the group, she smiled her warmest smile and put out her hand in a gesture of welcome. She turned and nodded to Apollo, who immediately understood what she was doing. Together they shook hands with each of the dancers, male and female, thereby erasing all memory of Apollo's presence or actions. Immediately, they began to move about the stage, stretching and twirling. Apollo grabbed his ballet bag, and the four exited the Palais Garnier.

Walking out into the Parisian night, Apollo leapt and pranced. "I'm so happy you found me! And look! Erebus and Nyx are preparing to blanket the night sky. Selene is beginning to show her bright, splendid features. How they contrast with the dark..."

"Quit it with the eloquence, Apollo. We're not in the 5th Century BC. Today's humans won't understand your gibberish," grumbled Ares.

"Well, pardon me for being educated. I'm sure you adore these mortals whose vocabularies are so limited. You can finally have conversations that you can understand," Apollo retorted.

"Why, you!" said Ares as he reached to strangle him.

Apollo twirled out of the way and laughed, bumping into Leo. "My apologies!" he sang out. He looked Leo up and down before raising one eyebrow. "Dear me, aren't you a pretty one?" He flashed a seductive smile and moved to caress Leo's flushed cheek before Athena caught his hand in midair.

"He's out of bounds, Apollo. For your information, so are all mortals. Please tell me you did not impregnate the ballerinas," pleaded Athena.

Apollo swallowed before answering. "Oh, sister, forgive me! I was not in control of my mind. In my oblivious state, I did not know the divine rules that bind us to the Council." Athena groaned. "But," Apollo added, "I did wear these disgusting things that I was given." He thrust his hand into his ballet bag, and brought out a box of condoms.

Athena inspected the package and exclaimed, "Ew! Do not hand these to me."

"Well, it's good he used them, Athena. These help prevent pregnancies, but their efficiency rate is around 96%," observed Leo as he read the box that Athena had tossed at him.

"Apollo. If we are still alive in nine months, you will personally take care of any love children you might have. Is that clear? Need I remind you that the Council is very strict about intercourse with humans? It's forbidden. Your memory is back. Do not let it happen again," declared

CHAPTER 15

Athena.

"Yes, Pallas Athene. My apologies," responded Apollo. Athena nodded as Apollo hung his head. Then he smiled. "I'm just so happy you found me! How did you manage that? And who are you?" he asked Leo.

"It's a long story, brother," Athena said with a chuckle. "Let's go somewhere private where we can both retell our adventures."

"I know just the place! You'll love their meat, Ares," announced Apollo as he hugged Ares' massive shoulders.

They headed south toward Avenue de l'Opera. Athena walked beside Leo, behind Ares and Apollo. His neck was still slightly pink; she would have to sit next to him in order to protect him from Apollo's charms.

A few minutes later, Apollo stopped in front of an upscale restaurant named Julian's. A long line of people were waiting to enter the renowned establishment. Apollo turned around and said, "Wait for me here. Let me talk to Pierre. I'll be right back." He strode into the restaurant, winking at the waiters. On his way in, he patted the host on the arm.

Athena noted that Julian's was a Michelin rated, 5 star restaurant. Only Apollo had the audacity to stride right in, completely skipping the line while only wearing tights and a light shirt. Ares crossed his massive arms over his chest. He was not very patient, but he didn't have to wait long. Within moments, the host approached them and, bowing and smiling, he waved for them to come inside.

The host led them to the back of the restaurant to a semi-private table, where a golden-haired man sat chatting amiably with a petite woman who was dressed all in white, and to a tall man who was holding a glass of wine. It dawned on Leo who the golden-haired man was. Athena shook her head. Apollo had quickly changed into a pressed gray suit, and he had combed back his wavy hair. Her brother was nothing if not fashionable.

"Mes amis!" he exclaimed. "Sit down, sit down. This is Miss Claudette, the finest chef in Paris." He beamed at the demure woman, who nodded her head respectfully. "And this is my good friend Pierre, owner of this restaurant."

Athena wondered how good a friend Pierre truly was, since Apollo had been in Paris less than a fortnight. Pierre was wearing a ring on his left hand's fourth finger. His skin didn't look tan around the edges, so she guessed that he removed it often. The man gazed at Apollo in wonderment. Athena sighed. *Another one of his victims.* "Good evening, Pierre," she said in a warm voice as she sat down gracefully opposite Apollo. "Miss Claudette," she said, bowing her head. The chef's eyes widened with adoration, and she blushed as she focused her attention on the Greek goddess. *Oh. This isn't one of Apollo's victims. She's mine.* Athena had seen that look before in a variety of women and even more men. Most of the time she was accustomed to it, but some humans and even immortals found ways to embarrass her. She hoped this would not be the case with Claudette.

"Ah, is this your family, Richard? I can see your parents have good genes," exclaimed Pierre as he scanned the group.

"Richard?" questioned Ares, wondering why Pierre addressed his brother by that name.

"It's a long story, my dear cousin," said Apollo with a wink. "But yes, our family does have quite an impressive pedigree." He smiled wickedly.

Athena saw that Leo was moving to sit down opposite her, but she held his arm and guided him gently into the seat next to her. Ares grunted and plopped himself down next to Apollo.

"Thank you for your hospitality, Pierre. It is one of my favorite qualities in people," sang Apollo. His melodic, seductive voice made Pierre's eyes gleam.

CHAPTER 15

"You're too kind, Richard. It is my pleasure to have you dine at my restaurant tonight," answered Pierre with a dreamy, faraway look. Apollo smiled and waved his hand in dismissal. Pierre bowed and took his leave, sipping on his wine while walking about the restaurant greeting guests.

"Well," said Apollo once they were relatively alone. "Pierre isn't actually the restaurant's owner. It belongs to Julian, his father. I met him last week at the opera. Such a nice man, very hospitable. Father would approve."

Athena and Ares exchanged glances. It was so typical of their younger brother to know everyone and everything. He loved parties and gossip. Even though he had forgotten his own name, Apollo could mysteriously find himself in the most advantageous of situations.

Athena cleared her throat. "Why did he call you Richard?" she asked, raising one eyebrow.

"Oh! Time to tell my story," Apollo announced. He straightened up and fixed his hair, winking at Leo. "I was following your tracks around London. A very fun and exciting place to begin my quest. I remember looking for you somewhere, when BANG, next thing I knew I was following music through the streets and ended up at a concert hall. Apparently, it was a closed recital. But you know how much I love music. I saw some ballerinas practicing their pirouettes, and I could not control myself..."

"I bet I know what else you couldn't control," interjected Ares.

Apollo ignored him and continued with his story. "I just had to dance with them. We danced and danced for hours. We had a jovial time. Afterwards, they asked for my name, and I told them I didn't know. They started calling me 'Richard Doe,' and it sort of stuck. They offered me a position in their group and I readily accepted. What could be more exciting than dancing through life and exploring the world?" He sighed, his eyes shimmering with joy and contentment.

"Wait a second," said Athena. "I think you missed a chapter here. How exactly did you get to Earth? And how did you find me? What happened at the hotel? How did you lose your memory?"

"Oh! My memory." Apollo rubbed his head. "I'm actually not sure about that. I just remember that Helios informed me of your residence, and then one day he visited me all flustered, and said you had vanished. He mentioned something about being attacked. I was livid, sister. Nobody attacks us Olympians. Before Father found out, I asked Hermes for his talarias, and promptly flew down to your rescue."

"That's very gallant of you," mentioned Athena.

"Thank you. You are my dear sister to be sure, and I wanted to know what had happened and who attacked you. My memory becomes fuzzy here. The only thing I can remember is that the entrance to your London hotel was near a river. I also remember feeling odd. Something made my skin crawl, like a cold hand reaching for my neck. Defensively, I tensed up, and the next thing I knew, I was following the sound of music through the streets of London." He gently rubbed his temples as if massaging the sensation away.

Athena's mind was in overdrive. So that's how he got to Earth – Hermes' magical winged sandals. The talarias were forged especially for him by Hephaestus and the Cyclopes. Hermes used them to travel around the globe and between realms. All of a sudden, Athena felt unsettled. What did Apollo mean when he said he tensed up? She was sure her brother had inadvertently used some kind of power that was unbeknown to him. Otherwise, how could he have protected himself against Ex Nihilo? If the timeline were accurate, Apollo landed on Earth merely minutes after Athena's "death" and Ex Nihilo's demise.

"Do you still have the sandals with you?" Athena inquired.

"Oh, yes. They are made of pure gold, you know. Very valuable and very attractive. I wanted to wear them on a special occasion," said Apollo, his voice rising melodically.

CHAPTER 15

Fantastic. "How many souls can the wings carry?"

"Just one. Hermes can transport more since they are his, but anyone else can only control them if they are traveling alone."

Hmm. There was one good thing about Apollo. He never lied. He simply couldn't. Athena corrected herself. Apollo could lie, he simply chose not to. As leader of the Oracles, his domain extended into prophecy and divination, and therefore, he valued truth above all else. She was disheartened by the news that the wings could only carry one being back to Olympus. She looked from Ares to Apollo, and back to Ares. The choice was clear. But how should she proceed? She must do so gently and subtly, so as not to arouse Ares' suspicion or ire.

"Good. That is wonderful news, Apollo. I am glad that Olympus will be protected soon enough. Father must be going mad with our absence. Athena continued in the same, superior tone, "It is about time that the strongest and bravest among us go back to guard our heavenly home."

Thinking, Apollo cocked his head to one side. He knew that Athena was not arrogant. He also knew that she possessed a powerful talisman that allowed her travel between realms. Athena could see the wheels turning in his head. He quickly glanced at Ares and then smiled softly. *He knows. Perfect.* She thought to herself. This was one of the perks of having a sibling who knew her so well.

"Yes, of course, sister. Olympus must be well protected and defended. Just like we did when the giants attacked us many eons ago. How will they cope in our absence?"

Athena and Apollo both looked at Ares, hoping that he would take the bait and volunteer to return to Olympus. Uninterested, Ares nodded as he was not fully tracking the conversation. Athena worked on another approach. As she did so, Apollo winked mischievously and stretched out his arms.

"Why, I do miss good old Olympus," commented Apollo. "We were having such fun before this commotion. I can picture Dionysus and Hephaestus having a grand time. Dionysus was so drunk that he tried to summon up the courage to flirt with Aphrodite, looking for a dalliance perhaps. Of course he could never get near enough to actually do anything. But now that you're here Ares, maybe Dionysus will succeed in his debauchery," Apollo drawled as if he were bored. At the mention of Aphrodite's name, Ares's attention was sparked and he became absorbed in Apollo's words.

"What did you say? Dionysus?" Ares demanded.

Apollo nodded disinterestedly. He looked at the menu and chewed on his bottom lip. "We simply must order tonight's special. I had it last week, and it's positively divine."

Athena watched as Ares's eyebrows furrowed, and then his frame began to shake. He was hooked. It was time to reel him in. "Ares, you should go to Olympus. You are the best to warn our family and protect our home."

If truth be told, Apollo and Athena could handle defensive strategies better than Ares. Athena knew that when she said "home," all Ares thought about was Aphrodite. Whenever Aphrodite was in danger, in order to protect his true love, Ares was at his most efficient and deadly. Plus, with Ares gone, traveling the globe would be more manageable. However, she would need to set some rules for Apollo if he were to stay. Things were only going to get tougher and deadlier as time went on. Athena was unsure what Ex Nihilo was planning, but she knew it was something nefarious.

"Yes," said Ares as he got to his feet. "Give me the sandals." Athena was shocked at Ares' efficiency. *Ares is right,* she mused. There was no time to lose. She gracefully rose, and Leo followed suit.

Apollo raised his eyebrows in surprise. "But I just ordered," he pleaded. "Can't we do this after dinner?"

Athena shot him an icy glare. If he were to team up with Leo and

CHAPTER 15

her, she would expect more alacrity and less hesitation.

"Fine," accepted Apollo. He looked toward the back of the restaurant where a waiter was hovering near the kitchen. "We'll take this to-go, please," Apollo said, as he followed his siblings and Leo to the door.

CHAPTER 16

Athena was glad she allowed Apollo to double back and wait for their to-go meal. It was one of the most delicious dishes she had ever had. Not that she needed much subsistence; she was very adaptable when it came to food.

"Wow, this dish is amazing!" exclaimed Leo.

"Isn't it just intoxicating?" Apollo said. "Makes your mouth water and your stomach gurgle."

Athena looked at her brother. Even though Apollo and she both resembled young adults, they were many millennia old. On her Finnish passport, Athena stated that she was twenty-four, the perfect age to travel the globe. She must obtain a similar passport for her younger brother. Would they share a last name?

Unlike Ares, Apollo and Athena were quite similar. They were both statuesque with perfect bone structure and beautiful, piercing eyes. Whereas Athena's were gray-green, like moss after rain. Apollo's were as golden as the sun, just like the rest of his body. His hair was slightly lighter than hers, but they could easily pass as siblings. She laughed inwardly; Athena looked more like Apollo's twin than his real twin, Artemis.

Glancing out the window, Athena took in the Parisian night. It was electric with people moving from place to place. Everyone seemed in a rush to get somewhere; *life must be very complex for these humans.*

CHAPTER 16

She wondered how different life was for each of them. Each human was unique; no two stories were the same.

A small movement caught her attention, and she scanned the street, looking for the source of her intrigue. Her gaze landed on the falcon she had seen earlier that night. It was focused on their apartment window. Locking eyes with the creature, she thought, *definitely mythological.* Falcons were very attentive predators, but Athena knew this particular falcon was for sure mystical. It had followed them across countries. It wanted something... or maybe it was looking out for them? The falcon had helped her twice already: by scaring the Spanish police officers away from her location, and the second by showing her where Apollo was. How did it know? And whose culture did it belong to?

"Brother," said Athena casually, "whose apartment did you say this is?

Apollo did not take his eyes off of Leo. "Oh, just some friends of mine. They'll be back in a week or so. They gave me their spare key."

Fantastic. Another of Apollo's conquests. "Am I going to have to track them down?" Athena asked, slightly exasperated.

"No need, sister. If either one got pregnant, I would be very surprised. They're men, you see," Apollo replied with a devilish smile. He reached over and started to pour some wine into his and Leo's cups. Leo refused with a shake of his head, and Apollo gave a sad sigh.

"Suit yourself; this is a 1978 Bordeaux. Dionysus would be so jealous right now."

"Apollo, if you could bring something with you from Olympus, what would you choose?" asked Athena.

"I brought my bow and arrow. Can't go anywhere without them. They're made of pure gold," he added. "I wish I could have brought my lyre, but it seemed unnecessary at the time. And it's a bit cumbersome. If I could keep Hermes' sandals, I certainly would. But it was better to send Ares back home. Poor bloke must be choking Dionysus at this very moment."

"So you wouldn't bring a pet?" questioned Athena.

"I don't think so. Hmm. If I had, I would have picked Python. He's a nasty fighter, but he prefers staying in the water near Delphi. Why do you ask?"

"There's a falcon following us. It's been helpful up until now, and I know you love falcons, so I wondered if he was yours. I am convinced it's mystical. Somehow he knows about us." Athena looked out the window at the falcon. It was in the same spot, unmoving. Its intense eyes were focused on them.

"I'm going to open this window," Athena said suddenly. Pushing the knob outward, she opened the window and reached toward the falcon, extending her arm in a gesture of welcome. The falcon did not move. It stared into the apartment. Apollo whistled softly; his melody was entrancing. The falcon cocked its head, extended its wings, and floated toward the open window. It landed on Athena's outstretched arm and adjusted its footing.

Apollo crooned and glided toward the window; he kept his voice low and whistled to the magnificent bird. Athena raised her hand to stroke the falcon's feathers and, aware of her every movement, the bird rapidly twisted its head.

"I'm not going to hurt you. It's alright," she whispered softly. The bird blinked and slightly bowed its head. Athena stroked its back with one finger. Leo shuffled closer to the window. The falcon sensed his presence and quickly turned its head toward him. Its eyes seemed to narrow, and it screeched.

"He's with us. He won't harm you," Apollo sang in his melodic voice. The bird, sensing that Leo was human, did not take its eyes off of him.

"What are you looking for?" Athena crooned, mostly to herself but partly because she felt that the falcon would somehow understand

CHAPTER 16

them. Unblinking, the bird turned and stared at her, then shifted closer and put a massive claw around the vegvisir that rested on Athena's neck. They all gasped as the arrows began to spin out of control. Suddenly, the arrow stopped and pointed south.

Athena turned to Leo, but he was already hurrying to get his map. He stretched it out beside the falcon, and Athena moved the necklace toward it.

They found their destination. She raised her eyebrows. *That's a pleasant surprise.*

Apollo chuckled loudly. "I'll definitely need a passport then."

"No way," said Leo. The falcon screeched loudly and flew off, vanishing into the darkness.

CHAPTER 17

That night, Athena dreamed. Recently, her dreams were full of memories; the happiest of her memories, but also, ironically, the saddest. Tonight she dreamed about her first day on Earth after she had been voted the Greek representative and had been sent on her precarious mission. Her dream was so vivid that she did not live it as a spectator; she saw it through her own eyes as if reliving each moment for a second time.

Tonight's dream started with Athena hugging her family goodbye. There were some tearful farewells and some encouraging words. She touched each of her weapons, making sure she carried everything she needed. Then, she securely attached her magical talisman to her arm. Her Father tenderly placed a blindfold over her eyes before sending her down on her mission. The blindfold was one of the Council's requirements for a representative's descent to Earth.

Athena felt a rush of wind through her hair and felt the clouds dissolving at her touch. Feeling the ground close in, she braced her knees and landed confidently. Many millennia had passed since she had been on this planet. She breathed long and deep, ingesting the flavors and scents around her. The air was cool and dry, and she could taste pollen, which indicated that she was in a large meadow. As she walked, her sandals squished into the soft ground, which meant that it was fertile. The wind was chilly, but it did not feel very cold, so she

CHAPTER 17

guessed they were in the Northern Hemisphere.

The Council's order gave no other instructions, apart from a summons that required that a representative be chosen from each mythology. Secrecy was of the essence; therefore, blindfolds were necessary for the first meeting on Earth.

Athena felt someone else appear beside her. Her new companion struck the ground heavily, but she heard no other sound, so they must have remained on their feet as well. *Athletic.* Athena was already done analyzing her surroundings and turned her attention to the figure next to her. She inhaled deeply to catch their scent. The god or goddess beside her emanated the scent of a forest. She inhaled again. Beneath the outdoorsy smell, she could sense another aroma, but what was it?

Two footsteps distracted Athena. She could not see, but was ready in case of an attack. She turned her head in the direction of the sound. She clenched her hand over her long spear. The footsteps were all but silent, as if whoever made the sound was not wearing shoes.

A deep voice cleared its throat. "You are summoned here today at the command of our great Council. I am your Council leader in charge of informing you of our current situation." The voice was heavily accented with distinct, clear notes. *Asian. This Council god is from India!*

Before leaving Olympus, Athena had conducted extensive research, and she had even pried her father's brain for the Council's identity and whereabouts. But she quickly realized that the mighty Zeus was as oblivious as she was. She was able to gather enough intel to know that the Council was very, very powerful and influential. She had already guessed, probably correctly, at half the members' identities. She knew that Zeus was not a member of the great Council, but she was sure that there was a Greek representative in the higher echelon; someone very clever, resourceful and intimidating. If not Zeus, there was only one other being that could forcefully represent the Greeks.

It had to be...

"You have been chosen and assigned a mythological partner in order to ensure your safety. There is a supernatural being who is wreaking havoc in our realm. This creature is very dangerous and will not hesitate to destroy you. We are tasking you with a very perilous mission. This divinity is out of control and out of our jurisdiction. We need you to uncover the identity of this unruly being and bring it to justice. It is of the utmost importance that you bring it back alive so that we may know the depths of its nefarious plan." The voice paused and moved closer to the blindfolded pair.

"There are various rules you must follow if you are to stay on Earth to complete your mission. Break any of these rules, and you will be held accountable by the high court. But most importantly, stay together. There is strength in numbers.

1. Do not show your powers to humans.
2. Do not influence or alter the human species in any way. You are forbidden to have sexual or romantic relations with them.
3. Do whatever it takes to adapt, live and survive.

Athena heard the rush of wind, and knew the Council leader was out of sight. She waited three more heartbeats before taking off her blindfold. She opened her eyes and blinked at the bright sunlight that illuminated the space around her. She was atop a mountain range with shin-high grass that shone green in the evening sun. She bent down and plucked a blade of grass, then holding it between her fingertips, she examined it. Straightening, she finally looked at her new companion. She controlled her expression as she gazed at the being beside her.

She was a goddess, and her appearance was wild. She wore a mixture of simple chainmail and animal skins, and her hands were covered in

CHAPTER 17

mud. Her boots were made of leather and rabbit skin. She had bright, almost white, long hair that was pulled up in braids. She wore an iron band as a crown that encircled her forehead. She had an untamed look about her, and Athena thought her hair seemed purposefully unkempt with wildflowers entwined in her many braids. Athena inhaled deeply, and was surprised that her companion's scent was of lavender and jasmine. Her eyes were a penetrating ice blue. She wore dark eye makeup that made her eyes seem like two glaciers drowning in a sea of blackness.

Athena scanned her companion for a long time. They remained quiet for several minutes, fixated on one another.

"Well, at least you're not a man." Breaking the silence, her companion spoke. She brought her hands up to her face and raised her left eyebrow. "I can take this mud off now."

Athena cocked her head to one side, studying this fascinating stranger.

"What?"

Athena shook her head. "Nothing." She looked around and said, "We must be somewhere in the Northern Hemisphere."

"This is Northern Europe. The Scandinavian Mountains," pointed out the wild goddess.

Athena nodded. She bent down and put her palm on the ground. Spring was coming to a close. Soon it would be summer. *Interesting.* "I wonder..." she murmured out loud.

Her companion crossed her arms over her chest, waiting for Athena to elaborate. Athena cleared her throat and said, "The explanation from our councilman was very vague. So this creature is wreaking havoc, but what kind of havoc? And if there is strength in numbers, why not send out more of us? Why not packs of four? Or two representatives from each culture?"

The wild goddess took a second to reply while she eyed Athena.

She chewed her bottom lip, and then seemed to make up her mind. "They don't know the identity of the culprit. It could be an inside job. Whoever is angering the Council could have divine allies here on Earth. It could even be one of us." She scanned Athena, daring her to deny her accusation.

Athena thought for a moment. "Good point." She took off her helmet and then extended her right arm toward her companion. "I'm Athena. Pallas Athena. Greek representative."

The blue-eyed goddess narrowed her eyes. She stared at Athena's outstretched hand for a long moment, then smiled and dropped her arms to her sides. She strode toward Athena, and grasped Athena's forearm in what she guessed was a sign of camaraderie.

"Freya. Norse."

CHAPTER 18

January 20th

Norse mythology encompasses the legends created by the North Germanic peoples. This began with Norse paganism and continued until the Christianization of Scandinavia and the modern Scandinavian folkloric period. Like many mythologies, the Norse culture is full of tales of deities, beings and heroes, ranging from the hammer-wielding, thunder-god Thor, to the one-eyed mighty Odin, to the vengeful goddess, Skadi. There's the mysterious god Heimdallr who, as legend tells, had nine mothers and could hear grass grow. In addition, there is the trickster jötunn, Loki. This half-giant is known for his various misdeeds across the Nine Worlds of the Norse cosmos.

Included is the beautiful, seidr-working Freya, who rode into battle to choose those among the slain who would feast with her and the Valkyries in the afterlife. In Old Norse society, seidr was a type of magic that was practiced and included awarding the user with the capability of predicting the future. An original member of the Vanir, an old branch of gods from the Norse realm of Vanaheim, she joined the Æsir after the Æsir-Vanir War; thus the Vanir became a subgroup of the Æsir. Along with her brother, Freyr, and her father, Njord, she was sent to join the Æsir as a token of truce between the warring groups.

History often overlooks the influence of women, and that is especially true in the case of Freya, who was one of the most important goddesses in Norse mythology. According to the Icelandic historian, poet and politician Snorri, her esteem was widespread. Freya held the honor of the highest of the Asynjur, and some argue that her status was almost on par with Odin, for she was so respected that she was granted first pick from those slain in battle. Freya took half of her chosen to the heavenly field, Folkvangr, while the remaining half traveled to Valhalla with the Valkyries, to feast with Odin in his unearthly hall.

Athena knew most of these facts since she had been busy researching those who either could join her as allies, or would become her enemies. But during her travels with Freya, she discovered more than just the summaries of Norse mythology. In retrospect, she could see that both her Greek culture and Freya's Norse background held many similarities. It was fascinating to hear and experience Norse culture through Freya's perspective.

Like Athena's own magical talisman, Freya brought some wonders from her own realm. She wore two necklaces; one was a magical stave called a vegvisir which could point the way to a lost traveler. It was a very useful tool that Athena was glad to add to her arsenal. The other was Brisingamen, a brilliantly golden necklace which allowed Freya to clear her mind and access future events. Like all divine beings who believe in prophecy, Freya accepted that the future was not set in stone and could be easily altered by the most minor of occurrences or events.

On their first full day together, Athena and Freya made camp at the base of the Scandinavian Mountains. Freya prepared a large fire and started to chant in Old Norse. Athena wondered if this ritual allowed Freya to access her seidr. Relying more on facts and events

CHAPTER 18

rather than on magic and prophecies, she remained skeptical as Freya chanted her incantations.

As the fire grew, Athena felt an odd shiver move down her spine. She tried to avert her eyes from the expanding flames, but before she could do so, she saw a movement in the orange glow. Freya sat down to better observe the rising flames while Athena clutched at her spear and focused intently on the blaze. Deep in the glaring heat, she could see their likeness. They seemed to be in a fog, but Athena confirmed that it was a reflection of them because she could see the clothes they were wearing.

There was something else. She could also see a black mass following them through the haze. As the images flashed by, she was first awed and then concerned about the significance of the vision. They were being attacked. Savagely.

"What can we do?" Athena asked as she broke the eerie silence.

"I'm not sure yet," said Freya. Her voice sounded far away as she peered into the flames.

Athena put her spear on the ground and sat with her legs crossed. She touched her fingers to her temple and tapped rhythmically as she pondered. What should be their first move? Her thoughts raced as she analyzed every viable option. She was looking for anything that would make it possible to survive and fight another day.

"Wait!" exclaimed Freya. "Go back, go back! What did you do? What did you think?"

"I was going through our options," Athena replied, narrowing her eyes at the roaring fire before her.

"Go back and move slowly through your ideas," Freya commanded. Athena closed her eyes and re-analyzed their options. Some ideas were really far-fetched and some were nearly impossible, but others were doable and practical. The flames shifted dramatically, signaling their solution.

"There! The flames don't show the attacker finding us in the near future. What were you thinking?" asked Freya.

Athena looked at her companion. Her eyes were brimming with anticipation and excitement. "We will act like humans and hide in plain sight. No magic, no spells. We won't leave a trail that it can follow."

CHAPTER 19

February 12th

After twenty-three days on the road, the goddesses developed a regular routine that kept them from influencing or interacting much with humans. Most importantly, it allowed them time to do research and strategize.

They traveled cross country until they were able to apply for their Finnish passports. It took very little of Athena and Freya's combined charms to obtain them. Soon afterwards they progressed through Sweden, and finally made their way into Norway. They planned to visit the Netherlands the following week, and agreed to extend their stay in Amsterdam by a couple of days. At this tourist hub, their presence would go unnoticed, yet they did not want to risk discovery. It was crucial to spend as little time as possible in towns and cities. The less people that noticed them, the better.

At first Athena wondered if Freya would be egotistical and self-serving, but she was the exact opposite. She was very professional and dutiful. Athena admired that Freya had a mind of her own. She wasn't subservient, but she would compromise. Even though she was very tough, she was full of mirth and cheer. Despite her cool, icy blue eyes, she was a very fiery goddess. Freya was energetic, easily excitable and prone to bursts of creative problem-solving. So far Athena was very pleased with her assigned partner.

They were in the Stormen Library in Bodø, Norway. The large pile of books that lay in front of them was equal to the height of their usual daily research. Athena was halfway done with her sixth book of the day when, suddenly, Freya slammed the manuscript she was reading shut, and groaned loudly.

"This is impossible! We've been reading these cumbersome books for days, and there's still no trace of it. Not a single clue," Freya said with a grimace. Then she crumbled the piece of paper she was writing on and hurled it across the library.

Athena calmly closed her book and leaned back in her chair, watching Freya's emotions play out. Her Nordic companion seemed very stressed. Her hair was tousled and messy. Exasperated, Freya rubbed her face, shoved the books aside, slapped the empty table before her, dropped her head, then covered it with her arms. Even though it appeared flawless to mortal eyes, Freya's skin was flushed and slightly irritated.

Athena had to admit that this task was maddening, even overwhelming. First, there was the constant threat of being attacked. Second, there was very little information available that could inform them of the whereabouts or background of the nefarious creature who was causing so much mayhem in their worlds.

In this situation, Freya and Athena were opposites. The more complex and frustrating the task became, the more Athena relished the challenge, knowing that even though it felt like she was not advancing, she knew that she was moving in the right direction. Instead of losing hope, she became fervently interested and more involved in the task. However, she had to admit that this was not the case with many of her peers. Each deity had a different coping mechanism and, if Athena was going to stay in synergy with her, it was important to find out what Freya liked to do to decompress. It was true they had traveled

CHAPTER 19

and researched non-stop for a few weeks now. Freya deserved a well-earned day off. In addition, Athena knew that one plus one was more than two, when two heads and two hearts wanted to reach the same goal.

"You're right. My eyes are starting to water," acknowledged Athena as she rubbed her eyes. "We should get something to eat and relax for the rest of the day."

Freya looked up from her slumped position and stared at Athena in disbelief. "You're not pulling my leg, are you?" she asked.

Athena chuckled. "No, I am not pulling your leg. What do you like to do for fun?"

Freya's eyes popped. She abruptly stood up and hurriedly stacked their books. "I have the perfect plan in mind. On my way into the library, I saw a flier. You'll love it. I promise." Cradling the remaining books, she jerked her head toward the exit.

Because Athena hesitated for an instant, she was nearly yanked to her feet by Freya. *She seems very excited,* Athena thought. Freya's skin was glowing, and she was more vibrant than she had been in days.

"Thank you!" exclaimed Freya in Norwegian as she effortlessly stacked the huge volumes and manuscripts in front of a confused-looking receptionist. She tossed her blonde, almost white hair from side to side as she prepared to escape from the library. Athena followed behind her, nodding at the dazed receptionist.

Stepping out into the dimming sun, Freya pulled on Athena's arm. "Come on! It should be this way. Eeek!" She squealed excitedly. Athena looked, trying to imagine where Freya wanted to go. They were heading south toward the city center. Athena could hear far away music, and was not shocked to realize they were heading in its general direction.

Freya skipped, almost danced, her way down the street. She was wearing a brightly colored knee-high dress with brown leather boots that showed off her strong, long legs. Her hair hung in loose braids. Her two necklaces reached down to her bosom.

Athena's outfit was very different from her partner's. She was wearing black jeans with black combat boots and a long white cardigan that covered the bronze armor that she always wore in public. As a finishing touch to her human outfit, she had decided to buy non-prescription glasses and tied her curls up in a high ponytail. Dressed in what she thought was typical of a student, she was confident that she could easily fit into a university crowd. Carrying her small Patagonia backpack that contained most of their research notes, currency and fake IDs, she followed Freya into the bar district.

The various pubs, bars and clubs played an interesting range of music. It varied from EDM, to hard rock, to 80s jams. Ignoring the music, Freya followed what sounded like medieval folk music down a time-worn street that was filled with rubble and into a small local pub. When Freya opened the door and stepped inside, her posture immediately relaxed, and it seemed as if her whole being was transformed by this small change of atmosphere. Ah, the power of music!

Athena sat down at a table near the exit and admired the musicians' instruments. They had drums, saxophones, violins and flutes. The music they created was truly intoxicating. From what Athena could observe, this music probably made Freya feel at home. Unconsciously, Athena fumbled with the ring on her hand which was also her aegis or bronze shield. She pictured the stunning beaches of Greece and the islands that surrounded her patron city, Athens.

"Would you like some mead?" asked Freya, who already held two cups of the amber liquid.

"No, thank you," Athena said. Freya shrugged and drained one of the cups in a single swallow. She smiled broadly and headed out toward the dance floor.

CHAPTER 19

Athena shook her head and opened her backpack. She took out her notebook and re-read her notes.

Species: unknown
Powers: rumors, unconfirmed
Culture: unknown
Allies: unknown
Enemies: Council of the Elders, Greek, Norse

Athena mentally added a question mark to where she had written Council of the Elders. *Who knows?* She looked toward Freya, who was dancing and singing along to the band's medieval music. She decided to delete the mental question mark next to Norse. During their time on Earth, her companion had been as loyal and attentive as possible. Athena prized herself on being able to accurately assess a person's character, and she saw that, even though Freya had flaws, she could be trusted.

"No, no!" A loud voice interrupted. "You said we would have some fun! No more research," yelled Freya over the song's drum solo. She closed Athena's notebook and shoved it roughly into the backpack. She tried guiding Athena out onto the dance floor, but Athena shook her head with a smile. Freya shrugged once more and took a long swallow of her second cup.

Sitting back down, Athena allowed herself to relax with the song's music. The old tunes created more energy than she had expected. Without thinking, she tapped her foot to the rhythm of the song. Freya twirled and sang with the rest of the pub locals, and soon the contagious energy spread like wildfire, reaching even the old couples by the exit. Within seconds, everybody was merrily singing and dancing to the drums and violins. *So this is a taste of Norse culture,* Athena realized. It was very similar to a Greek party; the floor was crowded with revelers who were dancing and singing.

This gathering differed from a Greek party, however. Most people here wore plenty of clothing. Usually, at Hermes' soirees, nudity was the main requirement. Normally, Athena stayed for her siblings' sake, lending a helping hand here or there. She pretended that their scandals and their embarrassments were beneath her, but inwardly she loved to observe the partiers and live vicariously through them. It was a win-win situation. Her image remained pure, yet her imagination was fed with plenty of tantalizing events.

Observing the dance floor once again, she saw that the locals were dancing a traditional one-two step. The women in the group would knit into a half circle in the middle of the dance floor, while the stomping men waited for them to retreat. As they did so, the men pushed into the circle, roaring with delight and dancing cheerfully. Some couples would interlace their arms and move in circles next to each other. Athena saw a giggling Freya join in. From the local crowd, a tall, bearded man approached Freya and started dancing with her, placing his hand on her hip.

A new emotion flared up in Athena. She took a moment to assess its meaning. Was she tired? She mused. *No, no.* It felt more like a stab in the pit of her belly. *Anger?* She thought not. Even though this feeling was unique, she was sure she had felt it before. *Hunger?* Never. *Wait.* This odd feeling did resemble hunger in a way, but not in the physical sense. She looked back toward the dance floor to where Freya and the locals were cheering and banging their cups together in merriment. Athena considered the bearded man who had approached Freya. He was regarding her with lust in his eyes. Of course it was lust. Who couldn't desire her? She was the light on the dance floor, the life of the party. The dancing continued, and as the men passed the women into the semicircle, the bearded man moved closer to Freya and whispered in her ear.

There it was again – that nagging emotion. Could it be suspicion? Athena definitely felt antagonistic toward this tall stranger, but she

CHAPTER 19

thought it seemed unfounded. Logic could not find the answer to this perplexity. What was this damned and incomprehensible emotion?

Oh, gods! Athena put her arms out to steady herself, even though her seat was perfectly sturdy. She took deep breaths, counting to five on each exhalation. *This can't be happening. It is not logical. It does not make sense.* She closed her eyes and tried to steady her racing heart. This was not the time to panic. *I must remain calm.*

"Are you alright, A?" Athena opened her eyes. Freya was looking over her, a worried frown on her beautiful face. Her blue eyes assessed Athena as she placed a tender hand on her brow.

"You seem a bit warm, A. Must be too crowded here for you. Let's go back," Freya said, trying to hide her regret.

"No," Athena finally managed. She reached out toward Freya and felt her skin tingle when she touched the Norse goddess' arm. "No, I'm alright. Just overthinking. Let's stay another moment. Keep dancing. It seems like a lot of fun. Don't stop on my account."

Freya's brows furrowed as she tried to peer into Athena's thoughts. For her part, Athena tried very hard to keep her mind completely blank, completely empty. She avoided any thought of Freya's white skin, her loose, untamed braids, or her rosy cheeks and soft full lips…

Freya shrugged and skipped back into the middle of the dance floor. Athena exhaled and straightened her posture, relaxing her muscles. She waved at the waiter and called, "I'll take a cider, please. The mellowest you have."

CHAPTER 20

February 26th

For the next two weeks, Athena kept her emotions under control. Whenever she felt as if they were bubbling up to the surface, she closed her eyes and counted to ten while forcing her hands to unclench. After their night of festivities, the goddesses had returned to their normal routine of research and discovery. They traveled to the Netherlands and stayed by the De Wallen area of Central Amsterdam, near canals that connected the city's districts. They were only a few minutes away from the Amsterdam Public Library.

To Athena's knowledge, Freya was unaware of her friend's newly discovered feelings. They continued with their cordial and respectful partnership as if nothing had changed. Just the other day, Freya had asked Athena if they might do something adventurous as relief from their studies. Athena was prepared for such a request, having booked two bikes to ride through the city. Outdoor exercise allowed Athena to clear her head and yet maintain a safe distance from Freya. They spent so much time together that any activity that brought them physically closer could weaken or obliterate her self-control. Today, however, Freya surprised Athena with a plan of her own.

Athena was busy in the library exploring what humans nowadays called the World Wide Web. Something in this fast-paced internet and its abundance of knowledge could lead them in the right direction.

Earlier, Freya had casually announced that she was going on a quick walk along the river that ran through the city. She mentioned something about wanting to clear her head, and Athena had no reason to suspect anything was amiss. As the hours flew by, however, Athena began to worry.

She had just made up her mind to go and search for Freya when the latter showed up at their usual spot in the library, carrying three large bags from Sephora, Miss Sixty and Mulberry. "We're going out tonight," she announced with a grin.

Athena smiled, but the gesture did not reach her eyes. Inside, she felt like running far, far away. "What do you have in mind?" she forced herself to casually ask as they left the library and headed back to their hotel.

"We haven't checked out the local scenery. There's a club that has the town buzzing. On my walk to the library, I overheard a group of young adults saying so."

Somehow, Athena felt that Freya was hiding part of the truth, but then again, Freya did love to party. It was as if she restored herself by absorbing the chaotic energy. Athena sighed inwardly. "Let's go then." How could she deny anything to this mesmerizing deity? No wonder her Greek family feared Eros so much.

Eros was technically Athena's first cousin once removed. He was known as Cupid to the Romans, and he was one of the gods most feared by the Olympians. His love-obsessive arrows were the cause of so much drama and pain. They were responsible for uncontrolled lust, mad infatuation and even desperation.

During his reign, Eros had many victims, including Athena's many siblings. Most famously, Eros struck Medea, daughter of King Aeetes of Colchis. She fell into an all-consuming and deadly obsession with the Argonaut, Jason. Her psychotic love led her to murder and dismember her younger brother in her ruthless show of devotion to her beloved Jason.

Athena shook her head. This was not her cousin's doing. Freya had a modest and subtle charm that entranced almost all who met her. Hell, even the Frost Giants from Norse Mythology lusted after Freya. She was independent, self-aware, honest, passionate, emotionally intelligent, self-respecting... in Athena's eyes, she was perfect.

Back at the Hotel Arena, a modern and well-located inn, Freya opened her shopping bags and tossed the contents onto her bed. Make-up, perfumes and leather outfits tumbled out. Freya scanned the clothes and then tossed a black shirt with elbow-length sleeves toward Athena. "With your figure, this will look great!" she exclaimed.

Athena blushed slightly and turned away from Freya's all-seeing eyes. She took off her cardigan sweater and held up the tight shirt to her bronze armor. "I'm not sure this will fit," she said, slightly confused.

Freya laughed heartily and crossed the room toward Athena. "No, silly. You won't need your armor tonight. I saw it foreshadowed in the flames." She chuckled as she made an undulating gesture with her hands. "Here, let me help you." Gently, Freya unbuckled Athena's back straps and helped her remove the heavy bronze armor.

Athena exhaled and forced herself to relax. She felt the tight fabric of the black shirt; it wasn't perfectly smooth, but that was to be expected with leather. The sleeves came almost to her elbows. It was a perfect fit. She placed her armband with her spear and short sword over the leather shirt. Athena smiled as she looked in the mirror. The black shirt covered half her neck in a sexy but modest sort of way. Freya seemed to have an uncanny sense of style. Athena's Aunt Aphrodite would be most pleased with her.

Athena turned to ask Freya for the rest of her outfit, but she stopped

CHAPTER 20

mid-sentence. Freya's back was to her as she was trying on her own outfit. She had chosen half-leather, half-denim shorts. They seemed like biker shorts, and they fit Freya's body impeccably. Her back was bare, and Athena noticed that she had ancient runes tattooed along her spine. Freya played with her hair before reaching over to grab a blazer that lay on her bed. Athena averted her eyes, pretending to be absorbed with reading the shirt's label. She turned when Freya called.

"What do you think?" Freya asked, a coy smile on her face. She was wearing a blazer that was shockingly whiter than her skin. She wore no shirt, but the fabric covered her chest as she twirled. Athena could not speak and did not try to, for fear that she would swallow her own tongue. *So much for ignoring Freya tonight.* It was impossible to look away. Her milk-white skin reflected youth and beauty.

"Here's the rest of your outfit. I'll do your hair and make-up next. Ah! Excited for tonight!" Freya squealed in her high, melodic voice. Athena took a deep breath. Apart from hiding from a murderous being, now she had to use all of the self-control she had gained in the eons she had been alive. *I do love a challenge,* she told herself.

Freya curled Athena's hair and then transformed it into a half-braid on the top of her head. She used very little of the makeup she had bought, for they both had magnificently clear skin. Her signature make-up move was the dark eyeliner that made each goddess's eyes sparkle and gleam. When she was done, Freya turned Athena's seat toward the mirror. Her grin was a clear sign that she was very pleased with her work. Instead of focusing on her reflection, however, Athena stared at the bottom of the mirror where there was a miniscule crack. From there she could see Freya's reflection. Athena watched Freya, who in turn was watching her. *How could someone like this exist?* Athena mused. *Was she real?*

"I don't think we're going to be very invisible today," said Athena.

"Look at you. You're stunning," replied Freya.

Athena's throat felt dry and she forced herself to relax.

"We're ready. Let's go." Without another word, Freya turned and, carrying a small purse, exited the hotel room.

Athena looked into the mirror. She saw her moss-green eyes, bright, wise and dangerous. But now she also saw something else... desire? Or was it fear?

The Warehouse Elementenstraat in Amsterdam was mostly raging electronic dance music, which did not bother Athena, but it was not her first choice of entertainment. Athena hung back as Freya explored every corner of the six-story building. Humans did find the most fascinating ways to entertain themselves. The line was long, but one look at both Freya and Athena, and the security guard opened the VIP entrance. Freya finished her exploration, turned to Athena and reached for her hand. "I think we should go to floor five! There are so many people dancing. It's exhilarating!" she yelled over the booming music.

Athena nodded and forced her heart to slow down as Freya squeezed her hand. Reaching the fifth floor, Freya immediately began to dance and jump to the pulsating rhythm. A DJ stood at the far end of the room, fist-bumping while she played with the controls on her monitors. The crowd seemed to be under her power as they jumped, screamed and relinquished control to the beat. Athena looked around at her surroundings including all the revelers, wondering where each person and each building block had come from. It fascinated her to understand that the world had become so globalized that stones from England, sand from Cairo, and plaster from Argentina could end up in a single building in Amsterdam, that in some instances was almost half a world away.

"I'm going to get some drinks! Want anything?" yelled Freya over the raucous noise. Athena shook her head, no. She was not worried about Freya, and for a moment, Athena felt released from the emotions

CHAPTER 20

she had been grappling with. But one look at the enamored humans fawning over Freya brought her mind back down to Earth, back to the feelings she wanted to bury.

Now she knew exactly what they meant. She felt jealous anytime someone approached Freya. She tried hard to hide her feelings; she had always thought herself a goddess of self-control. But she could see how powerful jealousy is. If anyone who was unworthy dared to approach Freya, Athena's rage would be so great, she would immediately break that being in two. She shuddered. For most of her life, she had frowned at such acts committed as a result of jealousy by her divine peers, but now it seemed that she was afflicted by the same disease.

A crowd was forming around Freya as she danced. Some humans got too close for Athena's comfort. She clenched her teeth and reminded herself that Freya was both powerful and old enough to set her own boundaries. As she looked around, however, she imagined herself dancing next to Freya. *Why not? I should take my chance... I can do this. I can do this.*

With one last deep breath, she strode toward Freya and her crowd of admirers. She was not much of a dancer, preferring to observe rather than participate. However, this music did not call for much rhythm. From what she could see, most humans just wiggled about uncontrollably and jumped every thirty seconds.

Athena decided to let go of a bit of her self-control. *10%.* She mimicked Freya, who was grinning while she danced. *This is actually kind of fun,* Athena reflected. The crowd around them pressed together, lost in the music, but whenever they got too close, Athena would flash her menacing glare and send them scurrying. As the music grew louder, she felt herself unwinding, and she allowed more of her self-control to vanish. *20%.* The minutes and hours seem to fly by as if one moment on this energy-filled dance floor was equivalent to fifteen minutes on the outside. The DJ turned up the beats per minute, and Athena kept dancing beside Freya. Her heart was filled with joy. Ecstatic. *30%.*

Athena decided to relax a little more. *40%. I'm still in control. I can do it.* She was not yet overwhelmed by Freya's intoxicating aura, or the way her body moved under the spinning lights of the club.

At first Athena did not allow herself to openly gaze at Freya's body, choosing to shift her eyes from one dancer to another. But now she found herself more often than not staring into Freya's face. She saw the crinkles next to her dazzling smile, and she saw her perfect white teeth that flashed brightly in the darkness. Freya jumped then reached out to steady herself, holding onto Athena's arms with her soft, tender hands. *50%*

"This is so much fun!" Freya yelled with a hearty laugh that sent shivers of happiness down Athena's spine. *60%*

Oh, gods! It was happening again, that overwhelming feeling in the pit of her stomach. She felt her skin burn where Freya still held her tight. Her nerves were aflame. Out of nowhere, a reveler bumped into them, breaking their small embrace. Instead of feeling grateful that her skin was no longer on fire, Athena's rage bubbled like lava, threatening to explode.

"Sorry," laughed the man as he stumbled, his breath reeking. As he looked for his victim, his eyes fixated on Freya's silhouette. He opened his mouth and slurred. "Those are some nice…" but Athena cut him off by slapping him across the face with such force that the man fell down, unconscious.

Abruptly, the crowd stopped dancing. Stupefied, they stared at the man. *70%.* Athena felt that her self-control was dissipating, and she feared she would retaliate if she lost her ability to restrain herself. She stepped over the unconscious man and strode down the stairs, exiting the building onto the street. Athena could count on one hand the

CHAPTER 20

number of times she had lost control, and she did not want to involve her other hand in the count. She paced down the sidewalk. After a couple of minutes, she stopped and placed her hands on the wall of a building. She sensed she was being watched, and she turned.

Freya strolled in Athena's direction. "Nice punch," she commented as she casually leaned on the building, bending her knee and placing her foot on the wall.

Athena groaned. "So much for not interacting with humans. Will he be alright?"

"I wouldn't worry about him. He's a pig. He deserved a nice whack in the face." Freya's eyes twinkled in a way that made Athena's heart melt.

"I'm sorry. I didn't mean to ruin our night out," she apologized.

"What do you mean, ruin? That was the highlight of my month! You tossed that man down with a mere flick of your wrist. I can't imagine receiving a well-deserved hit from you," Freya concluded with a chuckle. She looked down at the ground and then at Athena, moving her eyes slowly from her legs to her face, roving across every inch of Athena's body. *80%.*

Athena cleared her throat. "I would appreciate it if you would keep this incident between us, and not inform the Council of the Elders."

Freya harrumphed. She bit her lower lip, trying to find the right words. Athena's pulse quickened as she saw Freya lounging casually against the brick wall in the moonlight.

"I think there's a lot we can hide from the Council," Freya murmured. She moved toward Athena and touched her hair, fixing a loose strand behind Athena's ear. Freya did not pull away from their new-found proximity, nor did Athena want her to. *90%.* Up until this moment, she had forced herself to look away from Freya's mesmerizing eyes, from her lush, youthful body and from her skin that gleamed in the night. It was more than Athena could do to take her eyes off of her now.

    Freya closed the distance between them, inching nearer. Athena could feel Freya's breath on her face. It felt like a chilly gust of wind in the night. Her breath smelled of mint. Finally, Freya stopped mere inches from her lips. Alluringly, she traced her lip with her tongue. *100%.* The distance between Freya and Athena dissolved.

CHAPTER 21

April 29th

The Music City Center is strategically located in downtown Nashville, Tennessee, in the United States of America. Adjacent to The Country Music Hall of Fame and the Bridgestone Arena, this modern event center is a few blocks away from the hustle and bustle of Broadway Street which is the well-known hub for nightlife and live music. Apart from the many bars that tourists and locals visit in this famed city, there are numerous museums, professional and collegiate sports venues, and event centers that host a variety of lectures and concerts.

Demonbreun Street was packed with cars, ride shares and pedestrians who were making their way to the Music City Center. This evening's entertainment would include a highly praised and popular motivational speaker, and the atmosphere around downtown Nashville was bubbling. Scores of families, friends, and even some college students crowded around the inside of the Event Center to prepare for the highly anticipated affair. The waiting crowd hummed collectively as the attendees chatted and pondered how this evening would transform their lives. There were sodas and snacks available as well as adult beverages. The evening was shaping up to be splendid.

"What do you think Dr. Jackson will say?" was heard from a voice in the crowd.

"I wonder who the opening act will be!" wondered another.

"What if the special guest is someone famous?" giggled a young girl to her friends.

"It's already past 7 pm!" grumbled a sour husband to his patient wife.

"Maybe they're a bit tied up at the moment, darling. Don't worry, I'm sure

it'll start soon enough. Here, have some popcorn," the uncomplaining wife offered while smiling gently. Little did she know how right she was.

Dr. Jackson and his crew were indeed tied up, but the ropes that bound their bodies were not made out of human tardiness. In fact, every single human backstage was fettered and gagged with very real chains.

As Manisilat moved the last crew member into the tiny dressing room, she couldn't help but smile. "I'm sorry you'll miss the show, Doctor," she crooned as she beamed at the stupefied man lying chained in a corner. "It's to die for," she cackled as she locked the door.

Laughing maniacally, she made her way toward the stage. Before her turbulent arrival offstage, she had informed one gullible lighting technician that she was tonight's opening act, and to make sure her entrance was nothing if not dazzling. As she prepared to move up the stairs and onto the stage, she winked at the technician who was on the other side of the building in the lighting box.

"It's showtime," she whispered demonically. Throwing open the curtains, she strode toward the crowd, smiling and nodding at the clapping audience.

"Welcome! Welcome, my beautiful people!" she boomed, beaming at the many human souls before her. All they saw was a very attractive, sexily dressed woman with black leather tights that covered her curvy

CHAPTER 21

thighs. Underneath her leather jacket, she wore a tight V neck which allowed her to display most of her bosom to the crowd. Her nails were long and painted jet black, the same color as her beguiling eyes.

"Are we ready for an amazing show tonight?" Manisilat rumbled with her deep, powerful voice. These pathetic humans would never notice that she did not require their silly technology. Her voice was louder and more intense than their simple microphones. The crowd clapped and settled comfortably into their seats.

"Dr. Jackson is so very excited to meet you all tonight!" Manisilat laughed throatily and beamed at the gullible spectators. "Most of you don't know me, but I have traveled a long way to meet you. I cannot wait to see how our evening together unfolds." She wriggled her hands together in a gesture of eagerness.

Now... who to pick? Manisilat thought as she scanned the crowd. She noticed a couple in the third row who seemed to be trying hard to avoid eye contact with each other. She scanned the back of the room. A group of high school students on an outing were sitting together, throwing paper planes at one another while their teacher desperately whispered, trying to control them. She saw one young man near the middle of the spacious room who kept glancing to his right and scowling in his seat. *Got you.*

"Let's begin this evening by introducing ourselves. My name is a bit hard to pronounce." She winked at a group of young men in the audience. "So you can just call me Mani. Say it with me! Hello, Mani."

"Hello, Mani," muttered some voices from the crowd, not loud enough for her enjoyment.

"I can't hear you. What did you say?" she responded in a teasing, flirtatious way.

"Hello, Mani!" screamed the crowd.

"That's more like it. Hello, my beauties." Manisilat bowed and straightened slowly, making sure that her curves moved in just the right places. She needed her audience's undivided attention.

"You!" she said as she pointed at a middle aged man who was seated on the right side of the auditorium. "What's your name?"

The man pointed at himself as if to question her choice. Manisilat smiled and nodded encouragingly. The man cleared his throat and stood up awkwardly.

"Um. Hello. My name is Tom," he stuttered.

Manisilat peered at the man. He was of medium height with a typical southern beard and a bowl haircut that was most unflattering. *Low self-confidence, fear of crowds.* "Hello, Tom," Manisilat purred in her seductive voice. "Why so quiet? I promise, we won't bite." *Not yet.*

The crowd guffawed. Some yelled encouraging words, while others stifled their laughter at Tom's awkwardness.

"Tom," she whispered, making sure each syllable was enunciated. Her whisper was more of a whooshing sound, and it moved around the crowd, quieting it. "I want to share a secret with you. Will you share one with me?" Manisilat raised her eyebrow and peered into Tom's eyes. He gave the slightest nod.

"Like you, I have many fears," she lied. "And like most of you here, there are some things I love and some things I hate," she declared, putting emphasis on her last word. "For example, I hate failure." She looked around the room. "I'm sure half of you feel the same. Tom, what is it you fear?"

Tom was turning a ghostly shade of white, but Manisilat bore her eyes into his, denying him release. He stared mesmerized at her black eyes. "I fear public speaking," he said in a tremulous voice.

The crowd around him burst into laughter, and some yelled encouragement.

"Way to go, Tom!"

"You can do it, man!"

CHAPTER 21

But Tom was oblivious; he had become so mesmerized by Manisilat's stare. She blinked, releasing Tom from her deadly gaze. Tom shook his head and looked around in confusion. The person next to him patted him on the shoulder in an attempt to comfort him.

Manisilat turned to the couple she had spied earlier. "You!" she boomed as she pointed at a blonde girl who wore way too much makeup. Manisilat waited for her to stand. Once the girl did, she asked, "What do you love?"

"Hi, I'm Amy. I…" The girl stopped abruptly. She looked toward her boyfriend, then down at her feet. Manisilat tried to coerce the girl's eyes to move upwards, forcing her into her hypnotizing stare. Timidly, the girl looked into Manisilat's eyes causing her own to widen as she lost self-control. "I love my cat," she announced with no emotion.

The crowd cheered at the speaker's honesty. *Almost there.* Nervously, Amy sat down and looked away from her befuddled boyfriend.

Manisilat scanned the crowd and then pointed at the high school teacher near the back. "You!" She beamed at the stout lady who was trying to subdue her unruly pupils. "What do you hate?"

To her surprise, the teacher did not hesitate to stand up. With a loud bark, she yelled, "I hate it when my students don't listen to me!" This comment sent the crowd into a frenzy; most people were laughing openly.

Manisilat narrowed her eyes. She stared at the insolent fool who had ignored her scrutiny. She waited for the teacher to meet her penetrating gaze. Finally, the woman looked directly at Manisilat. *What do you truly hate?* she silently demanded.

The woman blinked and her posture slackened. "I hate both my students and my life," she said loudly, responding to Manisilat's wordless question.

The crowd gasped and for the first time that evening, the students became quiet. The silence stretched endlessly, almost painfully. *Got you now.*

"Thank you for your honesty. I'm sure a lot of us feel that way, don't we?" lied Manisilat as she scanned the room. Many people nodded, while others scowled and crossed their arms.

"It's normal to feel that way. Emotions are very important, but they do not control us. We control them," announced Manisilat. "For example, can we all clap our hands and smile? Come on! Don't be shy." The crowd did as she coaxed. The mood transformed from gloomy and depressed to happy and cheerful. "What about jumping up and down?" The crowd followed like sheep. "Can you scream at the top of your lungs?" The crowd yelled shamelessly, completely in her grasp.

Finally, she turned to the angry man in the middle of the room. "You!" Eager to express himself, the man's eyes met hers. "What do you hate the most?" whispered Manisilat as her eyes glimmered with repressed glee.

"I hate him!" the man screamed as he turned and pointed to an older man on the other side of the auditorium.

"Show me! Tell me how much you hate him," Manisilat demanded.

"I hate you!" the younger man bellowed at the top of his lungs as he lunged, then sprinted toward the older one. Fists raised, the two men collided and broke into a ferocious fight. Losing their self-control, the crowd began to yell. Collectively, every person except the two fighting men in the audience, peered into Manisilat's eyes.

"You!" Manisilat thundered. "Show me your hate!"

The crowd broke into pandemonium. Chairs were thrown, drinks flew through the air and fists met flesh. The audience was no longer human; they were savage, uncontrolled beasts. Within seconds the windows were shattered and a fire broke out. The event transformed into a riot.

Manisilat strode through the crowd, laughing and dodging flying debris. She shoved this way and that, forcing larger groups into bloody

CHAPTER 21

fights. As she reached the doors, she turned to survey her marvelous work. The Event Center resembled a war zone. Blood was flowing freely, and the fire was spreading dangerously. Manisilat opened the huge double doors and beckoned to her crazed followers.

"Come, my beauties!! Be free, spread your fire and your hate through the world!! Find your anger!!"

The horde of deranged humans turned at her command and charged out of the Music City Center, spreading their extremism and hate wherever they could.

CHAPTER 22

May 1st

Leo used his passport to fan himself. They had deboarded the plane just minutes before, and he was already starting to sweat. It seemed as if there was no air conditioning in the Cairo International Airport.

Leo shifted his feet from side to side as they waited to pass the immigration queue. They had not checked any baggage, preferring to carry their few possessions in their Patagonia packs. Leo was surprised at the amount of things that Athena managed to fit into hers. Back in Paris, he had watched in silent amazement as she neatly folded and added shorts, pants, shirts, long skirts, long sleeves, pairs of socks, jackets, blankets, books, first aid kits... basically anything she might require to travel the globe.

He now understood why they had bought so many items back in London on their first day of their journey. Not knowing one's destination required precise preparation. Leo felt that with his pack, he was well suited for hiking glaciers or trudging through the desert and that was what they were planning to do.

As the line inched forward, Leo guessed that they would need to wait another forty minutes or so before meeting their immigration officer. He hoped this border crossing with Apollo would be easier

CHAPTER 22

than that with his half-brother, Ares. Back then, moving from Spain to France, they only had to create a small diversion, but Egypt was a different ball game. Leo was curious to see why the falcon and the vegvisir had guided them here, and what they would accomplish in the land of the Pyramids.

Leo remembered how, back in Paris three days before, they had been eating the most delicious dinner when the falcon arrived with the most surprising news ever. He hadn't recognized the bird, but apparently it had been following them during their various escapades in Madrid... maybe even London. Sometimes he forgot who he was dealing with. His world had suddenly been transformed into a perilous adventure, as if he had been submerged in one of his childhood myths.

He didn't feel like the heroes of Greek mythology, those brave men and women with special strength, speed or abilities. In his new reality, Leo was battling the forces of darkness, and he was relieved that he wasn't alone. Athena had promised to stay by his side, and now they were joined by the mighty Apollo. Their presence diminished the pressure he felt. He was becoming more resourceful and self-assured, the longer he spent with the Greek gods.

Leo turned to look at his companions. Apollo was standing with his left leg casually extended in front of him; his right leg was supporting most of his weight. On his wrists he wore two small golden chains, one with a tiny bow and the other with a number of vertical lines that Leo now knew were actually arrows. He looked exactly like Michealangelo's statue of David. Leo's eyes widened in surprise. Even his hair had the same shape and curly form. The only difference between them, apart from David being made of stone, was that Apollo was wearing a maroon long-sleeved shirt with gray, tightly fitting pants and running shoes. If it were up to Apollo, he would never wear a shirt. The less clothes, the better.

Leo cocked his head as he looked at Apollo. *That's not entirely true,* he thought. Apollo loved to shop. He could spend hour upon hour staring at clothes and wondering out loud what colors and fabrics would mesh. Leo could not imagine how it had occurred, but in the short time Apollo had been on Earth, he had accumulated more than fifty pieces of expensive clothing. Athena had glared at the contents of his many closets in muted disbelief. Then, without another word, she turned to her younger brother and put up only one finger, which meant he could bring only one outfit with him.

Apollo had tried to argue, but one stony look from Athena quieted him. He was very disappointed when he had to leave his eight suits behind. His item of choice was a navy, three-piece suit that he reasoned he could easily pack. Leo recalled how Athena and Apollo had stared at each other for what felt like hours until Athena gave a shrug and allowed Apollo to pack it.

Now, the Sun God stood carrying his green Patagonia backpack that was filled with almost the same limited wardrobe as those of Athena and Leo. He had chosen the most vibrant colors; for example, one of his outfits consisted of neon shorts, a bright pink shirt and, to top it off, a lime green hat that contrasted outrageously with his honeyed eyes.

"Stop drooling," Athena said when she caught Leo staring at Apollo.

"Very funny," Leo replied.

Athena's gaze shifted toward the immigration officers. Almost all of the guards were male, and they seemed intimidating. Leo gulped and tried to stop his heart from beating so rapidly. Sensing what was happening to her companion, Athena took hold of his hand and gave it a squeeze, moving closer to him. "Relax, everything will be alright," she reassured him.

Immediately, Leo felt the tension in his body ease. His mind cleared, as if he were alone on a secluded beach, relaxing with a couple of his favorite books. He gave Athena a grateful smile.

CHAPTER 22

"Why do we have to travel like this? It's so inefficient," Apollo grumbled. Athena didn't respond; she just stared at Apollo. The latter groaned. "Agh. We could have found a way to get there hours ago. Instead, we're standing here in this hot, smelly place, lying about who we are and traveling like mortals," Apollo whispered in contempt.

Athena began to speak very quickly in Attic Greek, her words too fast for Leo to comprehend.

Apollo's stance hardened, his eyes widened. Athena continued speaking rapidly, her eyes boring into his. The tension between the siblings was palpable, and Leo started to wonder if anyone around them would notice their quiet, strained argument. Within seconds, however, Apollo heaved a sigh, and immediately replaced his petulant stare with a soft smile and a shrug. Casually, he caressed his hair.

"I'm honored to accompany my siblings," he bowed his head toward Leo, "to Egypt. I'm the official family chaperone, if you will. Plus, I haven't been back here in years. I wonder how it's changed since the old days." Athena raised one eyebrow, and released her grip on Leo's hand.

For the next half-hour, Leo and Athena filled the time by people-watching the crowd and the guards. Seeing as they were nearing the exit, she whispered urgently, "We'll have to split up when they call for us. Leo, you'll have to go alone while I go through with Apollo. Make sure you point to us when he asks you who you're with, just like we rehearsed."

Leo nodded and reached into his bag to take out his documents. *We're tourists. I'm with my friends. Her name is Alexandra Pallas, and his name is Phoebus Pallas. I got this.* Athena gave his hand one last squeeze and they parted, shifting into separate lanes.

Within a few minutes, Leo was signaled to approach the desk. He breathed deeply and made his way toward the officer, smiling and saying, "Good afternoon, Sir." The officer nodded once, not even glancing at Leo as he typed on his computer. He reached out for Leo's passport and quickly scanned it, squinting at his profile picture and looking through his recent travels.

"Why are you here?" the man said gruffly.

Leo gulped. "I'm here with my friends. We're tourists. We're going to the pyramids and all those, um, touristy places..." he trailed off awkwardly.

The officer looked up from his screen. He took in Leo's appearance from his huge glasses to his bucket hat. "Where is your group?" He asked.

"They're in that lane over there" Leo pointed behind him to the siblings. "Her name is Alexandra Pallas and his name is...." but Leo did not finish. He was interrupted by the man's whistling as his eyes widened in admiration.

"Those are your friends?" he asked.

"Yes." The man seemed to ignore Leo's last comment as he looked hungrily at Athena. Even though she was wearing a shapeless black, long-sleeved shirt with matching pants and a headscarf that covered most of her hair and face, there was no mistaking that with her tall slender body and the dignity with which she moved, she was a stunning woman. The immigration officer continued to ogle her, and Leo tapped his fingers to subtly catch his attention.

The officer composed himself and turned his attention back to his screen and Leo's travel documents. After what felt like an eternity, he eyed Leo with a slimy grin. "Good for you, Leonardo Clarkson," he said with a leer as he closed the passport and handed it back. "You have fun, eh? And keep her close, keep her head covered. Better for travel, eh."

"Um. Thank you," stammered Leo.

The man waved him off and resumed leering at Athena, smoothing his black hair with his hand while he completely ignored the other

CHAPTER 22

tourists in his line.

Leo walked off. This had not been as hard as he had imagined. He waited by the exit while Apollo and Athena cleared their immigration queue. Athena was standing behind Apollo, letting him do all the talking. In a relaxed stance with his hands resting by his sides, he was casually speaking to the agent.

The officer examining their papers seemed as intrigued by Athena as Leo's officer had been. He kept glancing past Apollo to stare at her in a most impolite manner. The siblings tried hard to ignore the officer, but Leo could tell that Apollo's patience was beginning to run out. Leo watched as the officer who had helped him left his post and joined the other agent. Even though he heard them commenting in Arabic, he was sure from their laughter that they were making off-color jokes about Athena.

Leo began to feel really warm, as if he were standing near a blazing furnace. Turning to look around, he saw that both siblings had tensed. He did not understand what the officers had said, but it was clear that both Apollo and Athena did, and they were not happy. Apollo's back became rigid. His fists tightened and his posture was menacing. Leo realized that the heat was emanating from Apollo. His bronze eyes were transforming, starting to blaze. It seemed as if in mere moments he would strike out at the officers. Leo held his breath, frozen on the spot.

Before anything could happen, Athena spoke up in a quiet voice. She caught the attention of the guards, who did not realize the anger with which Apollo's eyes were now burning. "Leo!" she called out. "We are almost through. Wait for us there, please," she said while she casually placed her hand on Apollo's shoulder.

The officers turned to stare at Leo, who could not leave even if he wanted to. They laughed again and gave Leo some approving nods. Absent-mindedly, they slid the siblings' papers across the desk. Apollo snatched them up and stormed out the exit without another word. Athena strode after him. Together, they followed Apollo to the street, bypassing baggage claim since they already had their backpacks.

Once out in the open air, they caught up to a fuming Apollo. "I can't believe they said that about you! I want to kill them," he yelled. Although his hands were still tightly clenched, his eyes were beginning to return to their usual color. Leo looked around, hoping that nobody had overheard them.

"Brother, do you seriously want to attack everyone who makes a sexist comment?" she asked.

"Yes! Those swine do not deserve to live. How dare they? I will crush them. I will blind them with my…"

"Then you'd better start attacking everybody, because those comments will not stop. Welcome to a day in the life of women. Just ignore it. It's not worth it. You said it yourself; they are below us. They are specks of dust. They are unimportant. Let's go."

She turned and headed towards the signs pointing to the bus stop. Leo followed her, and after a second, so did Apollo. Leo could hear his angry mutterings as they followed Athena across the street and out of the parking lots. "It's just so demeaning, having to pretend to be someone you're not, having to lie." Apollo shuddered as if lying was unthinkable to him. He continued in an irritated voice. "And those *vlakas*. Disgusting. They don't deserve my mercy."

Leo slowed down and decided to walk next to him as they followed Athena. He was right, of course. Being a male came with a lot of perks. It was easy to take life for granted. Women had it so much harder. Wherever they walked, they got leering and cat-calls. Leo admired those independent and strong women who traveled the world alone. It must take a lot of courage, guts and cunning to survive. *Maybe one day the world will truly reach equality,* he thought, but as they walked out onto the public street, his hopes dwindled.

CHAPTER 22

Leaving the Cairo Airport was almost as complicated as passing through immigration. They jostled their way through the crowd of locals who were either trying to sell to or con tourists. There were many men who approached them, yelling "taxi-taxi" or trying to intrigue them with pictures of the Giza Pyramids or city tours. Many got too close for comfort, but one angry look from either Athena or Apollo sent them scurrying.

That was not the case with one man, who instead of cowering, tried to intimidate them by standing right in front of Apollo. This did not work well for him since, already angered by what had transpired at the airport, Apollo shot him a murderous look. The man crumbled as if struck by hot pincers and covered his eyes, tears streaming from between his fingers. Apollo walked on, his eyes still burning with rage and indignation at this affront to his person. His anger that originated at the airport had not yet ebbed, and the fact that Egypt was not the most tolerant of countries was dawning on him.

Back in Paris, he had shouted in disbelief when Athena explained Egypt's stance with regard to women's rights and open sexual tendencies. Apollo had been used to freedom in all aspects of his life, but in order to blend in, some restrictions had to be put in place. "This is so different from the Egypt I remember," Apollo grumbled as they climbed into the airport bus that would take them through Cairo's streets and toward a second bus station.

Leo's mind raced through Egypt's history. In Ancient Egypt, women were considered equal to men, regardless of marital status. There were multiple famous and admired pharaohs who were women, including Hatshepsut, who was generally regarded as one of the most successful pharaohs of Egyptian history. Being a prolific builder, she commissioned hundreds of construction projects through Upper and Lower Egypt. Ancient Egypt had one of the longest histories of any country, tracing its heritage along the Nile Delta back to the 6th—

4th century BCE. In fact, the dynastic period in Egypt's timeline was longer than the creation and continuation of the West.

The centuries-old dynastic period shattered when Egypt came under Roman rule in 31 BCE with the suicide of the famous Queen Cleopatra. Four centuries later, Egypt's polytheism and religious views declined rapidly as Christianity spread throughout the Roman Empire. By 1517 CE, Egypt was absorbed into the Ottoman Empire, and then conquered by different European powers in the 18th and 19th century, whereupon it became an English protectorate.

Egypt finally gained independence in 1922, but British influence did not waver until well into the 1950s, when Egypt was then declared a republic. Even so, the country continued to face external and internal challenges from political unrest to terrorism and economic underdevelopment. Leo had learned in his world history class that Egypt's semi-presidential republic was a veil covering an authoritarian regime responsible for the country's problematic human rights record and its high gender inequality index.

Even after Athena had explained these facts, Apollo remained dissatisfied. The disabuse of his beliefs had been a huge blow, and Leo sensed Apollo's mounting rage. Apart from being lord of healing, music and dance, he was also known for his vengeful and oftentimes savage personality. Leo was grateful that Athena was keeping a close watch on her brother who, even as they exited the airport bus and walked through the Al Nasr station filled with harmless traveling foreigners, looked riotous.

Athena bought three one-way bus tickets to Saqqara. She preferred traveling in large crowds when they were in the city. Leo thought that in this way, she felt safer and less exposed. As they climbed into their seats, Apollo muttered under his breath, and Athena shot him a searching look.

Leo sat down and took his notebook out of his backpack. It

CHAPTER 22

was filled with useful information about Egyptian Mythology and architecture. He was not sure where exactly they were headed, but he wanted to be prepared. Beside him Athena stroked her vegvisir necklace. She seemed to be deep in thought, her fingers moving unconsciously through the arrows of the majestic pendant.

Leo opened his notebook. He had written some useful hieroglyphic translations and some demotic phrases. Ancient Egypt was pleasantly literate, using two written systems, hieroglyphics for sacred writing and demotic script for everyday reports and contracts. Fixing his glasses, he read his personal notes:

"Considered a cradle of civilization, Ancient Egypt
saw some of the earliest developments of writing,
agriculture, urbanization, organized religion and
central government. Iconic monuments such as the
Giza Necropolis and its Great Sphinx, as well
the ruins of Memphis, Thebes, Karnak, and the
Valley of the Kings, reflect this legacy and remain
a significant focus of scientific and popular interest...."

Leo closed from his notebook.

He surveyed his surroundings and marveled as they passed through bazaars and mosques. The city had an orange glow, as if it had been burned bronze by the sun. The houses and buildings shared that mirage, like a Saharan dust spreading through Egypt's capital. The farther they moved south from the city, the closer they got to the pyramids and the River Nile. The mesmerizing city was so different from what he was accustomed to. Egypt was truly its own unique world.

He felt both intrigued and scared by the magnificent country. For an academic like Leo, his childhood had been a bit difficult. He had been bullied by his classmates for his obsession with books and museums, and then a few years later, he had been tyrannized yet again because of his newfound secret that he was in fact attracted to boys and not girls. Apparently, in middle school there were no secrets, even if you did not tell a soul. The truth always found a way to wiggle out. Once his classmates discovered that part of him, the abuse and insults were endless. Leo had found solace in his books, burying himself deep in the characters' stories, by loving, hating, adoring, resenting and admiring them as he submerged himself completely in their development.

Growing up with an Italian grandmother meant that art, museums and music were constantly encouraged and ever present. They became a fundamental part of his personality and passion. He loved to cook which his "manly" father had considered effeminate. He loved to play music and sway to the rhythm of the melody. He enjoyed reading and writing poetry. The latter, sadly, had led to not one but two black eyes after the ruffians in his class searched his locker and found the incriminating evidence. Kids could be so mean. They confused honesty with cruelty. Their wounds left scars, scars that never seemed to heal properly, so any little word here or there could open them anew. Once he transferred to his new secondary school, Leo began working extremely hard to emotionally recover and improve himself. His mother was a source of inspiration for him as she rose to the challenge of raising a five-year old alone. Leo's father's abandonment was another laceration which only time and lots of patience could stitch together.

On their journey toward Saqqara, they passed the Giza Pyramids, and Leo pressed his face to the window, trying to catch a glimpse of the Giza Necropolis. Looking to his left, Leo could still see the city and the buildings that surrounded the outskirts of Cairo; when he shifted right, he saw the towering pyramids that were so famous. It was as if two worlds collided: Ancient Egypt, with its stretching sand dunes and next to it, modern Egypt, with its crumbling buildings and crowded streets.

CHAPTER 22

"Look at all that sand!" exclaimed Leo. "It goes on and on. The Sahara. Wow."

Apollo turned his head and his sulky expression transformed as he took in Leo's marvel.

"Did you know it stretches for more than nine million square kilometers? It's the third largest desert, preceded by Antarctica and the northern Arctic," said Leo as he pressed his face closer to the window.

Apollo smiled. "Ah, yes. My son accidentally burned this land," he reminisced as he stretched and rested his arms above his head.

Seems like he has calmed down, thought Leo. Apollo had the dreamy expression of someone about to tell a story.

"His name was Phaethon. He was my boy by Clymene. An Oceanid, you know. Most humans believed he was the son of Helios. I guess you can't really prove parentage. The boy was rash but brave. He wanted to prove to his friends that I was his father." He paused briefly, then dramatically continued, "I should never have agreed to his request. But what could I do? I barely knew the boy; at the time, indulging him just once seemed reasonable. When he asked to drive the Sun Chariot, I hesitated, but any son of mine could easily control my horses, so I granted his wish.

"Only those associated with the sun can control them, like Helios. I remember he laughed at Phaeton which only solidified my son's resolve. The boy started off well, flying level. Not too high and not too low. I'm not sure what happened; maybe he tried impressing the people below or maybe, like Icarus, he lost himself in the task, thinking he had full control...Young men," he glanced at Athena who was listening to his story, "and young women," he added, nodding in her direction, "can be reckless. Their youth masks their inexperience, and they think themselves invisible.

"Once the horses sensed a different rider, they panicked. Phaethon struggled to impose his will on them. He flew erratically, allowing the beasts to mark his way instead of the other way round. They flew too close to Northern Africa, and scorched the land with their radiant sun-filled energy. They would have continued to burn everything if Father had not stepped in. In the end, Zeus put a stop to Phaeton's madness by striking him down with a thunderbolt before any more damage could be done. Ah, foolish boy! How I loved him!" Apollo's eyes glistened with remembrance.

Their silence continued, but it was not uncomfortable. Leo thought of David and their relationship. He imagined what it would feel like to lose him. Leo was curious to see if their friendship would continue to develop. He allowed himself to dream of what their future could be.

The Sun God turned to his audience. "I don't know your backstory, mortal, but you're lucky, sister. You've never had to feel the pain of losing a loved one. It's blinding, like your soul is shattering into a million pieces. Day by day you try putting it back together, but never quite find all the pieces. You're broken, a shell of who you used to be." Athena's eyes seemed blank. Leo stared at her intently, but he knew he would never be able to read her.

He was touched by Apollo's words. He wanted to believe that Apollo was being truthful, but there was something in his eyes that did not reflect pain from the loss of a murdered son. This was a man full of contradictions. *Well, a god, not a man,* Leo corrected himself. From all the Greek myths he had read, Apollo could deliver people from epidemics, yet just as suddenly, he could launch with his arrows ill-health and deadly plagues.

Leo turned away from the golden-skinned god and looked out of the window, but he was distracted by a reflection. He realized the shiny objects were Athena's eyes. They had a faraway, expressionless look as if she were purposely closing her mind to those around her.

CHAPTER 22

Her jaw was clenched, and her hands were wrapped around the seat. Her casual posture seemed forced, and Leo felt uncomfortable just staring at her, but he could sense deep pain in her eyes. He could not look away. Was she thinking about the tasks ahead, or did Phaeton's story trigger some buried feelings?

Leo thought back to the last time he had seen Athena grow cold. Since she was sitting next to him, her body was close enough for Leo to sense the frostiness. He could no longer sense her usual radiating warmth. Her body seemed somehow chilled, almost corpselike. Could gods become statues at will? Apart from her intense and murderous stares when she was engaged in battle, the last time she had turned serious was when Leo had questioned her about her divine partner. He remembered his mental note never to ask her about that again. *What was that about?*

Leo opened his Egyptian mythology book, but did not take in the words. His mind kept drifting to David and their last conversation. He'd had to be very vague about his current whereabouts, and he felt uncomfortable not being able to tell David about his adventures. He was traveling the world and doing what he loved, but he could not share it with the one he most appreciated. Next time he saw David, if he ever did, he would tell him how he felt. He would be brave enough to do it.

Fears and doubt raced in Leo's head. *What if David didn't feel the same? Would their friendship be compromised? What if... What if...* Leo shook his head and resolved to keep faith. Whatever was going on between David and him was real. He looked out of the window at the Egyptian sand and felt at peace. He would survive all this, whatever lay ahead of them, just so he could see David one more time.

From beyond the bus, a lone falcon screeched.

CHAPTER 23

Thirty kilometers south of modern-day Cairo rests Saqqara, an Egyptian village in the Giza Governorate. It is the necropolis of the ancient capital of Memphis. Covering an area of 7 by 1.5 kilometers, Saqqara contains the oldest complete stone building complex known in history, the Pyramid of Djoser. This world-famous pyramid is sometimes called the Step Tomb. Compared to modern buildings, Djoser's step pyramid might not seem as impressive, but it set several important precedents since it was the first monumental structure made of stone. After Djoser, another sixteen Egyptian kings built pyramids at Saqqara. Pyramids were sacred buildings, and they included several important chambers that were not just graves; they were much more. They were monuments. They were tombs. They contained chapels. They were reminders of the glorification of life after death, for death was merely the beginning of a new journey to another world. They facilitated the rebirth of kings. And if kings could be reborn, who else could be?

Once the three travelers reached the archeological complex, they gathered their belongings and exited the bus. Leo held his notebook, partially because he could not wait to confirm his theories on Egyptian pyramids, but also because it gave his fluttering hands a task. His eyes feasted on the marvels before him. The glare of the sand and

CHAPTER 23

the sand-colored structures burned his eyes, but the ache could not extinguish his longing and curiosity. Together they explored the complex, marveling at the magnificent structures: the pyramid of Userkaf, the Teti Pyramid, the Pyramid of Unas, the Serapeum of Saqqara.

They walked toward The Southern Tomb of Djoser, past the step pyramids and up the white steps of the tomb, whose entrance was located thirty meters above the ground. It was easy to see why this was registered as a UNESCO World Heritage Site; the entrance to the pyramid had an imposing aura, as the sand surrounded the whole building, and the passageway was no more than a few feet wide. The steps and stairs erected by the ancients were completely paved, and there were more corridors to explore than seemed possible.

Leo remembered that when he was a kid, he thought the pyramids had been relatively easy to build, especially when he could stack ten blocks together with very little effort. But now, being inside this awe-inspiring structure was mind-blowing. The pyramids were hollow from the inside, with various underground corridors, hidden chambers and tombs that were blocked from the outside world. How could these constructions withstand more than forty-five centuries? The architecture was impressive, to say the least. Huge blocks of stone surrounded the subterranean vaults, undisturbed by the passage of time.

As the hours passed, Leo began to lose track of time, getting lost in the world of the ancient Egyptians. He could clearly envision them, the labor it took to build these monuments and the symbolism behind each composition. One of the vaults they entered was filled with hieroglyphics and beautiful decorations which shone brightly in the restored areas of the pyramid.

Leo was standing next to Athena, when he recognized a symbol marked in the old stone. It resembled the Shabaka Stone, a square incision surrounded by converging lines. Leo knew this symbol by heart since it was housed in the British Museum. The Shabaka stone was inscribed with Egyptian religious texts, but since it had been used as a millstone, the hieroglyphics had been damaged. This symbol, however, was very well preserved.

"I recognize this. It's a copy of the Shabaka Stone," excitedly whispered Leo. Athena looked around and, seeing that they were momentarily alone, she decidedly jumped over the divide and extended her arm toward the stone. She moved her hand over the symbol, barely touching the stone. Then she blew slowly over the surroundings of the symbol. Small hidden hieroglyphics started appearing in the dust-free stone. She caressed them tenderly with her fingers. The stone at the British Museum was eerily similar, yet unreadable. *Could this be a copy, or is it the original?*

As Leo began to read the symbols out loud, he heard shuffling steps. They turned in unison as a security guard made a beeline toward them. Apollo, who was lounging a few steps away, went to block the man.

"Quickly," said Athena, "take a picture of the inscription before it disappears."

Leo scrambled in his pockets for his phone and snapped three pictures before the security guard and Apollo appeared. They seemed to be in a one-way conversation, with Apollo asking general-tourist-like questions as the security guard ignored him. In his gruff voice, the guard said, "Step away from the stone, madam. It's forbidden to pass the yellow lines."

Athena made various apologies and pretended to have lost her way, signaling Apollo and Leo to follow her out of the man's earshot.

"Were you able to get a picture?" she asked as soon as they stepped into the dazzling Egyptian sunshine.

"Yes," replied Leo. "Look."

He placed his phone in between the siblings and turned up the

CHAPTER 23

brightness. The pictures were slightly blurry, but he was able to decipher most of it.

Leo began to read, "Thus Osiris came into the earth at the Royal Fortress, to the north of the land to which he had come. His son Horus arose as king of Upper Egypt, arose as king of Lower Egypt, in the embrace of his father Osiris and of the gods in front of him and behind him."

"Osiris?" asked Apollo.

"Yeah, Osiris. He was an Egyptian god. Foremost of the Westerns," replied Leo.

He turned to Athena, who had a puzzled look on her face. "Horus," she whispered. Then her expression transformed. "Is there any more?"

"Yeah, let me see," replied Leo. He turned his phone and zoomed into the stone's inscription. The lines he had read had come easily to him, since they were almost identical to the ones on the stone housed in the British Museum. After the first lines, however, the hieroglyphics were almost impossible to decipher, whereas this picture was crystal clear.

"It is there where the units wait for their eternal rest. There is no exodus. And thus from the earth, it is risen," he said slowly, making sure he was correct in his translation. "Above the ground in the mortal realm, into the temple of the ruler of the land of the dead." He closed his phone, replaying the words in his head. *What does this mean?*

"It is there where the units wait for their eternal rest?" pondered Apollo. His features appeared delighted at such a word quarry.

"There is no exodus," said Leo.

"Into the temple of the ruler of the land of the dead," muttered Athena. She paced up and down. "The land of the dead…I think I know the way. Let's get started." Not waiting to see if the others followed, she walked purposefully out of the complex and toward the bazaars.

Apollo shrugged, striding to keep up with his sister. Leo felt completely bewildered but followed anyway. Moments later, they caught up to Athena, who still had a pensive look on her face.

"You two, go and get supplies, enough to last us about three days in the desert. We already have headlamps in our packs, so get as much food and water as we might require. Let's meet here in an hour." Apollo and Leo went to get their supplies. Leo turned back just in time to hear Athena call out, "And stay together. Be careful."

It was the first time in a week that Leo had been separated from Athena. He had grown accustomed to her presence, and he felt a bit anxious to be without her. It wasn't as if he was weak. He knew he didn't have divine strength, but he also wasn't completely useless in a fight. Athena had a way of making him feel safe, comfortable, at ease. Leo wondered if her half-brother would have the same effect.

Exploring the Egyptian marketplace was unlike anything Leo had ever done. Every year he went to the Edinburgh Winter Market with his mother, eating hot fudge and trying delicious garlic fondue. Whereas Edinburgh was cold enough to freeze your bones if you were without a warm jacket, Saqqara's heat was so extreme that Leo felt as if his skin would melt if left exposed. The market was partially covered and there was a light breeze, but he could still feel the sweat beginning to trickle down his neck. Another huge difference between the markets was... well, everything. This Egyptian bazaar was filled with piles of spices, exotic fruit, drying meat, sacks full of nuts, jams, and cheese. The spices were built like cones, some measuring as high as two feet. The colors were splendid: bright crimson red, emerald green, dandelion yellow, every color and flavor of spice you could dream of.

The meat market was a long row filled with dried flesh that hung from the rafters. Next, there was a fish market with both live and dead fish to pick from. Some were already gutted; others had been caught

CHAPTER 23

that very day. There were also clams and shrimp, squid and crab. As they passed by stalls and continued, obtaining supplies here and there, Leo almost gagged at the salty smell. Apollo exited the meat and fish market, and, feeling relieved, Leo followed.

Once both were satisfied with their food packets, they had enough time to explore the rows of carpets, cushions, pillows, textiles, ceramics, lamps, lanterns, jewelry, everything that filled the stores around the bazaar. A multitude of cultures merged into one, a melting pot that created a fantastic market filled with wonder. Even Apollo was entranced by the merchandise: short damascus daggers, colorful kilims, and even a few snake charmers.

Leo checked his watch and saw that they had two minutes left to return to the meeting point. He tugged on Apollo's arm, and felt a warm sensation run through his hands where he had touched the god. The touch made him feel excited somehow, ecstatic almost, and he forgot about his earlier trepidation. *So this is what Apollo is like: carefree and light. Warm and exciting.* Being near Apollo made everything brighter. Leo's brain whispered an old wives tale. "If you stare into the sun, your eyes will burn and dissolve."

Unconsciously, Leo stepped away from Apollo, but as his lower body increased the gap between them, his upper body leaned forward, unable to detach from his aura. Suddenly, the loudspeakers from a nearby mosque summoned its followers for Asr prayer, alerting Apollo to the time.

"We'd better hurry. Athena will skin me like I skinned Marsyas." Apollo laughed as he began to stride toward their meeting point.

They hurried through the bazaar and reached the outskirts of the market to find Athena standing with, not one, but six camels. She was holding her vegvisir and looking straight at Apollo. "You're late."

Apollo inclined his head. "We got the supplies. Dried fruit, freshly baked breads, dried and salted meat, six gallons of water. Enough to last us four days and nights," he announced melodically. Athena narrowed her eyes. "I promise nothing will go to waste, Sister."

"It better not. Food sources are limited and…" She stopped mid-sentence as her focus shifted to Leo, who was staring at the camels while standing as far away from them as he could.

"Are we… Are we riding those?" he asked. Athena approached him, holding the reins of the first camel.

"Yes. Are you alright? It's ok to feel afraid at first," she whispered.

"No. It's not that. It's… Wow. We're riding camels through the desert? This is amazing. I'm… Wow."

Athena studied Leo, but since she could find no other explanation for his behavior, she placed her vegvisir inside her shirt and assumed her usual authoritative manner.

"Alright," she said, "Pick your camel. We have a long ride to Abydos."

"Abydos?" stammered Leo. Apollo started to laugh and moved toward the camels to slap Leo's back.

"I have no idea what's happening, but I know her." He shot a finger at his sister who was inspecting each camel and securing the supplies to their mounts. "She has a plan. She'll tell us soon enough." Caressing the nearest camel, Apollo whispered soothing words, and they seemed to instantly connect.

On the other hand, Leo was looking completely dumbstruck when Athena handed him the reins. "This is a good camel. Strong and fit. Do you need help getting on? We'll walk them to the edge of the sand dunes, and then ride the rest of the journey."

"I…" spluttered Leo, but he held onto the reins and followed Athena and Apollo into the Sahara. Athena had expertly tied the camels together from rear to front, and they formed a procession of six camels.

As they reached the sand dunes, Leo was wondering why they needed so many camels, when Athena whistled and all six camels

CHAPTER 23

kneeled. She moved to the front and stroked the lead camel. Leo looked out into the desert. It was a vast sea of sand; there was some brush here and there, but apart from that, there was nothing. *Where exactly are we going?* He opened his mouth to say something, but he had too many questions. He felt a warm hand on his shoulder and instead of feeling anxious, his fear turned to excitement. Leo noticed that Apollo was half-guiding, half-pushing him toward the third camel.

"Lock your knees in and sway with the movement. Don't fight it. Your camel will follow the route, so no need to guide him. Just enjoy the ride," said Apollo as he moved to mount his camel, the fifth in line. "Watch me. Step gently onto his hind leg and pull yourself up." It was easier said than done, but in the end, Leo was finally mounted on his camel with his pack secured and his water close by.

Athena adjusted her armband and covered her head with a silk scarf so that only her eyes were showing. She motioned for Leo to do the same, and he took his green silk scarf out of his pack. He mimicked her and felt immediately cooler. *This must be for the excessive desert heat.*

In one unhurried motion, she held onto the camel's back and raised herself into a sitting position, swinging her right leg behind her. After checking all her supplies and packs, she tapped her camel gently on the neck. The camel rose ponderously to its feet. Like the inverse of a falling domino, each of the six camels stood one by one until they were all on their feet and moving south across the Sahara, farther from civilization than Leo had ever been.

Parting from the Nile meant that the nearest water source would be lowly seasonal rivers and streams. More than 95% of Egypt's population depends on water from the Nile and, therefore, lives within a few miles of the river bank. It is incredible to note that this life-giving river is one of the longest in the world, stretching for more than 6,695 kilometers. It cuts through Egypt, Tanzania, Uganda, Rwanda,

Ethiopia and many more countries.

Ever since the building of the Aswan High Dam in 1970, the Nile no longer floods, but around 5,000 years ago, the Nile flooded so regularly that it was the main source of freshwater and transportation for the ancient Egyptians. It also provided them with fertile soil to farm since the nutrient-rich soil created thick and moist mud, perfect for growing crops in the dry desert land. The river was more than just a source of life... it was also a source of death. The river and its banks are home to razor sharp crocodiles, venomous snakes and powerful hippos. Ignoring their cute ears and chubby exterior, hippos are extremely aggressive and territorial. They are considered the world's deadliest mammal.... after humans.

Leo shook his head. *Homo sapiens. The marvels and tragedies that our species has imposed upon our planet.* As he looked out into the never-ending sand dunes, rocky plateaus, salt flats and dry valleys of the Sahara, Leo wondered how on earth a physically weak species was able to populate every corner of the planet from the deep jungles of the Amazon, to the inhospitable Artic, to the hottest desert in the world. He checked his phone and saw that the current temperature was around 37 degrees Celsius, or 98.6 Fahrenheit. He marveled at the fact that the highest recorded temperature in the desert was 58 degrees Celsius... 136.4 Fahrenheit.

Adjusting his position in the saddle, Leo again scanned the reddening horizon. The sand reflected an orange glow that was now familiar to him. He felt his eyes water as he fixated on the glare. Reaching into his pack, he took out a pair of UV sunglasses. He put them on, feeling respite from the intensity of the sun.

The hours went by and still they trudged on. The camels seemed content to sway and follow their course, moving up and down the sand dunes. It was shocking that the dunes could be as high as the Black Pool Tower in Lancashire back in England. From afar the dunes would

CHAPTER 23

be presumed to be around 70 feet high, but then just as suddenly, they would transform into huge mountains of sand. So stark. So simple. Each footstep the camels took created a momentary void in the artistic desert, but as soon as they moved on a short distance, the wind would erase the footsteps, repainting the perfect simplicity of the continuous sand, forever erasing their path within the dunes.

Leo's eyelids began to shut under the soothing sway of his camel's gait. He tried to open them, but the more he tried, the more his eyes would droop until he fell into the sweet oblivion of sleep.

Waking with a start, he opened his eyes and realized that many hours had passed. The sun was already low in the sky. *Must be close to sunset,* Leo thought as he rubbed his tired eyes. He felt for his glasses and found them in a corner of his blanket. Athena or Apollo must have unpacked his supplies for the night.

They had set up camp while Leo slept, and they had their blankets stretched outside of the tent they had purchased in London. The siblings were sharing a meal as they watched the sun dip below the horizon. There was nothing blocking their view. No cars or skyscrapers. No fog and no clouds. The view was crystal clear, even better than a painting. The sky was turning violet, with streaks of flaming orange and flashing scarlet.

Leo moved his blanket to sit down next to them. Empowered by the beauty and magnificence, all three were staring quietly, peacefully, at the sunset. Apollo passed Leo some bread, dried fruit, salted beef and a jug of wine. They ate in silence; the only sound that could be heard for miles and miles was the sounds of their chewing and the snorting of the camels nearby. Leo could even hear his own heartbeat, strong, steady, tranquil.

Then Leo noticed that there was no noise. No airplanes overhead, no construction. No screaming or yelling, no hustle, no bustle. Everything was silent. Everything was calm. For a moment, he felt like this was what life was all about. *This is how we find inner peace.* And he did feel at peace. He was aware of all his flaws and faults, but he loved them anyway. He knew he wasn't perfect, far from it. And yet he loved himself anyway. He knew that many did not approve of his life choices, but even so, enduring their humiliation and their derision, their sarcasm and their passive aggressiveness was nothing compared to what he was feeling now. He loved himself and he loved life. He smiled into the horizon and hugged his knees to his chest, feeling immense gratitude for being alive and for truly living.

CHAPTER 24

May 2nd

Her dream... It was so vivid, so real. Athena was standing by the window, gazing out at the new day. Happily she stretched and sighed. The sky was still dark, but the first rays of sunlight were peeking over the mountains.

"Agh," came a groan from the bed. Athena turned from the window and smiled at the bulk beneath the covers. Only her arms were visible as she held a pillow to her face. *Freya.*

"It's too early," moaned the Norse goddess. Athena crossed back to the bed and sat next to her. Gently, she held one of Freya's hands, caressing the smooth skin and tenderly kissing her fingers.

"Good morning," Athena whispered. A blue eye peaked out from under the pillow.

"It's too early," Freya repeated. "Let's sleep a while longer."

Athena continued to caress Freya's hand, running her own back and forth across her palm while playing with the outlines of her veins and her fingertips.

"That's not fair," said Freya. Her voice sounded more alert than before and Athena knew she would soon wake.

"What's not fair?" Athena asked, her tone measured as always, but somehow her voice was softer and more caring when talking to Freya.

"You. You can't wake me up like this. You'll make me want to stay in bed all day."

"We have a long day ahead; we're so close to finding him. I can feel it. If we get enough work done, we can come back early and sleep in."

"I wasn't talking about sleeping," murmured Freya as she sat up, her pillow and sheets falling unceremoniously.

Athena smiled before Freya leaned in for a kiss. Whenever their lips touched, Athena felt as if she were floating, as if no other feeling in the world could ever compare. Freya placed a hand behind Athena's lower back while the other rested lightly against her chest, feeling the rising and falling sensation of her breathing. After a moment they broke apart, their eyes still closed and their foreheads pressed together. Athena stroked Freya's cheek with her thumb. Almost in unison they stared into each other's eyes, one set gray-green, the other icy blue. Athena loved the outline of Freya's jaw, the skin around her mouth, her full cherry lips.

Freya smiled and opened her mouth to speak, but she hesitated. Instead of words, blood started to trickle, slowly at first but then faster and faster. Athena froze, her muscles tensed and her hands shook violently.

The scene around them evaporated, and Athena was transported to the day of the attack, to John Rylands Library, Manchester, England. To the origins of her worst nightmare.

Freya fell backwards and Athena caught her. She was kneeling down, holding Freya's head with her knees while she supported her back with her right arm. Athena's spear lay on the floor, momentarily forgotten, while her shield was firmly strapped to her left, creating a temporary barrier between them and the murderous creature. Suddenly, Freya's body felt heavy as if all the strength was ebbing out of her.

"No. No, please, Freya," Athena whispered as Freya looked up into her eyes. "Please. Stay with me."

CHAPTER 24

Freya smiled weakly, her eyes full of love. She raised a bloody and trembling hand to Athena's face. She tried wiping her falling tears, but Athena's helmet blocked her touch. Instead, Freya left a smudge of bright red blood that clashed against Athena's glinting armor.

"You'll find me," Freya murmured weakly, her hand falling and landing lifeless between their bodies. Her Norse vegvisir slid out of her cold fingers.

No. No. No. Athena clenched her jaw, and tears pooled in her eyes. She reached out to Freya's body and held her tightly as if this embrace could heal Freya's mortal wounds and bring her back to life. Even with her armor on, Athena could feel how icy cold Freya's skin was, and her tears flowed freely to mix with Freya's still blood. *Don't leave me. Come back. Please.*

Freya's body was like a lifeline for Athena, and she clutched it, unwilling to let her go. But she knew she was gone. One moment she felt the heaviness of her body, and Athena pressed her face against Freya's neck, but in the next Freya was gone. Vanished. Only air surrounded Athena now, air and Freya's blood on her armor.

From behind her shield, Athena heard a crackle of horrible laughter as the murderer triumphed in his latest massacre. The sound made Athena completely lose control. She screamed at the top of her lungs, a scream that was filled with so much pain she felt she would burst. The lights fluttered and shattered as she shifted in her crouched position ready to attack. Athena's forehead throbbed with emotion, and the only thing that held her mentally together was her fury and her thirst for vengeance. She twisted so quickly and threw her spear so rapidly that even the evil deity, who was standing more than twenty feet away, moved a fraction too late.

From afar the shot seemed like a miss, for the menacing creature was still standing, ready to attack. Athena raised her shield and charged, unsheathing her short sword from her mystical armband, ready for the confrontation. Ready to strike. Ready to kill. Ready for the end.

Instead, Athena and the deity glared at each other as Athena barreled toward it, her eyes full of pain, wrath, ferocity and murder. She raised her sword for the strike, but the deity vanished in a flash of electricity and lightning.

As soon as it dissipated, Athena fell to her knees, every muscle trembling with grief, shock and fatigue. In her anguish she did not notice that her spear had indeed grazed the deity before her, marking a single cut and drawing a thick, black liquid. Her spear quivered as it remained embedded in the stone wall, and Athena did not retrieve it. She was afraid to move, afraid of what she would see if she opened her eyes, afraid of the void that would confirm her worst nightmare.

Slowly, painfully, she recovered. She took one deep breath, then two, then five, then ten. She stopped counting until she regained control of her nerves. As if dreaming, she stood and turned her back to her spear. When before she would not dare look, now she could not look away. All her attention was directed to where Freya's body had lain just moments before. She was gone. Even the blood on the floor was gone as if she had never been there, never lost her life there. The only object remaining that marked Freya's existence was her Norse talisman: her vegvisir.

Athena bent down and picked it up in her quaking hands, trying hard to retain her self-control. And so she stood upright, sobbing harder than she had ever done before, feeling as if everything in the world had been torn apart, as if her insides would never heal, could never be pieced together, as if a part of her perished that macabre day....

"Athena! Athena! Wake up!"

She opened her eyes and drew her short sword from her armband, and in the darkness the sound of metal cut through the air. She turned

CHAPTER 24

as fast as the speed of light and aimed the point of the sword at the figure before her. As her eyes adjusted to the darkness, she realized with a start that it was her brother, Apollo. His golden hair tousled, his amber eyes worried.

"Hey, it's me. It's Apollo. Sister, what happened?"

Athena blinked and withdrew her sword, setting it back into her armband where it magically shrank in size and reattached itself.

"Sorry," her throat was dry and her voice was hoarse. "I had a bad dream. A nightmare, really."

"Oh. I thought so. You were sobbing and shaking, but your eyes were closed. I wasn't sure if you were being attacked." Apollo tried a half-reassuring smile and tapped her shoulder. "It's almost dawn. We can wake the mortal and head out early." He glanced toward Leo's sleeping bag where the youth was snoring contentedly. "I swear he could sleep through a tsunami." Apollo laughed and headed out of the tent, his pack already on his back.

Athena swallowed and dropped her head into her hands. She felt clammy and noticed her shirt was damp. *Just a nightmare. A terrible memory.* Changing clothes and packing, she headed out of the tent and trudged toward her camel. Kneeling beside it, she poured a handful of water into her hands and splashed her face. She leaned on her camel, then poured some water into a bowl and offered it to the gentle creature. The animal sniffed at the water and drank heartily.

After it had its fill, Athena fed the other five camels and brought water to them. They didn't need much; camels can survive up to fifteen days without water by using their humps as a storage for fat.

The entire group, including the animals, the deities, and the human, was well provisioned for the next few days. Apollo and Leo had over done their accumulation of food, and Athena was fine with their choice because she would rather not risk hunger when dealing with mortals. With Apollo's powers in her talisman, she would be able to heal any of Leo and Apollo's wounds, but she could not cure their hunger or thirst. Apollo would not be wounded by anything mortal, however. Only the mystical could harm deities. The only threat that Apollo and Athena needed to fear was another immortal or a horde of mythological creatures.

Involuntarily, she shivered. *You'll find me.* How was she supposed to find Freya? Where was she? Every day Athena held the Norse talisman, closed her eyes and envisioned Freya. And every time the vegvisir would spin out of control thereby affirming the fact that Freya was not in this realm. *If she isn't here, where can she be?*

The only thing that helped Athena escape her vicious mental cycle was focusing on her current labor. *I need to find Ex Nihilo. I will find him. Once I do, I will destroy him.*

Looking out into the early morning of the Sahara as the sun was rising, Athena heard the nearly imperceptible beating of powerful wings. A new presence was heading toward the camp. In this predawn hour, her ears worked better than her eyes; she, therefore, raised her arm without looking about. The swooshing of wings grew closer and closer until it stopped, and a majestic falcon landed on her extended arm. The falcon twisted its neck and stared at Athena.

Wordlessly, she took out her vegvisir, extending it to the bird. The falcon didn't move; its eyes remained fixed on Athena's. *So we're headed in the right direction then.* With one finger Athena stroked the falcon's elegant neck. She had a pretty good idea of what they would find in Abydos or more importantly... who.

"How was your journey?" Athena asked the bird. She got two blinks from its eyes in response. "Want some food?" One blink. Athena pulled out some cooked meat from her bag. She absolutely adored birds. She was especially fond of owls, and in ancient times she used to travel about with one perched on her shoulder. Both falcons and owls had better eyesight than she, especially at night, and falcons

CHAPTER 24

were incredibly fast. Some were able to reach speeds of 200 miles per hour. Owls, on the other hand, had their wings especially designed for silent flight. Athena observed this falcon's aerodynamic body and wondered what top speeds it could reach. Keeping the bird perched on her shoulder, she held the meat up to the falcon. It took the offering and tore into it with its razor sharp talons and equally powerful beak.

"Oh, he's back!" came a voice from the tent. Leo had finally woken and his curly hair was splayed in all directions. Cautiously approaching the bird, he walked over to Athena and the camels. The falcon continued with its feast, finishing its meat and sparing one intense glance at the teen. Then its head turned 180 degrees and focused on the rising sun. *Daybreak.* The falcon screeched once and jumped off Athena's arm as it flew fast and high toward the sun.

Packing up the tent and the rest of the provisions, they began the second part of their journey, making their way across the sand. Athena followed the arrows of her vegvisir so that she could be sure their path was true.

She didn't know if it was the bright openness of the desert or the quiet and solitude that the sand provided, but her thoughts keep shifting to last night's nightmare. She could picture those moments so clearly, could hear her own racing heart as she realized something was off. She could see the scattered papers she had left behind; the door being thrown open. She remembered the smell of metal as she adjusted her helmet. She remembered the sound of tearing as she ripped her clothes to reveal the armor she always wore. She remembered running as fast as she could through the streets that evening, not caring if any mortal saw her. She remembered feeling panic and dread when she entered the deserted library, the feelings of despair as she realized her fears were founded. She remembered hearing her pounding heart as she flew down the steps three at a time, remembered the agony as she saw Ex Nihilo strike once, twice, three times at Freya, destroying her with his venomous energy. She remembered sprinting to catch Freya, sliding on her knees to reach her before she hit the ground. Clear in her memory was the smell of rust, of blood, and the sizzle of metal on metal. Her vision became blurry with tears.... *You'll find me.*

Reaching into her pack, she took out Freya's passport. She touched its red cover and opened it to her favorite page. Freya was smiling happily in the picture. Her smile reached her eyes; her blonde hair was braided and hung loose on her left shoulder. Athena's fingers trembled as she caressed the picture. She didn't know how long she stared at the cover; it could have been mere seconds, but it felt like hours. She focused on Freya's picture, staring into her icy blue eyes, imploring her to move, to say something, to come alive. But she remained motionless, timeless and unchanging. *Just a memory.*

"Should we stop here for a break?" came Apollo's voice from afar. Athena brought herself back to the present, and looked at the barren desert. Raising her hand, she analyzed the position of the sun and realized they were very close to their destination.

"No. Let's keep moving. We'll be there in an hour," she replied without looking back. She clutched the passport in her hands and breathed deeply. For a brief moment she considered throwing it away, letting it drop on the sand and forgetting about it. It would be less painful. The document was only a couple of ounces in weight, but it felt so heavy in her hand. Her fingers loosened, and the passport inched down her palm. Then, just as the passport was about to hit the sand, she caught it and placed it in her pack. Some pain was worth carrying, no matter the weight.

They began the last leg of the journey to Abydos. In Ancient Egypt, the city was called Abdju. Renamed Abydos by the Greeks, it was one of the oldest Egyptian cities. The group made camp a quarter of a mile away from the Necropolis and after securing the camels, they

CHAPTER 24

proceeded on foot toward the sprawling temples.

As they approached the ancient city, they saw that the sand transformed into stone. They walked up the stone stairs leading to Seti's temple, which still had an intact roof. Athena marveled at the engineering of that era. With no machines, no bulldozers, no cranes, the Egyptians were able to perform astounding feats of architecture.

Back in Athens, the only structure built during her time that was still intact was her brother Hephaestus' temple. Her own father's temple had been destroyed by conquerors, and the city's populace had removed most of the remnants to build their homes. Of the original 104 colossal columns, only 15 remained. Athena shook her head. What was once the renowned largest temple in Greece was reduced to ruins and plundered for materials. Eighty-five percent of the temple was gone. But here in Abydos, the ruins seemed almost untouched. The vibrant colors that once adorned its facade were gone, dulled by the elements, yet it was the same in her precious Greece. The temples had faded to white or gray without any hint of the vivid colors that once depicted their adventures and histories.

Arriving at the Temple of Seti, the three entered through a gateway of columns that led to the Chapel of Amun Re. They studied the painted walls and symbols that filled the interior as they looked for a clue, something that would nudge them in the right direction. Athena was confident that she had almost solved the puzzle; she was just missing the last crucial piece, and she was sure the answer lay hidden within the city of Abydos.

The temple was built not long after Seti I became pharaoh in 1290 BCE, almost thirty-three centuries ago. It was completed after his death, during the reign of his son, Rameses II, often regarded as the most-celebrated and powerful pharaoh of the New Kingdom.

There were more than one hundred columns in the temple, and each column was completely decorated with hieroglyphics and paintings. Moving north through the hall of Nefertem and Ptah Sokar, Athena followed the beams in the first hypostyle hall as she read the hieroglyphics on the wall. Her excitement grew as she recognized that they were heading in the correct direction through the dark passageway and toward a chapel… The Chapel of Osiris.

Raised reliefs surrounded the chapel; they were some of the finest Athena had ever seen. Raised reliefs were a form of art in which images were cut into the surface. Reliefs were considered eternal, and for Egyptians, the decorations of tomb walls with reliefs or painted scenes reinforced important ceremonies and ensured that the royal memory would be kept alive.

Athena stopped outside the chapel to examine the paintings while Leo stood beside her. "Does this mean he's buried here? Osiris, I mean," he asked.

"Apparently so," Athena replied. One of the murals depicted Osiris' destruction and castration at the hand of his brother, Set. His member had been unceremoniously thrown into the Nile to prevent him from fathering a son.

"Ooph! How horrible," groaned Apollo. He crossed his hands over his groin. "I would kill whoever did that to me."

Athena thought for a moment. Osiris didn't end up killing Set, but he did sire a son who rose up and fought Set as a rival to the Egyptian throne. *Foremost of the Westerners, the king of the dead…*

She paced up and down Osiris' chapel. From the inscriptions on the wall, it was clear that he had a popular cult following. Osiris was the god of fertility, agriculture, vegetation, life, resurrection, the dead and the afterlife. *Why do all the clues point toward him, but not directly at him?* Athena walked into Osiris' hall. There was one scene of Seti making an offering to Osiris, another of Osiris and his sister-wife, Isis. The vegvisir pulsed inside her shirt. She was getting close.

They walked toward the end of the hall and entered an unidentified

CHAPTER 24

room. It was small and almost all of the reliefs were shattered. The paintings and illustrations were almost unreadable.

"Wow! This is crazy. Almost as intense as our Titanomachy," said Apollo.

"What? You can see it?" asked Leo.

"Yeah, of course," Apollo replied. He reached into his pocket and pulled out a lollipop. With a grin, he popped it into his mouth. Leo and Athena remained staring at him in amazement. "Why? You can't?" said Apollo as it finally dawned on him.

"No, we can't. What does it say? What is it?" Athena probed.

"Let me show you," Apollo said. Turning to Leo, he extended his hand. "Here, hold my lolly."

Athena turned back to check that no one had followed them into the room. She couldn't hear a sound and figured that they had a couple of minutes before any tourists or locals came wandering in. Nevertheless, she stood by the door, guarding it. She wanted no interruptions this time.

Apollo placed his hand on the wall and closed his eyes. Suddenly, his hair moved, but there was no breeze. Then, his hand started to glow. How could she have forgotten Apollo's healing powers? She stared expectantly as the room around them glowed as brightly as the sun, and images began appearing and swirling around them. The walls weren't being restored, but the images that had once lived inside the structure were glowing, coming back to life. It was the story of Osiris: his birth, his marriage to his sister, his death, his reincarnation, the birth of his son, Horus. There were more images floating around the hall: a baby Horus, protected by his mother; Horus growing and challenging his uncle, Set. There were more flashing images of their violent conflict: eighty years of war, a boat race, and finally Horus' triumph with his fist raised to the sky, unbeaten and unvanquished, restoring Maat.

Athena smiled and put her hand on Apollo's shoulder. He immediately opened his eyes and the images disappeared, all the light vanishing at once.

Yes. I knew it. It's him. Now it was time to find him. Where could he be buried? Surely his burial site would be unreachable to mortals.

"Wait. Is this what the stone was referring to?" Leo read the inscription. "Above the ground in the mortal realm, into the temple of the ruler of the land of the dead." He paused and fixed his glasses. "Does it mean we found it? And what exactly did we find?" queried Leo.

"Yes and no. We are closer to him than before, but don't forget the second part of the verse. "It is there where the units wait for their eternal rest. There is no exodus. And thus from the earth, it is risen."

"To him? Do you mean Horus?"

Athena smiled.

Leo covered his mouth with his hand. "Of course! You said each civilization or religion, per se, elected a representative. Who better than the one who restored Maat, the cosmic and social order? The literal ancient Egyptian concept of truth, balance, order, harmony, law, morality and justice!"

"Don't forget that it completed Osiris' resurrection," added Apollo as he leaned against the wall sucking his lollipop.

"Exactly. Now all we have to find is how to enter... enter..." Athena did not finish. She was recounting to herself the inscription on the Shabaka Stone. *It is there where the units wait for their eternal rest. Alright, so this place will be filled with mythical Egyptian creatures and soldiers. There is no exodus. We might not escape. And thus from the earth, it is risen.*

Athena closed her eyes so that she could concentrate. *From the earth, it is risen. So this divine tomb, palace or pyramid was beneath the earth... it will rise. How? Hmmm.* Athena said to herself. *Osiris was the Foremost*

CHAPTER 24

of the Westerners, the ruler of the land of the dead. Popping into her head was the image of the sun mixed with the darkness, the Egyptian symbol of death. *The sun rises in the East and sets in the West, and for the Ancient Egyptians, the word "Westerners" refers to the dead.* It clicked. She knew exactly where to go, and what was ahead of them.

Athena glanced at her watch; it was almost 3 o'clock in the afternoon. Less than three hours. "Nightfall. Right as the sun sets in the West. That's when we'll be able to see it."

"See what?" said Leo.

"The Temple of Osiris. The Temple of the Dead."

CHAPTER 25

"You're telling me that we are willingly about to enter a pyramid full of deceased, powerful, mythological forces from which we might never escape, and just to wake up some Egyptian god? Why?" asked Apollo as they paced while waiting for the Saharan sundown.

"I've told you. I don't know why," answered Athena. She turned back and saw that the falcon had rejoined their party, stretching its wings majestically on top of their tent. "But it's the missing piece of the puzzle."

Apollo was also staring at the bird, his expression showing his annoyance. "We're literally following some crazy bird across the desert," he muttered.

"It's not crazy. It's all connected," Athena replied. Apollo raised his eyebrows and shrugged. Athena retorted, "What else would you have me do? Dance ballet back in Paris? We don't have any other strings to pull. No clues, no evidence, nothing." She grasped her vegvisir and clutched it to her chest. *This is our only hope.*

"Aren't you afraid?" said Leo. "I mean, what is in there? What if we never leave?" Athena scrutinized him. She knew that it took great courage and bravery to face the unknown.

"Of course you two are fearless divinities. How could you be afraid?" he muttered.

CHAPTER 25

"No. We aren't fearless," said Athena. "There is no such thing. It would be equivalent to saying we are hungerless. You can't be fearless in the same way you can't just stop being thirsty. It's normal and natural. Fear is just another emotion. It's not something you can just wish away; it's something you work to face, and you work to conquer. You must learn to live with it and not let it define you."

Apollo guffawed and started snapping his fingers. "Hear, hear."

"It's true, Leo." She glanced at Apollo. "At least for me it is. I can feel fear and I can feel hunger. I will survive longer than you will without substance, but in the end, I need it too," finished Athena.

Apollo stared into Athena's face for a long time before smiling and saying, "Me too. I can be afraid as well. And I have been in the past. But I choose to face my fear, and I tell it to fuck off."

They laughed, and the atmosphere around them became more friendly and relaxed. Athena looked at Apollo and silently thanked him. Apollo nodded nonchalantly and opened a bag of nuts.

She did not want to bring Leo into a dangerous, unexplored territory, but leaving him outside would be even worse. She did not know how long they would be in the pyramid, but as long as the youth was near them, he would be safe. And he would be alive.

Athena beckoned for Leo to come to her. "Here." She reached toward her talisman and took out her short sword, then removed the ring from her right hand. As soon as it was off her finger, it transformed into her shield. "I saw you working my aegis back in London. You're a natural."

Leo's eyes widened as he held the weapons in his hands. "Are you sure?"

"Yes. I'm sure. I trust you." And it was true. She had come to trust this skinny mortal with all his quirks and flaws. He was good at heart, and he was loyal.

"Wow, you're going to make me cry," said Apollo sarcastically, but he smiled reassuringly. "You better not nick me with that sword, human, or I will fill you with arrows."

Leo gulped and turned to Athena in horror, but Apollo put his arm around him and tousled Leo's hair. "I'm kidding. But on a serious note, we should work on your stance before we head in. Look, mimic my movements and swing with your whole body, not just your arm."

Athena allowed the men their pre-battle routine while she went to water and feed the camels. After eating a light meal, she sat on the sand, crossed her legs and meditated. She visualized what she wanted to accomplish; her strong, rapid movements. *I am full of energy. I am powerful. I will succeed. I will master myself and conquer my opponents. I can do this. I can do this. I can do this.*

The air cooled as the sun dropped on the horizon. Athena stood up and clenched her fists, feeling the blood rush to her fingers. Then she touched her talisman and grabbed her trusty spear. As it lengthened, she balanced it, warming her body to the feeling of the weapon. There was a fluttering in her stomach, and she took in several deep breaths. It was normal to feel nervous; everything inside this pyramid, except for Leo, was mythological. And everything was dangerous.

With her free hand, she made sure her talisman was still attached to her arm. The last time she had not worn it, the manticores had severely injured her. *It'll be different this time. I won't be alone.* She looked to her brother, whose hair was flaming in the dusk; he too had taken out his weapons. His golden bracelets formed his golden bow and arrows; he did not need to carry a sling, as his left bracelet contained as many arrows as he needed. Seamlessly, in a controlled and powerful movement, he practiced setting the arrow on his bow.

Athena shook off her long-sleeved shirt and scarf, revealing her armor. Placing her pants and outfits carefully back into her pack, she put on her Greek leather sandals and laced them up to her calves. Then, she stretched out her cape and attached it to the top of her

CHAPTER 25

armor. Finally, she placed her helmet on her head. Fully clad in armor, she was ready for war.

The sun was almost gone as the last rays of light shimmered on the red sand. She stood next to Apollo and nodded once. He understood and moved silently behind her; with bow raised, he observed the outskirts of their camp.

"Give me your phone, Leo," Athena commanded. All traces of her warm nature were gone. She was authoritative and purposeful. Leo obeyed, unlocking the device at once.

"Are you looking for the picture of the Shabaka Stone?" he inquired.

"Yes, show it to me." He did as he was told. Athena held it with her left hand, her right clutched her mighty spear.

Kneeling down on the sand, she spoke in the classical form of Ancient Egyptian, speaking the incantations for the Temple of Osiris. As she did so, the ground beneath her feet began to shake. Athena stood and remained on the spot, unwilling to be intimidated. Suddenly, the sand before them broke apart, opening up a massive hole. The very top of a pyramid peeked out of the sand, then slowly, ponderously, raised itself out of the sand, stretching towards the heavens. Athena stood her ground, clenching her jaw and staring at the marble structure. It looked dampened, almost green with mold. Water and sand poured out of the structure as it continued its upward climb into the evening sky.

Finally, with a huge groan, the pyramid emerged from the underworld. Athena heard a screech and felt a flutter of wings behind her. The falcon had perched on her shoulder and the two stared intently at the pyramid. The bird turned its head and screeched once more, then jumped off Athena's shoulder and onto her spear. It placed its tiny foot on the sharp edge and slashed. Blood dripped from the wound, but the falcon did not hesitate; it flew toward the pyramid and placed its bloody leg on the dark, damp marble. A door materialized where the falcon had touched the stone. Flying back to Athena's shoulder, it screeched once more. Its injured leg was raised, but it did not seem to care; the falcon's attention was glued to the pyramid.

Athena breathed deeply and walked toward the door. She closed her eyes and pushed it with all her strength. Crackling like old bones after years of nonuse, the door groaned and creaked as it opened. The inside of the pyramid was pitch black, and it smelled like seawater. With the falcon on her shoulder, Athena entered first, followed by Leo and finally Apollo. She felt the nearby walls and realized they were slick and musty, as if this pyramid had been underground and underwater for centuries. She wondered when it had last been opened.

"Well, that wasn't so bad," said Apollo in his cheery voice.

As soon as he finished the sentence, the door swung shut behind them and locked them in the darkness. Twenty feet from them, a flame flickered, followed by another, then another, and so on until the chamber was filled with flames. Every time a flame came to life, a voice called out its name: Nephthys, Ma'at, Amun, Bes, Nut, Khonsu, Sekhmet, Bastet, Ptah, Anubis, Thoth, Sobek, Neith, Isis, Hathor, Geb, Set, Ra. The voices were shrill from misuse, but each was different in tone and aggression. Some were deeper than others, some were mere whispers, and some did not even sound human, more like growls or shrills.

"I take that back," commented Apollo as he raised his bow. Athena crouched low ready for an attack. Because of the total darkness, she hadn't noticed the inscriptions on the walls. Now they were everywhere. Athena replayed the Shabaka Stone's reference: It is there where the units wait for their eternal rest. There is no exodus. She looked around at the paintings, each a description of the rulers and gods of Egypt.

The falcon screeched and flew between the flames, lighting the pathway to the opposite hall. It stopped on the high archway before

CHAPTER 25

the antechamber and stared back at the group with its piercing eyes.

Athena adjusted her grip on her spear and slowly moved forward, watching each of the flames and their respective reliefs. The pathway was eight feet across, and it was slick with water. She took small, careful steps, and noticed that there was empty space from the pathway to the opposite walls, which were filled with the mystical flames and imagery. Unlike the colors in the temples they had visited previously, the colors on these murals had not faded over the centuries. They were lively despite the humidity and mold. Hathor's profile depicted a woman bearing a sun disk between two horns raised above her head. There were also images of her with the likeness of a cow, and one in which she appeared as a lioness. Athena noticed Ptah and Sekhmet's green skin, which was made musty by the swampiness of the place. She turned her head and noticed Sobek's flame which lit a statue of a mummified man with the head of a crocodile.

A shout made her quickly turn. Leo was staring at the bottom of the pathway with horrified eyes. "Did you hear that? What is it?" he asked, his voice trembling. Athena followed his gaze and realized that they were not alone. Making her way to the edge of the pathway, she peered over, and before her eyes had time to adjust, she heard a noise. At the base of the pyramid was a moat filled with green water, and there were animals moving around. *No, not animals.* She squinted at the dimly lit moat. She spotted a massive tail, over six feet long, but there was something shiny about the animal. She crouched lower and stared at the creature.

Without warning, it leaped out of the water and snapped its lengthy jaw. The creatures were more than twenty feet below the pathway that Athena now understood to be a bridge. The snapping provoked the other crocodiles in the lake, and now more than ten were snapping and swiping their scaly tails. Their skin was slimy, but not with water. Instead, they were so pale and dehydrated that Athena knew that they were dead, mummified creatures from the deep. As if to confirm her suspicions, one of the giant crocodiles leaped into the air and snapped at the group, revealing that half its jaw was decomposed and the skin that once covered its teeth was gone. Its eyes were creamy white, as if blind, but they could still sense the intruders.

Athena stood upright and clenched her spear. "Walk carefully. Do not look down. Keep your eyes straight and on that door." Following her own advice, she counted every step she took, ignoring the increasing sounds of ripping and snapping that rose from the depths of the pyramid.

When she was safely over the bridge and below the falcon, she turned around to watch Leo and Apollo make their way. Apollo was glaring at the walls of the pyramid with his golden bow raised high. He was walking slowly, allowing Leo to stay a few feet behind him. The teenager was trying hard not to look around, but his eyes kept wandering to the murals. Relief swept over Athena as she watched Leo follow Apollo's footsteps until they both reached the entrance to the antechamber.

The falcon jumped down onto Apollo's arm and turned its head to Athena. It raised its spindly leg and smeared its blood on Apollo's skin. It did the same to Athena, smearing her armor and shoulders, and then jumped onto Leo's head, dripping blood on his hair and face. Finally, it leapt back to Athena and clutched the talisman on her arm. Athena whispered her incantation, and the bird's leg was immediately healed. Gratefully, the falcon ruffled its feathers and attached himself to Athena's armor.

"Everybody good? Let's keep moving," she said, making her voice sound more confident than she felt. Either the falcon had noticed the mummified crocodiles' thirst for the strangers inside their holy temple, or they were about to face more threatening creatures. Athena opened the next door.

CHAPTER 25

The antechamber in front of them was large, its high vaulted ceiling reaching more than fifty feet. The inside was lit by enormous caldrons, and lining the walls were...

There was a collective gasp as they saw that what seemed to be statues were actually more mummified creatures. The falcon nudged Athena, who stepped forward keeping her spear at the ready. Every mummy on the wall turned its head in their direction, and as they approached the beasts, Athena saw that they were wearing armor. Rusty pieces of chainmail clung to their chests. Each had the chest of a man, but the head, legs and claws of a wild dog or a jackal. Athena could not help but gaze upon the scarred faces of the sentinels guarding the room while the creatures stared back at her and her companions. Their eyes were red, their skin was a dull orange with scars, jet black and brown, all over their bodies.

When they reached the middle of the chamber, one of the creatures took a step toward them. At once Athena raised her spear and Apollo loaded his bow. The creature turned slowly, baring its yellow teeth and sniffing at the group. Its movements were almost mechanical, and although its eyes were staring straight at them, it was clear that the creature could not see. It sniffed once more and returned to its position, its head high and its eyes unblinking.

Athena allowed herself a sigh of relief. She counted more than thirty-six of these creatures. Even though they were blind, the odds were in their favor.

The group continued to follow the falcon's nudging through two more chambers, one with creatures so wrapped in skins that it was impossible to tell what or who they could have been. Their khepesh, a sickle-shaped sword, shone brightly in their mummified hands.

The next chamber did not contain any visible creatures, but whenever they got too close to the side partitions, the chamber would rattle and roar with a piercing sound like chains being torn apart from behind the chamber walls.

Finally, they reached a massive opening that was flanked by two bird-like soldiers. In no way did the massive beings resemble humans. They were a hybrid species, each wearing a linen kilt that was so ragged that one touch would surely cause the cloth to disintegrate. Their chests, legs and arms were scaly and featherless, and they were so decayed that every time they moved, a putrid smell emanated from their bodies.

With his arm Apollo covered his nose and mouth, struggling to keep his bow and arrow at the ready. Leo gagged and raised Athena's shield to his face. At that moment the goddess decided that breathing was not a priority, so she did her best to distance herself from the creatures. She could endure any amount of physical pain, but the smell was so repulsive that she felt she would vomit if she continued to breathe in the fumes from these hybrids that had been dead for more than ten millennia. The disgusting creatures stepped aside as soon as the falcon approached; relieved, the group made its way into the last chamber.

Athena was grateful to see that there were only two more of the species inside the room, and they both were far away, guarding an enormous slab of stone that seemed to protect a tomb. A massive depiction of a man with the head of a bird covered the top of the slab. *Finally, Horus. We're here.*

The falcon flapped its wings, hopped onto the tomb, and tapped the top of the stone with its beak. Apollo lowered his bow and moved toward the tomb, examining it with his hands. "There's a small opening here." He withdrew a hand filled with mud and muck. "We need a key or a hook."

Athena searched the room, looking to see if the key was resting nearby. For a second, she had a horrible feeling that they had forgotten to bring the key. The falcon flew from one side of the chamber to the

CHAPTER 25

other, then it repeated its tapping on the tomb. Athena walked toward one of the fires that lit the room and lifted it from its palette that was shaped like a bird's wing. Then, while walking around the room and scanning the perimeter, she saw it, and her heart missed a beat. There was a small lake, similar to the moat they had seen at the entrance of the pyramid, at the base of the wall opposite the tomb... and below the dark, murky waters shone a bright golden key.

Oh, Gods. She crouched next to the dark lake and squinted her eyes to see any other movement apart from the shimmering key, but it was pitch black, and the water was not clear. Instead of seeing into the depths of the lake, she saw her helmet reflected on the surface of the water. Placing the torch down beside her, Athena stood up and removed her helmet, and then her cape.

"What are you doing?" asked Apollo, approaching her from the other side of the chamber.

"The key to the tomb is down there, so I'm going to dive into the depths and retrieve it."

"You're not serious. That water is foul, and who knows what creatures could be down there."

Would you like to volunteer in my place? Athena thought bitterly. She wished nothing more than to stay on dry land and above the acrid water. But the truth was that Apollo, with his arrows, would be better able to defend from above; here he easily could protect the tomb and Leo. He was the better swimmer, but Athena was more adaptable and resilient. She would survive longer in this malodorous lake.

"It won't take long. I'll get the key while you get ready for whatever might come at us. This is Egyptian territory. As soon as we open the tomb, we'll be safe." *I hope.* Athena looked into her brother's eyes and squeezed his shoulder. She then turned around, steadied her spear and plunged into the water.

The water was thicker than normal, more viscous than usual. As she swam toward the shining key, she could feel moss and algae around her. It was like an underwater kelp forest. Getting closer, she used her spear to clear her path downward.

When she was a mere few feet away, she stopped suddenly, sensing something massive stir beside her. She turned in the direction of the movement and gasped, expelling air. A colossal hippopotamus was striding through the seaweed. Sniffing at the water, it moved away from Athena.

As Athena swam toward the key, she encountered dark, thick liquid. She attempted to swim through the murky water, but as soon as her hand moved over it, she realized with a start that it was the falcon's blood emanating from her armor. The reddish substance, her only protection from the mythological creatures, floated away. The hippopotamus had stopped its retreat and was moving slowly, ever so gradually in her direction.

Athena accelerated and stretched her hand out for the key. At the same time, the hippopotamus finally sensed the intruder, and it charged at full speed toward Athena. The stagnant soil rose up, and Athena was unable to grab the key. She moved out of the way of the rushing hippo and again tried to grab the key. It turned and, unable to swim or float, it used its bulk to barrel through the water.

Athena knew she was in trouble. Hippos were extremely dangerous and territorial, and she was a foreigner invading its home. Running out of oxygen, she tried to grasp the golden key even though her vision was impaired by the flying debris and disintegrated bones that littered the lake's floor. Finally, her fingers clasped something solid and cold.

She turned toward the rushing hippo and waited for it to close in. Then, with a massive effort, she pushed herself away from the lakebed the moment the animal opened its mighty jaw, which was almost four feet across. She heard the snap of its incisors as they barely missed her feet. Swimming as fast as possible, Athena broke out of the water

CHAPTER 25

and accelerated to the edge of the lake, back toward the light and the tomb. She could hear the snorting and huffing of the hippopotamus behind her and tried to keep her head clear, thinking only of the key in her hand and how she would soon be on land. *One more stroke, one more stroke, one more stroke.* She crashed into the stone steps leading out of the lake, and with the help of her spear, she attempted to lift herself out of the water. She was a second too late, however, and felt the incisors of the hippo scrape her armor and cut into her leg.

As soon as she was free, she saw three arrows fly into the hippo's snout. Dripping water and blood, she ran toward the flames, where a frantic Leo was waving at her. Athena slowed for a second before she felt a mass collide with her. All the air rushed out of her as she crashed into the stone floor, then she heard a snap and knew her spear had shattered on impact with whatever had attacked her. From the floor she could see the top half of her spear, and she reached for it as she was hit again by the rushing beast. This second strike made her lose her footing, and the key flew from her hand.

"Get the key! Get the key!" she screamed as she heard the creature race toward her for a third time. She was finally able to see it clearly, and realized it was one of the guardians of the tombs. The scaly hybrid was indeed a combination of a man and a bird. Without wings but with sinuous and powerful arms, the beast attacked again as Athena braced herself. They collided against each other and crashed into the wall.

The sentinel screeched in her face, its breath so disgusting that Athena preferred swimming in the hippopotamus-infested lake than being pinned to the wall by this creature. They wrestled each other, Athena holding its neck and beak away from her face with all the might she could muster. Then, out of the corner of her eye, she saw Leo tearing toward the tomb holding the key in his hand while Apollo kept arrows flying in all directions aimed at the creatures that were piling into the room.

"Come on, come on, come on! Open it! Ahhhhhh!" Athena, her adrenaline pumping, yelled into the hybrid's face. With one hard squeeze, she snapped its neck, causing the creature to screech in anguish, but it kept fighting; an aggravating problem when dealing with the undying. It punched at the wall beside Athena's head, and dodging, she barely avoided the blows.

A light suddenly radiated through the hall and filled the entire chamber with an explosion that sounded like stone crashing into stone. Athena spun toward the light, and there beside the now broken tomb stood a tall, lean dark-skinned man. His legs were spread apart in a powerful stance; his sandals were blue and red, matching his linen toga that covered his abdomen and upper legs. On his ankles, wrists and biceps shone blue and gold bracelets. He wore the symbolic Double Crown of Egypt, which was adorned with a cobra in its center. The magnificent falcon was resting on his shoulder.

He raised his hands in command and at once, every creature in the chamber ceased their attack and bowed down. Feeling around for more injuries, Athena touched her neck and steadied her beating heart. She locked eyes with the man, pulled herself together and straightened her posture as she walked toward him with as much dignity as one could when covered in slime, blood and muck.

She reached out her hand to the man and he looked at her intently. His eyes were soft brown, almost the same color as his flawless skin. The falcon stayed on his shoulder, and both their eyes moved in synchronization.

"Thank you for helping me. We have a lot to discuss," said Horus.

CHAPTER 26

May 3rd

It was a lovely day in Brisbane. The weather was a balmy seventy degrees Fahrenheit, the humidity was lower than normal, and there was zero chance of precipitation. The rainy season had finally ended, and the Australians were delighted that they would not be afflicted by any more tropical cyclones.

Brisbane is one of the cities included in the Queensland area of Australia. This three million square mile country is just short of equaling Europe's land mass. It is the sixth largest country following Russia, Canada, China, the USA, and Brazil. Mainland Australia is divided into six territories: Western Australia, South Australia, the Northern Territory, New South Wales, Victoria and Queensland.

Robert Sharma was working late analyzing the monitors that lit his face. An employee of the Queensland Fire and Emergency Services, he was one of 4,000 front-line officers and auxiliary staff. His shift had officially ended two hours earlier, but there were so many reports that he was stuck at work on a Friday night.

Robert clicked on the screen and closed the report he was reading. *Four more to go.* He sighed heavily. His thoughts kept shifting to activities he could be enjoying if it weren't for his co-worker, Brett, who had decided to take his vacation that week. *Out of all the weeks in the year, he had to pick this one.* Robert's workload had nearly doubled because of Brett's absence.

Angrily, he tapped the next report and checked the number of pages. *Twenty-five.* "No!" he grunted out loud as he hit the monitor with his hand. There was little chance that he would be able to join his friends at the movie. He had been waiting eagerly to see it, and had only waited until Friday because Penelope was joining their group.

He had a substantial crush on Penelope Suarez, a fellow Queensland Fire and Emergency Services employee. She was the current acting director, and Robert counted the days when he could pass by her office and say a quick hello. Once a month he enjoyed a glorious fifteen-minute meeting with Penelope, during which they discussed that month's reports and developments. Robert had not yet wracked up the courage to ask her out. He felt it would be uncomfortable and unprofessional to do so at work. He figured that one day they might meet in a casual setting where he could inquire about Penelope's current dating life.

Robert's pulse quickened when he imagined how their conversation might evolve: "Oh, I'm single now; looking for my perfect man, someone strong and brave and smart like you." He put his hand on his head and sighed happily.

As his hand slipped, the motion brought him back to his senses. He shook his head, trying to focus on the report he was reading. He noticed that he had read the same page three times without absorbing any meaning. He groaned. Robert reached over and drained his coffee. If he skimmed the rest of the reports, he would be able to finish before the movie started. He would have little time to freshen up, but he could change his shirt and put on some lotion. Plus, if he skimmed the reports, he could always catch something important and just finish properly reading them over the weekend.

He opened the next report. Cost of 1.2 million Australian dollars.

CHAPTER 26

That sounds about average. Blah, blah, blah, early start to the bushfire season. That was normal, he thought. Nothing out of the ordinary. He skipped the last three pages and opened the next report. 22,550 square kilometers. Smoke from recent fires moved to the South Pacific Ocean. *Not my problem.* His spirits lifted as he imagined meeting up with his friends and casually sitting down next to Penelope.

Robert opened the last report and began to rapidly skim it. There didn't seem to be anything out of the ordinary, but just as he was about to close it and submit his hours, something caught his attention – one sentence in the middle of page six. He blinked and shook his head. He read the sentence again. *That's not possible.* It must have been an error, just a silly human error by whoever typed this report. He looked at his watch and saw that he had a couple of minutes to spare before showtime. *I'll just read this last report. I'm being paranoid; it's totally fine.*

Robert clicked on the print icon. Finally, the fourteen page report was in his hands. He licked his thumb as he turned the pages. Even though his mind screamed for him to remain calm, his pulse raced. *Oh, no. No. No, nooo.* He finished the report and grabbed his calculator. *These numbers are off; it's a mistake.* He waited breathlessly for the calculator to confirm the error. But as the numbers appeared on the tiny screen, Robert's heart dropped.

With trembling fingers he reached down into his pocket and called the only person who could right this situation.

"Hello?" came a female voice.

Robert was panting, his voice barely audible. "Penelope. We have a problem."

"Yes, we do, Robert. It's nearly 10 pm. Are you coming? If this is work related, why are you calling me on my cell phone? Just send me an email and I'll…"

But Robert cut her off. "We have a code 19. 2219." Robert heard silence on the other end of the line. He could hear Penelope's breathing as she whispered, "Oh, my God."

700 miles away, Mangkukulam was walking through an expansive New South Wales forest. He felt completely at ease. He loved exploring nature. Unlike his fellow demons, Manisilat and Manggagaway, he preferred avoiding humans as much as possible, choosing instead to wander through deserted pastures, empty forests and uninhabitable deserts. His favorite form of dark magic was transformation. Seeing the before and after effects of his presence brought him close to ecstasy.

Full of perverse mischief, he strode among the green trees native to South Australia. He crunched the weeds and moss that grew underfoot. His eyes widened with pleasure as his focus landed on the various creatures inhabiting the woodland. He counted three bird nests perched high on the topmost branches with little chicks chirping for their parents or for food. He stopped walking and put his orange stained hand on a massive oak. He inhaled deeply and smiled his slimy, hair-raising smile.

"Oh, my dear friend," he whispered to the oak in his cold, dead voice. "After today you will transform. You'll become something entirely new, something you've never been. After today you'll be nothing but ashes." He cackled as he looked up at the massive tree. The leaves seemed to sway mournfully, pushing away from Mangkukulam's poisonous air.

The wind was blowing eastward, so he started walking west. The further he trekked the more powerful the wind became, as if trying to race away from him. He blew a kiss to the invisible force. *My unwitting, unsuspecting lover.* With a snap of his fingers, his hand became a fiery beam of energy. The orange and red flames reached hungrily for the lush vegetation like a needy child reaching for its mother.

CHAPTER 26

Nonchalantly, Mangkukulam stroked the massive oak trees around him. He began to sing a shrill, off-key song that made the birds take flight in terror. To the beat of his deadly tune, he shrieked after them, "Say goodbye to your homes." He cavorted through the forest, raising his voice as he began to hear the creak of the falling trees behind him and the lamentation of the animals running for dear life. The more destruction that was left in his wake, the more his fire intensified and the more his insanity was fueled. The smoke was quickly blanketing the sky, spreading dangerously into the nearby human settlements. *Soon they will realize what is happening. And soon they will waste their efforts trying to contain the enormity that is Mangkukulam.*

He whooped and squawked as the wind raced farther and farther away from him, spreading his destruction in the opposite direction. In a frenzy, the animals who were in his path ran as his shrill song brought tears of blood to their eyes. Yet in their panic they collided against the massive wall of fire and debris in Mangkukulam's wake. He walked on, burning and killing as he went, until nothing was left alive behind him.

Raging uncontrollable fires could last for days, and Mangkukulam's energy wasn't dwindling. On the contrary, he was gaining more and more adrenaline as the acres continued to burn. The miles of casualties skyrocketed to unprecedented heights. Nothing could deter Mangkukulam from his purpose. Nothing.

On his destructive journey south-westward toward the state of Victoria, Mangkukulam did not encounter a single human. He saw buildings collapse and heard the terrified screams of those trapped inside, but he saw not one human. That was, until now.

In the middle of the fourth night of the conflagration, he heard a whirring sound coming from the sky which the rising flames illuminated. That caught Mangkukulam's attention. It was an air tanker that was closely followed by two helicopters. Mangkukulam smiled at the man-made machine. *What could those puny specks of dust do to contain my ferocity?* After further inspection, however, his smile transformed into a snarl. The air tanker was releasing some sort of material from its base, and miraculously some of the fires were being subdued.

Mangkukulam's yellow teeth were bared. Time to release his wrath on his first human victims. He clapped his blazing hands, and the flames spread across his frame. He raced to the tallest tree and hugged it so tightly that the tree snapped where his searing skin embraced it. With his entire might, he lifted the broken tree and threw it toward the air tanker. It flew across the night sky like a meteor about to collide with its target. At the last moment, the massive air tanker swerved, but not before its tail caught on fire.

Mangkukulam raged as his tree missed the air tanker, but he was quickly comforted as he realized that the tanker's near miss meant an exact bull's eye on the unsuspecting helicopter behind it. The metallic machine plummeted to the ground in an explosion of smoke and debris. Within seconds Mangkukulam reached the site of the helicopter's collapse. Most of the machine had been crushed or burnt, yet there was a small black box which had survived the intense crash. Mangkukulam could hear faint noises coming from the tiny box. With a snap of his fingers, his flames were extinguished, and as his curiosity mounted, he opened the box and waited.

"5466. Can you hear me 5466? Over."

Mangkukulam raised his eyebrow and was about to crush the tiny black box with a kick when he heard another voice.

"Any survivors 5466? Can you hear me? Over."

"I can hear you 7898. This is the Q-6 base. Do you have eyes on 5466? We lost signal moments ago. Over."

"No signal from 5466 here either. Air Tanker 23 is returning to base. The tail end of the aircraft has been badly damaged. Over."

CHAPTER 26

"Crikey! What is going on with these fires! They are out of control. Return to base immediately. It is not safe anymore. Over."

There was silence from the radio. Mangkukulam waited for the static and the signal to ebb, and his patience was rewarded.

"Currently flying over the south side of the fires. I can't believe it. Must be twelve million acres already. It's rapidly spreading toward eastern and north-eastern Victoria. Over."

"That's not the worst of it. The fire department is estimating that more than a billion animals will die. And most of our endangered species will be driven to extinction. There is nothing we can do."

The voice coming from the static-filled radio sounded severely depressed and agitated. Mangkukulam stayed glued to the little black box, his energy renewed and his spirits at an all-time high. On his return to Earth, his first global fire had been across the Pacific Ocean in California, but that fire had only destroyed about four million acres. He had been pleased to hear that it was described as a giga-fire, but now he wanted to dwarf that catastrophe. He wanted to cause complete mayhem. He wanted chaos. And most of all, he wanted even greater destruction.

As if on cue, the clueless operators continued their dreary reports. "We've declared a state of emergency across New South Wales and have recommended Victoria do so as well. The Australian Defence Force has been mobilized to provide air support and manpower. I just hope these fires die out soon. I can't even fathom what would happen if they spread north toward Queensland. They had an unusually dry summer and the consequences could be catastrophic. Over."

Mangkukulam's eyes almost popped with anticipation. He had never thought that humans could be remotely useful to him. He considered their intelligence to be limited. And he had been right on one account. They were so oblivious, so lost in their own grief, that their horrifying future was incomprehensible. A malevolent idea wormed its way into his devious mind. He looked north, toward the sprawling trees and the fleeing animals. Stepping over the black box, he started running, changing his direction from South-East straight due North.

The Queensland Fire and Emergency Office was filled with employees. Many had been roused from their homes; some wore nice evening outfits, while others were wearing their pajamas.

Robert had already printed forty copies of the report and the machine kept pouring out more by the minute. Penelope was standing by the room's monitors reading and re-reading the report. She would sometimes close her eyes, and Robert could see her lips silently moving as if she were arguing with herself. She grabbed the nearest calculator and tapped furiously. After reading the numbers on the screen, she would swallow and resume her silent argument.

After what felt like an eternity, she addressed her staff in her authoritative voice. "Can someone tell me if this is feasible?"

"There is little probability of the fire spreading north toward us from New South Wales," came a voice from the front of the room.

"We should issue a warning!" someone shouted from the back.

"Seems like the dry conditions could combine with the southern fires," yelled another person. "But if the brushfires don't spread into the state of Victoria, we should be able to survive without the magnitude of damage explained in this report."

Penelope frustratingly rubbed her temples. "Do we or do we not declare a state of emergency?"

Robert fidgeted in his seat, rubbing his palms together. He would open his mouth to speak, and then close it just as suddenly. The silence stretched across the room. Nobody had the answer.

Suddenly, the ring of a lone telephone shattered the unsettling quiet.

CHAPTER 26

Penelope straightened and answered. "This is Officer Suarez. Copy." Robert and his fellow officers held their breath. Penelope's face was becoming paler by the second. "Copy. I understand. Affirmative. Over."

Robert heard the line click, but Penelope did not put down the phone. She seemed to be steeling herself. Her hand began to shake slightly as she finally hung up. "The fire is approaching Queensland. We need to evacuate."

Robert's mouth was dry. He glanced around the room watching as the bombshell hit his fellow officers. Most were stunned. Others seemed dazed as if they had been slapped across the face. Robert looked at Penelope. He remembered how he had felt just a couple of hours before, daydreaming about a movie. Now, Penelope stood frozen, her eyes unblinking. Silent tears streamed down her cheeks, tears that scorched Robert's heart, tears that could never save the Australian countryside.

CHAPTER 27

May 4th

Officially known as the National Capital Territory (NCT), Delhi is a city and union territory of India. New Delhi, the capital of India, is situated in the northern part of the country. In the last census, the National Capital Territory's total population was recorded at over 16.8 million while the total population of India was 1.38 billion people, about 17.7% of the population of the entire globe.

In the bustling city of Delhi, Manggagaway exited the New Delhi Railway between the Ajmeri Gate and Paharganj. She made her way down the streets, taking in the scents and sights of the city. She was wearing an immaculate gray suit and carried a small briefcase that contained various medical instruments, a white physician's scrubs and forged medical certificates. These had been relatively easy to obtain. With a bit of money and a bit of persuasion, humans were quite malleable.

The first thing Manggagaway always noticed when she explored new cities was the noise: the honking of horns, the screeching of cars. She heard the rumble and commotion of the city, a sleeping tiger roaring to life. But the tiger never truly slept, never truly rested. It was always on the prowl, always on the hunt for new prey.... and so was she.

Out of the four agents from the Kasamaan, Manggagaway was smaller than both Mangkukulam and Manisilat. Her skin was white as snow, in contrast to the other three. Similar to Manisilat, her hair was black as ink, but hers was neat and well kept, perfectly straight and perfectly brushed. She was the most focused of the four and the most fastidious. She walked with purpose; she was on a mission and there was nothing that would stop her.

Manggagaway continued her route across the city, crossing streets and intersections, passing cars, motorcycles, cyclists and pedestrians. As she approached her destination, she allowed herself a moment of observation. Her dark eyes missed nothing. All around her the humans were on the move, hurriedly shifting from place to place. Most of them were self-absorbed; their eyes were glued to their smartphones or to billboards on the walls of buildings. They passed children begging in the streets without so much as a glance. There was no compassion in their eyes. Their only motivation for hustling through the day was to survive long enough to rush into the next morning.

This was the third city Manggagaway had visited on Earth, and each of these metropolises had confirmed her suspicions. Tolerance was not a dominant characteristic of humans. Whether it was differences in skin color, language, or even something they called politics, humans found riveting ways to destroy one another. Her fellow demon, Manisilat, would be thrilled at their inhumanity. Manisilat thrived on chaos, she was a homewrecker. And Manggagaway? Well, Manggagaway loved contradictions.

As she continued studying the humans passing by, she saw that what united them also destroyed them. Humans were so creative. They created imagined realities for themselves, and stuck to those realities with such force that it ended up consuming them, so much so that there was real power there, as real as their little brains could manage. The corners of her mouth raised in a hint of a smile.

As Manggagway moved farther along, she came across a piece of paper on the road. She reached down and grabbed it, noticing with delight that it was an Indian rupee. She examined the money that she held between her fingers and traced the outline of the bald man whose face was plastered on the paper. Expressionless, she neatly folded the bill and ripped it into four perfect squares. Then she returned it to its original position on the ground. Money was one of those commodities that humans thought held power. They were utterly consumed by it. They were capable of the most wicked behaviors in their pursuit of it. In the end they would even die to amass it, to store it, to hide it away. *All that effort for some paper.* Paper that could unite, and paper that would surely divide.

Manggagway was not going to attack the humans with an ineffective weapon that held no real power. She was going for a shot straight to the heart, for a mortal wound. And the best part was that she knew it would not even be a challenge. In the past, humans were required to have great mental skills. It was essential for their survival. They were physically weak creatures, easily overpowered. But banded together, they were a force to be reckoned with.

But now, even the imbeciles got to survive. They were allowed to pass on their unremarkable DNA, and instead of creating more powerful, more adept and smarter generations, they left their weak, pathetic offspring in their wake. This was what Manggagway had to deal with. Not even a challenge. But she knew the real defiance would come later.

As if on cue, and just as she reached the doors of a tall, elegant building in the city center, the group she was looking for assembled. Entering through the double doors, she followed the group across the lobby and into a meeting hall where she was approached by a man who introduced himself. "Dr. Way, it is a pleasure to meet you. I am Bhim Ghosh from the Delhi Pollution Control Committee. I hope you are not too tired from your long journey."

Manggagway shook hands with Ghosh and nodded. "Thank you for the welcome. Your country is very pleasant. Shall we start?" She faked a foreign accent so that Bhim would not realize how flawlessly she truly spoke his language.

"Of course. Follow me," said Bhim as he gestured towards the front of the hall.

As Manggagaway scanned the few people attending the conference, she was intrigued to see women in the crowd and in such a position of power. One was wearing a shapeless red dress, adorned with green lace. Although her head was covered, Manggagaway noted that the woman was possibly in her early forties with two or three children. In both dress and tradition, India was a conservative country. This person was an anomaly, far more dangerous than any man at the conference. It was time to make her first move.

Opening her briefcase and retrieving her white uniform, she attached a medical badge to her pocket. It read, "Dr. Man G. Way, John Hopkins University, MD". Carefully tying her hair back in a low bun, she approached the desk where the teleconference would be publicly shown. The cameramen and photographers had already finished setting up their equipment. Although she had never set foot on the American continent, some fake identification records and diplomas were enough to convince people of her pedigree. *The right words falling on the right ears.*

She started her teleconference with an assertive and dogmatic attitude, making sure she dropped an accumulation of information and facts that were incontrovertibly true. "I am a representative from the United Nations, sent here to process many major health issues around the world. As you all know, the World Health Organization

(WHO) is conducting education and research programs as well as publishing scientific papers and reports for standards for disease control and health care."

As she spoke, Manggagaway allowed herself multiple glances in the direction of the attendants. She specifically focused on the Delhi Pollution Control Committee. They would be aware of most of the facts and, if driven to it, could provide information refuting Manggagaway. She needed them on her side.

The real scientific report from WHO stated that in 2014 Delhi was the most polluted city in the world, and since then they had tried to find endless ways to drive down the damning figures that were evidence of the corrosion of Delhi's environment. In 2018, India's Ministry of Earth Sciences published a research paper attributing almost 41% of PM2.5 (fine particulate matter) air pollution in Delhi to vehicular emissions, 21.5% to dust and fire and 18% to industries. After the report was published, there were several clashes between the scientific community and the Indian Automotive Manufactures, who lobbied against the report. Further on, an environmental panel appealed to India's Supreme Court to impose a 30% tax on diesel cars, but no action had been taken to penalize the automobile industry.

In the previous days, while touring the city, Manggagaway realized that most of Delhi's residents were unaware of the alarming levels of air pollution and the health risks associated with it. They walked around without face coverings and inhaled the deadly gasses that were carelessly being added to and trapped in the Earth's atmosphere.

To add to her delight, not only was India suffering from air pollution, it was also being devastated by water pollution. She estimated that around 70% of the surface water was unfit for consumption. Each day, at least 40 million liters of wastewater entered the rivers and water bodies. There was little to no treatment. Their water supply was contaminated by sewage, runoff, solid waste and plastic. Manggagway

CHAPTER 27

loved it; she thrived on their desperation.

Quietly ignoring all the troubling facts, she rambled on with made-up figures. She praised the local governments and private companies for their grand efforts in their fight against pollution. She reminded the audience of the $140 million dollars that had been spent on the project, most of it falling into corrupt hands, but she made no mention of that in her speech. Toward the end, she claimed that the WHO was most impressed by the country's effort, and they would consider awarding them an environment grant that would allow them to completely eradicate both air and water pollution by 2050. Manggagaway's insides glowed. At this rate, by then most of the population would be poisoned and dying.

Finally, she turned directly to the attendees and opened a forum for questions. Time for the second round. Time for the pawns to be moved into their spaces. As she predicted, one of the first hands to be raised was that of the woman wearing red. This woman would not only be thinking about herself; she would be thinking of her children and possibly grandchildren. Anything that tied humans to an outside force gave them more alternative solutions, more reason to question their realities.

"Dr. Way, you stated that the Yumana's levels of fluoride, nitrate and arsenic have decreased dramatically over the past years. Do you have any proof or physical evidence for this claim?" asked the woman in a tone that questioned Manggagaway's outrageous claims.

Arsenic. She debated which she preferred most: Arsenic or Lead. Both were highly toxic, and posed intense threats to public health by causing a variety of diseases. Before answering, she thought about the man who had escorted her into the hall, Bhim, from the Delhi Pollution Control Committee. She weighed the risk versus the reward of her next move.

"Great question. The WHO worked in conjunction with the Delhi

Pollution Control Committee. Without their efforts and without their long lasting battle against climate change, Delhi would not have been able to defeat this plague. I want to personally thank them." She looked directly at Bhim, who seemed mildly shocked and intrigued. "And I also wish to thank the Association of GSD. The GSD supplied most of the infrastructure required for a project of such magnitude. Without them, India would be heading into chaos and a massive environmental crisis."

In reality, the GSD, a government-run social development organization, was one of the most, if not the most, corrupt organizations in Delhi. They had been accepting grants and perks from the same industries that were causing massive discharge into the Yamuna River. Their factories were responsible for the rising level of ammonia, which was a toxic foam that covered the river. Of course, Manggagaway knew all of this. *Check.*

The woman seemed to be unimpressed with Dr. Way's response. She raised her hand once more and when Manggagaway nodded, she stood upright. Her voice was clear and strong, but Manggagway was not paying much attention.

Her focus was directed to Bhim. She was powerful enough to break into the man's head. She went through his memories, his starved and powerless childhood, his tiny and crowded apartment in the city's center. She went through his longings and his desires. She weighed his future possibilities against his present path. She showed him how to escape his misery, how to gain the upper hand in a downward spiral. She showed him the cost of his dreams, the cost that would be paid with paper. Paper that was useless and purposeless yet compelling and addicting, as coveted as power. Everything had a price. And this price was the Earth.

The woman finished her questions and her probing, but instead of answering, Manggagaway waited. She waited for her pawn to move,

CHAPTER 27

to pounce, to make his choice.

Bhim rose from his seat, his eyes ablaze with new found hope. It was not hope for the country, nor for the environment, but for himself. "I can confirm Dr. Way's claims. The Yamuna waters are healing. Soon they will return to their 20th century splendor: clear, blue and able to provide safe drinking water to the community of Delhi and New Delhi."

There was scattered applause and sighs of relief from the crowd as they swallowed the lies that Manggagaway had force-fed them. A foreigner claiming their problems were solved was one thing, but that claim backed by one of their own was better than gold. *Check-mate.*

Many hands were shaken, and there was some discussion on what was to be done next. Manggagaway allowed them their moments of counterfeit triumph and exited the building, making her way across the city. As she walked, she seemed to notice more exhaust in the air than before, more trash on the streets, more precious resources drained and lost forever. It was as if Earth knew it was being defeated and was on the road to complete devastation.

There, there. You don't have much time left. The end is near. Be tranquil and enjoy your last sunsets. Gone were the days when she could only attack a handful of humans. The world was now so populated that she could go after thousands, even millions. The thick blanket of noxious haze that burned humans' lungs and eyes settled about her, and the burning sensation felt like the sweetest of triumphs.

As she walked along the shore of the Yamuna, Manggagaway remembered another river she had visited earlier, the Ganges. She smiled, allowing herself a taste of victory. More than 500 million people depended on the Ganges. She pictured the muddy, polluted water and the people and animals that bathed and drank from it. She lived for this. She lived for the sickening pestilence, for the plagues. She lived for infections and contamination. Long, long ago, she erroneously had been called a healer. But in reality, she was so far from being a healer. She was a killer.

CHAPTER 28

May 5th

The seat beneath Leo felt hard and sturdy. *I'm not dreaming. This is real.* He kept clutching the chair with both hands to remind himself that he was awake, to bring his mind back to the present. Only a few days ago they had been camping in the Sahara, searching for mystical pyramids in the desert sand, and now he was seated at a table with not one, but three gods.

Leo's eyes kept drifting to Horus', and then back to his tea. He squeezed the chair once more before reaching for his cup. His hand was slightly trembling as he brought the lukewarm liquid to his lips. The minute sound caught Horus' attention and he turned his head toward Leo, whose cup shook so violently that his tea threatened to spill over. He would have to get used to Horus' gaze, the four eyes peering at him from all directions.

Instead of choosing a material object as his talisman, Horus had chosen the symbol for which he was most known – his eye. The Eye of Horus symbol, a stylized eye with distinctive markings, was commonly believed to have protective magical powers. It constantly appeared in ancient Egyptian art, and was one of the most common motifs for amulets. Leo chuckled, then thought to himself. *Oh, the irony.*

The Egyptian deity spoke quietly. "Does something amuse you, human?"

Leo turned his chuckle into a cough and shook his head. "I…" He cleared his throat. "My apologies. I did not mean to offend you."

"Then, pray tell, what was your meaning?"

Leo looked to Athena before replying to Horus. She sat motionless across from him, her eyes guarded. She gave the tiniest and barely perceptible nod. Leo cleared his throat once more before answering. "I laughed because I found it very clever that you chose your eye as your talisman. In modern times it is associated with well-being, healing, and protection. It is very popular, found in art, clothing, buildings, video games; it's even tattooed on human bodies. It's fascinating to me because it is also a symbol of your history and your mythological journey." Leo steadied his nerves as Horus continued with his inexpressive stare. Finally, Horus returned his attention to the table, but the falcon on his shoulder remained staring at Leo, his eyes black and glistening. *Not just a falcon. It's Horus. It's still him,* Leo reminded himself.

When Leo first heard how Horus had chosen his talisman, he was in complete disbelief. He had always read and incorrectly assumed that talismans must be inanimate, like Athena's armband or the Norse vegvisir she carried with her. In all the volumes of history that he had ever read, not one mentioned a live animal being used as a talisman, but then again, there were so few records from ancient times that were still accessible and intact. He thought about the famous Library of Alexandria, regarded as the capital of knowledge and learning, and how it had gradually declined over the years, suffering after the purge of many intellectuals, the accidental burning of part of it by Julius Caesar during the Roman Civil War, and the lack of support and funding that contributed to its eventual demise. He wished he could have had one month, one week or even a day inside those walls,

CHAPTER 28

running his fingers across the old pages of papyrus and the thousands of volumes that were now forever lost to humans. As if reading his thoughts, Horus commented in his temperate voice, "There's much more that humans don't understand, and unfortunately, never will." He straightened his back and reclined in his chair, exhibiting poise and silent power.

"I still cannot comprehend how you can see through all of them," Apollo said. In contrast to Horus, Apollo lounged casually, his legs parted and his arms resting on his chair and on that of his sister. Between his fingers he nonchalantly twirled his golden bracelet that in a second could transform into his bow and arrows. His eyes, however, were devouring the Egyptian god's attire and whole being. Leo understood the non-verbal communication that Apollo's posture implied. He was relaxed, yet vigilant. His hands were resting on this valuable possession, sure to kill if either he or his sister were threatened. On the other hand, Athena sat to Horus' right, directly across from Leo, and her posture was stiff and unanimated; her face, which seemed to be carved out of stone, evinced no emotion, no hint of the thoughts that lurked behind her gray-green eyes.

"On the contrary," replied Horus, "my range of vision is magnified. Instead of having a small, frontal binocular visual field, mine is expanded twofold." He did not sound pedantic or arrogant. In fact, Horus had a calm and intellectual demeanor, although he was still imposing because of his general aura and especially because of his attire.

He was wearing his traditional robes, if they could even be called robes. *More like a kilt or a long skirt*, Leo mused. They were black with golden threads; his belt was thick and made of solid gold with natural stones embellishing it. His sandals were of fine leather and were woven across his feet and calves. His chest was bare, but he wore a golden necklace that resembled a half-disk and covered most of his shoulders and upper body. He was extremely well built; his tendons flexed at any sudden movement, and he had a hint of a beard. However, apart from his natural grace and posture, he still retained some bird-like tendencies. His head shifted quickly without any movement from his body, and he paused just before using his hands, as if adjusting himself.

"That must be an advantage on the battlefield," said Apollo testily. Horus turned his head, as did the falcon that rested on his shoulder.

"There are many advantages. You see, we Egyptians have a special connection with our animals. We are as one, fused together with an unbreakable bond. I live through him, and he through me. Neither of us can live without the other, and yet we may survive long enough to resurrect the other. It is a sacred bond."

Leo could not contain his curiosity. "I've read that there used to be domesticated dogs and cats at the royal courts, but were there more animals?"

Horus turned his head again, his eyes staring. He paused for a moment before answering. "We kept a variety of pets: baboons, monkeys, fish, gazelles, lions, mongeese, snakes, falcons of course, and even hippos." Leo gasped. "Yes, indeed," continued Horus in an academic way. "Hippos and crocodiles, while dangerous to humans, were under our divine control and protection. The latter were kept as sacred animals in the temples of my friend, Sobek. We had a close relationship. The Lord of the Waters, he liked to be called. He is very ferocious indeed – loyal but ferocious." Horus trailed off, lost in his memories. The siblings exchanged a knowing glance, and Athena clenched her jaw.

"Horus," she announced in her strong, reassuring voice. "We need you to tell us what happened. Why did you look for us? What are you doing here? And, how were you attacked?"

Horus turned his head and stared straight at Athena, his four eyes, two human, two animal, unblinking. Athena returned his scrutiny. Leo held his breath, not wanting to disturb the two titans.

At long last, Horus spoke. "I will tell you all I know. Do you promise to do the same?"

"That is for me to decide afterwards." Athena's response was curt and businesslike. "For now, please commence."

Horus' expression did not change. He lowered his right arm, and the falcon hopped gently onto his forearm. Horus stroked the bird with his long fingers. He seemed to be weighing his words. Then, he began his tale:

He was chosen by the Egyptians to represent them under the Council of the Elders. He acknowledged that he would not reveal his partner's identity, for they were under an oath of allegiance. The partnership had not lasted long; within a few days, they were immediately attacked and taken hostage. Horus described how he had sensed danger mere moments before their ambush. His falcon had also alerted him to the sudden change in magnetic fields, and Horus was sure they would be crushed. He sent his falcon away to fly to safety and scout from above.

Horus admitted that his memory had been tampered with, for in his original form he could only recount certain visions and senses. The few recollections that he could accurately recall were the sounds of screams, the metallic screech of bars, and the feeling of cold metal that was fastened around his neck while he was in captivity. When prodded further by Athena, he admitted that he did not know who his captors were. They rarely spoke in his presence, and he was blinded the moment he was captured. He did not know how or when he had lost his sight, but his loss did not affect or trouble him, for he had already suffered that calamity during his rebellion against his uncle, Seth.

"What did they want from you?" asked Athena.

Horus raised his hand to his neck. "They wanted my talisman. I remember being searched. I remember my partner's indignation as they tore it from her. Our talismans keep us safe in the physical world; without them we are vulnerable. She was incarcerated, and so was I. Their methods of extracting truths were most ingenious, and, dare I say, oftentimes effective. But I was safe, at least for a time. As long as my falcon was free, I would not crumble. The days turned into weeks, however, and I grew weak from our separation."

Horus closed his eyes and clutched at his neck. "It came for me one day. I felt its presence. It tried to break me, but it was in vain. You can't break what isn't whole. I was protected because I wasn't truly there. My mind was with my falcon, and so was my soul and my drive. It got angry, very angry. I can't tell if it meant to destroy my body, or if it was an action driven out of rage, but he finished me off."

There was a long pause in which nobody spoke. Horus kept his eyes closed, and his falcon cooed into his chest, placing its face close to his master's heart. Horus dropped his hand from his neck and stroked the bird. When he opened his eyes, they were glossy with joy and love. It was clear that Horus adored and revered his falcon more than anything in the world.

When Leo saw Horus' expression, his thoughts went immediately to David. He looked away from Horus and his eyes fell on Athena. Her expression was no longer stony; another emotion emanated from her eyes. Leo was taken aback, for instead of pity or sadness, her eyes seemed filled with hope.

"My falcon rescued me. He followed Ex Nihilo's scent throughout the world and found you. I owe you," he inclined his head to them, "my life." Horus took the time to appraise each of them, his eyes scanning them like X-rays. He straightened his back and rested his frame on his chair, placing his hands on the table with his palms down. "Now, how do we take this devil down?"

CHAPTER 29

Athena could not help but smile. There were a lot of positives from Horus' story. It would have been very hard for him to lie to Apollo, for he could sniff out lies faster than a Greek Harehound. Athena believed him, and she was grateful that he would be a potential ally in their war against Ex Nihilo. Still, she remained silent as she observed him. There was a difference between respecting and trusting someone. It was a big leap for Athena; she could count on one hand how many people she trusted. Two of them were in this room: Apollo and Leo. Her thoughts shifted to the third person she trusted more than both of them combined. Her smile vanished. *Freya.*

Horus had mentioned that they had been attacked quite suddenly and effectively. Athena was not surprised. She recalled how Freya had lit the fire back on their first day together on Earth, how the flames had shown them a swift and coordinated attack. They had thwarted that ambush by using Freya's magic and intuition and Athena's cunning. She replayed their first conversation, how Freya had guessed that there might be foul play at hand.

Every day that passed, Athena became convinced of the same. Something was not adding up. The more she pondered the situation, the more Athena was sure that someone was betraying them. Someone powerful enough to be included as a member of the Council of the Elders. What was their endgame? What were her enemies planning, and why was it happening?

Athena reviewed her mental notes on Ex Nihilo, and updated them according to recent discoveries.

Species: unknown.

Powers: Controls electricity. Can induce severe memory loss in immortals. Capable of fatally wounding them. Ability to travel great distances undetected.

Culture: unknown.

Allies: unknown.

Enemies: Greeks, Norsemen, Egyptians and another unknown culture.

She did not know whether to put the Council of the Elders on the list of allies or the list of enemies. For the time being, she placed them in their own bubble filled with question marks.

Again, Athena scrutinized Horus. She thought of the possibility of his being a spy against her. It would be the ultimate inside job, for she had been the only deity to have stood up to and wounded Ex Nihilo. For all Horus' talk of being imprisoned, he could be hiding part of the truth. Athena's eyes turned to her brother. He returned her gaze, and she could see in his eyes that he believed Horus, that there were no falsehoods in his tale. She relaxed her posture and resumed studying her mental notes. She was narrowing down Ex Nihilo's powers; both Horus' and her own encounters attested to that. She was sure now that it was Ex Nihilo who had tried to attack Apollo. Why he hadn't succeeded was another matter. *Unless...*

She gasped. *Of course!* She stood up and walked about the room, tapping her finger on her temple. Her mind buzzed as her thoughts raced. *What had Apollo said back in Paris?* He had found her hotel, the Royal Horseguards in London, and was entering the building when he felt a chill. She closed her eyes and pictured the scene. Apollo had tensed, had somehow protected himself, and then right afterwards, he

CHAPTER 29

had lost his memory and so had the staff in the hotel. But something was missing, something important...

She turned rapidly and addressed her brother. "Apollo, you haven't seen Ex Nihilo, have you?" she asked inquisitively, catching him off guard. Apollo blinked and shook off his surprise.

He thought for a moment and then shook his head. "No, I never saw him. Not directly at least. But I do have a clear picture of him from the accounts that you, Leo, Ares and Horus have given me," he replied. "Why?"

Athena's eyes glowed. She could feel the adrenaline rushing through her veins and knew that she was getting close. She approached the table and put her hands on the back of her chair. "Ex Nihilo isn't working alone. He has allies."

"But how do you know?" Now it was Leo's turn to be puzzled.

"Apollo came to Earth mere minutes after I was attacked by Ex Nihilo. He must have been extremely vulnerable in that state. That would have been the perfect time for an attack against him, unless..."

"Unless he had someone on the sidelines keeping guard," finished Horus.

"Exactly. Apollo wasn't attacked by Ex Nihilo. His strikes are coordinated and ruthless. If he destroyed me only moments before, why not take down another god? A possible explanation could be that he isn't powerful enough in his current state, but we have seen him and he is fully capable of complete mayhem and bloodshed. Therefore, someone else was there to intercept Apollo. Someone who specializes in altering memories."

"That someone altered my memory, as well!" exclaimed Horus. He stood up and paced around the room, his falcon hopping off his shoulder with a shriek.

"Yes! That someone, *or something,* has been closely involved in every attack. But why?" Athena sat down and put her hands on her face, thinking. *Why would someone so powerful need an ally who could alter memories? Why would they need to in the first place?*

"Horus. You said that when you were imprisoned, you were searched for your talismans first, and then taken into confinement. Is that correct?"

"Yes, that is how I recall it. My memories get blurred after that."

Interesting, thought Athena. One thing was certain: Ex Nihilo was after talismans. But there was something that didn't add up. The Council had said it was a slaughter, that they were being destroyed. Yet, in Horus' recollection he remembered hearing screams, multiple screams, in fact, and from different sources. What if Ex Nihilo wasn't interested in killing first and asking second? What if it was the other way around? That would be confirmed with both Horus' and Apollo's accounts. He had kept Horus until he was of no more use. He could have easily destroyed him, but he controlled himself. *Well, at least long enough to keep Horus a prisoner.* Athena remembered that Ex Nihilo had lost control before, back in the Royal Horseguards when she had set her trap. She could understand now that it was fury that drove him to annihilate her; not something thought-out and planned. The planning was done by another... by both of them? By one of them? Athena was not sure yet, but she felt the warmth of knowledge surging through her veins. This was what she most enjoyed: The thrill of solving a mystery. The thrill of a challenge. The thrill of the chase.

It seemed that Apollo's thoughts were moving in the same direction. "So there's two. The one who can alter minds and Ex Nihilo. He does the dirty work, so to speak, while the other lurks behind and plans. Do you think they're from the same culture?"

Athena was pondering Apollo's last remarks when Leo joined the conversation. "I doubt it. Their modus operandi is too different. They don't act together. The first time you were attacked, Athena, it was only by Ex Nihilo, not by the other one. If it had been both, you

CHAPTER 29

would not have retained your memories. Same as the second time. I think… I think that it came to the hotel in London when it sensed Ex Nihilo's demise. It must have inadvertently run into Apollo and quickly defended itself. It must not be as potent or deadly as Ex Nihilo, for it didn't harm Apollo; just set him off course for the time being."

"Who is it, and what are they hiding?" added Horus.

Athena cleared her mind. "On the contrary, Leo. Whoever has been altering memories is extremely capable. I was able to cure some of Apollo's amnesia, but not all. And Horus," she turned to him, "remember back when we were leaving the pyramid, when I healed you in case of any unseen injuries? If you had had mild amnesia, my restorative touch would have cleared it, but it didn't. Both you and Apollo have serious mental blanks." She bit her lip before continuing. "We're dealing with something far more dominant than we thought. Something that wants to keep its identity a secret."

Apollo banged his fist, leaving a knuckle-sized dent on the table. Horus' falcon rapidly turned its head. "The Council, those traitorous bastards."

"We don't know that. Also, we are under strict rules that must not be disobeyed," Horus replied with a concerned glance at Leo. Then he spoke in an ancient dialect, directed at the immortals in the room. "How can you say this in front of him? You are breaking an order."

Athena raised her voice, using the same language. "The mortal fused a blood oath with me, he's trustworthy. In any case, he probably understands what we're saying. He's been studying ancient artifacts and cultures for most of his life." She looked at Leo, who was blushing, confirming what she had just said. They had only known each other for a few weeks, but she trusted him completely. He was the first person to whom she had involuntarily opened up.

She had been in a very vulnerable state when they first met, and he had been comforting and caring ever since. Back in London, she had almost chopped his arm off when he tried to console her, yet instead of angering her, his gesture had touched her somehow, in a way that very few mortals ever had. She did not feel the need to hide herself behind a mask when she was around him, and she had slowly come to like his presence in their group. He had never asked anything of her, no magic potions or unlimited wealth. Without hesitation he had signed up for a very vigorous and demanding task. Even though she often felt her hope in humanity dwindle, there were still a few humans who were willing to risk it all for the greater good.

Horus' face was impassive, a sign that Athena had learned to associate with him being deep in thought, but she could tell he was unconvinced. She waved to Leo to come to her side. He obeyed, and she reached for his arm, then waved her hand over his palm, producing a burnt tattoo of snakes moving about in his hand. Leo's face seemed to turn green. Horus' eyes, his and his falcon's, examined the intertwining snakes. Satisfied, he again sat down at the table.

Apollo approached, and looking over Athena's shoulder, he commented, "You're bound to us now, mortal." He flashed his brilliant, self-assured smile. "Don't look so pale. We're the good guys."

Athena waved her hand again and the snakes disappeared. "Leo," she said in her most soothing voice. "You're doing an excellent job. You're strong and brave. Never forget that. We will protect you like you've protected us." Leo smiled, and tears filled his eyes. Athena sensed that these words of affirmation meant more to him than all the awards in the world.

Clearing his throat, he said, "I'm going to get some food. Would any of you like something from the cafe?" Horus and Athena shook their heads in response, but Apollo asked for some snacks and fruit. Leo nodded and walked out of the apartment.

As soon as the door closed behind him, Horus turned to face Athena. She knew he wanted answers. "We haven't broken any rules." Her

CHAPTER 29

face reddened before her next sentence. "He's just our friend, nothing more. I did not force him into the blood oath; he wished to join me on the quest. He was the one who woke me after I was attacked by Ex Nihilo. I have felt his attempts to destroy me. And I, too, wish for revenge. Leo saw him, Leo faced him, and he did not cower in fear. He's brave and he's bright; more so than he himself knows."

Horus slowly nodded, his movements ever graceful. Then he closed his eyes, breathing deeply. "Do you really believe the Council is involved?"

Athena sighed. "There's foul play, Horus. Either there's something they're not telling us, or there's someone who is playing them. How else could you explain your blitz? It's too coincidental. You couldn't have used that much magic to link you to an area so soon. They knew you'd be there, and they knew you weren't alone. You are an almighty deity, and yet you were overwhelmed. Only someone extremely ancient and tremendously experienced could have coordinated that onslaught." She finished, allowing her mind to swirl through possibilities and outcomes.

Apollo sat beside her and pursued his lips. "I am still unclear as to why they are abducting deities. I thought they were just stealing talismans. Why go to all the hassle of incarcerating them? And how many are there anyway?" He grabbed a glass from the table and turned it in his hands.

"I can't be sure," Horus responded. "Being down there, no light, just darkness. It was disturbing. It was chaotic."

Athena walked away from the table. She looked out the window into Cairo's busy streets. There was something she was missing. Ex Nihilo had purposefully woken and provoked Ares to attack her. He could have done it for many reasons: to harm her, to stall her, to evoke discord, to start a civil war between them, to cause mayhem and chaos...

You'll find me; Freya's last words to her. Is this where she was meant to go? There were too many questions and not enough answers. Athena clutched at the wall drapings, pretending she could grasp hope in the same physical way.

A sudden thought hit her like a thunderbolt. If Freya could see the future, had she seen her demise? Had she planned it so that Athena could escape? Was that why she gave her her vegvisir before passing on? Her throat felt tight and heavy. She had not allowed her mind to drift to such a distressing level, but Athena could not help it now. She had looked everywhere for Freya, had spent hours glued to the vegvisir, but to no avail. There was only one place where she could be, the one place that the vegvisir could not reveal yet. She was quite literally in the most dangerous place on Earth.

Athena felt like screaming at the top of her lungs, to scream and scream until her voice would break, until her pain ebbed away into nothingness. She wanted to mount a rescue mission, but she did not know where to go. She wanted to search every grain of sand, every droplet of water until she found Freya. She wanted to put her hand on Freya's, to hold her tight and never feel alone again.

The doors to the apartment opened and, carrying snacks, bread and fresh fruit, Leo walked in. He absentmindedly placed them on the table in front of Apollo and continued to read the newspaper he was holding. Athena remained by the window, her back to them, allowing free reign to her silent tears.

"What are you reading?" asked Apollo.

"Huh?" answered Leo. "Oh, me. Agh, man, I know we're in the middle of a crisis, but this, too, is horrible. There's been another global fire. This time it was in Australia. It says here that an estimated 46 million acres were burnt, over 5,900 buildings were destroyed, 34 people were killed, and over 3 billion animals perished. Some endangered species were even believed to be driven to extinction. It

CHAPTER 29

was even worse than the United States' fire that occurred only a few days before. How brutal. It just seems so unprecedented, so... chaotic."

Athena's ears perked up. There was something buzzing in her brain, and it wasn't pain; it was more of a sixth sense. *Chaotic.* She hastily wiped away her tears, strode over to the table, took the paper from Leo, and read it carefully. Her eyes, which had been watering moments before, were now brimming with excitement. She felt like a bloodhound chasing her prey. She had caught the scent, and now she was on the hunt.

"I'm sorry, but why are you grinning? This is terrible news," said Apollo disgustedly.

Athena's heart raced; she had not felt so alive, so close to her goals, as she did now. "Look!" She threw the newspaper down in front of the group. Horus peered curiously at the paper. Leo sat dumbfounded. Apollo shifted away from Athena, repulsed.

"I can't believe you're excited about this. It's the most disrespectful, heinous and..."

"Do you think it's their doing?" interrupted Horus. His eyes, too, seemed filled with new energy.

"Them? You can't be..." said Apollo, but he caught himself and took the paper from the desk, reading it over and over again.

"Oh, my gods! You're right!" exclaimed Leo. He jumped out of his seat and put his hands on his head. "We found them!"

"I believe we found one of them," said Horus, who was reading over Apollo's shoulder. "As you said before, human, this is their modus operandi."

Athena could have shouted in triumph. She was so excited, her mind swirled with possibilities.

"We've got them now!" Apollo cried out as he threw the paper down on the table.

"I don't want to be a party pooper, but how exactly do we have them? We don't know where they are, or where they'll strike next," questioned Leo with some resignation in his voice.

There was a moment of complete silence when each of them thought furiously. Leo absentmindedly played with his curls. Horus rested lithely on the chair, tapping his fingertips. Apollo paced back and forth, murmuring to himself. Athena closed her eyes and meditated. She tried to position herself in this evil creature's shoes. Someone so despicable that they would willingly and readily destroy so much life and beauty. *If I were them, where would I go? Where could I cause even more destruction and more mayhem?*

The answer struck Athena like a powerful tsunami. "I know where they're going." She smiled widely. "And we'll be there to ambush them."

CHAPTER 30

May 6th

During this time of year, the island of Luzon in the Philippines was extremely hot and humid. The average temperature was above thirty-three degrees Celsius, with horrendous thunderstorms expected and heat strokes guaranteed. Near Mount Cagua, in the northern part of the island, stands the Fire Mountain Volcano; unbeknownst to the four lost hikers, the volcano was not asleep. On the contrary, it was very much awake.

The lost souls continued on their doomed trek up the mountain in search of high ground. Sixty meters below them, deep in the mountain's caves and crevices, an agent of chaos walked alongside her cruel master. They were vile and evil beings, so much so that the hikers' fear of exhaustion and dehydration was the least of their problems.

Hukluban and Ex Nihilo made their daily inspection across their wicked realm, Kasamaan. Quietly, they surveyed each of their caves and each of the passageways. Hukluban's stunted walk was a deception that only Ex Nihilo and his agents were aware of. Hukluban was a shapeshifter, capable of altering her form into whatever she desired. Why she dressed in rags and assumed the physical appearance of a hag was privy only to Ex Nihilo who knew that, if Hukluban had had a soul, it would have been a clear reflection of her: frightful, ghastly, empty and ruthless. Just like him.

In the darkness, Ex Nihilo and his pupil heard a scream from one of the caves. The cry was full of pain, despair, and torment. Hukluban didn't even turn around; she was completely apathetic as she continued hobbling through the blackness with her wooden cane in hand, displaying no interest or regard for the sound. Ex Nihilo was pleased. The millenniums of rest had not changed his agents. They were still as malicious and destructive as ever.

The walls of the open cavern they were approaching were lined with red, glowing brightly in the darkness. They resembled gushing wounds, or blood splattered across a battlefield; yet the true brightness came from the lava of the active volcano. But this was no ordinary lava; it flowed around Kasamaan, filling it with a savage warmth, heat and despondency. Ex Nihilo's Kasamaan was metaphorical for his own dead soul that could feel nothing. The Kasamaan's walls beat strong and steady, with the rushing lava resembling the heart that Ex Nihilo would never want or have.

It was here that Ex Nihilo decided to stop and communicate with his minions. He closed his eyes and accessed the minds of each of his horsemen. First, he spoke to Manisilat, the destroyer of homes, of love, the bearer of unrest and doom. Manisilat answered his call with a screech of delight.

"Master, I am at your service, always."

"Manisilat," Ex Nihilo replied in his emotionless and chilly voice. Next, he called Mangkukulam, the only male agent. He was the fire that consumed the world, the prince of famine and deprivation.

"My lord," he purred. Lastly, Ex Nihilo reached into Manggagaway's mind. She was his second in command, his most trusted servant. She was the queen of sickness, the sovereign of pestilence and pollution. She accepted his invitation and remained silent, ever present and ever

CHAPTER 30

vigilant.

"Update me. Manisilat, you first," commanded Ex Nihilo.

"Yes, Master. I have infiltrated a continent across the sea. I've filled the humans' hearts with hatred and loathing; they are set to self-destruct. I felt the pull of anger, and I sensed the potential for annihilation. I've heard of their new weapons, capable of immense damage. I will ignite the flame on the kindling. I will lead them to an inevitable civil war. The chaos will be magnificent and horrifying." Manisilat laughed shrilly, clearly pleased with her work.

"What are these weapons you speak of?" asked Mangkukulam.

"The mortals call them nuclear bombs. They are capable of yielding ten tons of trinitrotoluene or TNT, a highly explosive material," Manisilat could not contain her mirth; she laughed loudly and triumphantly as she explained her findings to the others. "They are so powerful; a single bomb can annihilate cities. Anything near the blast would be immediately eradicated, and those close to the radius would experience great pain and lasting damage."

Ex Nihilo trembled with jubilation. He had underestimated humans, thinking them unpleasant and weak creatures, not worth his notice. But now they had become unwilling and unknowing pawns in their cosmic games. "I'm satisfied, Manisilat. Continue on your path." In the background, Manisilat's shrieks and chuckles could still be heard. "Mangkukulam," commanded Ex Nihilo.

"My lord," repeated Mangkukulam. "I am attacking the sources of life for these humans. They rely on their surroundings for existence, these places called forests and habitats. I am depleting them of such necessities. Without fauna, the temperature of the planet will begin to rise and rise until it matches my own. Then, I will be able to burn through anything and everything in my path. They depend on oxygen for their survival, and I will take it from them."

Ex Nihilo considered the slow game that Mangkukulam was

planning. "What say you, Manggagaway?"

"Master, I offer advice to my comrade. Attack them where they will hurt the most. If you plan on steadily depleting their resources, then swiftly take their largest supply and do it with deadly force. They will scramble to minimize their losses, and we will strike while they are disconcerted and divided."

"Good, Manggagaway. You understand, Mangkukulam?"

"Yes, my lord. I will make my way across the world to their most important resource. I will commence at dawn."

Ex Nihilo was satisfied. He could see the outstanding progress of his agents and knew that they would succeed. He did not need to ask Manggagaway about her advancements. Manggagaway was poisoning resources as she traveled the globe, already affecting more than one billion people with plagues, epidemics and sickness. She had targeted the most populated and unsanitary locations, wreaking more unseen havoc than the humans could possibly foresee. It would be too late when they finally realized their downfall. They would try to patch up their raging fires and floods with band-aids. Ex Nihilo laughed maniacally; his plan was working and there was nobody who could stop him... except...

"Have you encountered any difficulties?"

All three of his agents responded in the negative. Ex Nihilo considered their responses. The Greek woman was a problem. She was close on his trail. In his garden of destruction, she was a thorn challenging his deadly paradise. He turned to Hukluban and dismissed his agents, allowing them to resume their ruinous tasks.

"We must plan ahead. We must find her and put an end to her." *Her and her little human friend.* Ex Nihilo bristled with anger at the thought of them and their crusade against him. He was reserving a special place in his torture chambers especially for them. As he considered the next move, he noticed that Hukluban had raised her eyes in surprise to

CHAPTER 30

the ceiling. She sniffed the air and turned to Ex Nihilo, her expression expectant. Ex Nihilo dismissed her, and Hukluban departed the cavern. Ex Nihilo was unconcerned. Hukluban was his most deadly of agents, and allowing her free reign to pursue her prey gave her the ability to hone her skills, especially if her prey was foolish enough to wander so close to her lair. He glided away through the darkness, pondering and planning.

On the top of Mount Cagua, four lone hikers sighed with desperation as they finished their last drops of water. Filled with dread, one fell to his knees and pounded the ground. They had gotten lost by following a wrong trail, and for the past thirty-five hours, they had not been able to find their way. It was as if this part of the island was cursed; nothing was thriving. There were springs, and the water appeared clear and potable, but upon further inspection, it was highly poisonous. Hiding behind the facade of perfection, it seemed to be a beautiful oasis when in reality, it was just an illusion.

"I can't do this anymore," said one of the hikers. She dumped her pack on the ground and began to cry. She knew that crying would only lead to further dehydration, but she was so sick that no real tears flowed; her eyes were irritated and dry.

Another hiker dropped his pack and surveyed the mountain, holding on to hope, unwilling to accept defeat. His lips were chapped and cut, his arms were peeling, and his vision was blurry. But still he believed. He trusted he would find a solution and escape this nightmare.

He turned to the crater's edge and spotted a faraway figure. He wiped his eyes and squinted into the sunlight. *I see something,* he thought. He covered his head with his hands, shielding his eyes from the glare. *Yes! There's someone over there!*

"Hey!" he yelled with all his remaining strength. "Help! Help us!

Please!"

The figure he had spotted did not move, and for a second he feared it was just a rock. His heart dropped for a split second, but then the figure moved and turned in their direction. "It's a person! We're saved, we're saved!" he told his group.

The figure he saw was stooped and carried a staff. It was staring straight at the four wretched humans who were begging for life, for safety. The group realized with alarm that it was an old woman with wrinkled, weather-beaten skin. They lifted their arms in salute, waving desperately to catch her attention. Slowly, the figure raised her right arm, moving it ponderously over her head. The group watched in silence as horror spread through their bodies. Then, instantly their hearts gave out.

From far away Hukluban stared at her newest victims. She lowered her arm and turned away from the bodies that were sprawled on the ground, returning to Kasamaan and her cavern of pandemonium.

CHAPTER 31

May 7th

The Amazon Rainforest, the world's largest broadleaf tropical rainforest, covers most of the Amazon Basin of South America and extends into more than nine nations including Colombia, Peru and northwestern Brazil. The Basin encompasses more than seven million square kilometers, of which five and a half are completely covered by the rainforest. Wet tropical forests are the most species-rich biomes in the world, and as the largest in the Americas, the Amazonian Rainforest has an unparalleled biodiversity. One in ten known species lives in the Amazon, constituting the largest collection of living plants and animals species in the world.

Apart from housing two and a half million species of insects, tens of thousands of plants, and around one hundred thousand invertebrate species, the rainforest is also home to many crisscrossing rivers, including the Amazon River, the second longest in the world at four thousand miles in length – the equivalent distance from New York City to Rome.

Life in the Amazon is far from glamorous; the rainforest contains several predatory creatures including the black caiman, jaguar, cougar and the giant anaconda. Electric eels and piranhas hide below the surface of the murky-brown waters, and around the trees various species of poison dart frogs are ready to pounce at the earliest opportunity. Besides these killers, there are many dangers, invisible to the naked eye, that prowl about the forest. Numerous parasites and disease vectors, including Malaria, Yellow Fever, Dengue Fever, and the Rabies Virus that is spread by Vampire Bats, have permanent lodgings in the Amazon.

As the group searched for a place to camp deep within Brazilian territory, Leo adjusted his long-sleeved shirt and tried to cover as much skin as he could. They had been in the jungle for less than four hours, yet Leo was already desperately looking forward to his next shower. The above thirty degree weather combined with more than ninety-seven percent humidity transformed the jungle into a deadly sauna. Instead of removing layers, Leo kept adding clothes. The moment he heard a mosquito buzz around his ear, he decided to wear his thermal gloves. Throughout the trek he kept his ears covered with his hands. He was sweating so profusely that every minute or so he had to adjust his long curls that threatened to block his vision. When they finally stopped in a small clearing, Leo put down his pack and rifled through it, looking for another item he could wear.

"Want some help?" said Apollo. He sauntered over to Leo and opened his own pack. He took out a gray beanie and helped Leo place it on his head. Casually, Apollo cleaned Leo's dampened and foggy glasses. He gently brushed his curls out of the way and hid them beneath the beanie, then replaced his glasses. Apollo looked toward Horus and Athena whose backs were turned as they inspected the trees and the surrounding area in the clearing. Seeing that their attention was elsewhere, he winked at Leo before he strolled off to set up a perimeter.

Absent-mindedly, Leo adjusted his now freshly cleaned glasses and pretended to be absorbed inspecting a nearby tree. He was uncertain about how he felt about Apollo. He had a level of attraction toward him, but then again, who didn't? The man was a stunning magnet, electrifying those around him. On the other hand, this magnetism made Leo feel uncomfortable.

He was immensely gratified that no one in the group could infiltrate his fantasies, especially when they were out of his control. The dreams had commenced after their long overnight flight across the Pacific Ocean. Leo had sat down next to Apollo, with Athena and Horus deep in conversation in the row in front of them. Unlike his time with Ares on the train to Paris, Leo had felt completely at ease with the golden Apollo. They had discussed music and poetry, history and art; genres that were, unfortunately, not considered masculine in today's era.

The more he spoke with Apollo, the more he wished the world could become more open and respectful of all, regardless of culture, upbringing or sexual orientation. It was wild to think that only a few millennia ago, the concepts of masculinity and femininity were so different from today. There were pros and cons to each, and Apollo and Leo eagerly discussed them.

Leo remembered a paragraph from Yuval Noah Harari's book, *Homo Sapiens*. "In democratic Athens of the 5th century BC, an individual possessing a womb had no independent legal status and was forbidden to participate in popular assemblies. They could not benefit from a good education, nor engage in business or in philosophical discourse.

In direct contrast, in modern-day Athens, women can be elected to public office, make speeches, design jewelry, cars or software, they can have a public or private education, etc." Even though they are still quite underrepresented in politics and business, they are not as restricted as they were in times past.

Despite the fact that many modern Greeks consider being attracted to women only an integral part of being a man, Yuval has noted that, in fact, there were many ancient cultures who viewed homosexual relations as not only legitimate but even socially constructive. Ancient

Greece and Ancient Sparta were the most notable examples, including works such as the *Iliad* and the *Odyssey*. Leo's favorite example was that of Queen Olympias of Macedon, who was one of the most temperamental and forceful women of the ancient world. It was rumored that she had her own husband, King Philip, killed, an action that would surely shock today's society. But she did not object when her son, Alexander the Great, started a relationship with his childhood friend, Hephaestion. Leo shared with Apollo that his own mother had not had the same reaction as that of Queen Olympias. However, she still unconditionally loved and cared for Leo.

A sudden movement from the top of one of the branches in the clearing brought Leo back into the Brazilian Rainforest. He realized with a jolt that it was a serpent slithering down the branch. Its skin was bright green, and its eyes were yellow with a black slit in the middle, dividing the eye vertically. It coiled and uncoiled toward Leo, focusing its attention on him.

"Beautiful, aren't they?" commented Apollo from behind him. He strode past Leo and stretched out his arm to the snake that slithered onto his limb. "This is an Emerald Tree Boa." With a smile he added, "Non-venomous." The snake, almost five feet long, coiled itself around Apollo. It seemed to be attracted to his heat as it explored his chest and shoulders.

"Did you know that if a snake licks you, you could acquire second hearing and second sight?" Apollo stroked the boa and looked at Leo, whose expression was somewhere between nauseous and intrigued. Apollo laughed heartily. "My son, Asclepius, used to have snakes roaming around his dormitories and shrines where the sick and injured slept. He believed they had healing properties." Apollo ran his finger across the snake's body. "His rod is still used today, I saw it back in Paris."

"Did it have one snake or two?" asked Leo. Apollo cocked his head.

CHAPTER 31

"Well, if it had one snake then it was definitely the Rod of Asclepius, but if it had two snakes, then it is the Caduceus," Leo explained.

Apollo's eyes glinted. "No wonder my sister chose you." He placed his arm back on the tree, and the snake slithered toward the foliage. He made a move toward Leo, but Athena appeared beside him.

"Brother," she said, "would you be so kind as to gather kindling with Horus? We need plenty for the ambush." Apollo looked from Athena to Leo, giving him a side-eyed glance.

"As you wish." He strode off toward Horus, who was waiting for him in the middle of the clearing.

Athena sighed and peered at Leo. He felt she was x-raying him with those all-seeing eyes of hers. He hoped she could not imagine the emotions that were battling inside him. He thought she was going to scold him for standing around being unproductive, but instead she asked, "How are you?"

"Me? I'm fine. Thanks. Um, how are you?"

Athena smiled. "I'm well. Thank you." She continued studying him, and Leo could see she was choosing her next words carefully. "I hope this weather is not affecting you too much."

Leo looked down at his ridiculous attire and chuckled. "I'm surviving. Just trying not to get eaten alive by these mosquitos." Growing up in the UK meant that Leo was not accustomed to this type of humidity being mixed with the hot climate. His summers in Salerno were more like this Brazilian heat, yet in Italy he could enjoy an ice cream while on the beach, then take a dip in the clear blue water to refresh himself. It was not like this jungle, where he was in constant vigilance and avidly avoiding any pool or river.

"If you want to make some calls or have some time to yourself, feel free. I am almost done with the preparations." She squeezed his shoulder before walking off.

Leo nodded absentmindedly before reaching for his phone which was inside his travel pack. He sat down on the ground and stared at his screen for a long time before turning it on. After a pause, a single bar popped up in the right hand corner. Leo swallowed. He half-wished he would not have had any service abroad, especially this deep in the jungle. *I guess this is a sign.* He scrolled through his missed calls and saw his mom had tried to reach him a couple of hours before. He swallowed and started a text message to her: "Hey mom! I'm all good. Super busy with a project. Talk to you later."

After pressing "send," he continued to scroll through his unread messages until he finally dialed the number that had been on his mind for most of his journey here. *David.* He put the phone to his ear and exhaled, listening to the ringing on the other end. *Maybe he's busy and won't pick up.* Checking his watch, he noticed that it was nearly three o'clock. Even though they were separated by more than five thousand miles and an ocean, London was only three hours ahead of Brasilia. David's voice sounded on the other end of the call, and Leo caught his breath.

"I was starting to get worried. What's up, Leo?" asked David.

Leo managed to smile, but he still felt a bit uncomfortable. A lot had happened since he last saw David. There was so much to say, and so much to hide.

"Nothing much. I'm just hanging," he managed to finish awkwardly.

"No kidding. Why didn't you tell me you were going on vacation? I took over Dupont's class until the end of the term. I'm concerned about you. You've been awfully quiet and mysterious. I was beginning to think that whatever had occurred to Dupont had happened to you, as well."

The twig Leo was holding in his hand shattered as David's last comment hit close to home. He hadn't mentioned to David that Dr. Dupont had been murdered. How could he? He had made an unbreakable blood oath to Athena. The terrifying image of Ex Nihilo

CHAPTER 31

back at the British Museum re-surfaced in Leo's mind. Its ruthlessness and savagery sent shivers down Leo's spine. If Ex Nihilo had finished off Dupont without so much as a second thought, what would he do to him who was actively conspiring and planning his demise? Leo felt like throwing up.

"Hello? Are you there?" David called.

"Yeah, I'm here, sorry. I'm getting bad service."

"Ok." There was a strained silence as Leo clutched the phone to his ear while David breathed on the other end of the line.

"Are you still in London? Or did you go visit your family abroad?" David asked.

"Actually, I'm traveling with Alexandra." Leo was terrible at lying and hoped David would not hear the quaver in his voice. "She wanted to backpack through Europe. We've been, um, bonding lately."

"Oh, yeah. Your half-sister. That's nice to hear. Where have you visited?"

Leo took a moment to answer, then said, "Madrid. We went to Parque del Retiro and stayed there a couple days. We also went to Paris and visited the Opera Garnier. She's been showing me part of her world, and introducing me to her friends and family. It's been quite the experience."

"Well, that's exciting. I'm sure her world must be different from yours. Do you get along well?"

Leo looked at Athena who was organizing the campsite, preparing for the upcoming ambuscade. "Yeah, surprisingly so, we do. We have a lot in common. Our personalities complement each other." He was quiet for a moment while he compared David to Athena. They each had a lively mind and a healthy appetite for ideas. They were always searching for new solutions, believing that sheer willpower and intelligence could achieve even the most challenging of goals. Both of them were also extremely independent. Their characteristics were visionary yet decisive, pioneering yet private, and curious yet determined. Whereas Leo was guided by morality, David and Athena relied heavily on logic and reason… similar to Apollo.

Leo wiped his forehead and shook his head, clearing his mind and focusing back on his conversation with David. "I've been helping her with her job a little, it's really demanding and stressful. That's why I've been off the grid the last couple of days. I'm sorry, David. I should have called earlier or sent a message. Thank you for taking over the class."

"Not at all. I quite enjoyed the challenge. Some of the papers were very intriguing, although others were downright boring."

The conversation got lighter and David chatted excitedly about his summer plans and his upcoming new classes for the fall semester. The friendly banter made Leo feel more relaxed.

After half an hour, David returned the conversation to the last time they had seen each other in London. "You still owe me a coffee, Clarkson. The fact that you've escaped the UK doesn't mean you'll get to avoid that. I'm looking forward to it."

Leo felt a warmth pulse through his veins. "Me too." He was working up the courage to make it an official date. But before he could, David interjected, "You can invite your sister if you want. I want to hear all about your trip. What did you say her line of work was?"

Feeling deflated at the missed opportunity, Leo answered, "Oh. Um, she's…" He scanned his surroundings for an idea. "She studied Environmental Engineering. Recently, she's been researching the Amazon rainforest."

"Now that is interesting! You two do have a lot in common."

"Why's that?"

"Well, you very well know that the name *Amazon* is said to arise from a war Francisco Orellana fought with the local indigenous tribe, the Tapuyas. Custom decreed that women were expected to fight

CHAPTER 31

alongside men, and therefore Orellana derived the name from the Amazons of Greek Mythology." David paused before adding, "as described by Herodotus and Diodorus."

Leo laughed out loud. "You are such a nerd, David. But what does that have to do with me?"

"Correction, *we* are such nerds. Admit it, you loved my soliloquy. Anyway, you're completely obsessed with Greek mythology and, let's be honest, any mythology." David's chuckle could be heard through the phone, but Leo remained pensive. Was David more astute and observant than Leo realized? Was he getting close to the truth, or had Leo accidentally spilled some important information? He quickly checked his hand and flexed it, wondering if the invisible snakes would start eating him from the inside for betraying Athena's secrets.

"Leo? I lost you again."

Leo snapped back from his reverie. "I'm here. I'm just..." He stopped. He heard footsteps and turned to see that Horus and Apollo had rejoined their party. The three gods huddled close together and started an intense discussion.

"I have to run. I'll talk to you soon, okay?"

"Yeah, alright. Take care, and don't be a stranger."

"I won't. I promise to call again soon." Leo debated for a second then said, "David, thank you for being my friend. It really means a lot to me. And..." his words caught in his throat. He opened his mouth to finish his sentence, but the words wouldn't come out.

"I know. I'm thankful for you, too. And take care. I mean it. I want my free coffee." David's voice was warm and tender; it soothed Leo. He felt his eyes tearing up, and he hoped this would not be the last time he spoke to David. He kept the phone close to his ear, waiting for David to hang up, unwilling to do so himself. Finally, a few moments later, the call ended. Leo put his phone back in his pack. Then he stood up and joined the group in the middle of the clearing.

Athena's face was impassive, carved out of stone. Her eyes flashed the color of steel: dominant, relentless, unforgiving. Apollo opened and closed his fists, bracing for a fight. His whole body seemed to burn with anticipation, and his golden hair rustled in the wind. Horus' mouth was locked in a tight line. His dark eyes were all-seeing, focused and attentive. All three looked at Leo as he approached them.

"Get ready," said Horus. "They're coming."

CHAPTER 32

Athena spread out the maps on the ground in front of the group. One of the maps depicted the green zones of the South American Rainforest. Another one showed the various trails that crisscrossed the basin where they were currently located, and the last one was a satellite view of the recent deforestation of Southern Brazil and Bolivia. From her perspective, the most efficient way of starting a mega-fire would be to start in the south by the state of Mato Grosso, and follow the wind and streams upwards toward the northern states of Roraima and Pará. The combination of the wetlands and the savanna plains was perfect for the raging fire that her enemies were planning, and they would not expect any opposition. Athena and her squad were primed for the ambush.

Back in Egypt, Athena had figured out that the Australian wildfires had not been caused by a natural disaster. They had the rotten reek of a demonic presence. She realized that that level of chaos could only be the result of Ex Nihilo's savagery. She also knew that an ambush would be an unexpected trap that could allow them to at least ensnare Ex Nihilo, or even defeat him.

"Is everybody clear on his mission? We can't afford any mistakes," she stated.

The others nodded. Athena took a deep breath. "Horus, what do you see?"

Horus closed his eyes. When he opened them again, they had rolled back, and all that was visible was the white of his orbs. The miniscule movements of his eyes indicated that he was connected to his falcon, who, while soaring below the clouds, was transmitting a vision of their surroundings. "The fire has advanced about ten miles since our last reconnaissance. Its trajectory remains northwest."

"Apollo, light our pit. Let's draw them in." Her brother gave a thumbs-up, and within moments their campsite fire roared with inky smoke that rose through the trees. "Here, put these on." She handed out tactical earpieces she had purchased before this trip. "With these in our ears, we'll be able to communicate with each other."

Apollo tapped his earpiece and examined it from all angles. Horus held his in his hand and stared at Athena, as Leo adjusted his earpiece. Athena was already wearing hers, and she spoke in a slow, hushed voice, covering her mouth. "Leo, can you hear me clearly?"

The youth said, "I hear you. They're working." Apollo shrugged and put his in, while Horus cautiously did the same.

"Hello? Hello?" Horus said in a higher than normal voice.

Apollo covered his ears and said, "You don't have to be so loud. We can hear you just fine." Horus turned to Athena, awaiting her next command.

"It's crucial that once we engage them, we must not break ranks, no matter what happens." She stared into their eyes, searching for any protest.

Horus spoke up. "They will want to divide us; that's how they operate. If we stay together, they will not find a weak spot. This is critical."

"Are we ready?" Athena asked.

Apollo smiled. "Let's do it."

Leo cleared his throat. "Yes, we can do this." He sounded eager. *His heart rate must be quite high. I can sense his adrenaline*, Athena

CHAPTER 32

thought. She glanced at Apollo, and saw that his energy was palpable and contagious, although she and Horus remained immune. The latter solemnly bowed his head and spoke in an ancient dialect, the translation being, "May the gods be with us."

With that, the group scattered and advanced toward their positions. Horus wore his black shendyt, his upper body uncovered but for his golden regalia, and Athena had on her battle armor and full arsenal. She had given Leo her cape to wear, and Apollo had redressed him to make him appear less human and more god-like. Leo remained in the clearing, tightly holding on to the Khopesh that Horus had lent him. The Egyptian sickle-shaped sword resembled a battle ax except for its sharp, curved head. Apollo remained with him, explaining how to use the weapon both defensively and offensively. Like a sniper, hidden atop the trees with his bow and arrows, Apollo's position would be directly above Leo. Athena and Horus walked toward their station in companionable silence. Once they were far enough away from the campsite, however, Horus took off his ear piece and stared intently at Athena. Quietly, she did the same.

"Does he know?" Horus questioned.

Athena shook her head. "No."

Horus' eyes stared deeply into hers. "You're ruthless." Athena's gaze remained fixated on him. "That's why we might win." Without another word, Horus walked off.

When he disappeared from sight, Athena flexed her arms. Reaching for her talisman, she secured her spear and short sword before attaching her aegis to her arm. She stared at her helmet for a long time, peering at her distorted reflection in its bronze surface. She looked into her own eyes while the sounds of the rainforest surrounded her – water rushing by in a nearby stream, a nut crashing to the ground, tree leaves rustling in the soft breeze. She placed her helmet on her head, ready for battle.

On the plane ride across the Atlantic, she had devised and discarded more than a dozen tactics and maneuvers, rating their efficiency and odds of survival. There were only two plans in her mind that had higher than average possibility of success, and only one in which the odds were in their favor. She had tried to find other solutions and bypass this one plan, but she was unable to come up with another with such favorable probabilities. She had an intuition that if the group stuck to their precise strategies, they might all survive... *might*. She thought of all that had happened, everything that had been sacrificed, the losses that had created a void in her. And she knew... she just knew. She was willing to do anything and everything to triumph.

Athena reached her tactical position and waited. The only sounds were those of her surroundings. She looked skyward through the dense vegetation and breathed deeply, trying to smell smoke. When she couldn't sense anything, she put her earpiece back in. Apollo was just now leaving Leo's side and climbing into the branches of a tree. She could hear his grunting as he scaled the trunk.

"Do you see anything, Horus?" she asked quietly.

Horus was silent for a moment. Athena wondered if he had misplaced his earpiece until she heard his voice through the device. "Three miles away, the trajectory has changed by a fraction." Athena held her breath and anticipated the confirmation. "It's heading northeast now, directly toward us."

Determination spread across Athena's face as she began warming up her muscles. *The trap is set; time to charge.* She adjusted her grip on the spear. She sheathed her short sword for the charge, the better to hold on to her main weapon. She half-knelt on the forest floor. *Father, give me strength. Look after us,* she prayed. She felt the soft ground beneath her fingertips, the motion reminding her to stay present, to neither look ahead or glance back. Her mind cleared; her objective was plain, visible, unfettered and confirmed. With one last exhale, she

CHAPTER 32

broke into a run.

Racing in a southwestern direction, she flew through the trees, her footsteps so quick and light, they mimicked the movements of her half-brother, Hermes. She was lithe and agile, jumping over rocks and fallen logs, flying by the animals that inhabited the Amazon. After three-quarters of a mile, she started to smell smoke. In another half-mile, she saw rising flames. Frightened animals darted toward her, sprinting away from the wall of fire that was coming closer, growing taller by the second, consuming the lush vegetation. She blinked to keep the smoke out of her eyes. She needed to time this assault well; there was no room for error. Finally, she felt a presence nearby; a demonic presence. *Got you.*

She slid to a stop, crouching and keeping an eye out for sudden movement. Like a panther stalking its prey, her footsteps were silent; the twigs beneath her feet did not even crack.

At last, she saw it, running wildly through the forest. Its skin glowed orange, but it seemed papery, scale-like. It was laughing, enjoying the chaos and destruction that it was causing. It shot a bright flame directly into a massive Sumaumeira tree that was almost 150 feet tall. The tree burst into a fire-storm, consuming itself from within. The evildoer chortled and continued on its path of ruin. Athena watched as the tree snapped in half and crashed onto the forest floor.

Athena seethed and baring her teeth, she growled. With a flick of its wrist, this pestiferous villain had destroyed the more than five-hundred-year-old tree. There was no remorse in its orange eyes; no compassion for the life that the ecosystem had lost; no understanding of what it had done. The recklessness of the action and the lack of empathy made Athena's blood boil.

The creature stopped laughing and turned to where Athena had been standing only seconds before. After an agonizing pause, it pivoted toward the smoke that rose from the group's fire pit. Intently, it analyzed it, then charged toward the fumes, its cackle of malice drifting behind him.

Hiding behind one of the remaining Sumaumeiran trees, Athena exhaled. *That was close.* She had sensed the wretch's intent just moments before it happened. She gave silent thanks to her intuition; she would need all of her senses on high alert tonight. Moving out of the debris, she followed the creature's footsteps, staying a quarter-mile away. She could still hear it chanting and screaming. Part of her wanted to block out the sound, but she needed to analyze as much of the creature as possible. If she could decipher the dialect, she would be able to identify which culture it belonged to.

For the next four minutes, the only things she heard were its sing-song and the noises from her earpiece. When they were close enough to the campsite, she put her hand over her mouth and said, "Less than a minute. So far it's just one creature with firepower."

Athena's mind raced. She fought hard to keep her head clear and present; she needed to remain focused. Anger, frustration and anxiety had no place on the battlefield. These emotions would only hinder her. She needed to remain loose and free. This seemed contradictory but was essential for triumph. When she was a hundred meters away from their clearing, she began to run at full speed, closing the distance between herself and the brute. *Fifty, forty.* She breathed deeply as her heart pumped in her ears. *Thirty, twenty.* She moved her spear to her right side and felt its wooden grip. *Ten, nine, eight, seven, six, five, four, three, two, one!*

Their clearing was a wide semicircle with the fire pit on the far side of the field. A lone figure stood in front of the rising flames. He was tall and slender, his hair was untamed, his face was streaked with mud and blood. He wore black boots with black pants and a navy sweater. A red cape was draped over his shoulders, and he held an Egyptian Khopesh at the ready. Athena did a double-take before she realized

CHAPTER 32

that this was Leo, and not a random stranger. Apollo had done his job to perfection; it was time to do hers.

The orange creature hissed at Leo as it rubbed its hands together, building up a great ball of fire. Right before it shot it, a massive gust of wind bellowed from behind Leo. The wind knocked the creature to the forest floor, and it hit the ground with a bone-cracking thud. *Horus.* Athena had been cautious about allowing her group to use magic, but now that they were all in the clearing, there was no holding back. Now was the time to use all of their power and strike the first head off the hydra's shoulders.

Lightning fast, the creature popped up and laughed. It pointed a scaly finger in Leo's direction. "You can't stop me. Step aside and surrender!"

Leo remained rooted to the spot. Horus moved into the clearing and stood next to Leo. The creature's laugh faded, but its eyes were hungry and assessing. "So be it."

Before it moved, six arrows shot down from the sky. The being flinched and tried to protect itself with its arms, but the arrows hit their marks. The beast roared in fury, losing itself completely to madness, as its body transformed into pure fire from which emanated a scorching heat. With a boom like a thunderclap, it sent flames across the clearing, attacking ferociously. Horus raised his arms, his muscles clenching with overwhelming strength as he swiped down, sending powerful wind in the creature's direction. It fell backwards, landing in a crouching position and snarling.

Athena saw her chance and pounced. The wretch's skin resembled scales, bringing to mind an Amazonian caiman. Although ferocious, the caiman was not an alpha predator, it had an enemy: the jaguar. Like the jaguars that inhabited the territory, she moved in for the kill.

As the creature dodged to avoid Apollo's arrows, Athena rose and hurled her lethal spear. At the whooshing sound, it instinctively turned, but it was too late; the spear pierced its shoulder. The throw had been so forceful that the spear continued flying until it hit the tree behind.

Trapped, the creature bellowed trying to pry itself free. Each time its skin touched the spear, its hands burned. Confused, the creature stopped fighting and looked in horror at its hands. Just as she had with Freya's vegvisir, Athena had coated her weapons with the blood of Ex Nihilo. It was a sure way to fight fire with fire. The creature would not be able to free itself without excruciating, even lethal pain. The poison would soon start consuming it from within. Its eyes blazed red and it hung its head in distress, screeching in a desperate plea. Its skin was no longer on fire; it was reverting to its scaly orange glow with puncture wounds oozing a lime-green paste.

Athena unsheathed her short sword and charged the creature. She raised the sword and prepared to bring it down across its neck, severing its head from its body. The red and orange glow from the inferno surrounded Athena, while the lush vegetation encircled the dying creature. Its eyes were full of incredulity and panic, while hers were filled with revenge and bloodlust.

A flash of electricity shot down in front of Athena, meters away from the speared beast. Blasted backwards, she landed on her knees in the middle of the clearing. She stood up, the hair on the back of her neck rising. She was staring straight into the face of the being she most despised. Ex Nihilo had come out to play.

CHAPTER 33

The ground around Ex Nihilo sizzled with electricity, and the smoke from the blazing Amazon surrounded the group like a veil, transforming the clearing into a death-dealing showdown. Ex Nihilo glared at Athena with a look of pure poison that would shatter anyone's resolve. But not hers. She wasn't alone this time; she wouldn't face him with stacked odds. She stood her ground on her own terms, not on his.

Ex Nihilo made a move to advance, then hesitated. Athena sensed a presence, and knew that Horus had come to stand beside her. A sudden movement on her other side signaled that Apollo had joined them. Leo took up the rear as he lifted the Khopesh. They assembled, forming a wall that would not crumble. The only sound that could be heard was the grunting of the speared creature next to Ex Nihilo. It wrestled, trying vainly to free itself, all the more widening its shoulder injury, which was turning black. Its veins were visibly pulsating with the befouled liquid that had entered its system.

Ex Nihilo spared one glance at his companion, and then turned toward the group. His gaze was reserved specifically for Athena, and she knew that she was his true enemy. No words were needed to reveal the hatred that passed between them. Athena had humiliated and emasculated Ex Nihilo, denying him his true form and degrading him to a mere adulteration of his former self. Ex Nihilo was behind the conspiracy to destroy that which she held dear. He was the mastermind behind so many assaults on this frail and beautiful planet; behind the abduction of so many of her kind. But even worse, Ex Nihilo had taken something far more precious from Athena. It was not her soul, nor her dignity, but her heart. She would not rest until she brought him down; until she took everything he valued and crushed it beneath her feet. Her mission was to find his plans and destroy them.

"Stay together," she whispered. The group tensed in anticipation. "Three, two, one."

All three deities attacked at once. Apollo shot his arrows rapid-fire, one after the other. Horus raised his hands to the sky and brought them down, channeling all his energy into the wind around them. The ground shook with the newly formed hurricane that encompassed them. The trees trembled violently, and the debris around them rose dangerously, swirling faster and faster until it resembled a massive tornado.

Ex Nihilo remained still and unyielding. He raised his slimy hands and formed a great ball of electricity, his hands twisting and curving to increase the voltage. Athena stared incredulously as the current gained energy by the second. The rays transformed into solid purple streaks, capable of delivering more than fifty thousand volts of electricity. But it was not the voltage that could paralyze or even kill them, it was the high quantity of current that surrounded them. Hearing the sizzle, Athena knew that Ex Nihilo was about to strike with devastation unlike anything she had ever faced.

"Look out!" She screamed, turning rapidly and extending her arms to push the others down. Her aegis crashed onto Apollo's chest, and he collided painfully with Leo. Horus was too far away to be completely shielded, and he was struck by one of the electric shots that had managed to avoid Athena's short sword. He screamed in agony as his skin was seared. When he opened his eyes, his white orbs were

CHAPTER 33

crisscrossed with purple lines. The current flowed through Horus, making its way to his wind-induced tornado which exploded in a fury of wreckage.

Still holding her sword, Athena covered her head with her arm. With the other, she protected Apollo. Thankfully, Leo had used her cape as a shield, protecting most of his body except for his hands, which were covered in red gashes. The green rainforest which had previously surrounded them had been transformed into a gray, dust-strewn hell with fiery red conflagration. Athena struggled to take in her surroundings. Horus was kneeling beside her, his head hung low and his breathing shallow. His hands were clenched over his heart as sweat poured down his face and puddled on the ground. She reached over and pressed lightly on his skin. She closed her eyes as her amethyst glowed brightly, trying to heal him. Horus coughed and shivered, but he remained in his crouched and defenseless position, his breathing coming in painful gasps.

Athena stared in horror and disgust at Ex Nihilo, who seemed completely unharmed and untroubled. She did not want to test his energy, as she was unsure how long it would take him after such a discharge to recharge and attack again. But as she was studying him, she saw an opening where she could attack. The temptation was so great that she crouched low and analyzed her options. *There! I can make it. I can end this!*

But as she prepared to strike, she heard an almost imperceptible noise and squinted to see through the smoke and drifting ashes. At first glance there seemed to be nothing hiding in the destroyed vegetation, but Athena knew she was not imagining a barely visible silhouette hiding behind the foliage. With a gasp, she locked eyes with the being. Who or what it was she could not tell, but clearly those orbs were black pools of madness and mayhem.

Time seemed to stop momentarily as her senses went on high

alert. A falcon's shriek sounded from atop the Amazon's umbrella. Another movement, this time from her right, alerted her to yet another presence in the clearing, hiding behind the destruction. A piercing scream erupted behind her. It was Leo. He was flat on the ground. His eyes were closed, and his arms covered his head and ears as he sought protection. At the same time, she felt a third movement nearby. Apollo had risen to his feet and was darting toward Ex Nihilo, readying his bow and arrows, emanating light and power.

"Noooo!" Athena screamed, twisting in his direction. He must have seen the same opening she had; the same opportunity for a swift and efficient strike. But he had not seen the two creatures lurking in the shadows, awaiting their unsuspecting prey.

"Apollo! Stop! Nooo!" she yelled, but to no avail. Apollo was already letting loose three arrows at Ex Nihilo. She dashed forward, raising her sword as she tried to catch up to him. But just as his arrows flew, the two creatures who had been hiding pounced. The one on the left shrieked as it rushed at Apollo, catching his attention and causing Apollo to jerk to a stop and, quick as lighting, adjust his weapons in its direction.

But he had not accounted for the second creature, who rushed at him at the exact same time as its companion. It was slighter than its counterpart, yet they shared the same ferocity. Just as Apollo let his first arrow fly, the second figure reached him, jumping onto his back and burying its small, white fingers in his golden hair, causing Apollo to miss his target. The first creature crashed into his midsection, colliding against him so that he fell backwards in a heap. Athena expected them to hit the ground with a crash, but instead all three disappeared in a storm of energy, the flash blinding Athena.

She ran past the spot where her brother had been and stopped abruptly, wildly searching. She swiped at the gray cloud that signaled their departure, waving her weapons in despair. A laugh caught her

CHAPTER 33

attention and she turned rapidly, raising her aegis. Snarling, Ex Nihilo bared his blackened teeth and rested a slimy, peeling hand next to the speared orange wretch who was sputtering black ooze. He raised his hand and snapped his fingers. A flash of energy shot down from the sky and evaporated both Ex Nihilo and his minion, leaving behind Athena's impaled spear, a hellish inferno, and her shattered plans.

CHAPTER 34

Leo's blinding pain disappeared as soon as Ex Nihilo vanished, although an excruciating headache remained. He clutched at his head in anguish, waiting for the pain to dissipate. Slowly, he began to relax his fingers and straighten his back. Finally, he raised himself onto his hands and knees. He took ten steadying breaths before opening his eyes. He felt as if he had been punched in the stomach. His chest hurt but the steady throbbing of his head was beginning to ease. He looked around, feeling disoriented, until he remembered that he had put his glasses in his pocket.

Sitting down on the ground, he reached into his pants and took out his battered glasses. The left side of the frame was cracked, while the right side was slightly bent. He winced as he put them on, realizing that his palms were raw. He heard a sob and peered into the distance, trying to make out the figure that was standing by a burning tree. He took a sharp breath and realized that his chest pain was due to the smoke filling his lungs. He tried to stand and promptly fell down. He began to crawl toward the figure, his palms dripping blood.

"Athena," he managed to croak, but she didn't hear him. Horus was kneeling on the ground, his eyes closed and his hands clutching at his chest. Leo cracked his jaw, trying to alleviate the throbbing in his ears. He felt as if his eardrums had ruptured in the explosion.

Athena remained in the same position as before, utterly immobile.

CHAPTER 34

He groaned and attempted to speak again. "Athena," he wheezed, a little louder this time.

Her head snapped up, but she did not turn around. Her shoulders were rising and falling, and her arm hung by her side, still holding her sword. After several agonizing minutes, she screamed so loudly that Leo's heart caught in his throat. The scream went on and on, until she raised her sword to the sky and brought it down in front of her, impaling the ground. She dropped to her knees, holding the top of the sword with both hands, her aegis discarded. Her head was resting against the hilt of the sword, her sobs barely audible.

Leo raised an arm in her direction, trying to comfort her even though she was far away. As he did so, he felt a drop of water fall on his palm. More drops fell from the sky. The precipitation turned into a steady rain, and Leo lay face up on the ground with Athena's cape around him. He stared at the clouds gathering overhead, the water caressing his wounds. The fire began to subside as the rain erased the scorching heat and cured the wounds that had been inflicted on the Amazon.

Leo closed his eyes and allowed the water to encompass him, feeling as if this sweet release from the smoke and the torment could hold him forever in a state of blessed contentment. He heard Horus groan. The god raised himself to his feet, his energy restored by the rain. He walked over to Leo and extended his hand. Leo took it, and Horus helped him hobble toward the kneeling Athena. On their slow walk across the clearing, Horus' falcon flew down through the rain, landing on his shoulder.

When they were a couple of meters from her, Leo looked around and started to ask, "Where is...?" Sadly shaking his head, Horus stopped him. He helped Leo down, settling him next to Athena. The falcon flapped its majestic wings to shake off the water. Horus rested his arm on Athena's shoulder, and she flinched at his touch.

"It's my fault," Athena whispered. "I should have warned him. I should have done more." She was still wearing her helmet, but Leo could see that her eyes were red and filled with tears. They seemed distant, as if reliving her earlier anguish. "I saw them. I should have warned him. I shouldn't have brought him here. I made a mistake. I was wrong." Her breath caught in her throat. "I knew it was dangerous, and I still led us here. I led him here. I've lost him." Athena hung her head, her tears spilling onto the already soaked earth.

Horus remained quiet, his expression despondent. Leo felt so much pity for Athena. He had never had any siblings, but he could imagine the sorrow she must be feeling over Apollo's demise. Siblings are a part of you, so often allies in this strenuous yet wonderful life.

Leo looked at Horus, who was standing with his head hanging, his hands resting on his belly. The left side of his once-smooth chest was now crisscrossed with angry scars. The pattern resembled the tree of life, the scars protruding and growing from his battered heart. The veins on his neck were inflamed, rising up to his earlobe like streams across a river. His falcon, sitting atop his shoulder and resting its head against his neck, crooned and caressed him.

"Are you alright?" Leo asked.

Horus raised his hand, silencing him. The gesture was not unkind, as he bowed his head in acknowledgement of Leo's concern. Leo understood that Horus was respecting Athena's grief, allowing her to mourn.

Athena continued sobbing, mumbling to herself, "It's my fault. It's happened again. I can't do this. Not again. Please, not again." Around them, the rain crashed down with even more force.

Leo removed his glasses and put them in his pocket. He didn't need them in this downpour. He began to clean the mud from his face. Every stroke of his hand reminded him of how gentle Apollo had been when he dressed him; his bright smile and his golden eyes twinkling with delight. But now, Apollo was gone, dragged away to a hellish underworld. Leo's sodden hair hung across his face, the water pooling down his nose and onto the now drenched ground. He felt the soft fabric of Athena's majestic cape and unfastened it from around his neck. His navy sweater had burns and tears across his ribs, but the reddish gold cloak was completely undamaged for it was impervious to the fire that had raged across the now saturated battlefield.

Struggling, Leo stood and approached the kneeling Athena. Tenderly he attached her cape to her armor. She was so lost to the world that she didn't seem to notice his presence. He sidled behind her, clutching his side. One of his ribs was broken; any movement sent intense pain shooting through him. He examined his ripped sweater and saw that his skin was purple from a massive abrasion. He hoped the injury would not cause him to bleed internally.

Horus was still standing vigil, deep in thought. Raindrops cascaded down his body and pooled around his sandals. He seemed to be carefully assessing his next move, his eyes studying Athena. Ultimately, he stepped forward toward her, his soles splashing.

Gently he held Athena's elbows and raised her to a standing position. She did not object to his touch, but her breath came in jagged gasps as if all the air in the world could not satiate her need for oxygen. Horus removed her helmet and placed it on top of her skewered sword. He held her face in his large hands, his fingers lightly brushing away her tears. Her hair had been dry, but now the rain skidded down her face, soaking her dark, golden hair and giving it a metallic sheen. Horus raised her face so that their eyes could meet. They looked at each other, wordlessly communicating their sorrow. So many words unsaid, so many feelings unexpressed.

Finally, Horus embraced her, hugging her tightly to his chest. Her face rested in the crook of his neck, while her cheek pressed against the unharmed side of his chest. She sobbed, her tears mingling with the falling rain. Horus rested his jaw against her head, stroking her long hair. The falcon on his shoulder crooned and moved closer. Leo wiped tears from his eyes.

They stayed there for a while, Horus stroking Athena's hair while she wept. Leo wondered if Athena had ever been consoled in this way. She was the type who never shed tears; the type who would never show weakness. He knew that tears were a natural biological process. Releasing them was a healthy way to heal the body.

Athena shouldered so much responsibility. She was always expected to come up with a solution, to never falter. He understood from all his Greek texts that Athena was believed to fear nothing, but their recent encounters made him realize the opposite. She cared so deeply about those she cherished that she was afraid of failing them, afraid of not protecting them. Leo sensed that Apollo's abduction was not the only thing she was mourning. She had probably been carrying so much on her shoulders that this was the weight that tipped the scale.

Leo groaned, his chest felt tighter and his breathing became difficult. Painfully, he stretched out his arm and slowly bending his knees, he sat on the water-drenched soil. The movement caught Horus' attention; he scrutinized Leo with penetrating eyes.

Horus untangled himself from Athena and held her shoulders. "It's not your fault," he said firmly. Athena looked utterly bereft. "It's not your fault," he repeated. Athena's chest heaved as she struggled to breathe.

"It's not your fault," Horus said a third time. He cupped her face and his eyes bore into hers. "You couldn't have stopped it. There was nothing you could do." Athena opened her mouth to protest, but no words came out.

"Listen to me," Horus said more forcibly but not unkindly. "You didn't do this. It is not your fault. We planned the best we could, and we were defeated." Athena flinched at the last word as if she had been

CHAPTER 34

stabbed. "We did everything we could. He's not gone. We will get him back." Athena's eyes filled with tears, and Horus gave her shoulders a small shake. "Listen to me! He's not gone. He was taken, just like I was; like so many before me. They have him, but we will get him back." Leo was surprised by the sudden passion in Horus' voice.

Horus continued. "We will not stop until we succeed. This is a long marathon, a long journey. One lost battle will not define us. It is just an illusion, a worthless perception. A mirage we will shatter." Entranced by Horus' words, Athena stopped crying. She no longer looked completely devastated.

The rain was slowing to a steady drizzle. "You're not all-seeing, Athena. None of us are. You couldn't have foreseen this. We planned as well as we could, and these were the cards that we were dealt. Now we must make our own fate and write our own destiny. You know as well as I that loss is part of this game; every day, we win and we lose. You're lying to yourself if you don't admit your failures and faults. If you've never faced a setback, then you're ill prepared for this war. You have to stand up and admit your losses. I dare you to look me in the eye and say you've never lost."

Athena's usual fire was beginning to shine in her eyes. Horus continued. "We get back up and fight. It's what we do. We lose battles, but we win the war." He squeezed her shoulder. "Are you with me?"

Athena reached for her weapons. She seized the short sword and sheathed it. Then, she put her hand on Horus' chest and said in a determined voice, "I am with you." As she spoke, the mist vanished, and the sun began to shine on them once again.

"Good," replied Horus. "Now fix the boy. He's dying."

Athena turned to Leo, who was on the ground, clutching his abdomen. She strode forward and touched his cheek. "I'm sorry." Leo waved his hand in dismissal, groaning as he smiled weakly, but her words stuck in his brain. They seemed deeper than he had expected, as if she was apologizing not only for his physical harm, but for something far more consequential. Athena closed her eyes and healed him, her violet amethyst shining brightly.

Leo felt his chest expand as his broken and bruised ribs re-attached themselves. The burns on his hands disappeared, and his skin became smooth once more. Leo took his glasses from his pocket and held them out to Athena. She smiled as she placed them on his face, instantly restored. She moved toward Horus and touched the crisscrossing scars on his chest and neck.

Horus placed his hand over hers and gave her a sad smile. "There are some things that can't be fixed. The shot was well-aimed, and hit me right in the heart. I'm lucky to be alive." Athena traced the lines across his body, the scarlet scars contrasting vividly with the chocolate brown of his skin.

"Let's get out of here before it gets dark," Athena said as she moved to retrieve her spear. She stopped, analyzing the tree that had imprisoned the orange wretch. Horus and Leo approached and followed her gaze across the tree's base. The orange creature had not made it out intact; his left arm and part of his shoulder were still attached to Athena's spear that was lying on the ground. Athena bent down and touched the green and black liquid that was seeping from the appendage. She lifted her fingers to her nose, sniffing the secretion. Raising her hand to the sun, she examined its effect on the fluid.

"I have good news," Athena said with a victorious smile. "I know who they are." She looked at Horus and Leo, her smile widening. "And I know exactly how to find them."

CHAPTER 35

May 8th

Apollo heard his own breathing before he realized he was finally awake. He opened his eyes slowly; his head was pounding. Gingerly, he massaged his scalp. His fingers came away with some dried blood. *How long have I been knocked out?* The last thing he remembered was staring into someone's yellow, piercing eyes. After that he felt a sensation as if the eyes had been bottomless pits, a never-ending cycle of falling but never hitting the ground.

He tried standing, and heard the rattle of the chains that bound his hands and feet. He tugged at them and knew he would be able to easily break the fetters. Iron, steel, titanium; these materials were like paper to a god like him. He looked around at his surroundings; the light was dim, but he could make out the grim outline of the cave that imprisoned him. It was dark and dry, and the walls were maroon, as if they had been burnt numerous times. The cave was small, no larger than five square meters. There was a steel gate at the end, making it resemble a cage.

Apollo stood, moving his body gracefully in order to avoid interlocking his chains. Once he was upright, they were almost taut. He stepped forward and heaved. The irons crunched and groaned as he forced his powerful body to fight against them. Instead of being attached to the cave walls by hooks, they appeared to have been inserted straight through the wall, affixed to an invisible force. Apollo heaved again, and the shackles protested. When he readied himself for a third try, his head seemed to go blank and he stopped, feeling a sharp pain in the back of his neck.

"I would avoid that if I were you," said a low, loathsome voice.

"Who's there? Show yourself," Apollo commanded.

"I doubt you'd like that. Last time I came, you passed out... again."

Apollo struggled against the chains, but they held fast. "What do you want? Who are you?" he demanded.

A cackle came from the darkness. Deep and menacing, it made the hairs of Apollo's arms stand up. He stopped struggling against the shackles. Never having felt this sensation before, it was foreign to him, but somehow there was a familiarity. *What's happening?* The oddest feeling coursed through his body, and his head began to spin.

"If we keep this up, maybe you'll remember. It might take some days, maybe weeks, but we have all the time in the world".

Apollo was sure he had heard this voice before, but at the same time, he felt as if this was their first meeting. He felt like throwing up; his stomach churned with acid.

"Be careful. You don't want to burn through these chains. Last time you tried, you didn't stop screaming for days." The voice sounded amused, taunting him.

Apollo's temper flared. *I'll prove you wrong. I am majestic. I'm made of fire. I am a god.* He heaved with all his force against the chains. They moved slightly, but they did not crack. He struggled and roared, willing himself to push one more time, but to no avail. The chains barely even moved.

Then came maniacal laughter, a laugh so harrowing that Apollo could not control himself any longer; he summoned the rest of his resources and pushed against the restraints. He became so consumed

CHAPTER 35

with escape that for a moment he was aflame, fire burning through him. Still, the chains did not move. They were indestructible, unyielding. Apollo's head was ablaze, and he could not handle the temperature any longer. He collapsed on the ground, his muscles aching, his eyes burning.

A movement made Apollo look up. He immediately wished he hadn't. Ex Nihilo glided in through the gate. His figure brought shivers down Apollo's spine, and suddenly he realized why he felt so weak, so afraid.

"Ah. You remember? Good. I was getting tired of our little game. I must congratulate you," said Ex Nihilo. His voice displayed no emotion, but the sound made Apollo want to hurl. He looked at his shaking hands and realized that his wrists were burnt and bleeding, and that many of the scars weren't fresh. He noticed with despair that his scars were overlapping and crisscrossing his skin; some were light and fading with age, while others were dark and fresh, and some had recently ripped open.

"You won't get away with this. You can't keep hurting me," Apollo spat.

"Hurting you? Me? No. No, no, no. I'm not really hurting you." Ex Nihilo pointed at the rusted and soiled chains around his neck. "You see, these shackles are bound to you, but the one that is injuring you... is yourself."

Apollo glared at Ex Nihilo and held his gaze. "I don't believe you," he snarled.

"I don't care if you believe me or not. Why would I, when you don't even believe in yourself?" As Ex Nihilo spoke these words, a weight dropped in Apollo's stomach. He immediately felt detached from himself. *This can't be happening. It's not real.* He stared incredulously at the fetters that held him. They were made of steel, an easily breakable material for him.

Ex Nihilo laughed, filling the room with an icy chill. "Why should I fight you when you are fighting yourself?"

Apollo's body felt heavy; he felt completely powerless. His breathing was erratic, and he was having a hard time keeping his thoughts clear. His mind started gnawing at him from within, filling him with anxiety and dread. He closed his eyes and tried to control his spiraling emotions. Ex Nihilo crouched in front of him and placed his scaly hand right below his neck. He couldn't touch Apollo, but he could zap him with electricity.

Ex Nihilo forced Apollo to raise his head and stare into his cold eyes. Apollo obliged, trembling uncontrollably from head to foot. His eyes were puffy with anguish, and when he looked into Ex Nihilo's face, he couldn't see clearly. The only image he saw was his own golden irises staring back at him. He would have preferred to stare into a void, into a black pool of emptiness. What he saw in his eyes terrified him and shook him to his core.

Apollo could see his self-belief draining away. *How? Why?* But he knew how. He knew that he had been fighting this battle far longer than he could remember. He was spiraling slowly down into a hole that he himself had built. His strength was the first to ebb; the concrete walls with which he had protected himself were turning into sand; he was drowning in despair.

Apollo did not realize it, but Ex Nihilo was gone. He had left him to fight a war alone, a war with himself, a war he had lost over and over again. His memories came rushing back, and he remembered every time he had woken up and tried to break the chains. He had searched for freedom from the restraints, for an escape. He had fought and screamed, bled and struggled. But now, as he lay broken and shattered on the floor, he realized that his true enemy was himself.

CHAPTER 36

May 10th

From above the clouds, the island of Luzon was a dark green and brown mass in the midst of a sea of blue. As the little plane descended closer and closer to the island, the vivid colors of the Philippine Sea brightly contrasted with the beige beaches and silvery rock formations. Light blue transformed into emerald green, and the sea's crystal clear transparency created a reflection of the greenery around it.

If these were the colors Athena could distinguish while she was wearing polarized sunglasses, she wondered what they would be like up close. The stunning colors reminded her of the Mediterranean Sea back in her native Greece. The steep rocks, the caves and the thousands of islands brimming with sea life, were some of the similarities between the Philippines and her homeland. She found it curious how alike these two places were, and yet one was her haven, while the other was the residence of her most hated nemesis.

Athena tore her gaze from the window and inspected the Twin Otter, their skydiving plane. It was a fast, strong aircraft, capable of carrying more than fifteen people on two long benches. The twin engine turbine jump plane, with the wing high and out of the way, had a wide door which would allow for an easy exit. She had chosen this method of transportation because it was the easiest way to get close to the massive Cagua Volcano that was located in the Cagayan Valley. In addition, it would help them save energy and time by avoiding long hikes in the scorching heat.

Athena looked out of the window once more, and saw that they were close to their target. She secured her pack and attached the parachute rig to the outside of her gear. Since she was wearing her talisman, she didn't need a chute for this descent. But since they were pretending to be tourists, she figured it would be best to keep up with appearances until the plane was out of sight of Luzon.

She turned to Horus and raised an eyebrow. He gave her a silent thumbs-up and began to prepare for the jump. The plane was far too noisy for conversation. She stood up and grabbed three of the human helmets from the cabin, passing them back to Leo and Horus. Then, she approached the pilot and handed him four bills totaling a thousand Philippine pesos. She signaled that this would be their stopping point and he winked as he accepted the cash. Money most certainly did not buy happiness, but it had many benefits. A thousand Philippine pesos was equivalent to around twenty United States dollars or seventeen Euros. What could get you a meal in Europe or the US could buy you three solo skydiving tickets and one discreet pilot's silence.

Athena headed back to the wing and nodded to the group. They had agreed that she would be the last to jump, after Horus and Leo, who would jump together. As Leo was neither an immortal nor an experienced skydiver, Athena and Horus had agreed that one of them must jump with him in order to ensure that he would survive the 16,000-foot dive. Horus had volunteered to take him, as one of his powers was wind manipulation. If something went awry, he could propel himself and Leo onto land, or teleport them far enough away to avoid any attacks.

Athena would have preferred that they avoid magic so as to not

CHAPTER 36

draw attention to themselves, but she reasoned the skydive would be as safe as any plan. How could Ex Nihilo recognize them from that distance? With their get-up and costumes, they looked exactly like modern-day adventure junkies, not deities. Athena decided that she would no longer call him Ex Nihilo; she would now address him by his true, evil name... Sitan.

After their last battle in Brazil, Athena had noticed three distinct clues about their enemies' possible backgrounds and identities. A quick two-day visit to the National Library in Rio de Janeiro revealed exactly what they were looking for. The massive library was the largest in Latin America, with more than nine million books.

Leo's eyes had been as wide as saucers when she described what they needed to uncover. Athena wanted to validate her suspicions by obtaining information. She used inductive reasoning instead of deductive reasoning to develop her plans. She preferred creating a theory instead of testing one that already existed. She was a thoughtful tactician, and she waited until both Horus and Leo had confirmed her own conjectures before meticulously carving out a plan.

All three of them had acquired the same information through different paths. Leo discovered an old Portuguese book about the findings and travels of Ferdinand Magellan, a sixteenth-century explorer who was best known for having planned and led the 1519 Spanish Expedition across the Pacific Ocean and to the East Indies. Although he was killed during the voyage, he nevertheless had discovered an inter-oceanic passage that to this day bears his name. His crew completed the first recorded European circumnavigation of the world when they returned to Spain in 1522. His body was never recovered after the Battle of Mactan in the present-day Philippines, and Leo found various indications to suggest that something nefarious had occurred on the islands during that period of time. The European perspective that Leo investigated was full of conquest and territorial expansion.

On the other hand, Horus delved into the surviving native narratives which depicted the fight for the preservation of indigenous culture, the struggle to maintain Philippine identity, and the divide and conquer tactics that led to colonial rule.

A combination of their research provided them with a clear and distinct picture of their enemies. It unveiled an ancient Filipino mythology in which an evil leader was followed unscrupulously by his four destructive henchmen. The first agent was a creature called Manggagaway. She was able to transform herself at will into a human, and she was primarily associated with diseases and pollution. The second was called Manisilat, and she thrived on social destruction and chaos. The third was Mangkukulam. He had the elemental ability of Pyrokinesis which allowed him to create, control and manipulate fire, flame and heat. The group had realized that this was the speared wretch who had set the Amazon ablaze.

The fourth and only one they had not yet faced was Hukluban. She was a shapeshifter, capable of changing herself into any form she desired. She was certainly the most deadly, skilled at killing mortals by simply raising her hand. Many times Athena wondered why she had not come to the Amazon showdown. Furthermore, her name had given Horus headaches; his unconscious had been sickened at the sound. Athena mentally noted that, if they ran into Hukluban, she must be the first to be taken down. Athena would personally target her... if her master was absent.

The leader and overlord of these four horsemen of pandemonium was none other than a dark Filipino god, Sitan. He was the guardian and ruler of the Kasamaan. According to the Portuguese narrative, Sitan was a parallel to the monotheistic Satan, with the Kasamaan being the Tagalog version of Hell. He was feared and reviled as a malicious and destructive entity, the embodiment of evil. The last

CHAPTER 36

surviving scriptures of native Filipinos limited his power to tempting, ruining and corrupting mankind, but Athena knew better. She knew he was near-omnipotent and that, besides his underlings, he had powerful allies.

Athena would not rest until she unmasked her foes and defeated them, and she was grateful she had Horus by her side. Their challenge was not easy. They were facing the lords of famine, pollution, pestilence, war and death, and they needed all the help they could get. There was only one place where they might find allies and take back the stolen talismans… and that was exactly where Apollo was being held prisoner. *Hell on Earth.*

Athena turned back to the group in the Twin Otter. Horus was adjusting Leo's suit. The youth looked excited yet tense; his hair was pushed back into his helmet, and he was fixing his glasses so that they would not fall during the jump. "Are you sure I'm not too tall? Will you be able to see alright?" Leo yelled as Horus fastened the belts around his chest.

"I'm fine," Horus replied, giving Athena a side glance. Athena smiled. Sometimes Leo forgot he was dealing with immortals. He had proved himself useful more often than not, and he had been extremely helpful during their exploits in Brazil. Athena cocked her head. He had been a little too obliging. In the last couple of days, she caught him staring at her and then quickly looking away, the blush creeping up his neck making him appear guilty. He was hiding something, or maybe he felt accountable for what had happened in Brazil. Athena shook her head and cleared her mind. *Focus on the present. Stay in the moment. Breathe and believe.*

Horus gave her the thumbs-up, and instructed Leo to sit down. When he did, Athena opened the side door. The wind whirled around them and Leo's head snapped back. Athena could see his mouth moving, but she couldn't hear what he was saying. Horus nodded to

Athena, propelled himself forward, and jumped off the plane. Athena moved to take their vacated place in front of the door. She sat down on the edge of the plane and exhaled. She moved her legs out in front of her, but the wind immediately swung them to the right more forcibly than she could have expected. She gripped the inside of the door and readjusted herself, bringing her legs back into the plane. From a distance she could see that Horus and Leo were making a beeline for the top of Mount Cagua. She closed her eyes and exhaled again. *Let's go.*

With a huge surge of adrenaline, she scooted to the back of the plane and charged the open door, throwing her arms out in front of her in a swan dive. She moved through the air like a bullet, propelling effortlessly through the clouds. This was the most wonderful and thrilling sensation in the world. The wind brushed her skin and her hair flowed against the current as she moved her arms back and held them tight to her sides, making herself more aerodynamic. She did not want to land away from her target, and with her new streamlined pose, she was beginning to catch up to Horus and Leo.

Athena debated not opening her parachute; the intoxicating feeling of the skydive was pulsing through her system. She felt invincible. She felt free. Even though she was technically falling and losing altitude by the second, she felt as if she were soaring through the air. Propelling at 120 miles per hour had never felt more liberating. There was only one other sensation that could parallel or even compare to this one…

That thought reminded her that she needed to open her parachute. She was only a couple of hundred feet off from her deployment point, and she easily glided toward her target, landing in an open stance with her boots leaving deep imprints on the ground.

As soon as she touched land, she immediately changed into her battle uniform. She knew that there would be no people around the base of Cagua, and she had no time for modesty. She changed rapidly,

CHAPTER 36

donning her armor and full weaponry before making her way toward Horus and Leo. They landed fifty feet away from their target zone, and when Athena reached them, Leo was leaping and running in circles with abandon.

"Did you see that? Wow! That was amazing. I can't believe it!" Leo exclaimed. Filled with adrenaline, he began pacing up and down. Athena put a hand on his shoulder and forced him to control his excitement. "Yes, you're right. We should focus! We are on a mission!"

Horus' face was expressionless, but Athena could tell he was enjoying Leo's display of emotions: happiness, euphoria, jubilation, and ecstasy – sensations that go through one's brain during a jump. It was an overload seeing the world from an unconventional perspective, noticing Earth in the most vivid of pictures, smelling the crisp, clean, fresh air, hearing the sound of the loud rush of the wind, the peaceful quiet that follows the chaos.

"Come on," said Athena as she exchanged a knowing glance with Horus, and they began their hike up the volcano's crater. Athena led the way, checking her vegvisir to make sure they were on route. After a few minutes up the slope, Leo caught up with her.

"Hey," he awkwardly commented. Athena merely raised one eyebrow in acknowledgement. Leo cleared his throat. "You know I trust you, right? Like, I'm in. Fully in. Whatever you need, I'm there." Athena clenched her jaw and waited for Leo to continue. He seemed to be debating how to phrase his next words. "You might have said something. Back in Brazil, I mean." Athena remained silent until Leo added, "In your sleep."

Her head shot up. "It wasn't weird or wild. It was just..." Leo trailed off. He ran a hand through his curls and sighed. Athena maintained a neutral expression. Had she accidentally let it slip that she had used the boy as bait; that she had chosen to put him in an extremely vulnerable position to enhance their odds of survival? And worst of all, had she let slip that she didn't feel any remorse, that she just felt disappointed that her plan had gone awry?

Leo gulped and peered at Horus who was following in their wake, but far enough away that he was out of earshot. Leo leaned toward Athena and whispered, "You kept saying over and over, 'You'll find me.' The first night, I thought you were having nightmares, but the second..." Athena forced her expression to remain calm and undisturbed. She prided herself in her self-control, but clearly her mind was in disarray.

For the last two days, she had felt an increase in flutterings, and she was not sure if it was eagerness or if it was anxiety. She and Horus agreed that they had to infiltrate Sitan's dominion, that they had to break into the Kasamaan; most importantly, so they could rescue Apollo, and in addition, they could rescue the other deities that were trapped in the hell-hole. They reasoned that the liberated deities would join them in an attack against the darkness.

But Athena had another motive that she was keeping secret. She was dying to see Freya again, to see her smile and to hug her tight and never let go, to tell her how much she loved her and how much of a void her absence caused. She absolutely adored her brother and would do anything to free him, but her love for Freya was... she couldn't find the right word. It wasn't as if her heart had been taken over by Freya. It was more like her heart had expanded, as if it had grown so much that there was more space for her to love. However, Freya occupied her daily thoughts. She was ever-present in her dreams. She was the burning candle in the obscurity of her nightmares. She was the light in her world.

Athena had always considered herself a strong, independent woman. And she still was; there was no refuting that. But Freya had added something to her otherwise lukewarm existence. She had cut through her defenses like steel through paper, through fortifications Athena

CHAPTER 36

had never known she had. She hadn't looked for love. She had been so content in her own world, but when Freya crashed into it, there was no going back.

Athena forced her tone to be casual, but when she spoke, her voice was barely higher than a whisper. "I want to get my partner back." She did not say anything else. She could not. She had swallowed her feelings for so long that she would not allow them to resurface; not here in this foreign jungle, not on this trek into enemy territory. Not here without *her*.

Leo nodded thoughtfully. He was silent for a long time. When they finally reached the top of the crater and stopped before the jungle's end, he reached out and patted her armored shoulder, giving her a reassuring smile. Horus observed the exchange from afar. Then his eyes rolled upward so that only the whites were visible as he visualized the field from his falcon's perspective.

"It's deserted," he commented as he walked toward them, his eyes cloudy and still far away. Athena nodded and shrugged off her pack. She retrieved an old, battered book she had borrowed from John Rylands Library in Manchester. She would return it once her task was completed. And if she didn't succeed… Well, there would be no need to return it. The written word would be the last thing humans would concern themselves with if her squad failed.

Holding her vegvisir outstretched in her hand, she knelt on the jungle floor and opened the book to the page of mystical incantations. Athena had learned a lot from Freya's seidr, a form of Norse magic. She handed Horus a small tube in which a lime-green and blackened liquid pooled. It was Mangkukulam's blood, and they were going to use it to break into the Kasamaan.

She wasn't as expert at sorcery as Freya was, but she had been able to ensnare Sitan once, so she was confident she could do so again. She read the Runes on the page and then closed her eyes, chanting in Old

Norse. She heard Horus open the tube of liquid and could feel the pull of the spell working. Mangkukulam's blood formed itself into a three-dimensional hand. Still holding the vegvisir in her palm, she turned it sideways and the floating hand mimicked her movement. She stood up slowly, her movements controlled and concise. The vegvisir turned slightly, and she followed the arrows in the direction they pointed. She stepped over a smoking hot spring with sky blue and shamrock green moss.

The vegvisir began spinning wildly, signaling the entryway. Athena stretched out her palm while Mangkukulam's floating hand did the same. Without touching the ground, she forced his buoyant hand to press against the rock. As soon as it did so, the hand vanished and a stone vault opened in front of the group. Athena exhaled as the outside layer of the Kasamaan was unlocked before them.

She turned to the group and nodded solemnly to each. Then she looked up to the sky and closed her eyes for a second as she felt the sun's rays on her skin. She prayed it would not be the last time she saw daylight as she started the descent into the elusive cave of chaos.

CHAPTER 37

Athena descended into a dark and rocky crevice that was completely black; all the light had been extinguished. She felt around the walls, and counted twelve wooden tapers. She heard footsteps directly behind her and recognized Leo's shallow breathing.

"Do you have your phone with you?" Athena whispered. For a second she thought he hadn't heard her, but then came the sound of a zipper. Approaching him, she touched his chest then traced his outline down to his outstretched hand. She pressed the phone's button, and a low light came on. Using the phone for guidance, she circled back across the crevice, and noticed a gaping hole in the farthest corner of the inner cave.

It was large and murky, but she could see light at the bottom of the pit. Taking her vegvisir out from under her armor, she closed her eyes and imagined Apollo. She pictured his dazzling smile and his bright, golden hair that matched his radiant eyes. The vegvisir's arrows swirled in the darkness and stopped, pointing down into the abyss.

There was no going back now. Athena walked over to where she sensed Horus and Leo stood, bumping into Horus, who had been shadowing her. The sound of her armor colliding against his skin drew a gasp from Leo. Athena tensed, but it seemed that they had infiltrated the first level undetected.

Holding Leo's hand, she guided him to the entrance of the pit. She felt a gust of wind and knew that Horus had summoned his falcon. Although his eyesight was eight times better than Athena's, the falcon's vision was not adept in the dark. Athena wished she could summon an owl, but she surmised that the mythological falcon would be superior.

The bird flew down into the pit in an effortless dive. Horus placed his hand on Athena's shoulder as he explored the cave through his bird. "There's light at the end of the chasm. It's around a thirty-meter drop. I'll use the wind to decelerate us," he said.

Athena nodded, and then she remembered that he couldn't see her. "We'll jump together. Hold my hand."

"Wait." Horus moved to her other side and spoke to Leo. "When we land, press down on your nose with your hand like so." He motioned in the dark. "Breathe out to help equalize your ears. Use gentle controlled pressure."

"Ok," whispered Leo. "Like scuba diving."

"Scuba diving?" Horus asked Athena. He took Leo's hand in his, while holding Athena's with the other.

Athena shook her head. "It's a human activity."

Horus counted, "One. Two. Three."

The three jumped into the pit and plummeted down. The chasm was transformed from complete darkness into glowing bright and dark red lines. Since Horus had used his powers to manipulate the air resistance, they did not land abruptly, or in Leo's case, fatally.

Athena handed Leo his phone and took out her spear, holding it in front of her before stepping forward to explore the cavernous entryway. The walls seemed to be filled with lava, yet instead of being warmed, Athena felt an icy chill. Physically, she felt intense warmth, yet mentally she experienced a frigid despondency.

"Stay close," she commanded the others. They moved forward to

CHAPTER 37

explore the Kasamaan, their tension building. After a while, Horus stopped walking and his eyes rolled back. Athena and Leo stood frozen, waiting for his instructions.

"It appears to be deserted. I can't see or hear anything," he announced.

Athena doubted that Sitan was orchestrating a premeditated ambush, as their arrival in the Kasamaan was unpredictable. This was the opposite of a Trojan horse. They were fully armored and dangerous, clearly wolves in wolves clothing, walking directly into the jaws of their enemy. That was the brilliance of the plan... or so she thought.

Guided by the vegvisir and the falcon, they continued to explore. They approached a set of warped, splintered stairs that led them deeper into the recesses of the cave. As they progressed further, the lava coursed within the walls, growing ever stronger.

As they descended, the only sounds that could be heard were Leo's footsteps. They reached an extensive, dimly-lit, rocky alley. Suddenly, Horus stopped, and turned to face one of the many gates lining the alley. Some were made of steel, others of iron, stone and wood. Horus' eyes were glued to one on his left, the one made of stone. Athena raised her spear and approached the tiny grotto. It was less than five square meters with barely enough space to stand upright. She tapped the walls with her spear. Claw marks gashed the stone, frenzied and feral. Leo followed her into the grotto, squeezing himself in while craning his neck.

"This place gives me the creeps. It feels horrible," he commented as he looked around at the walls with aversion. Athena agreed. The sensation of being stuck in a constricted space with distress and pain as your only companions was the true evil of this prison. It made her stomach churn. She turned to exit, and saw that Horus was still frozen in place. Unable to tear his gaze away, he was staring numbly into the alcove.

Athena approached him and touched his chest gently. "Horus?"

He seemed to snap out of his dream, exhaling shakily. "This is where I was held," he said in a cold, dead voice. He raised his hand and caressed his neck. His agonized expression revealed that he was reliving that time of incarceration.

"You're free now. It's going to be alright," Athena began to say, as she tried to imitate the soothing tones he had used with her back in the Amazon. But when she opened her mouth to speak again, she heard a loud sob from one of the other grottos. They turned their heads in the direction of the sound. *Apollo.*

Horus, Leo and Athena tiptoed forward, trying to make their footsteps inaudible while waiting for another sound to point them further along. They paused before another sob steered them to the left side of the alley, to a steel-gated alcove near the back. Athena inhaled. A feeling of determination spread through her body. She was about to free her brother from this heinous place, from this... She stopped.

Horus and Leo did not notice her hang back as they continued. She inhaled again. *That can't be right.* So far every grotto had been empty, and the only sounds in the alley were their breathing and the sobbing. Athena pivoted to the cavern next to her. The door was made of wood, and its hinges were rusty with age. She pushed it open. As soon as she entered the alcove, a familiar scent wafted around her like a veil. Lavender and jasmine. *Freya.*

Athena lowered her spear and inspected the prison where her lover must have been locked up. She touched the red gashes of lava on the wall, but instead of a sensation of fire, a chill spread through her body. When she closed her eyes, she could smell the sweet scent of her dear friend, her darling ally, her beloved. Her eyes filled with tears as she clenched her fists, her wooden spear crunching under the pressure.

A wave of madness overpowered her. She was about to lose control and completely destroy the cave, when an inscription on the wall caught her attention. She squatted low to read the engraving. It was roughly carved with a red, black liquid outlining the words.

> **When death**
> **takes my hand**
> **I will hold you with the other**
> **and promise to find you**
> **in every lifetime**

Athena dropped to the floor of the cave, her knees scraping against the rocky ground, her cloak cascading. She lifted a trembling hand and caressed the words on the stone wall, her tears pooling beneath her helmet. Her spear lay forgotten by her side as she traced the unevenness of the engraved words with her fingers.

Sweet memories flowed through her mind. She remembered Freya sitting next to her on a train, reading Rupi Kaur's poem from "The Sun and Her Flowers." She had looked up from the pages and smiled at Athena, her grin spreading bewitchingly to her eyes. The memory brought fresh waves of fondness, anguish, respect, grief, admiration and love.

Had she been too late? Was this the place she was meant to have found long ago? *You'll find me.* What was there to find now? Freya was long gone from this prison. Her scent was fading; her last remains were the words on the wall. Athena punched the stone. Then, laying her head against the heated enclosure, she sobbed hysterically. *I'm sorry. I'm sorry. I promised I would find you, but I was too late. I'm sorry, Freya. I'm so sorry.* Athena took off her helmet and rested her forehead against the engraved words, her tears washing away some of the dried liquid.

Suddenly, she realized that the poem was engraved with blood,

Freya's blood. That was why she had been able to distinguish the smell. It was a reminder of her worst nightmare.

Athena drew in a shaky breath and wiped the tears from her eyes. She read the inscription again. *You'll find me.* Her broken mind grappled with possibilities. Maybe she wasn't meant to find Freya. Maybe Freya was meant to find her. "You'll find me," she whispered.

"Athena?" Leo had dashed into the tiny alcove and was staring at her. He noticed the poem on the wall, his eyes popping with sudden understanding. He turned to speak to her but stopped as he caught sight of her tear-streaked cheeks and the dried blood on her face. Athena hardened her expression and, standing shakily, repositioned her helmet and grabbed her spear. She kept her eyes locked on Leo's, afraid that if she averted them, she would shatter emotionally.

"There's something you should see," Leo said, his voice grave as he exited the cramped grotto. Athena turned to see Freya's last words. Kissing her hand, she caressed the stone.

"I promise to find you in every lifetime," she vowed. She turned and followed Leo.

CHAPTER 38

O*h, shit.*
Athena gaped at the maps and spikes on the wall. They were full of markings and notes. The entries ranged from population tabs, to pollution levels, to highly vulnerable natural areas, to possible strikes for a nuclear holocaust. Athena could not believe her eyes. Even the theoretical radioactive fallout of a worldwide mass detonation had been calculated.

This was even worse than she had imagined. Sitan's fight was no longer with deities; he was planning to bring utter destruction to the world. Had that been his aim all along? To incapacitate as many supernatural beings as he could, before moving on to even more nefarious plans? Athena saw that the numbers and lettering varied, which meant that more than one had planned and plotted on this board.

"Where's Horus?" Athena asked Leo.

"He's with Apollo. He instructed me to show you this. His falcon spotted the doorway and alerted him." Leo was pale, the blood drained from his face. "Athena, you don't think this is possible? I mean, this can't happen."

Athena surveyed the board again and frowned. She wouldn't lie to him. This was not the time for false faith. They needed to face the truth, and accept the challenge. "Some of this is already happening.

Sitan and his crew might be trying to make it worse, but some of these things," she waved at the board, "have been occurring for years." Her eyes roamed the details on a map: habitat loss, deforestation, unsustainable human practices, global warming, water scarcity.

Another map had numbers and statistics methodically arranged on its border. There were areas in the oceans where "Dead Zones" were written in bold letters, next to a reminder to keep adding boat fuel, pesticides, sewage and plastic waste to propagate the pollution. This was repeated on land, following major rivers and lakes. A third map depicted human growth and population. Fifteen cities were encircled, including Tokyo, New Delhi, Shanghai, Moscow, Mexico City, Cairo and Karachi. Some countries were completely underlined with bright, neon ink, including Argentina, Poland, Serbia, The United States, and Turkey. The words "Divide and Conquer" were written on the page.

The board made sense now. Sitan was going after the world's weak points. He was looking to crack that which was already splintering. His agents must be in charge of the different areas: social, political, geological and geographical.

Athena approached the map on the left, the one with neat handwriting. Two blue pins dotted India's Yamuna and Ganges rivers. This was the work of Manggagaway, Sitan's agent of pollution and pestilence, which was organized, calculated and tactical.

Athena moved to the next map, the one dealing with social issues. The handwriting was wild and reckless, but the meaning did not escape Athena. "Divide and Conquer" was Manisilat's motto: destroy, split, fractionate and let the humans exterminate themselves. They just needed a push, and mistrust would dismantle their society.

The geographical map was clearly Mangkukulam's. His brazen destruction was what had first alerted Athena to their devilry. There were smudges across the fraying paper. The west side of the USA, and most of eastern Australia, was smeared and scorched, as if his hand had

CHAPTER 38

clawed at his past misdeeds. Athena wondered how Mangkukulam was faring. He had suffered a grave injury; the poisoned spear tip was ironic, since it was his own master's munition.

She progressed to the last map, which only had two symbols. It had thirteen Xs strategically placed around the globe, and sixteen Os in seemingly random locations, one in London and another in Manchester, England. She saw one near the Swiss Alps, another in Tahiti, a third in Montana, a fourth in Banff in the Canadian Rockies, and a fifth in Brazil. She double-checked the last one. *Brazil!*

Tearing her gaze from the maps, Athena looked at Leo. "Is your camera working? If so, take a picture of every detail."

Leo tapped his jacket pocket and said, "Already did. I have videos and photos of this entire place." Athena nodded. Her eyes were blazing with anticipation, a shred of her old optimism having returned.

The huge metallic door swung open and Horus burst in, half-carrying, half-dragging Apollo. His hair was dirty and unkempt. His clothes were soiled and filthy. He had cuts and bruises all along his wrists, neck and ankles. Athena dashed forward to help Horus. She took hold of Apollo's shoulder and raised him. It was no easy task; he was almost entirely limp. She touched his face and gasped. His wounds were not healing, no matter how much she attempted to restore him. "What have they done to you?" Athena asked as she brushed his hair out of his eyes.

Apollo glanced up at his sister, his golden eyes completely dull. His usual dazzling aura was absent, replaced by a somber, detached demeanor. Athena stared at the purple and dark red contusions on his neck. The injury appeared to have been caused by being chained and strangled.

Horus thrust a roughly carved wooden box at Leo. The motion made him almost drop Apollo, and as soon as Leo took the box, Horus bent low and swept Apollo into his arms. If Apollo's eyes hadn't been open, Athena could have sworn he was unconscious. She continued brushing his hair back, counting his injuries.

Leo placed the chest on the ground and opened it. "Oh, my gods!" Athena could see the treasures inside the wooden box. She kissed Apollo on the forehead before kneeling down next to Leo and grabbing one of the beautifully carved metal pieces. It was a talisman. She rummaged through the chest, her eyes wide as she realized what they beheld. Leo was holding a resplendent amber necklace, turning it this way and that as he analyzed it.

Athena stared numbly at the necklace. It was Brisingamen, Freya's torc. She took out her vegvisir and placed it next to the necklace. The runes and coloring were similar, the bronze shimmering in the dim glow of the cave. Leo and Athena exchanged knowing glances. She squeezed his hand, uniting the necklace and vegvisir.

At that moment, Horus' eyes rolled and he shuddered. Athena snapped to attention, raising her spear. Horus' eyes refocused. "Someone's here. We need to leave." He gathered Apollo in his arms. "Now."

Athena and Leo put the talismans back into the chest. Leo stood and hugged the wooden box, unwilling to let such a discovery out of his sight. Athena dashed toward the door and held it open as the others exited the main cave. They moved quietly to the uneven stairs and up to the higher level, following a route to the chasm that led out into the Philippine sun. They were only fifty feet away from the exit when they turned one of the corners and came face to face with a wrinkled old crone. She was standing alone in the principal opening, her gnarled hands clutching a cane.

"Leo, close your eyes! Don't look at her!" Athena ordered, realizing that this seemingly harmless creature was Hukluban, the shapeshifter. Her appearance was just an illusion; she was extremely savage and lethal. "Get them out," Athena said to Horus. Her tone invited no

CHAPTER 38

dispute. Her eyes remained focused on Hukluban as she weighed the hag's every move. "Horus, do it. You can't help me and protect them both. Get the talismans out of here. I'll meet you outside." Horus struggled as he tried to carry Apollo and guide a sightless Leo toward the chasm. Athena knew that in order to fully defeat Sitan, they needed to regain control of the talismans. They needed to rob Sitan of his dark advantages and level the playing field. She would face a thousand enemies in order to get back that which had been taken from her.

From the other side of the stony crypt, Hukluban's head twisted in Horus' direction. The creature raised her cane and sent a rock flying in their direction. Athena sprinted to deflect the blow with her aegis. The stone shattered and pebbles rained down harmlessly around her. Athena raised her spear to draw Hukluban's attention away from the others. She remained close enough to protect them, but far enough away that they would not be the main target.

Hukluban twisted her decaying head to the side. An ear-splitting groan thundered across the cave as her bones cracked and then reformed themselves. Her figure expanded until she almost reached the top of the cave. Her hands, now transformed into massive paws with huge claws, dropped ponderously to the ground, shaking the foundation of the Kasamaan. Hukluban had become a terrifying, gigantic beast with razor-sharp teeth. Drooling as she growled, her acidic saliva hit the ground and cracked the surface.

Athena charged, pivoted and jumped, protecting herself with her shield. She held it high above her face as she slashed and struck at Hukluban's new form. Athena knew she had to strike first; there was no time to be defensive, not when she needed to buy time for the others to escape. She slammed into Hukluban's limbs, cutting tendons, to prevent Hukluban from flattening her with her enormous paws. The creature roared and spit acid at her, spraying it across the vault. Athena knelt and waited for the secretion to spill around her, her aegis protecting her from its effects, but as she waited, Hukluban turned her rage on the others.

"Nooo!" Athena yelled. She used her shield to smash one of Hukluban's paws, shattering her bones. Hukluban lifted her head in distress as she missed the group by mere feet. The acid hit the cave walls and began to seep into the rock, forming cracks as it was absorbed.

Raising her spear high, Athena continued her attack, but Hukluban retaliated with a forceful smack. Athena crashed into the vault's floor, her armor scraping the hard ground. Immediately, she rotated, turning to see where her spear had landed, then she reached for her short sword. It had fastened itself to the far wall behind Hukluban's head.

Athena dashed forward, sliding and dodging out of Hukluban's grasp. She ran at full speed toward her spear. Hukluban's massive head followed her every move. The beast opened her mouth to snap, but Athena had reached her spear. She swiftly unhooked it from the wall, bringing it down in a lethal arch against Hukluban's face. She struck one of the monster's eyes, and cut into her mouth. Hukluban boomed in agony as Athena repositioned herself for a new assault.

As she assessed where else to strike, Hukluban's shape shifted once more; this time her whole body disappeared. Athena searched for her, keeping her spear high while her shield covered her side. But at that moment, she felt a violent punch that knocked the wind out of her. She turned to face whatever had struck her, and received another punch, this time to her head, making her lose her balance. She lunged, barely holding herself upright. She refocused and scanned the cave, but saw nothing.

Another blow, this time to her hands made her almost drop the spear. She twisted upwards and spun the spear around her body in a

CHAPTER 38

circle. She thought hard as she defended herself from the next strike. She closed her eyes in order to heighten her other senses. She heard a movement from behind her. She counted her turns and stopped suddenly where she sensed the enemy was.

Athena bounded forward and struck with her spear. She felt the tip collide against a solid form, but then it was wrenched away. Athena sprang with her arms outstretched. Her fingers closed around skin, and she squeezed tightly. Athena kept thrusting, forcing whatever creature she was strangling against a wall. She would know where she was the moment they struck the cave's stones. Sure enough, her knuckles smacked against the wall, and the creature shuddered.

Athena continued to press and squeeze with ferocity, the emotions of the day surging through her body, pumping her with adrenaline. She opened her eyes to glimpse Hukluban's new form. The darkness made it hard to decipher what form the creature had chosen, but it resembled a transparent ghoul. Her teeth were inverted and protruded, and her hands, which were clutching Athena's forearms, were swollen and red. Her dark eyes were starting to roll as her appearance was solidifying. Hukluban was losing control of her senses.

She kicked at Athena, but the goddess took the blows, forcing herself to stay strong and unmoving. Hukluban opened her mouth and shrieked, sending high-pitched waves across the cave. The walls shook and the structure of the vault became vulnerable.

Athena remained immobile as rocks fell around her. Her knuckles were bleeding from forcing them against the stone, but she did not care; she was consumed with this task. Hukluban realized her intent, and raised her ghoulish legs to Athena's chest and pushed with all her remaining strength. Athena staggered backwards, rocks crashing down around her. She reached for her short sword and unsheathed it, then lunged forward.

But Hukluban was no longer there. In her stead was a goddess, and her appearance was wild. She was wearing a mixture of simple chain mail and animal skins. Her hair was almost white, pulled back in braids, and she wore an iron half-crown. *Freya?*

Athena lowered her sword as her eyes focused on the image of the Norse goddess. Freya smiled and opened her arms wide, approaching Athena for an embrace. Athena felt tears fall down her cheeks as she strode forward to close the distance between them, her eyes were full of hope, tenderness and love.

"Athena," Freya began, but her words cut off. She looked down at her abdomen and stared in disbelief at the sword that impaled her. Her eyebrows furrowed as her icy blue eyes met Athena's. Savagely, Athena retrieved her sword, the blood rushing out of the gash on Freya's stomach. If she hadn't been wearing chain mail around her chest, Athena would have stabbed her in the heart. She watched as Freya fell down to her knees, staring incredulously at her fatal wound. Athena had aimed well, striking at the abdominal aorta. The ruse was up: Hukluban would bleed to death.

Just as Athena had surmised, the fake-Freya's eyes became cloudy. Her skin went from soft and youthful to wrinkled and withered. Athena, her eyes burning with hatred, lifted her sword to cut off Hukluban's head. As she started the motion, Hukluban shrieked once more and transformed herself into hundreds of bats. They bled profusely as they flew frantically around the cave, splattering the place with hot liquid. They crashed against the cracks on the stone, further fracturing the structure.

Athena's eyes widened in alarm. She charged over to where Horus, Apollo and Leo were exiting. Horus was carrying both, propelling himself upwards toward the sky. The ground around Athena started to violently splinter and disintegrate, the cave collapsing in on itself. Athena bolted toward the chasm, frantically trying to reach the exit.

CHAPTER 38

Horus' falcon swept down around her as it tried to help. The falling rocks were now the size of boulders. Athena knew there was only one recourse left. She tore her armband from her arm, and threw it at Horus' falcon. As she did so, the stone she had been standing on fragmented, and she fell backwards into the abyss. The falcon flew down, and catching her talisman with its claws, accelerated upwards and away from the collapsing Kasamaan.

Athena saw the bird safely disappear before she plummeted down head-first. Then she was falling, falling, falling.

CHAPTER 39

Leo opened his eyes against the blazing sun. His head was spinning, and his throat burned as he vomited. He collapsed on the sand and allowed the waves to wash over him, cleaning his face and soothing his aching head.

Horus knelt next to him. He wiped his brow with his hand, and then scooped up salt water. He cleaned Leo's shoulder, and repeatedly splashed water on his face. Leo raised himself onto his hands and knees. He cupped some water and splashed his mouth to wash away the smell of vomit. He felt relief, even though the salt was burning his tongue. Sitting heavily on the sand, he let the water wash against his legs. He covered his head to shield it from the sun while he watched the turquoise water crash against the white sand. "Where are we?" he asked Horus.

Horus continued cleaning his wounds while he replied, "El Nido, in Palawan."

Leo looked around, seeing tall rocks jutting out from the vegetation. His heart missed a beat as he remembered the phone in his jacket pocket. He crawled away from the water to sit cross-legged by Apollo and the wooden chest. As he took out his phone and touched the screen, the device came to life. Thank the gods, his phone was intact. It held so many clues; every detail in his last pictures contained crucial information.

CHAPTER 39

A drop of blood hit the screen. Leo raised his hand to his forehead, and felt a gaping wound on the top of his head. The water had cleaned some of the blood, but now that he was on dry land, the wound was pulsating. His sticky hair was plastered to his face. He wondered where Athena was, and if she could help him.

Apart from the three of them, the small beach was deserted. The gray-black rocks were studded with green and yellow wildflowers. Reaching up to the sky, the broad palm trees were imposing. The only sounds on the island were the waves crashing against the rocks, and the swinging of the palm trees in the breeze. There was no sign of the goddess.

"Where is Athena?" Leo asked as Horus continued to bathe himself in the water and brush the sand and soot from his hair. Horus either chose to ignore Leo, or was taking his time to respond. Horus continued to scrub vigorously before making his way to Leo. He kneeled in front of him, assessing his head injury. Then, he stood up and strode toward Leo's backpack, which lay a few feet away. He opened it and retrieved one of the first aid kits. Horus dampened a towel with alcohol and cleaned Leo's cut, then sutured the gash with a needle and thread. Leo considered Horus' unspoken words and his actions. *Where was Athena?*

The last thing Leo had seen was the scorched and darkened walls of the caves. He had kept his eyes shut, for fear Hukluban would kill him. *Who prevailed?* Leo could not imagine Athena's defeat, but he had heard the screeches and felt the heat from whatever beast Hukluban had transformed into. He remembered the sensation of burning liquid that had sprayed them while rocks crashed down. His only thought as they escaped the Kasamaan was to hold onto the chest filled with talismans.

Horus finished stitching Leo's wound and sighed. He lowered his head mournfully as his hands dropped to his knees. Leo saw Horus' falcon before he even heard him approach. Some of his feathers were ruffled and battered, and he was carrying something between his claws. *No.* Leo sucked in his breath, his mind going blank. Horus raised his head and extended his arm. His falcon glided to a stop, perched on his forearm, then dropped Athena's armband into Horus' hand.

Leo's chest constricted. *No, no, no. It can't be.* She had been standing right next to them only a few minutes before. Athena, his mentor, had never backed away from a fight. His ally, who always found a solution. His friend, who never gave up. She couldn't be gone.

Horus' expression was muted, and his movements were restrained. Leo stared into Horus' eyes, eyes that had seen too much. Horus reached across Leo to the wooden chest and opened it, placing Athena's armband on top of the talismans. He sat back, closed his eyes, and raised his face to the sky.

Behind him, Apollo groaned and stirred weakly. Wearily, Leo stretched his hand toward the chest, his fingers millimeters from the slender leather armband carved with Greek serpents intertwined around an amethyst. His mind flashed back to when he had first met the goddess; the panic he had felt beneath her intimidating and all-seeing gaze. It was also the first time he had faced Sitan, the first time he had felt the chill of his presence.

Leo's eyes roamed across the chest to where Athena's vegvisir entwined with a beautiful, amber necklace. He picked up the necklace and inspected it. At first sight he had discovered who it belonged to, but now another deeper meaning struck him. This was Athena's divine partner, the one who had been brutally attacked before her eyes. Leo knew that there was more to this story than met the eye. His gut screamed at him to seize the vegvisir and find Athena; to find the deities whose talismans had been stolen.

Horus was standing directly behind him, scrutinizing his every

CHAPTER 39

move. "Do you recognize these?" he asked. Leo nodded, recalling his first full conversation with Athena back in London.

"It's why..." Leo couldn't say her name. "That's why she enlisted me." Horus took the vegvisir in his hand and closed his eyes. Whatever he was imagining made the instrument spin.

Leo studied the remaining talismans. There were an even number of artifacts. *That doesn't seem right.* He thought back to what Athena had said, about two representatives always traveling together. If he added Horus' falcon to the calculation, the resulting number would be odd, which meant there were some talismans missing.

Horus grunted and Leo looked up at him, puzzled. *What is he looking for?* Horus bent down and examined Apollo's wounds. Apart from the many contusions, he had some fresh acid burns across his lower back. Leo recoiled at the sight of Apollo's neck injuries. A faint silhouette of metal was etched deep into his golden skin, and the contrast was ghastly.

Questions spilled out of Leo. "Can't he heal himself? He's the god of medicine, for crying out loud. Didn't he create the armband? That's part of his power, isn't it? Who could have done this to him?"

Horus patted Apollo's shoulder before answering. "Some wounds cannot be healed so easily. Mental wounds can have longer effects than physical wounds."

"What type of torture did they use? Was that what happened to you, too?" Leo did not have the courage to voice his last question: Will this happen to Athena, if she somehow survived?

Horus' touched his own neck, which was injury-free. "They don't torture you; you torture yourself. That's the irony and true evil. You self-destruct. When locked in the Kasamaan prison, you lose your sense of self, and eventually forfeit your sanity."

Leo's fears for Athena intensified. He knew she must be saved. He inspected Apollo's wounds with a new resolve. "Will he be alright?"

Horus placed his palms together and said, "Apollo will heal, but it will take time, patience and a lot of self-love. The mind is incredibly powerful. It can be one's greatest foe, yet it can also be a powerful ally." Leo bit his tongue as he pondered Horus' last remarks.

"We'll stay with him," Horus added. He never commanded, unlike Athena whose voice could project when she was in an authoritative mood. "We can help him heal, support him, keep him safe until he recovers his full strength."

Leo swallowed. "Should we go back to London?"

"No. That's too dangerous. Sitan knows where you live. We must go somewhere different; somewhere he can't find us. Did you recognize all the talismans? Can you tell me who they belong to; from what cultures, and from which geographical areas?"

"Most of them," Leo said as he rummaged through the priceless artifacts. "And I can identify the unfamiliar ones through research and study."

Horus nodded. "I need a complete list of all the ones you know, and you need to start as soon as possible on those you don't."

Leo reflected on how much had occurred that led up to this moment. He recalled the improbability of his current path. There were too many what-ifs, and so many unknowns. It all started when Athena found his essay on "The Mystical Elements of Ancient Cultures," which led her to seek out Dr. Dupont and ensnare Sitan. What if she hadn't read it? What if the Manchester Library hadn't published it? What if she hadn't invited Leo to come along? Would he be the same person he was now? What would have happened to his relationship with David had he chosen to remain in London? Did he regret all the travels, all the beauty, and all the loss he had seen so far?

In the past few weeks, he had never felt so alive. He pictured his small dorm room in London, currently locked and abandoned. He imagined going back to King's College and to the British Museum.

CHAPTER 39

Part of him longed for security and stability that came with being a student. But the other part – the dreamer, the adventurer who longed for excitement, the one who was fighting to stay with Horus and Apollo, to find Athena and to bring down Sitan and his minions – craved the thrill and the sense of accomplishment that only a trip filled with uncertainty could bring. A journey not only paved with sweat and tears, heartache and setbacks, but which was also filled with joy and discovery.

Most of all, Leo wanted to help Athena; no matter where she was, he was going to stand by her, as she had done for him. She had opened the doors to her world and invited Leo in. He was not about to turn his back and desert her. He would continue her fight against Sitan and against the forces of darkness that had taken her. He would not give up; her courage and her bravery would live on through him. Good will conquer evil, and justice will prevail.

Leo resolved to be strong when faced with adversity. He looked at Apollo, who seemed helpless and defeated. He knew how much he would need to sacrifice to help him heal, to help him thrive once more. Leo was still holding the amber necklace. The warmth of the gemstone filled him with resolve.

"Okay. I'll get on it." Leo placed the necklace back in the box, and stood to face Horus. "So what's the plan?"

Horus waved his hand over the chest. "Let's start by waking our colleagues. We'll form a coalition. There must be a reason why these talismans were under guard and locked away. We won't be alone the next time we face Sitan."

"Where will we go?" Leo asked. They would need somewhere he could access the internet. A library would be preferable, but safety was most important. He stared at Apollo's limp figure and steeled himself. *I can do this. I believe in myself.*

Horus placed a hand on his shoulder. Two pairs of eyes looked directly at him; the immortal ones and the avian ones. Leo's entire body pulsed with energy. He flexed his hands, feeling the blood rush to his fingertips. *I'm in. I can do this. I believe in myself.*

"Somewhere mystical," Horus answered, his eyes unblinking. "Somewhere magical." His falcon screeched. "Somewhere they would never dream of finding us."

And with that, they embarked on their next quest.

Acknowledgments

I would like to express my appreciation to some amazing individuals who played pivotal roles in the creation and development of this book. Their unwavering support and dedication were the fuel that kept me going throughout this journey.

Thank you to my friends and family, to JA, Lynette, Sara, Magda 2, 3 and 4, Javi, Matt and Mike. Thank you for taking a chance on me, for giving this story a home and for our wonderful friendships.

Marty, you were the one who saw the potential. You gave me confidence and hope when I needed that belief the most. Your encouragement, feedback, endless enthusiasm and cheering have truly touched my heart, both on and off the court.

Tia Daryl, your dedication and support were nothing short of amazing. Your keen eye for detail, positive energy, and countless hours spent helping me refine this manuscript made all the difference. Your contributions transformed it into something I am truly proud of. This odyssey would not have been the same without your unwavering faith in its story. Thank you for believing in Athena, Leo and me.

And to those whose names may not be listed here but whose support has been no less significant, thank you from the bottom of my heart.

You are the unsung heroes of this adventure, and I am profoundly grateful for your roles in bringing this story to life.

Printed in Great Britain
by Amazon